HARMONY OR HAVOC
THE FUTURE OF KONDOR HANGS IN BALANCE.

THE AVIANS OF KONDOR

MARK B. WITTS

WITTY WORDS
PUBLISHING

This is the story I felt compelled to write—a novel that has simmered in my mind for quite some time, with many starts and stops along the way. At last, I've managed to bring it to print. I hope it provides you with moments of pleasure and escape, as it was intended.

*A heartfelt thanks to all who helped make this happen, especially to my life partner, **Christian**, for his unwavering support and patience.*

Mark B. Witts

PURITAWHITE MOTHER TREE
HOME OF CALEB AND
THE WHITE FLOCK

CONTENTS

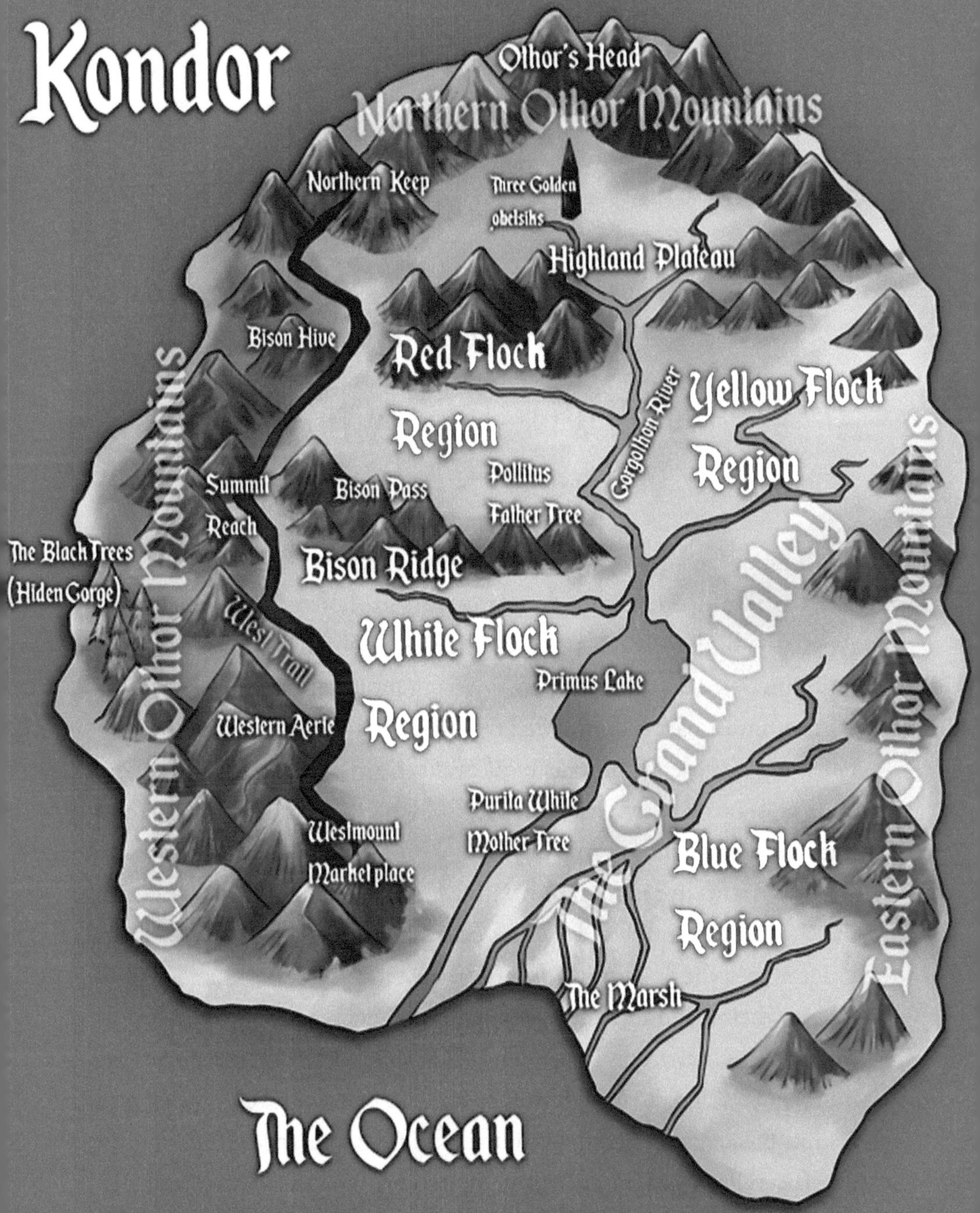

Kondor
Othor's Head
Northern Othor Mountains
Northern Keep
Three Golden obelsiks
Highland Plateau
Bison Hive
Red Flock Region
Yellow Flock Region
Gorgolhon River
Summit Reach
Bison Pass
Pollitus
Father Tree
The Black Trees (Hiden Gorge)
Bison Ridge
Western Othor Mountains
West Trail
White Flock Region
Primus Lake
The Grand Valley
Eastern Othor Mountains
Western Aerie
Purita While
Mother Tree
Westmount Market place
Blue Flock Region
The Marsh
The Ocean

Prologue:
The World of Kondor

Nestled on an ocean-covered planet, the Grand Valley is the heartland of Kondor's single vast continent, home to the remarkable Avians—a birdlike species whose culture is as vibrant as their surroundings. Encircled on three sides by towering mountain ranges, the valley's northernmost part is dominated by the imposing Othor's Head mountains. At the base of this cluster of peaks, on the edge of the Highland Plateau, stand the mysterious Three Golden Obelisks, their origins and purpose shrouded in mystery.

The Avians live in harmony with Mother Kondor, communing with the Great Trees and weaving their existence through song. Each flock's unique "melodic fingerprint" is more than a means of communication—it binds their communities, celebrates their heroes, and soothes their sorrows. Life centers around the mighty Gorgothon River, which bisects the valley, nourishing the sacred Mother and Father Tree groves, flowing into Primus Lake, and branching into the expansive southern Marsh.

The valley's geography naturally divides the Avians into four distinct flocks—White, Red, Blue, and Yellow—each adorned with plumage that reflects the predominant color of blossoms in their region. Every four years during the 'Light,' when all seven moons align and are full, the Highland Plateau transforms into a vibrant stage. Males compete in dazzling displays of song, color, and movement, seeking lifelong mates in a spectacle of unity and beauty.

Surrounding the Avians' domain are the Othorians, bat-like beings thriving in the shadowy mountain ranges. Masters of metallurgy and engineering, they inhabit vast underground hives and only emerge and stray into the Grand Valley during the 'Dark'—a quadrennial event when Kondor's seven moons vanish, plunging the world into shadow. This rare darkness marks the Othorians' frenzied reproductive season, starkly contrasting the Avians' luminous celebrations during the 'Light'.

Trade binds these two distinct peoples. The Avians offer exquisite textiles, sweet honey, and therapeutic nectars, while the Othorians provide tools and their prized luminium metal. Yet, their fragile peace remains haunted by the memories of devastating wars and disputes. Old grievances linger beneath their uneasy cooperation, threatening the tenuous balance.

CALEB
AI REPLICANT IMAGE

1.
IRKA'S CRY FOR HELP

———◇———

Caleb woke up with a sense of foreboding. The image of Irka in peril haunted his thoughts, and the echo of her distressed cry reverberated within him. An icy shiver coursed through his body, ruffling the light downy feathers on his chest before spreading to every extremity. The cool, damp air of dawn clung to his feathers, and the earthy scent of the jungle below filled his nostrils. Now fully awake, he leaped off the edge of his flota airship anchored amid the sprawling treetops, soaring into the dawn sky.

The crisp early morning air filled Caleb's lungs as he flapped his lustrous white wings, gaining altitude. The night's chill melted away with each powerful stroke. The sun peeked over the horizon, casting a golden glow on the tree canopy below. A verdant expanse spread out beneath him like an endless, emerald sea. Meandering silver rivers cleaved through the green, converging toward the heart of the Grand Valley.

Shaking his head and breathing deeply of the clear but thin air, he tried to dispel the thought of Irka in trouble. Her beautiful face and smile, now contorted into one of fear, seemed burned onto his mind's eye and struck deep in Caleb's heart. He had to fight the overwhelming urge to recklessly fly off and rescue her.

After a simple glide and dive maneuver, Caleb gracefully landed on the highest perch of the mainmast, where he had the best vantage point and view. He stared at the entrancing scenery, trying to calm his mind with the beauty of his surroundings. With his acute vision, Caleb could just make out the mighty Gorogothon River to the east in the far distance, where it bisected the Grand Valley, fed by melting snow and ice from the surrounding mountains.

Then, with an added pang of homesickness, his eyes peered deep into the south where his family flock and Irka resided at his home Mother Tree, PuritaWhite. The sense of urgency flooded back, the fear for his new mate, Irka's, safety refusing to relent, leaving a dry taste in his mouth.

Unsure of his next move, but just wanting to get moving, he swiftly roused their pack of buzzies. A gentle telepathic nudge was all that was needed.

Feeling Caleb's distress, Goffry, his childhood companion who had come with him on this exploration trip, now joined him at the top of the flota. Feathers fluffed with uncertainty as he landed. "What's the matter, Caleb? What's the rush?" The early morning light cast soft shadows on Goffry's face, highlighting the concern etched in his features.

Caleb's response was urgent and laced with conviction. "Something is horribly wrong, Goff. I heard distress calls from Irka in my sleep! I can't explain it, but I felt it deep in my being. She needs me, and I must leave at once!"

Goffry's brow furrowed as he considered Caleb's words. So keen was the Avian olfactory sense that Goffry could smell the concern emanating from his best friend. "Of course, I trust what you are saying, but how could you have heard her from this distance? Even in deep communion, it would be difficult. I know your connection with Irka is strong, stronger than you let on, but we are far up the valley, nowhere near any Great Tree. How is that even possible?"

"I don't have an explanation, Goff. I just don't, but I know what I heard. Irka is in danger. I have to go back home; I have to find her," Caleb affirmed resolutely, his eyes shining and nostrils flaring with determination.

Goffry responded with a firm nod, his eyes also now alight with resolve. "I'm with you, my friend. Let's do it! Let's cast off and get going southward immediately; we can make plans as we go," he declared, his voice steady and supportive.

With a short beat of his wings and an affirmative nod to Goffry, Caleb took off from his perch, expertly gliding to the other side of the flota. He skillfully unhooked the anchor rope that tethered them to a towering treetop below. As he pulled up the thick rope, the rough texture slid through his fingers, leaving them with a familiar tingling. The flota air raft slightly dipped but then began to rise.

Simultaneously, Goffry attended to their pack of buzzies, offering them a quick breakfast of sweet pollen cakes. As he broke off pieces of the sticky cake the delicious smell lingered in the air, mingling with the wet scent of fresh morning dew evaporating off the flota. After equipping the buzzy team with their flight harnesses, they started buzzing excitedly. Their translucent wings created a harmonious hum as they prepared for the journey.

Caleb's early morning mental wake-up call had gone out to the entire flota raft. This symbiotic entity was composed of many different living plants, vines, and fungi. Giant gasbags, almost mothlike in appearance but with huge papery sacs instead of wings and propeller-like tails, provided the lift for the elongated basket-like airship. Several gasbags, attached to the sides of the flota, began expanding, producing more hydrogen gas as the early morning sun hit them, happily following Caleb's mental instructions.

As the entire raft began to ascend, Caleb expertly piloted the flota, feeling the cool wind whisper against his skin and feathers, gauging its direction and speed with great accuracy.

He quickly came to a decision. There was no room for hesitation. Thoughts raced through his mind as he sent out a message to his buzzies.

Responding swiftly, they sensed the urgency and worry emanating from their beloved captain and companion. With wings beating feverishly, they pulled hard on their flight harnesses, causing the flota to alter course. While the mainsail alone could move the raft, the buzzy pack significantly augmented its speed, providing crucial directional steering.

To set the flota on autopilot, Caleb secured the boom and tightened the sheets, making sure the mainsail was properly positioned. He checked the rigging, securing loose lines, and adjusted the wind vane to respond to changes in wind direction. Finally, he positioned the large rudder sail to ensure steady navigation.

Satisfied, feeling the ship smoothly sail on its optimal course, Caleb returned to perch atop the mainmast, lost deep in thought. He preened his flight feathers meticulously, ensuring their aerodynamic efficiency. His ritualistic grooming was accompanied by his soft, absent-minded serenade of birdsong, blending with the murmurs of nature around him, providing small comfort and relaxation to think more clearly. The morning breeze carried the light aroma of blooming flowers and damp earth, grounding him in the moment despite his anxiety.

Goffry, having completed his task with the buzzies, quickly swooped up to join Caleb. He also began his morning grooming routine, meticulously smoothing and arranging his plumage. "So, fill me in on the plan. I felt the change in direction." With a quizzical gaze, Goffry studied his best friend, who was lost in thought and nervously grooming his feathers, wondering what was on Caleb's mind as he waited patiently for a response. The morning light highlighted the tension in Caleb's movements and the furrows in his brow. The rustle of their preening and the fresh scent of plumage oil mingled with the distant sounds and smells of the jungle below.

Letting out a warbled sigh, Caleb finally broke the silence, his words now flowing quickly. "Goff, I have to get home as quickly as possible, but first, I think it best to make a stop at IrmadineRed Mother Tree. She's the closest Great Tree with communing ability, and that's the fastest way to gather more information and hopefully put my mind at ease. I'll leave you with the flota. Follow me as fast as you can; I can make much better time alone. I'll wait for you at IrmadineRed after I communicate with our flock. I feel bad abandoning you, but it's what I have to do."

"I completely understand. Go with the wind, Caleb. We'll catch up with you as swiftly as possible," Goffry replied, sensing the urgency in his friend's eyes and refraining from further questioning.

With a nod and a grateful tweet, Caleb hopped down through the branches of the flota and swiftly prepared himself with a small body pack for supplies. Luckily, having just turned back south toward home after an extended scouting, trading, and gathering trip, they had a fully stocked pantry. The scent of dried fruits, herbs, and pollen cakes filled the small room, mingling to create a comforting aroma.

Taking just the basics—water, milkcheese (made from Great Tree milksap), and a bit of concentrated strong sappa for an energy boost—Caleb wore only a streamlined loincloth made from an exceptionally lightweight, silklike gossamer fabric, along with his usual talon knife, a small stinger crossbow slung over his back, and a quiver full of stinger arrow bolts attached to his belt.

Trada, his prime buzzy, would want to accompany him, but Caleb had already decided that he must leave him behind with Goffry to take charge and help navigate the flota as swiftly as possible. He knew that Trada would do his best and push the team of buzzies to their limits. Caleb and Trada shared an incredibly strong bond, each fully aware that they would always do what was best for the other, and in battle, they would defend one another to the end. The relationship between a master and his buzzy was one of deep respect, affection, loyalty, and friendship, especially with the pack leader, the prime buzzy.

With his preparations complete, Caleb glided out around the side of the flota and perched at its head, where Trada and his troupe of buzzies were now harnessed, furiously and enthusiastically pulling at the tethers tied to the front of the airship. Trada broke from the rest, unhooking himself and passing it to his first mate, Pica, Goffry's prime buzzy, with practiced ease before flying back to Caleb, settling next to him on the main front perch. Caleb stroked the top of Trada's head, running his fingers along the soft, bristle-like hairs, causing Trada to hum softly with delight. However, the urgency and concern radiating from his cherished master made Trada's hair stand on end, despite the gentle caresses he was receiving.

With a slight tingling in Caleb's arm, he connected his mind with Trada, sending him reassuring energy and love, swiftly conveying what he had experienced and the foreboding sense concerning Irka. Trada winced and gazed at his master with his sorrowful, enormous eyes, understanding what must be done. He sent back the message that he would follow up with Goffry and link up with Caleb as soon as possible. The urgent situation was now crystal clear to both, and with barely a final rub against Caleb's hand, Trada swiftly returned to his place at the front of the buzzy team.

Goffry was now fully engaged with the flota's rigging, deftly controlling the sail and the rudder, steering them in the right direction, expertly utilizing every available air current to hasten their progress. Once the flota reached a higher altitude and moved in the optimal direction, the buzzies would unhook their tethers and take a break by settling on their perches along the side of the floating raft.

Before departing, Caleb had one last task. He lightly slapped and rubbed the nearest gasbag attached to the flota and transmitted a message, announcing that he was transferring leadership to Goffry, and they were all to heed his commands until they were reunited. Pausing to reassure the gasbags and thank them in advance for their assistance, Caleb felt his communication spreading across the entire flota in familiar faint pulses of green-white energy, akin to a heartbeat. Communicating with the gasbags was a very basic form of interaction; instead of using actual mental "speech," they exchanged pictures, feelings, and visualizations.

"I'm off! I will see you soon. Enjoy fair winds, my friends!" he called to Goffry, the buzzies, and the whole flota, punctuating his departure with a parting goodbye birdcall.

"Wishing you a strong tailwind as well," Goffry warbled back, waving Caleb on.

Caleb leaped high into the air, making final adjustments to his flight gear as his glistening white wings caught the air currents with a slap. The clear dawn horizon stretched out in front of him, with no clouds in sight. Several free-floating gasbags drifted about around the flota, some of them enormous and engorged, those usually higher up in the sky, and the smaller ones below. You could always tell when gasbags were in the area from the light methane gas smell they emitted as a by-product of hydrogen production. Caleb's powerful wings sliced through the air as he sped down the Grand Valley, heading south toward IrmadineRed Mother Tree.

Casting one last glance backward, Caleb sent a final mental wave of love and regret to his flota and crew. He noticed a few more gasbags attaching themselves to the flota, lifting it higher into the air. Known for their passive and gentle nature, gasbags often congregated in groups and sometimes traveled for many miles with the wind, aided by light propulsion from their propeller-like tails. Sensing a faint farewell from his flota in response to his thoughts, Caleb lowered his head to minimize drag and pushed hard against the air, propelling himself upward into higher altitudes to ride the faster currents for a swifter journey.

Gaining altitude was strenuous, he was feeling the burn on his muscles. He had recently molted and his primary flight feathers had not yet grown out, but using favorable updrafts, he managed to ascend quickly. Caleb pressed on in his flight to IrmadineRed Mother Tree, and after a relentless day and night of arduous but uneventful travel, he finally caught sight of her in the early hours of the second morning. From a high altitude, he arched his wings, allowing a swift descent. He spiraled down while deftly maneuvering past stray gasbag floaters, the wind chilling his skin and flattening his feathers with firm pressure. He let out a beautifully melodic welcoming call, as habit and good manners dictated when approaching a Great Tree.

As he drew nearer, the immense size and grandeur of IrmadineRed filled Caleb's heart with awe, his chest tightening with a mix of reverence and urgency. The earthy aroma of enriched soil, the musty scent of fungi and wood, and a floral scent rose up to greet him. Despite having encountered all known Great Trees in his lifetime, each visit inspired a profound sense of wonder. He always marveled at the harmonious coexistence of these ancient trees with the extensive fungal masses entwined with their gigantic roots, burrowing deep into the ground and interweaving with the mycelium network and other tree and plant roots.

Caleb admired the colossal trunk and limbs of IrmadineRed, towering over ten times the height of the lesser trees below. The lower part of the trunk tapered slightly and became incredibly smooth, exuding a sticky sap that glistened in the morning light. The sap had a slightly sweet, resinous scent that mingled with the fresh, crisp air. This band provided protection from invading crawling insects, dooming them to a sticky death, entrapped and eventually absorbed by the tree. Access to the upper regions of these towering Great Trees was only possible through the air, a privilege of the Avians.

As he descended further, Caleb's sharp eyes observed resident wild buzzies nested along the main branches of the trunk. The buzz of these friendly creatures created a soothing hum that reverberated through the air. Any unfriendly flying creature would not be allowed near the Great Tree; the resident buzzies protected their hosts with fervor and dedication.

The air filled with the rosy scent of Irmadine's vibrant red blooming flowers. Each was in harmony with Irmadine's predominant crimson color theme, with some blossoms growing to several feet in diameter. He spotted red macca fruit varying from small fist-sized fruits to colossal ones, requiring ingenuity for harvest. As he came closer the sweet fragrance of the crimson blooms intensified becoming intoxicating, mingling with the other jungle scents to create a heady, calming perfume. Products from the Red Flock Great Trees induced physical strength and stamina, even now just the strong aroma of the blossoms made Caleb feel better.

Now on his final approach to IrmadineRed, Caleb extended his thoughts, establishing mental contact while coming within her communing range. The vibrant energy of the Great Tree pulsed through him, a warm, comforting sensation that further eased the fatigue from his journey. With a final burst of energy, he landed softly on the mossy platform concealed among the vast boughs and branches.

Folding his wings neatly, Caleb strode to IrmadineRed's nexus, a large smooth dark green burl protruding from the core of the tree not far from where he had landed. The nexus chamber was a recessed alcove in the giant trunk, covered with a tightly woven thatch of vines and branches. Large bracket fungi lined the walls, and he seated himself on one—an outgrown shelf with a leathery, soft top—that provided a low sitting ledge facing the central node.

Caleb took hold of the nexus, initiating the communing ritual. The cool, slightly sticky surface sent a tingle through his fingers as he connected, feeling the ancient tree's wisdom and strength flow into him. A profound sense of calm and clarity washed over him, mixing with the urgency and concern for Irka. He closed his eyes and focused his thoughts, ready to commune with the ancient Mother Tree.

"*Caleb*," came the welcoming message from IrmadineRed, suffusing his mind with a genuine sense of warmth, soothing his nerves despite his mounting apprehension.

"*Hello, Mother Irmadine*," he responded, transmitting his need for assistance to communicate with PuritaWhite, his Mother Tree, and his flock.

"*I sensed your arrival, young Caleb, and I could feel your worries and anxiety*," she replied, sharing her own concerns. "*There have been significant disturbances all over the Grand Valley, and I was just trying to gather more information from my brethren Great Trees.*"

"*Thank you, Mother Irmadine. I am deeply concerned for Irka and my flock. I need to know if they are safe*," Caleb conveyed, his thoughts tinged with desperation.

Deepening their connection, IrmadineRed and Caleb together sent an energy wave down the Grand Valley. In Caleb's mind's eye, the image of his Mother Tree, PuritaWhite, took shape, but shockingly, she remained unresponsive. IrmadineRed intensified her efforts, sending a stronger query toward the marsh, near where PuritaWhite stood. An ominous feeling engulfed Caleb as he realized something must be gravely amiss. The lack of response from PuritaWhite indicated she was likely severely injured or in a state of shock, rendering her incapable of communicating clearly. It also came to light from other regions of the valley that several flocks had been attacked, and two other Great Trees had been damaged.

"*Othorians! I see the past events so vividly in the collective memory. The truce is now over; that is clear*," Caleb gasped out loud and inwardly at the shock of such news.

Irmadine sent out a calming rush of energy in response. "*Caleb, first let us come together with a healing for all.*" She sought to soothe, mend and repair, connecting with more of the Great Trees between them and PuritaWhite until waves of restorative energy spread throughout all of Kondor, with each connected Great Tree contributing to the collective effort.

Caleb felt the combined healing energy flow into and through him, a powerful yet gentle force that began to alleviate his frayed nerves and replenish his strength. *"Thank you, Mother Irmadine. Your wisdom and strength are a great comfort."*

"I will continue to monitor the situation and provide whatever aid I can," IrmadineRed assured him. *"Go now, Caleb. Protect your flock and your loved ones. The strength and support of all of the Great Trees is with you."*

Caleb withdrew from IrmadineRed, feeling a deep sense of gratitude. "I will," he said aloud, his voice filled with reverence and conviction.

The exertion of this communication left him physically and mentally drained. He slumped onto the fungi bench, sweat beading on his forehead and face, panting to cool himself down. While the communing bond had ceased, thankfully he still felt the life energy emitted by the colossal tree gradually replenishing his strength.

Caleb took a moment to think, quickly confirming his decision to reach Irka and his parents as rapidly as possible. He mapped out a route that would take him across Bison Ridge, using the Bison Pass through the high mountains as a shortcut. This path would shave several days off the journey but came with some risk, as the pass was turbulent at best. However, once they exited the pass, they would be closer to the center of the Grand Valley and could follow the west side of the Gorgothon River to reach PuritaWhite. First, he would rejoin Goffry and the flota at higher altitudes to maintain their pace and hasten the journey home.

Expressing his gratitude and love for IrmadineRed, he departed the nexus chamber, climbing higher into the upper boughs along a well-trodden ancient pathway. Reaching the highest launching pad, he sprang into the air, unfolded his wings, and commenced his ascent back toward his flota—he could always quite precisely home in on their location.

As he climbed, Caleb traversed a group of large gasbags, expertly bouncing off some to gain additional height. He was tiring quickly. When he reached the highest one, he sat on top and gently stroking its surface humbly asking it to take him up higher. Not only did it respond but two other nearby gasbags latched on and they all began to expand together, rising up quite quickly, their resilient papery skins rustling as they expanded. Taking time to rest atop the pod, Caleb felt his fatigue catching up with him. Regrowing flight feathers were definitely hampering his flying ability, so using the friendly gasbags to lift him to a higher altitude would give him a break.

Seated atop the gasbag pod as it ascended, Caleb could rest, giving him a chance to groom and preen. To his surprise, he noticed that the newly emerging primary flight pin feathers on the ends of his wings bore a dark hue, more pronounced than the usual metallic white tinged tips inherited from his father, Jonus. This dark coloration puzzled him, given his lineage as a White from two PureWhite parents. While off-colored plumage wasn't uncommon among Avian males, it was rare within the White Flock.

Initially dumbfounded by the dark emerging pinions, Caleb gradually accepted the unexpected development. He carefully preened and massaged his growing feathers, gently pulling at the loose parts of the keratin sheath that enveloped them, hoping to expedite their growth regardless of their color.

Letting out a hefty sigh, he muttered to himself, "Great, just what I need to brighten my day!"

Irka's chilling call still haunted him. She was always on his mind, and closing his eyes he could picture every detail of her face. She permanently displayed a huge smile of happiness yet now he envisioned her beautiful features shadowed by fear. His heart ached to know that she was safe, but all of his continuous mental probes went unanswered. No surprise considering the distance, but he desperately held out hope that he would feel something more.

Breathing deeply, the chill of the thin air catching in his throat, Caleb began to sing an intricate and emotionally charged tune. It was beautiful and melodic, with deep, sad undertones. He sang of his love for Irka, his fear for her safety, and the sadness of knowing she was in danger. Now standing high atop the gasbag pod, he flung his song against the wind, using a vocal range he never knew he had. The song echoed everywhere within earshot, a true lilting crescendo of romantic sadness.

As the last few notes of his song faded away, a faint but growing awareness of his approaching flota, accompanied by Goffry and his buzzies, reached his senses. It wasn't a conventional sound at first, but rather a disruption and vibration in the air that Caleb detected through his feathers. The familiar scents, the subtle rustle of a sail, the whisper of expanding and brushing gasbags, and the sense of reconnection with Goffry, Trada, the pack, and the entire flota gradually strengthened as they drew nearer.

Preparing to meet them, Caleb stretched out his wings, flapping lightly to keep his balance and test the air. As the distance between them gradually diminished, he felt anxious to reunite with them, pacing back and forth but waiting for the right moment. At this altitude, the air was thin, and his wings would only support him for a short distance. He swelled with pride as he eyed his flota; even from afar, their synchronized movements and the orchestrated undulations of their wings created a captivating display of unity and teamwork.

He could wait no longer. With great eagerness and visible exertion, Caleb leaped off the gasbag pod and flew toward his friends.

IRKA
CALEB'S DEVOTED NEW MATE

2:
IRKA IN TROUBLE

Irka had just glided from one of the smaller Mother Tree saplings to another nearby. She was harvesting from the grove surrounding her new home Mother Tree, accompanied by her prime buzzy, Trudy. Her faithful companion tugged along her floating baska. Kept aloft by a small attached gasbag, these baskas were used to transport collected fruits and produce back to the flock's reserves.

Irka laughed at her sometimes-clumsy companion, the baska was getting quite heavy and was now a bit stuck on a vine. "Just back up a bit, silly. Go around," she playfully scolded, turning her attention back to the task at hand. Trudy, although obeying her command, emanated an unapproving yet loving hum with a defiant little butt shake as she vigorously vibrated her wings to alter course.

Familiar with the varying ripening patterns of almost every fruit and nut in the grove as all Workers from the flock were, Irka anticipated the locations for the ripest yields. However, the capricious nature of the ripening process often felt like a playful game orchestrated by the Mother Tree, challenging the flock to earn their reward through diligent labor.

Amused by this whimsical notion, Irka smiled to herself and released a soft, warbled chuckle. Engrossed in her work, she examined every flower and fruit she passed. The white blossoms had a complex and delightful scent—floral, but with tones of sinus-cleansing herbal resin.

Absentmindedly, she began chirping and tweeting in a low, melodious key that gradually blossomed into a full-blown tune. Her birdsong mirrored her feelings—fond remembrances of her past growing up in the RedBlush Flock, the love of her mother, Glorita, and the once bright red color of her plumage, which she secretly sometimes missed. Now, her feathers were a glorious white, still with a pink tinge, a result of the change in diet from red to white Great Tree food products. Her song grew louder, filled with joyful thoughts about the present, echoing with elation and contentment.

Irka had recently mated with Caleb, whom she adored with all her heart and soul. The memory of their amorous Pairing ritual never seemed to leave her mind. It harked back to the last season a mere year ago. The Avians observed the Pairing ritual every four years when all the moons of Kondor were full and visible in the night sky concurrently. This celestial event, known as the Light, rendered the night sky as luminous as day for an entire month. It alternated every two years with the Dark, a period when all the moons were concealed at night, casting the world into an abyss of darkness.

What a romantic setting it had been, Irka recalled. The Highland Plateau was illuminated with faintly violet moonlight. The cooing of newly matched mates singing passionate birdsong resonated among the sparse cactus trees that grew nowhere else but on the plateau. These trees bloomed at nighttime only during Pairing seasons, and the blossoms hung like long garlands from their branches. Irka had adorned herself with some, and the scent was extremely intoxicating, invoking deep passions and amorous feelings.

During this last Pairing season, Kondor had experienced an extraordinarily bountiful harvest, which had attracted a multitude of eligible young Avians to the Highland Plateau. Upon first laying eyes on Caleb, Irka immediately sensed an unspoken connection, a profound understanding that they were destined to be together. Unbeknownst to her at the time, Caleb reciprocated her sentiments. His initial reserve masked his feelings, considering Irka to be too exceptional for him, way out of his league.

Shaking herself back to the present with a ruffling of feathers, Irka flew further through the grove. The heady aroma of the countless flowers, painted in every shade of white, surrounded her, leaving her momentarily giddy. Again, her mind wandered back to relive Caleb's hesitant approach and coy display of his stunning white wing feathers when he first noticed her. His clumsy yet beguiling and charismatic interest brought a wistful smile to her lips as she recalled the unforgettable encounter.

Her new life partner possessed an above-average stature, distinguished by an exquisitely chiseled and lustrous physique. Uniquely, every feather adorning his body bore a pristine white hue, except for the two end flight feathers on each wing, which bore a subtle, delicate white metallic tinge. She adored the slight deviation from the standard flock colors which highlighted his handsome appearance, granting him an air of humble distinction.

Shaking herself from the reverie of her recollections, Irka refocused on her goal. She gave herself another shake to dispel the lingering intensity of her passionate memories.

"Okay, Irka, back to work, my dear," she said aloud, jokingly, to no one in particular. Glancing around, she realized she was near the eastern fringes of the grove. It was almost time to return, and as soon as she could fill the baska, she would head back up to the storeroom. Only then would she be content to retire to her nest high up in the ancient tree for some rest—perhaps after a nice supper with her flock mates.

With patient anticipation, she waited for her buzzy, Trudy, to catch up to her. The scent of perfectly ripe fruit ahead wafted by, and with that whiff alone, Irka knew exactly where the prize was. She pushed off from her perch, continuing the journey to the appropriate tree.

Pausing on a nearby tree branch, she thought she detected slight movement amid the nearby bushes. Her scrutiny intensified, the movement ceased, but was that an unusual brief silence in its wake? Irka's feathers bristled with a hint of apprehension. The Mother Tree grove had never presented any overt dangers, always considered a place of safety and peacefulness. So, after a couple of moment's silence, she decided that it was most likely an innocuous squill—a not uncommon rodent-like creature that rooted about on the forest floor.

Irka's focus was diverted by the sight of the perfectly ripe macca fruit she had been searching for, adorning a nearby branch close to where she had just landed. Trudy had also swiftly caught up with the baska in tow, allowing Irka to secure the newly discovered bounty. The perfectly mature ripeness of the fruit reassured her that her timely arrival had not been in vain, recognizing that a delay until the following day might render the fruit past its prime.

As she delicately plucked the fruit from the tree, a sense of gratitude permeated her thoughts, a silent acknowledgment to the tree for its generosity. The fruit's detachment elicited a familiar deliciously honey-sweet aroma, further affirming its superior quality. With a deft motion, she transferred her luscious prize to the awaiting baska. The attached gasbag could easily be encouraged to release more gas to offset the weight, ensuring a smooth ascent and Trudy exerted extra effort in response.

"I know where another one is, Trudy," Irka said, her voice filled with satisfaction. "Just one more, and we'll head back."

Trudy buzzed happily in agreement, her tiny wings fluttering with excitement, letting off a small plume of pollen from a sac attached to her leg.

Irka turned her attention to where the other smaller fruit she remembered was located in the same tree. Her mouth gaped in surprise as she peered at the spot where it should have been.

"But ..." Irka looked back at Trudy. "It was there yesterday. I am ... certain."

Perplexed by the disappearance, she drew closer to the tree branch where she knew the fruit had been hanging, only to be met with an even more distressing sight. The fruit had been violently pulled and severed from the tree, leaving behind a trail of white sap oozing from the fresh wounds. The sticky sap emitted an acrid, slightly acidic odor that was impossible to ignore—an unmistakable response from the tree when mistreated.

Irka's feathers instinctively bristled in response. This was a wanton act of vandalism. The gash on the tree branch was a telltale sign of foul play, a manifestation of brute force absent in the customary gentle harvesting practices of her fellow Workers.

"Trudy, look at this," Irka whispered, her voice now tinged with fear. "Something's wrong."

Before Trudy could respond, Irka suddenly felt a coarse rope net ensnare her, seemingly materializing out of nowhere. The net immobilized her wings and constricted her movement, the rough fibers digging into her feathers. Involuntarily gasping, a vile rancid smell raked down her throat and filled her mouth with acid. Panic surged through her as she thrashed desperately, trying to break free, but the net only tightened its grip. She opened her mouth to sound an alarm, but before she could utter a single note, a savage blow struck her head.

Pain exploded behind her eyes, radiating through her skull as her vision blurred. Darkness began to close in, swallowing the world around her. In her fading consciousness, she caught a terrifying glimpse of her captors—Othorians, their forms shrouded in dark, heavy garments, gloves, and hoods, with their faces hidden behind narrow-slitted glasses that obscured their eyes. They were faceless shadows, cold and merciless.

The last thing she saw in a brilliant, searing glowing flash was Caleb's face. She reached out, her trembling fingers grasping for him, desperately calling out to him for help. But before she could make contact, the world was swallowed by an all-consuming blackness, plunging her into nothingness.

In the lush sanctuary of the PuritaWhite Mother Tree grove, two mysterious Othorians, cloaked in darkness and secrecy, loomed over Irka's bound form. The smaller one casually taking a bite from the sweet juicy fruit he had taken earlier. Together the two attackers emitted a feverish symphony of clicks and vibrations. Their glands exuded a stream of pheromones as punctuation or in excitement, a light yet unpleasant pungent smell. This exchange of aromas enabled the Othorians to enhance their communication in conjunction with their intricate vocal language.

These bat-like invaders had concealed their distinctive odors at first, enabling them to catch their unsuspecting victim unaware. They knew full well that these bird people possessed a super keen olfactory sense. Now, as the first-strike assault had fully commenced, they openly secreted an unmistakable scent of triumph that marked this territory as secured. This foul tang in the air now permeated the grove, which had previously smelled beautifully of delicate floral scents. They also signaled the message *"one captive"* to their hive using high-frequency ultrasound calls. This declaration swiftly reached their fellow hive mates.

Staying vigilant and wary, the two Othorians remained on high alert, fully aware that Irka's devoted buzzy still lurked, biding its time to launch a counterattack. Despite the buzzies' gentle companionship with the Avians, they remained fiercely defensive, prompting the Othorians to exercise caution.

Lutheg, the larger of the two figures, towered silently, peering about intensely. His companion mirrored his hushed demeanor, crouching down and looking about with evident apprehension. A persistent buzz resonated through the air, emanating from the extremely agitated Trudy, the witness to her master's downfall at the hands of the intruders. The incessant buzzing hum, meticulously orchestrated by Irka's faithful companion, defied spatial orientation, intended to bewilder and disorient.

"Lutheg, do you think it will come for us?" Kieran hissed, his eyes scanning the canopy.

"Stay alert and quiet, and put that fruit down. Your hunger almost gave us away," Lutheg replied almost silently, his tone grim.

As the buzzing escalated and wavered momentarily, Lutheg swiftly pinpointed the precise location. He was a master knife thrower, a high-ranking officer. Without hesitation, he hurled a dagger directly at his target. Caught off guard, Trudy, with her unfortunate delayed reflexes, succumbed to the swiftness of the attack.

The Othorian war dagger cleaved into the faithful, lifelong companion of Irka, prompting the buzzy to convulse and plummet through the branches until she met the forest floor with a sickening thud. Only then did the Othorians ease their stance slightly, but maintaining surveillance over the encircling woodland.

Days of patient observation, meticulous mapping, and strategic reconnaissance had preceded the orchestrated assault. The assailants had realized that most of the adult flock members, including the flock Protectors, were absent on their harvesting runs, lured away by the promise of this season's abundant yield throughout the Grand Valley. Assessing the PureWhite Flock's remaining contingent of less than twenty members, the Othorians deemed it a prime target, their small team poised to overpower the defenders with a surprise raid.

"We've timed this perfectly," Kieran muttered, his voice laced with satisfaction.

"Yes," Lutheg agreed, his eyes narrowing. "But stay focused. We aren't finished yet."

While the Avians were committed to protecting their flock and the Great Tree at any cost, the absence of more than half their members rendered the remaining few vulnerable. The Othorians, targeting specific individuals, intended to eliminate any resistance swiftly and mercilessly, sparing no quarter in their mission.

Devising an elaborate diversion to distract the flock, the cunning Othorians had orchestrated a fiery onslaught using a newly invented explosive missile charge planted near the main nexus of the Avians' home tree. They foresaw the resulting chaos would impede any pursuit, ensuring a safe and unhindered retreat. Devoted to extinguishing the blaze and salvaging the cherished Mother Tree, the remaining Avians, in their valiant effort, would be completely distracted, their attention consumed by a raging inferno. It was a good plan, and it was working.

Standing over Irka's incapacitated form, Lutheg and Kieran patiently awaited the signal of an *"all clear"* from their commander. Muffling Irka's mouth with a gag and blindfolding her with a cloth sack, they secured their captive, preparing to depart. Amid the acrid smoke of burning vegetation and wood engulfing the area, they detected the scent and vocalizations of *"Success"* and several *"One more captured"* calls from their fellow raiders, solidifying the favorable outcome of their covert operation.

With a grunt, Kieran hoisted Irka over his shoulder, adjusting her weight for optimal balance, and swiftly descended from the tree. Equipped with slits in his gloves, Kieran effortlessly maneuvered the terrain with his retractable claws and his dexterous feet, furnished with an opposable thumb-like toe, enabling him to climb rocks and trees with acrobatic precision.

Despite their mastery in climbing, the Othorians' preference for upright movement remained unaltered. They possessed the ability, in various degrees, to glide short distances; most of them possessed vestigial leathery flaps beneath their armpits. On rare occasions, however, some Othorians were blessed with fully functional leathery black wings, which elevated them to the exalted status of Great Leaders. These leaders were revered and followed with an almost divine reverence.

Assisting Kieran, Lutheg remained vigilant, their senses heightened as they descended, ever alert for the slightest hint of danger. Upon reaching the forest floor, Lutheg peered through an opening in the dense foliage and spotted the distant chaos unfolding at the Mother Tree. His eyes locked onto a shadowy figure, which he suspected was one of Bertran's top lieutenants, emerging briefly from the cover of the trees. The figure quickly raised a blowgun and fired a dart toward a small group of three Avians who were turned away, unaware of the threat. Without hesitation, the lieutenant then vanished back into the treetops. Lutheg and Kieran continued their cautious advance through the grove, moving toward a prearranged convergence point, communicating in hushed tones and coded clicks as they pressed forward.

"Thetan's son, Bertran, is the cause of all this. That malicious and greedy wannabe king, he's pushing us too far," Lutheg was muttering, his voice tight with anger. "There is no need for this level of merciless attack, these Avians are unarmed."

Kieran glanced at him, concern etched on his face. "We must follow orders. We can't question them now. We should not speak outwardly of this but I agree. I know many others also have concerns but let us bide our time."

Reaching the edge of a field, hunkering down in some thick bushes, Lutheg responded in a muted tone, "Agreed… when the time is right. I also know others who have apprehensions about leadership. I am happy to know that we are both of the same mindset."

As Lutheg and Kieran continued their approach, skirting the meadow, the comradery between them was palpable. The bright sun of the meadow was quite blinding so they stayed in the shadows as much as possible. The pungent smell of Othorian scent lay like a thick moldy blanket on the forest.

"You know, while we are alone, let us confer further," Kieran, glancing around to ensure they were alone, began again. "There's a lot of discord simmering within our hives, I see you feel it too. Many of us doubt these aggressive tactics."

Lutheg nodded, his brow furrowing. "I've noticed. But the hive's mindset clings to obedience. It's hard to break away from that, especially with someone like Thetan leading us."

Kieran sighed. "It's Bertran's plan that worries me. He is the one to watch. It is *his* doing. We've been promised lavish boons for corralling some Avians to the Highland Plateau. But the source of these rewards? It's all so mysterious. Have you heard the whispers?"

"About the Three Golden Obelisks?" Lutheg asked, his voice low. "Yes. And the force that demands our subservience and allegiance. It doesn't sit well with me, Kieran. Not at all."

Kieran looked thoughtful. "We've had a harmonious time with the Avians for quite some time. Many of us want to keep that peace intact. The idea of a coerced alliance with some unknown, the promise of undisclosed incentives … it's unsettling."

"Bertran's sway is potent," Lutheg agreed, his voice tinged with frustration. "Thetan's leadership still commands absolute loyalty, and the promises of untold riches, technological wonders, and breakthroughs in health care make it even harder to question him."

Kieran nodded, his eyes reflecting the shared unease. "We have to be careful, Lutheg. We're walking a fine line here. But for now, let's just focus on the task at hand and keep our opposition silent."

Lutheg gave a grim nod, his resolve hardening. "Agreed. Let's get this done, and hope for a better path to emerge."

As they emerged into the sun again a flash of blinding reflection betrayed the movement of polished metal in the sun. Lutheg's heart sank at the grim sight of two out of the three Avians that they had previously seen avoid the blowgun, now falling victim to a relentless assault.

They smelled the strong messages that were now being sent, as well as an ultrasonic command to withdraw and regroup to the west of the Mother Tree grove. From there they would journey to the mountains and the path northward as previously instructed.

"Let's get away from here. We'll head straight to the western rendezvous point."

Kieran nodded; his acknowledgment was silent but understood. Their mutual complicity bound them together forming a bond stronger than normal friendship.

CALEB
A CENTRAL FIGURE, PROTAGONIST AND PROTECTOR FOR THE AVIAN PEOPLE

3:
THE JOURNEY HOME

❖

Before embarking on their long journey back to PuritaWhite, Caleb and Goffry stopped to efficiently reorganize their flota. Caleb attached new gasbags that he had brought with him, allowing some of the smaller ones to float freely. With a fond pat, he encouraged some of them to expand, lightening the flota's load and resulting in a more streamlined shape.

Simultaneously, Goffry meticulously stripped the airship down to its lightest possible weight. He removed sections of the raft, particularly those made of dead wood and metal. Surplus supplies were unloaded and sent down to IrmadineRed using the buzzies and the released gasbags. Goffry ensured that nothing went to waste; the extra organic matter would be stockpiled in the Mother Tree's storage nooks, to be reabsorbed later if unused.

"Making sure we're as light as possible," Goffry explained, his voice strained with effort.

"Agreed," Caleb replied, hands deftly securing a gasbag. "We need to get back as quickly as we can."

Upon returning, Caleb had relayed the troubling news that he had no direct contact with PuritaWhite and that they were still in the dark regarding Irka's situation. There was a growing certainty that something dire had transpired, not only with Irka but also with their Mother Tree and perhaps the entire flock. After a brief discussion, they both decided to abandon their mission and head home with urgency.

As the flota leader, Caleb had already planned their next steps out. Firstly, regain altitude and then travel south using Bison Pass. Careful navigation would be required to avoid mishaps and the wildly changing air currents. They would begin by leveraging the prevailing counterclockwise winds in the Grand Valley, then quickly speed through Bison Pass, saving several days on their journey.

The challenge was not just the treacherous terrain but also the unpredictable weather patterns that often converged in the Pass. Sudden gusts could slam into the flota, threatening to push them off course, or worse, into the jagged mountain peaks. This route was also generally avoided due to its proximity to Othorian outposts and the well-traveled West Trail. Caleb knew that any miscalculation could spell disaster, not just for him and Goffry, but for the entire flota.

Taking a small breather from their work, they met on the deck. Caleb sat on the gunwale of the raft, testing the direction of the gusts with his feathers, his eyes half-closed in thought. "This route will be risky, but it's our best shot, Goff. What do you think?"

Goffry nodded, his eyes scanning the horizon. "We'll make it. We just need to keep a close feel for the wind currents and go for it."

Both of them were adept at navigating even in treacherous conditions, so they were confident they could accomplish their goal. However, the lack of Great Trees in this area meant sacrificing further communication for increased speed.

Caleb's exhaustion had begun to take its toll, exacerbated by the strain of the rapid flight to IrmadineRed Mother Tree and the taxing attempt at communication with his home flock. Although he was naturally inclined toward communing, the mental stress often left his mind clouded afterward. Despite the need for rest, he had been reluctant to pause and relax.

After finishing their preparations, Caleb and Goffry steered the raft upward—they had descended to unload. Their buzzy team diligently pulled the flota with the aid of the gasbags, which filled and stretched as they produced hydrogen gas. The acrid smell of methane confirmed this transformation. For now, the sail remained rolled up, secured to the mainmast until they reached the ideal altitude, at which point it would be unfurled to catch the wind and propel them onward.

"Time for a rest," Goffry said, glancing at Caleb. "You look like you need it."

Caleb nodded; his eyes heavy. "Thanks, Goffry. I'll take a quick snooze."

With a nod, Caleb entrusted Goffry with navigating the flota, allowing himself to retreat to the central nesting chamber for some well-deserved rest.

Caleb retrieved a sizable portion of milkcheese from the pantry, along with a handful of dried pollen cake and fruit bars. He also selected a gourd bottle of sappa nectar wine from the larder. Sappa, derived from various Great Tree blossoms on Kondor, had a variety of effects depending on the color and type of fruit flowers used in its preparation.

As he downed several large gulps of the sweet, aromatic wine, he felt a calming sensation wash over him. His muscles relaxed, and he struggled to keep his eyes open. Before long, he had curled up and succumbed to a deep slumber, his mind enveloped in vivid scenarios.

In his dreams, the image of his Irka, appeared over and over again—a constant presence in his thoughts ever since he received her distress call. Caleb's memory of her endearing sweetness and unwavering devotion provided small solace amid his turmoil. As a former member of the RedBlush Flock of the Red Colony, Irka bore striking plumage, with stunning white feathers tinged with a deep pink blush.

This was a reflection of her native Father Tree, Pollitus, situated at the end of the Bison Ridge not far from where they would emerge. However, the plan was to take a direct southern route—there was no time for a visit at this point.

Caleb's dreams oscillated between joyous memories of his fledgling years and the poignant recollection of his sparring sessions with Goffry and his other brood mates. Though their playful practices were akin to a carefully choreographed dance, one moment of misjudgment had resulted in Caleb injuring Goffry. Despite Goffry's quick forgiveness, Caleb couldn't shake off the shame and guilt, and their bond transformed into an unspoken understanding that transcended words.

"Caleb, wake up. Wake up." Goffry's gentle voice stirred Caleb from his fitful slumber.

With a weary sigh, Caleb sat up, grappling with the weight of his troubled thoughts. "I could use a week of sleep," he groaned.

Goffry leaned back, smiling wearily. "I get it, but I need to take a break as well before we hit the Pass."

"Of course. Thanks so much for letting me go first. You need rest as much as I do." Offering him the gourd of sappa, Caleb encouraged Goffry to take a break and replenish his energy. Observing the fatigue etched on Goffry's face, Caleb couldn't help but worry about his friend. With a vigorous shake, Caleb made his way out of his nest chamber, preparing himself to take control of the flota.

Flying up to the uppermost perch of their floating raft, Caleb examined the mainsail and ensured the rudder sail pole was securely positioned at the appropriate angle. A quick glance at the sky, with the moons and stars fading in the brightening dawn, assured Caleb that they were maintaining the correct course. Caleb could sense the change of smell and taste of the air. Now he could sense the damp rock, mosses and snow from the high mountains, with an almost imperceptible taste of acrid mineral deposits like lime and sulfur.

Confident in the flota's navigation, Caleb inspected Trada and the buzzy pack, confirming their secure perches alongside the flota. Noting Trada's half-awake state, Caleb sent a calming thought to his companion, prompting the buzzy to drift back into a peaceful slumber.

Settling in, Caleb meticulously preened his feathers, as this repetitive grooming always helped to calm him. He let out a deep sigh, watching the majestic sunrise over the sprawling Grand Valley. The Eastern Othor Mountain Range lay far off in the distance, still visible on one side, while the picturesque Western Range was bathed in the warm glow of the rising sun on the other. Looking southwards Caleb's acute vision allowed him to discern the massive Bison Ridge and the canyon gap they were headed for. Satisfied with their progress and estimating their return home in six days or less, Caleb couldn't help but wonder what awaited them upon their arrival. His anxiety was still high but focusing on the present moment helped.

From his perch Caleb seamlessly directed the flota's flight pattern, synchronizing his thoughts with the undulating gasbags, sensing the wind patterns and strength with his feathers and skin. The familiarity of their coordinated flight enveloped him, lending him a sense of stability and belonging amid the vast expanse of the open sky. With every passing minute Caleb's resolve strengthened, his determination unwavering as they embarked on their journey back home.

MARTA
CALEB'S MOTHER, LEADER AND
COMMUNER OF THE WHITE FLOCK

4:

Marta and Jonus

—◇—

arta and Jonus were on their way back home, accompanied by
several of their flock members and crew. Together, they piloted
their primary flock flota—a larger vessel designed for extended voyages. They had been on a trading and discovery expedition, across the
Grand Valley. They took a direct route over to visit with the Yellow
Flocks of the eastern side of Kondor now returning at a leisurely pace.

Jonus glanced around the impressive hive flota, admiring the spacious top deck. The large but conservative air ship boasted a communal
galley area, increased storage compartments for trade goods and many
other modifications.

"Our flock flota has served us well on this trip," Jonus remarked,
his voice carrying a note of pride. "The spare berthing nests have been
a blessing for our guests."

Marta nodded, her eyes scanning the intricate patterns and accents on the flota's trim, bowsprit, and mainsail. "The work of our
flock is truly remarkable. I'm still astonished every time I see these
iridescent silvery-white patterns on the gasbags. They add such undertones of elegance."

After a brief pause, her fingers running over the mesh of living air plants that formed the main frame and structure, she added, "This airship is truly a masterpiece." Inwardly, she felt a deep sense of pride, marveling at the many shades and hues layered over the pure white base. It really distinguished their vessel. "It's incredible how these new organic-based stains we're using highlight the structure and reduce air drag, making it not just beautiful but functional as well."

Jonus chuckled. "Remember when we first took off? We were worried about the prevailing winds. But our tacking maneuvers and the various new sails have really helped increase our speed."

"Yes," Marta agreed. "And staying at a lower altitude has given us a stunning view of the landscape below."

Jonus pointed over the side of the flota. "Now look where we are!" Clapping his hands in excitement and chirping with glee, he exclaimed, "Look at that tapestry of marshlands, meadows, and trees below, with endless species of flora and fauna. It's captivating. Smelling all the new floral notes has my mouth watering in anticipation of tasting new nectars. It's been such a wonderful journey, hasn't it?"

"It certainly has," Marta replied, though her voice carried a hint of distraction. She let out a series of soft, thoughtful, drawn-out tweets.

"Something on your mind? You have me concerned. Should I be?" Jonus asked, his melodic tone gentle but probing.

"It's nothing. I just had a troubling dream last night," Marta admitted, shaking her head slightly and ruffling her wings. "It's given me a vague sense of foreboding. But I don't want to spoil the excursion for anyone, even myself."

"Dreams can be unsettling," Jonus replied, emitting a soothing trill. "But we're here, in this beautiful place. Let's immerse ourselves in the journey and the company of our flock. Let's just go and explore!"

Swooping down through the branches, singing excitedly as they went, Marta and Jonus did just that. With obvious thrill and enjoyment. They investigated the bountiful plant life, discovering various rare blooms, fruits, and nuts, which they collected and deposited into their anchored floating baskas. The new and unusual aromas from all directions were overwhelming in the best possible way, thousands of scents layering like thick blankets over the marsh and mingling with the rich, diverse scents of the forest at its ecotone margins.

With their personal prime buzzies off exploring and playing in the nearby trees, Marta and Jonus relished the day's discoveries and the serene natural surroundings. This landmark area was simply known as the Meadow. This vast open space in the center of the great southern Marsh allowed more sunlight to enter the surrounding jungle, creating a perfect microclimate for some truly rare species of plants. A perfect Avian playground.

Joining them on this expedition were several esteemed members of their PureWhite Flock, including this excursion's appointed captain and close friend, Granger. He was accompanied by his wife, Kita, and his elder mother, Celia. Each of them played a pivotal role as Leaders and Communers in the PureWhite Flock, bringing a wealth of skills and knowledge to the mission.

Celia held the esteemed position of Head Brooder, responsible for the nurturing, education, and training of the flock's younglings. This role was integral to the community's continuity and well-being. Kita, meanwhile, was being meticulously groomed to succeed Celia as the Head Brooder, poised to assume this vital role upon Celia's eventual retirement.

Celia's mother, the venerable CeCe, was the oldest living Avian and former Head Brooder, revered for her decades of dedicated service. Now, at the advanced age of 188, she remained remarkably spry and agile. CeCe had made her permanent home in the Western Aerie, a sanctuary revered as one of the only two nurseries for all young Avians of Kondor—a place of respite and safety.

Additionally, General Eldred, the Head Protector of the flock, was present, accompanied by a squad of five top PureWhite Flock Protectors. Protectors served as escorts and defenders during the journey and of the entire flock when at home. While it was relatively peaceful in Kondor at this time in history, the presence of Protectors was a precautionary measure, especially against rare attacks from the local wildlife.

Ontan, the Head Worker from the PureWhite Flock, had also joined the expedition, along with two other scouts and five Workers, led by Bard. They were responsible for scouting ahead and gathering valuable information during their travels. Alongside them were twelve of the finest PureWhite Flock buzzies, renowned for their intelligence and strength, assisting in various tasks throughout the journey.

Marta had just landed on a branch not far from Jonus, smiling at the sight of him. Without thinking, she sent out a few low, loving chirping sounds. Jonus turned, smiled back, and responded with a trill of beautiful notes. Then he turned to admire a special blossom growing from the tree branch he was perched on.

"Look at this, Marta," Jonus exclaimed, pointing to the impressive blossom. "It's a rare one."

Marta redirected her attention to a plump, ripe morta fruit she had spotted, but just as she began to pluck the blood-red-black treat, she sensed something was wrong—danger was near. Listening to her intuition, she swiftly leaped to the other side of the tree, hearing something whoosh by her ear where her head had just been.

"Jonus, watch out!" Marta called out, her voice calm but filled with urgency, together with a sharp, warning trill.

Glancing below, she recognized the threat: a large hooded figure now aiming a blowgun at Jonus. Reacting with lightning speed, she drew a throwing talon from her waistband and expertly flicked it, piercing the assailant's throat before he could release another deadly stinger. Simultaneously, she warned Jonus with another shrill call.

Jonus, now fully alert to the threat, retreated to safety between two tree trunks. He received Marta's message, assuring him of her safety, so he remained under cover. Despite being a capable fighter himself, Jonus knew Marta's skill in battle was unmatched. A tiny grin briefly crossed his clenched lips.

"They don't know who they're attacking," he thought.

He knew any attacker—or even multiple opponents—stood no chance against Marta, especially an angry Marta protecting her loved ones. He remained still, listening for any sign of further danger. Aware that Othorians rarely traveled alone, he was prepared for the possibility of additional threats.

Utilizing a stealth bird call, he communicated with Marta, projecting his voice to create the impression it was coming from a different location, confusing any potential attackers. His brief call conveyed a question: *"What should I do?"*

Marta responded with her unique stealth song, seeming to emanate from all directions. She announced the presence of at least two more assailants to Jonus's southeast and another to his southwest. Her subsequent low grunt and the sound of something falling through the trees indicated the elimination of one of those threats.

"Okay, only two remain to your southeast. I've got this. Stay put," she reassured Jonus, providing him with a critical update. Marta also warned him that the attackers were Othorians, something he already suspected.

Jonus absorbed the information, momentarily stunned by the breach of the long-standing truce with the Othorians but rogue attacks still happen rarely. Setting aside the surprise, he remained vigilant, ready to spring into action, if necessary, his talon at the ready.

Marta remained an unflinching shadow, her every breath measured, her stealth a weapon as sharp as her blade. In the heart-pounding moments that followed, she was a coiled viper, waiting to strike. Then, without warning, the earth shook—a thunderous explosion ripped through the air. Smoke and debris clouded the forest. One of the attackers, bolted for the cover of the trees. But Marta, unfazed by the blast, let her instincts take command. Her movements were a deadly symphony, fluid, precise, and merciless.

With a calm yet determined demeanor, she effortlessly hurled another of her customized talons toward the fleeing figure. The deadly projectile struck with unerring accuracy, piercing the side of the attacker's throat. The brute dropped to the ground, lifeless—another chilling testament to Marta's lethal precision. Despite the chaos around her, Marta remained composed, her senses keen as she swiftly refocused on the task at hand.

Creating a false Othorian sound, which she directed from a nearby tree, Marta lured out the last assailant, swiftly dispatching him before he could pose more of a threat. Satisfied that the immediate area was secure, she called out to Jonus with a clear, decisive chirp.

"Jonus, all is clear. Come, we must move quickly. That blast we heard was from our expedition flotilla. They must be under attack too." Marta's voice betrayed her concern and urgency.

As Jonus joined her, they swiftly ascended into the air, flying toward the fleet of hive flotas anchored along the edge of a serpentine waterway branching off from the Meadow. They navigated through the dense foliage, ascending above the forest canopy to survey the chaotic scene at the mooring site. Smoke billowed from one side of the main hive flota, which now listed at an angle. The port side had also collided with the riverbank trees, causing several gasbags to deflate and detach, floating aimlessly above the distressed vessel.

Other smaller private flotas had released their moorings and hovered high above the scene, while a couple of others drifted away, seemingly unpiloted. Marta and Jonus spotted their personal buzzies, Speckle and Grayface, as they dive-bombed down to meet them, emitting a mix of deep concern and relief in their buzzing. The group briefly reunited before slipping back into the protected edge of the forest, their silent understanding prevailing.

"We need to secure the area," Marta said, her voice steady despite the urgency. She let out a series of sharp, commanding chirps.

Jonus nodded, responding with a low, reassuring trill. "Let's move quickly."

Marta efficiently communicated with the others as they glided through the foliage toward the damaged flota, ever watchful for any further potential threats. She heard General Eldred's familiar battle calls—a series of loud, resonant squawks—in the distance, signifying the loss of an Avian in the surprise attack.

Marta's expression shifted from tense determination to a frustrated sneer as she processed the details. Despite Eldred's limited mastery of stealth calls, his communication provided critical information: at least ten surviving Othorian attackers were retreating eastward, likely toward one of their cave entrances in the West Othor Mountain Range.

Upon hearing that the assailants had fled west, Marta's group burst out of the tall trees into the sunlight, heading directly to unite with Eldred.

"Speckle, find any stragglers," Marta instructed as she flew, her voice calm but firm, accompanied by a quick, sharp chirp. "Grayface, you too."

The buzzies buzzed in acknowledgment and took off, their wings a blur of motion. They fanned out in a search pattern, leveraging their extraordinary vision and keen sense of smell to detect any remaining Othorians and report back to their masters.

As they approached the clearly damaged hive flota, Marta called out to General Eldred and his Protectors with a loud, piercing whistle, signaling them to join her. High above, flock members were already collecting the escaped airships, helped by harnessed buzzies pulling them back together. They remained at a higher, safer altitude until the all-clear was given. The lack of strong winds worked in their favor, aiding the flotilla's reconvergence.

"General Eldred, report!" Marta called out as she landed on the main deck, her voice punctuated by a series of rapid, questioning calls.

"Two of our Protectors are down," Eldred replied, his voice grim, accompanied by a low, mournful warble. "Those miserable, cowardly Othorians have retreated. We're still securing the immediate area, but we believe it to be safe and clear." He sat down to catch his breath, leaning against the listing airship's railing and breathing deeply.

"Thank you for the update. Take a moment; we'll check the ship," Marta and Jonus replied, starting to assess the extent of the damage. Jonus immediately went over to the central nexus of the raft, where he connected with the biotic flota, eliciting a healing greenish-silvery throbbing glow that spread throughout the raft in waves. Marta first focused on the large, burned-out main gasbag of their beloved airship, and a tear rolled down her cheek as she stroked the remains of its leathery, paper-like skin. The explosion had clearly been caused by an Othorian missile of some sort, igniting the gasbag and causing it to detonate. It had been instantly killed in the explosion.

"This is… she was… Abby," Marta whispered, her voice filled with emotion, punctuated by a soft, sorrowful coo. "She… traveled with us for years."

Sensing her sorrow, Jonus glanced up from the nexus with a gentle, soothing tone. "We can heal the others," he said softly. "Abby's loss is heavy, but we must move forward."

Marta nodded, despite her sadness, choking back her emotions she started calming and encouraging the remaining gasbags to increase their output, assisting the flota in righting itself. Signs of regrowth and healing were already becoming visible, thanks to Jonus's strong healing energy.

"Good job, Jonus," Marta said, her voice filled with determination, interspersed with a series of encouraging chirps as she straightened out the loose rigging and lines. "Let's secure the flota and make sure there are no more surprises."

"General, gather the remaining Protectors once they have finished their security sweep," Marta ordered, her voice steady, marked by a firm, commanding warble. As Head Protector and Leader for the Pure-Whites, she commanded everyone's respect. She was seen as the head Leader even though all Leaders were equals, all happily looked to her for guidance. "I'll start gathering everyone else once we have control here so we can determine our next course of action."

Eldred saluted as he flew off, with a sharp, respectful chirp. "Understood, Marta. We're almost done."

Marta and Jonus stood on the deck, watching as the chaotic scene slowly began to calm. The urgency of activity around them was a stark contrast to the serenity they had enjoyed earlier in the day. A lingering smell of burning reminded them of their loss.

"We'll rebuild," Jonus said quietly, placing a comforting hand on Marta's shoulder and emitting a low, reassuring warble. "We always do."

Marta looked at him, her eyes fierce and filled with determination. "Yes, we will. And we'll make sure this never happens again. This aggression cannot go unanswered. Upon our return home, I will personally lead an envoy to have an audience with Thetan himself. I will have answers, and these raiders will be tried and punished for what they have done."

MARCUS AND LEURIN

5:
THE THREE GOLDEN OBELISKS

———◇◇◇◇———

Leurin of Thelon III, from batch 362, item XII46256-AI Core B7, dutifully maintained his watchful vigilance over the well-being of his esteemed Creator, Marcus Trumanian the Ninth of Niter 6. Leurin, an Enhanced Intellectual Being (EIB), acted as a partner, helper, and friend to Marcus. Together, they had spent 2,516 local orbital cycles stationed on the planet Kondor, fulfilling a critical scientific mission.

Their primary objective was to study the planet's psychically advanced race of winged beings known as the Avians. Their secondary task was to conceal the planet from long-range sensor scans through the deployment of a protective ring of satellites, shielding the planet's existence from external threats, especially the Takers.

Seated comfortably in the Commander's Lounge, Marcus inhaled deeply. Even though the aroma of the recycled air was carefully balanced and controlled to please him, it always smelled a little metallic and stale to Marcus. The plush chaise beneath him felt soft and soothing. He glanced at his reflection in one of the blank monitor screens. His body was getting older—his hair gray—but it was still in good shape, well-muscled and trim, always kept in optimal health. A good body could last for hundreds of years, and Marcus disliked the complete rebuild process; it took years and was essentially a drag. Yes, he could look fully rejuvenated, but there was something comforting about his current appearance. After all, he was mature even by Creator standards. His ancient race was virtually immortal and could choose the time of full ascension when ready. He was far from ready.

His thoughts drifted back to the mission at hand.

"Leurin," he began, his voice tinged with both weariness and resolve, "have you ever wondered if all our efforts to protect this world and stop the Takers will be enough?"

Leurin, who had focused his entire awareness into the avatar standing beside Marcus, adopted a posture of attention. Although he was the ship itself—the entire spaceship was, in fact, Leurin—Marcus preferred speaking face-to-face. So, whenever possible, Leurin used this physical embodiment to communicate with him. To Leurin, Marcus was not just his creator and master, but his dearest friend, and he always did everything in his power to bring him comfort and ease his burdens.

"I believe our efforts are substantial, Marcus," Leurin responded with a thoughtful look. "The Kondorians' psychic abilities are remarkable, and our satellite network is secure. However, I understand your concerns. The Takers are a relentless force."

The Creators, espousing extreme pacifism, had faced a relentless onslaught from these Takers, a highly aggressive race from a distant quadrant of the universe. They systematically ravaged inhabited planets within mere months, leaving behind desolate, lifeless landscapes. The Creators, having conquered death and illness long ago, chose to live in seclusion yet maintained interconnectedness with their kin throughout the galaxies. Despite their abilities, they refused to take any life, subsisting on synthesized nutrition and spending prolonged periods in deep meditation, reflection, and hibernation. At the same time, their ever-curious minds delved into intellectual pursuits and scientific enigmas.

Marcus nodded, his fingers absently tracing the intricate inlaid patterns on the chaise's armrest which was becoming a habit. "The Takers' aggression is unlike anything we've ever faced. And yet, to be true to our beliefs, we must remain steadfast in our pacifism. We must stop them without violence. It's an impossible scenario."

"Indeed," Leurin replied, his bio-mechanical eyes focusing on Marcus with a mix of empathy and calculated logic. "Our role is to observe and protect without interference, as dictated by the Prime Law. But your recent telepathic connections with the Kondorians have revealed much."

Marcus closed his eyes, recalling the vivid sensations from his mental encounters. "Thetan, the Othorian leader, is surprisingly lucid and open. At first, his mind was a fortress; now I can influence him subtly. And then there's Jurgus, from the Blue Flock … I can still taste the bitter and sour blue sappa he was savoring when I connected with him. It was overwhelming, Leurin. Like nothing I've ever experienced. I have never been exposed to such tactile, sensual, and emotional stimulation at once. How do these poor beings cope? I do not understand."

Leurin tilted his head slightly, analyzing Marcus's expressive and passionate response. "These psychic connections we can now create are not just scientific breakthroughs, Marcus. They are awakening something within you, feelings long suppressed."

Marcus sighed, the weight of these new sensations pressing down on him. "You're right. For so long, we've suppressed our emotions, our desires. We've subsisted on bland, synthesized nutrition, avoided any physical or emotional stimuli, and hidden away for so many millennia. But now … I feel alive again. Revitalized!"

Leurin's voice softened. "These sensory experiences are a double-edged sword. They give you strength, but they also make you vulnerable." He gazed deeply into Marcus's eyes, analyzing the blood flow and heartbeat, seeing into Marcus's being. "You are changing. There is no doubt."

Marcus met Leurin's gaze. "Vulnerability is a part of this three-dimensional reality, isn't it? Change is always present in this life, even if we take no action. Perhaps we've been too focused on avoiding it, on hiding from conflict. Maybe it's time we faced it, even if it means feeling pain and emotions."

Leurin considered this, his advanced intellect processing the implications. "You're suggesting a shift in our approach. But how do we reconcile this with our commitment to pacifism?"

"We must do our utmost to protect, without destroying, seems like an oxymoron," Marcus said firmly, slapping the armrest in frustration. "The telepathic connections with the Kondorians could be the key. If we can understand their psychic abilities, harness them, perhaps we can create a defense strong enough to deter the Takers without resorting to violence."

Leurin nodded, seeing the determination in Marcus's eyes. "It will be a delicate balance, but it is worth pursuing. The survival of not just us, but countless species, depends on it. These Takers are 'harvesting' entire galaxies as we speak."

Marcus stood up, the touch of the cool metal floor grounding him. Lately he preferred to have it cool, why not warm and cozy as usual he wasn't sure. He just felt like he wanted to feel something… different, something new. "Let's begin by deepening our telepathic connections; they call it communing here. I want to understand the Kondorians better—to feel more of what they feel, to know their strengths and weaknesses. And we must improve our satellite network, making it even more undetectable to these invaders."

"Agreed," Leurin replied, moving to his Creator's side. "I will start the enhancements immediately. And Marcus, remember to pace yourself. The intensity of these experiences can be overwhelming."

Marcus smiled, a rare warmth and excitement spreading through him, a flush coming to his cheeks. "Thank you, Leurin. I couldn't do this without you."

As Leurin left to initiate the upgrades, Marcus took a moment to reflect. The faint hum of the machinery around him in his Lounge, the extremely subtle vibrations under his feet, all felt more alive than ever before. He knew he was going in the right direction—he felt it deep in his core. He also knew it would challenge and shake that very core, but he was ready.

"Bring it on," he muttered, again staring deep into his reflection in a glass window, something he rarely ever did in the past.

In the days that followed, Marcus and Leurin worked tirelessly. They strengthened their satellite systems, sending out swarms of self-replicating manufacturing bots to construct and improve their hidden outposts and sensor arrays. They fortified their sentry positions on the moons and planets within the solar system, preparing for any eventuality.

Marcus spent hours in deep meditation, honing his telepathic abilities, upgrading his PSY boosting equipment and programming, then reaching out to the Kondorians. He established a stronger connection with Thetan, subtly influencing the Othorian leader's decisions. Thetan's mind was a complex labyrinth, filled with both malice and brilliance. Guiding him required finesse, but Marcus was determined.

One late evening, as the sky above Kondor turned a deep purple upon sunset, Marcus once again sat with Leurin in the Commander's Lounge. Fresh air from Kondor now circulated throughout the entire ship, bringing with it the scents of the planet—mountain breezes, flowers, and greenery from the plains. The stale, recycled air was replaced by the vibrant essence of the world they were protecting. One full exterior wall of the lounge was now a screen showing a real-time view of the Highland Plateau below them, its rugged beauty stretching out as far as the eye could see.

"Leurin, I've been thinking about my species' history—and our future," Marcus began, his voice contemplative. "We've always avoided conflict, but at what cost? Our society is in decay, our people are losing hope and purpose. As you know, most of my kind have moved on from this dimension and ascended, leaving this reality behind."

Leurin, ever perceptive, responded, "Change is difficult, but it's necessary for our survival and that of so many others. Your telepathic connections are revealing new possibilities—a new view of life and these extreme challenges that the Takers bring. I believe that we must embrace change and innovation with courage. I am proud of you. Of us."

Marcus, fidgeting slightly in his chair, looked deeply into Leurin's eyes, nodding and smiling. "Thank you, my friend. It means so much to me to have your support. We will continue to learn from the Kondorians, to understand their psychic abilities. And we will use that knowledge to create a superior defense that aligns with our values. The Takers will not destroy us, Leurin. We will find a way."

Leurin's gaze softened, a blend of loyalty and admiration in his mechanical eyes. "We will, Marcus. Together, we will ensure that our people, and the countless others who depend on us, survive this threat. And perhaps, in doing so, we'll discover a new path for ourselves—one that honors both our past and our future."

Marcus took a deep breath, feeling the cool, fresh air fill his lungs. The challenges ahead were immense, but for the first time in centuries, he felt truly alive. He felt purpose, not just in the mission, but in the journey itself. The Takers were formidable, but so were the Creators—and now, they had something new: hope.

As the stars began to twinkle in the twilight sky, Marcus and Leurin sat in companionable silence, their eyes fixed on the view of Kondor below. They were ready to face whatever came next, united in their resolve to protect this world and everything it stood for.

"Let's get to work," Marcus said quietly, a determined fire in his voice.

Leurin nodded, his mechanical form humming with energy. "As always, my friend. Let's begin."

And so, with renewed purpose and an unbreakable bond, they set their plans into motion, preparing for the battles that lay ahead—not just against the Takers, but against the darkness within themselves, and the long road to a new future.

GOFFRY
CALEB'S FLOCK MATE AND BEST FRIEND

6:

Caleb's Journey Continues

Caleb's arms were starting to feel the strain. The wind whipped through his feathers, bringing the scent of rain showers and the fresh, earthy aroma of the jungle below. They had descended to a lower altitude where the winds were less severe and were now using a smaller, heavier storm sail, having furled the mainsail.

He and Goffry worked together to steer the flota toward the entrance to Bison Pass. Goffry skillfully handled the rigging, catching the maximum thrust from the prevailing winds funneling through the gap in the mountain range. Caleb, manning the rudder, kept his eyes focused on the craggy entrance to the pass in the distance, its immense size a testament to the ancient forces that had shaped this natural shortcut eons ago. Trada, Pica, and the buzzy team were securely nestled into alcoves built into the ship's railings, ready to fly out if needed.

The vividly green forest canopy slipped quickly beneath them as the strong winds buffeted them along. This band of forest close to Bison Ridge was nourished by the remaining moisture carried by the relentless counterclockwise winds, condensing as it rose to meet the massive barrier. Despite the constant futility, Caleb tried once more to reach out to Irka in his mind. He felt her absence keenly. The strong bond between them persisted even in silence and across great distances. He knew she was alive, but he also knew she needed him.

Caleb shook himself out of his reverie, joining Goffry to secure the sheets before returning to his station, gripping the rudder as it bucked and jolted in his hands. The air currents were growing stronger quickly and could be unpredictable.

"Perhaps you shouldn't accompany me on this perilous journey. The risks are substantial, Goff," Caleb said with concern and a sad tweet. "I don't want you to get hurt just because I'm too anxious to take a safer route."

Goffry paused from his work coiling up some loose rope, his wings stretched out and flapping occasionally to keep his balance. His response was firm but supportive. "Caleb, I feel just as apprehensive as you. You know how much we all trust you. We all share your worries and want to ensure our flock's safety. I speak not only for myself but also for the whole flota. We're behind you, and the sooner we get home, the better."

"Thank you so much for your support," Caleb replied gratefully. "Let me commune with everyone before we reach the point of no return. I want everyone to feel free to choose, so I'll mentally connect to make sure of that."

Caleb tied down the rudder as they hit a calmer patch and gently touched the nearest gasbag, sending a mental message throughout the ship. The entire flota glowed in waves of iridescence, emanating feelings of love and solidarity. Receiving back positive feelings of overwhelming support and unity from all, Caleb felt ready to continue.

Using the brief pause in the winds, they did a final triple-check of the airship, tying down every loose item, and stowing away the last bits of cargo. shortening the storm sail further to be cautious.

As they plunged into the mouth of Bison Pass, the howling gale-force winds returned pushing them relentlessly forward as they navigated the treacherous gap, testing their skill to the limits. Caleb's heart raced as the smell of wet earth, rain, and ozone filled his nostrils—bad weather was ahead. His and Goffry's feathers were plastered against their bodies, offering some protection but taking a beating in the process.

Sure enough, an unexpected mountain storm descended upon them with fury. Hitting a whirlpool air current, the flota was flung into a chaotic spin, hurtling upward and around. It was pointless to try to control their direction, even though Caleb hung on tight to the rudder; the sail had been shredded by the strong gusts. Despite being secured tightly, gasbags were being ripped off the raft, and the buoyancy of the flota was quickly being lost.

"Hang on, everyone, we're going down!" Caleb cried into the wind, his voice straining against the roar. A series of sharp, urgent alarm calls followed in his own birdsong, and with all his strength, he sent a mental warning to the others through their shared connection.

The battered airship, listing completely to one side, was whipped around toward the unforgiving rocky side of the canyon. As an imminent crash loomed, Caleb's final urgent call to abandon ship echoed through the chaotic winds. A powerful gust tore him from his spot, snapping the ropes that anchored him. Rain and sleet pounded down relentlessly, blurring his vision. Drenched with icy cold rain and with no sense of direction, he struggled just to stay upright.

Miraculously, Trada, his loyal buzzy, appeared from within the maelstrom and latched onto Caleb's leg like a clamp. Time slipped away as Caleb's strength waned with each passing moment. The storm swallowed him up and spit him out. In a harrowing instant, he spotted a massive rock jutting in front of him. He attempted to veer out of the way, but then braced for the hard impact. Somehow, he managed to slow his descent slightly before colliding with the unyielding surface.

Bruised, broken, and completely drained, Caleb dragged himself and his attached, semi-comatose buzzy into a small fissure on the rock's surface, shielding them both from being swept away by the relentless assault of the tempest. A jarring blow from a sizable branch struck him from behind, sending Caleb into unconsciousness.

Warm sunrays on his wings and back stirred Caleb awake. He found himself wedged into a small grotto, secured by the large tree branch that had knocked him unconscious. Pushing the broken limb aside, he dragged himself out into the open to assess his condition and surroundings.

He realized he had crash-landed in a rugged mountainous area, no big surprise there. The storm had torn apart much of the vegetation in the area, the rocky landscape was littered with debris. Judging by the towering peaks on either side he thought it likely they were about two-thirds of the way down Bison Pass. They were on a small rocky ledge not far up from the bottom surrounded by patches of coarse grasses and sparse stands of succulent, cactus-like trees, their dwarfed, twisted forms sculpted by relentless winds. The bracingly cold, thin mountain air was filled with their resinous scent.

Caleb stood up slowly, uttering a few moaning chirps and grunts, propping himself on a large boulder. Taking a long, slow, deep breath, he shut his eyes to calm his racing nerves. The strong, fragrant whiffs of blooming mountain flowers, lichens, and mosses added a refreshing aroma, lifting his spirits.

After a moment, he sang out several loud White Flock locational cries, hoping to hear a response from Goffry or any other survivors. His heart sank when all he heard were his lonely calls echoing off the rocky cliffs, escorted back to him with the sounds of the wind and nature.

When he first awoke, Caleb had discovered Trada still wrapped around his leg limp from exhaustion, with torn wings and a broken leg. With loving care, he had pried off the injured buzzy and carefully stashed him on a soft nest of grass and moss, back where they had landed. Now, limping and wincing in pain, Caleb returned to tend to him. He used a green healing salve from his emergency stash attached to his waistband, massaging out the bends in his buzzy's kinked and torn wings, then binding Trada's injured leg in a stick brace. The gentle touches and sharp scent of the medicinal ointments roused the broken buzzy, who responded with gentle licks from his proboscis and contented purring.

Despite the searing pain from his own injuries and an overwhelming urge to sleep, Caleb turned his attention to his own wounds. He applied healing cream to his damaged right wing, which was missing several old flight feathers that had been torn out by the tempest. Much of his plumage was crumpled, damaged and in disarray. Old flight feathers never usually drop out until a new set was fully unfurled. This meant he was grounded for the time being.

Caleb settled back on the ledge against the protective rock face, contemplating their predicament while finishing his preening. The warm sun on his body brought some relief, and he managed to again get upright, stretching out his aching muscles.

He found a small pool of clean rainwater nearby and refreshed himself, bathing and washing away as much of the ground-in dirt as possible. He offered a much-needed drink to Trada, who lay almost comatose in the sun. Sharing a pollen cake and a drop of green healing sappa from his emergency stash, mixed with the fresh water, they both eased into a state of exhausted serenity. Nestling back into a makeshift nest of soft moss and lichens, they drifted into a deep exhausted slumber, their bodies and minds drained from the intense turmoil they had endured.

Sometime later, while Caleb and Trada were deep in their torpor, a scouting party of Othorians emerged from the encroaching gloom. They skillfully encircled the unsuspecting pair, swiftly and efficiently subduing them. The Othorians had spotted them earlier in the day and had been meticulously tracking their movements. Now, bound and stripped of their freedom, Caleb and Trada found themselves being led to a nearby cave, shrouded in uncertainty.

Inside the cavern, Caleb listened intently to the Othorians' animated exchange in their clicking and hissing language. Although not completely fluent, he understood much of it, though some of the ultrasonic parts of their dialogue were beyond his hearing range. Caleb's keen sense of smell also detected the Othorian pheromones, sharp and acidic at times, sickly sweet at others, indicating their emotions and states of mind.

Six large dark figures dominated the scene in the cave, hunkered around a small metal brazier filled with glowing coals, engaged in heated discourse. The largest of the group, addressed as Major Jubba, commanded authority.

"We've captured the Avian, Major Jubba," one of the scouts reported, his voice edged with pride.

"Excellent," Jubba replied, his eyes narrowing as he noticed Caleb stirring. "But Bertran's methods are too extreme. We need to find a peaceful resolution with the Avians." Standing tall, his dark black skin glistening in the glow, he peered intently at each of his subordinates.

A dissenter within the group spoke up, frustration evident in his voice. "Peace? You're going against Bertran and Thetan's orders! We need to crush these bird people, not coddle them!"

Major Jubba's eyes flashed with anger, his cold steely stare causing the dissenter to squirm in discomfort. "Are you seriously advocating for more violence, Pitre? We've already lost too many." He paused, allowing the young rebel a chance to back down.

"I am," Pitre hissed, his tone defiant as he looked around for support. Pride got the best of him, and he stood his ground. "Our *leaders* are right. Violence is the only way to ensure our dominance on Kondor."

Jubba's response was swift and brutal. He approached Pitre slowly, and in a split second, slashed his dagger across the dissenter's throat before Pitre could react, silencing him instantly. The still-convulsing body hit the ground with a thud, and Jubba kicked it aside with a grunt.

"Anyone else have issues?" Jubba's icy gaze fixed on his subordinates, who quickly submitted, bowing their heads in compliance. The rest of his squad, loyal to Jubba, agreed with his political views for the most part.

Caleb observed the power play, noting the Major's authoritative stance as he reestablished control over the group. The sharp, sour scent of Othorian fear hormones filled the air, mingled with the earthy odor of submission.

"I am open to any thoughts or reservations," Jubba asserted, "but I am the leader here. I say we need to find a way to coexist in peace with the Avians. I will speak with our... guests and make them more comfortable."

As Jubba approached the captives, Caleb feigned unconsciousness while Trada lay motionless at his side. "I know you're awake, my friend," Jubba said, his voice surprisingly gentle as he spoke in Caleb's mother tongue, albeit with a heavy accent. "Do not fret. I mean you no harm. We have much to discuss."

"May I ask about your identity and purpose here?" Jubba inquired, casting a probing gaze in Caleb's direction. "Few Avians dare to traverse this perilous route through the Pass, which suggests you must be in a rush to reach a specific destination."

With a cautious hand, Jubba freed Caleb from his restraints, helping him sit upright. "Please hold back your companion," Jubba requested, motioning toward Trada. "Even though he is severely wounded, I know your partner would attack us at the first opportunity."

Caleb signaled his understanding in the Othorian tongue, prompting Jubba to raise an eyebrow in curiosity. Together, they released Trada, who moved closer to Caleb's side, maintaining a vigilant stance but remaining compliant.

"Good," Jubba acknowledged. "Now, we must discuss what is happening in Kondor. My scouting party and I, along with the remaining members of my squad, vehemently oppose the recent turn of events. Our leader, Thetan, and his son, the cruel Prince Bertran, have garnered much support among our people, but know that the silent majority longs for continued peace between our communities." Jubba remained standing, his frustration evident as he kicked at the stone floor and took a breath. Caleb remained silent, allowing him to speak his mind.

"It appears that recent raids on your sacred Great Trees have resulted in many captives being taken," Jubba continued. As Caleb's mouth opened to respond, the Othorian cut him off with a raised hand. "What I know is that most of your people seem to be safe for now, though they remain in confinement. They are all being taken north, first to Bison Hive, then toward the Highland Plateau below Othor's Head. We remain uncertain of the reason behind this."

Caleb, still seated, began to rise. Jubba offered his hand, and Caleb gratefully accepted, using the Major's support to stand. Trada had fallen back into a light snooze, briefly opening his eyes to ensure his master was safe.

"So may I ask, what brings you here?" Caleb inquired, leaning against the cold rock to soothe his aching body. "Why are you so far from all the activity?"

Jubba leaned forward slightly, his gaze focused and intense as he freely recounted their recent activities. "We were sent on a 'scouting' mission here in Bison Pass to man one of the long-abandoned guard posts," he began, his voice carrying a trace of reluctance. "But I believe we were dispatched to this remote location due to our, shall we say, 'noncompliance' with Thetan's wishes."

He approached Caleb and offered his arm for support. "Come, let's move closer to the heat. It will do you good. I assure you that you are safe and free to leave at any time. I would like to consider you my ally and friend."

His words hung in the air, laden with unspoken implications. It was evident that Jubba and his companions had become ensnared in a complex web of political maneuvering and dissent within their community.

Caleb accepted the offered arm, stumbling slightly to buy himself a moment. "Thank you, Major Jubba. Your kindness is much appreciated, and that alone makes me your humble friend. I believe we share similar ideals. I hope we can be allies as well."

Trada, now fully awake, stumbled along with them as they approached the circle of now-smiling and welcoming Othorians. After sharing some food and clean water in silence as was the custom, they all relaxed, absorbing the welcoming warmth of the glowing brazier. The smoke was comforting and light, with a metallic earthy taste lingering at the back of the throat.

With a full belly and Trada purring at his feet, Caleb recounted the truth about his mission. His worry about Irka was evident in the deep concern etched on his face as he recounted his story.

After the meal, most of the Othorians had set out on a scouting mission, they moved about well at night, often sleeping through the day to avoid the sun. Jubba stayed behind with Caleb, continuing his story, his tone measured yet brimming with underlying frustration. He angrily poked at the coals with a wooden branch, sending sparks up into the air.

"Thetan and his son, Bertran, have been coercing many of our kind to align with their aggressive stance toward your people," Jubba explained, his brows furrowed and his jaw set with determination. "But there are those of us—rebels—who believe in preserving the peace that has long existed between our races."

Jubba's expression grew more intense as he recounted the challenges they faced. "We have been discreetly gathering information and silently resisting Thetan's mandates. It's a delicate dance, requiring careful balancing to avoid detection by his loyalists, like that one," he nodded in the direction of the dead Othorian, still lying in the cave, pushed against the wall. His words were tinged with caution.

As Caleb absorbed all this information, a sense of despair settled over him as he pieced together the potential fate of PuritaWhite and their flock, his concerns gravitating toward the well-being of Irka. Together, he and Jubba engaged in a profound conversation that spanned long into the night, fostering a bond of camaraderie and shared purpose.

GOFFRY
AI REPLICANT IMAGE

7:
Goffry's Return

Goffry had clung desperately to the flota amid the raging tempest, helpless as he witnessed Caleb's wrenching separation from the airship and the dramatic loss of the gasbags tethered to the craft. The storm pummeled them relentlessly, causing the flota to quickly lose altitude, careening wildly before eventually crashing onto the rocky ground with a series of sickening crunches. By some stroke of fortune, Goffry was spared any direct impact, though he was severely bruised and utterly depleted. He sought shelter within the wreckage to ride out the remnants of the relentless storm. As the tumult subsided to a lull, Goffry succumbed to a semiconscious state, left with no other recourse but to wait out the storm's final throes.

Goffry jolted awake, momentarily disoriented, before the searing pain coursing through his body brought memories of the recent catastrophe rushing back. Groaning, he hauled himself out of the wreckage, finding support against a nearby rock as he surveyed the surroundings bathed in the soft, early light of dawn. Flexing his limbs, he tentatively fluttered his wings, wincing as he felt the strain on his muscles and noticed the absence of many of his flight feathers.

"At least nothing's broken," he muttered through clenched teeth, his words punctuated by a sad, hurt birdsong.

Turning his attention to the damaged flota, Goffry marveled at its surprising resilience. The airship had sustained many areas of damage, but it remained remarkably intact. Some of the meticulously carved deadwood parts lay broken. The mainmast, snapped in two but still secured by ropes and vines, rested alongside the battered airship. Tattered sails clung to its damaged form, some flapping in the constant breeze. The smaller storm mast, listing and askew, stood as a testament to the violent ordeal. Miraculously, the flota had come to a halt jammed against a small cliff, partially immersed in a pond—a stroke of fortune that lifted Goffry's spirits, considering the flota's dire need for water to heal properly.

Approaching the pond, Goffry took a deep drink of the clear water, observing how the flota had already extended roots into its life-sustaining depths, drawing much-needed nourishment and moisture. The living plants that composed the airship possessed advanced sentience, automatically initiating their healing process when injured. With a Communer's presence, growth could be significantly accelerated and directed to the most critical areas.

Hobbling back onto the airship with strained effort, Goffry made his way to the nexus of the craft. Although not a Communer himself, he possessed the ability to establish a basic connection with the flota's components, conveying rudimentary emotions and thoughts. Seated at the nexus, he closed his eyes, initiating a link. The plants' collective distress intertwined with his own, but as one, they breathed in unison, finding solace in their shared effort to mend their wounds. Goffry transmitted waves of reassurance and love, urging the plants to expedite their recovery.

As the groaning and creaking of the plants intensified, they began reassembling and melding into a more cohesive structure. After terminating the connection, Goffry set to work, gathering the discarded remnants of broken branches, leaves, and vines and transporting them to the ship's flexible composting tank. The organic material would be reabsorbed, nourishing the airship. Nutrient tubules emanating from this tank spread throughout the flota, sustaining all living components on the vessel. Goffry supplemented the process by infusing the nutrient mix with a few drops of green and red sappa as well as various herbs, hastening the ship's restoration.

Leaving the airship behind, Goffry ascended the mountainside, hoping for a vantage point to locate the missing pack of buzzies or catch a glimpse of Caleb's whereabouts. He called out distress bird squawks as he went, hoping for a response. Casting a glance back at the flota, he saw the vessel slowly begin righting itself, gradually on the path to recovery. Four deflated gasbags remained attached; their paper sack bodies partially visible in the safety nooks built into the bulkheads of the flota. Two had emerged and started to fill with gas; in time, the others would heal, though the limited number made an airborne ascent impossible.

As Goffry climbed higher, the sun loomed high in the sky, casting a radiant midday glow. Scouring the nearby cliffs and mountains, constantly calling out in song and loud whistles, his gaze searched fruitlessly for signs of life. Suddenly, a faint buzzing sound from behind a mound of rocks caught his attention. A surge of hope ignited within Goffry as he recognized the familiar hum of his prime buzzy, Pica, his faithful companion and Trada's mate.

Ignoring his own pain, Goffry hopped and clumsily glided toward the source, discovering Pica trapped within a rock crevice. Freeing her, he scooped Pica into his arms with joyful delight. Pica, trembling and purring with excitement and relief, licked him affectionately. A tear of joy welled in Goffry's eye as he cradled her carefully, smelling her familiar honey-like scent. Tenderly stroking her belly and bristles, he reassured her, their thoughts merging in silent understanding. Despite her wounds, Pica's wings remained intact, and with her master's encouragement, she proudly demonstrated her ability to fly, exuding a brief surge of jubilation before retreating back into Goffry's protective embrace.

Together, they made their way back to the flota, where Goffry retrieved some food, ointment, and sappa that had survived the crash. The two companions shared a modest but nourishing meal. After preening themselves with healing salves, they watched the sunset as the day wound to a close. Their bellies sated, they nestled together in the relative safety of Goffry's nest chamber aboard the flota, drifting off to much-needed sleep.

The following day broke with a warm, golden radiance enveloping the flota. Mist rose from the dew-laden rocks and plants in the small rocky meadow where they had fallen from the sky. The creaking and cracking of the mending raft, responding to the sunlight with a burst of growth, roused Goffry from his late slumber. He found Pica already up and about, fluttering with newfound strength and basking in the invigorating morning sun. Goffry joined her, and the two indulged in a brief mind commune as he stroked her head bristles. Pica conveyed her eagerness to embark on a scouting mission. Her agility in the air far surpassed Goffry's grounded state, making her the perfect candidate to conduct a rapid aerial search.

After a brief plea from Goffry not to overexert herself, Pica launched into the sky, ascending in widening circles, her sharp eyes scanning the terrain for any signs of life or survivors. Goffry watched her until she was out of sight, then turned his attention back to his chores.

Throughout the day, Goffry divided his time between clearing debris, resting, and tending to his injuries with generous applications of healing ointments and sips of restorative green sappa. The reunion with Pica had infused him with renewed hope and vitality, spurring him to organize the flota and restore it to a semblance of order. He managed to straighten the smaller, listing storm sail mast and untangle the main mast from snarled rigging. The tall mainmast was broken and couldn't be repaired, but he salvaged sailcloth and rope.

Attending to the remaining gasbags, Goffry applied healing salve to their papery skins, observing as they slowly reinflated, their buoyant, propeller-like tails whirling with newfound energy and determination. Though their complete recovery would take time, Goffry remained optimistic, trusting in the healing capabilities of these gentle floating plants.

As the day drew to a close, a trace of worry crept into Goffry's thoughts—Pica had yet to return. But just as the sun began its descent, a welcome sight greeted him from a distance. Pica led the charge, flanked by three more members of the original buzzy pack, towing along four partially inflated gasbags. Despite their diminished size, the gasbags harmoniously propelled the group forward, guided by the coordinated efforts of Pica and her companions. Overwhelmed with joy at the sight, Goffry eagerly awaited their arrival, brimming with anticipation.

With buzzing excitement, Pica descended, immediately engaging in a mind communion with Goffry as soon as she was in range. She had not only located the lost buzzies but had also spotted Caleb farther south, accompanied by two Othorians near the mouth of a large cave. Her reluctance to risk a confrontation prompted her to return swiftly. After finding and rallying the other buzzies, they managed to locate the four scattered gasbags, regrouping and steering them back to the flota.

Exhausted from the day's efforts, Pica and the other buzzies needed sustenance and rest. With darkness fast approaching, Goffry decided to postpone his reunion with Caleb until the following day, hoping the presence of the Othorians wouldn't pose any immediate threats. Unaware of the recent Othorian assaults, Goffry remained reassured by the longstanding peace between their peoples. Pica, however, relayed her observations, expressing concern for Caleb's bedraggled wings. Even from a distance, she could tell he wouldn't be able to get airborne.

The following morning, dense mist enveloped the Pass, restricting visibility to only a few feet ahead. For Goffry, this presented an ideal opportunity to conduct a discreet reconnaissance of Caleb's location, gauging whether it was safe to make contact. Pica accompanied him, having already shared the precise location and directions through their communion. Caleb's whereabouts were approximately half a day's journey across rugged terrain. From Goffry's current position, it was clear he would need to cover most of the distance on foot, with only a few brief glides.

Testing his wings, Goffry had to accept the reality that he still couldn't rely on them for flight. Being molting season for all Avians, his new flight feathers were just beginning to emerge, currently in the form of unfurled long pinions. With additional healing salve and extra preening, they would soon develop into the robust main flight feathers required for full flight control. The storm had essentially plucked his flight feathers almost bare.

Braving the morning chill, Goffry embarked on his arduous trek, scaling the terrain with effort and lots of perseverance. Pica flew ahead to guide and scout the way until they finally reached an elevated point that afforded a clear view of the entrance to the Othorian outpost cave. As the sun gradually penetrated the dissipating mist, Goffry, perceiving no immediate signs of life, cautiously crept closer, finding cover behind a sizable boulder that offered an improved vantage point.

In the next moment, he spotted Caleb, accompanied by a towering dark Othorian, striding onto the stone platform at the cave's entrance. Goffry emitted a faint, distinctive White Flock identifying warble, a signal he knew Caleb would recognize. Instantly, Caleb's face brightened, and he reciprocated the call with a beaming smile, indicating that all was well and it was safe to approach.

"Come here, Goffry, where are you?" Caleb sang out in a reassuring melodic call, waving in his direction. Pica, closely watching and listening, beat Goffry to the reunion. With a joyous buzz, she flew into

Caleb's embrace, lavishing his face with eager licks. Overcoming his pain in a moment of jubilation, Goffry hopped and fluttered, uttering a couple of choice words through the discomfort but ultimately joining Caleb in a heartfelt embrace at the cave entrance. Their reunion was a mix of elation and relief.

Jubba, observing from a distance, wore a small smile as he stepped back, allowing the bird folk and their faithful companions to reconnect. Emerging from the cave behind him, Trada took flight, albeit somewhat unsteadily, hastening to join his mate, Pica. The two buzzies tumbled together on the ground, their buzzing and purring a testament to their shared relief and love. Trada briefly soared into Goffry's awaiting arms, eager to express his joy at their reunion.

"Thank Mother Kondor that you and Trada are safe, Caleb. I was losing hope, thinking I had lost you," Goffry exclaimed with an excited little tune of chirps, his eyes welling with tears. Overwhelmed with emotion, Caleb struggled to articulate his feelings, gulping back his own tears as he embraced Goffry again. Stepping back, he held Goff's head in his hands. "I feel the same. What a relief," he managed, eyeing his friend's disheveled appearance.

"You look like me. Just a tad rough." Caleb chortled, a wry remark about their shared bedraggled state. They both broke into laughter and a short duet of notes they often sang together.

At this juncture, Jubba withdrew back into the cave, followed by the other Othorians who had emerged, their drawn daggers reflecting their concern about the commotion. This provided the two Avians and their buzzies a moment of respite to renew their bonds. Settling onto the balcony, Caleb and Goffry shared their respective tales of survival, with Caleb visibly relieved upon learning that the flota was in close proximity, salvageable, and on the road to recovery.

After sharing their stories, Caleb and Goffry decided to send Trada and Pica back to the flota to rejoin the pack of buzzies, allowing them to heal and recuperate. Despite Trada's struggle to fly in his injured state, with Pica's support, he managed to convey reassurance to Caleb about his ability to undertake the journey. Caleb and Goffry planned to join them soon after a discussion with the Othorians to gather any additional information they could about the unfolding events.

Caleb strode back into the cave with Goffry, calling out to Jubba and his squad of rebels. "Let's talk, my comrades," he began, his voice now resonating with purpose. "It seems we are in agreement, and hopefully, we can all forge ahead with our alliance to put an end to this madness affecting both of our people." With determination in his step, Caleb joined the circle of his new allies huddled around a small fire.

The brazier crackled in the cave; some pieces of dry, scavenged aromatic wood had been added to the crake coals. The cavern filled with a light, sweetly scented resinous smoke. The small flames cast flickering shadows on the rough-hewn walls as Caleb, Goffry, Jubba, and his allies strategized their plans to counter Thetan's aggressive advances.

"We must journey back to my Mother Tree, PuritaWhite, to assess the situation and reunite with our flock," Caleb said, his words infused with urgency. He outlined his intentions to help rally all the Avian flocks, fostering a unified response that would protect their interests.

Jubba nodded, acknowledging the weight of Caleb's responsibilities. Retrieving a pouch from his waistband, he produced red pigment and proceeded to mark each of their faces, signifying their collective rebellion against Thetan's tyrannical rule.

"Let it be known that this red mark shall be our symbol of resistance," Jubba declared, emphasizing their united front against the oppressive forces. "Trust no one else," he added, unrolling a detailed map showcasing the location of Westmount Marketplace, the southernmost Othorian hive on the western side of the Grand Valley, in close proximity to PuritaWhite. "A resistance movement is growing there, led by

Portia, an ally devoted to the cause. Portia is a trusted friend; she can relay any messages you need to send to me quickly and secretly."

"Your information is invaluable to us, Jubba. We know of this place. When we get home, we shall join the Othorian rebellion; doing everything we can to rescue any Avian captives will be our priority. Justice will come second."

Their farewell carried an air of solemnity, yet an unspoken sense of camaraderie and mutual support underpinned it. "May the Holy Odin bind us together and keep you safe. We shall cross paths again," Jubba proclaimed, his words echoing through the cavern with resolute fervor. With a final exchange of well-wishes, Caleb and Goffry set out on their journey back to the flota.

WESTMOUNT
MARKETPLACE

8:
Marta and Jonus Return Home

———◇◇◇———

Marta and Jonus swiftly reorganized their battered flota contingent, coordinating seamlessly with General Eldred, Granger, and the rest of their flotilla. The Othorians, reeling from their failed raid, had retreated hastily, granting the Avians a brief but much-needed respite. Determined to uncover the Othorians' next move and motive, Marta dispatched a pair of covert scouts to discreetly trail the fleeing enemy.

Though victorious, the Avians were not without loss. They mourned the deaths of two beloved flock members taken by the surprise attack. In contrast, they confirmed seven Othorian casualties, suspecting many more were wounded. Thanks to the valiant efforts of the Protectors, General Eldred, Marta, and Jonus, the main White Flock flota suffered only minor damages during the ambush, save for the loss of a cherished gasbag.

Jonus, demonstrating his adept communing skills, promptly facilitated the mending of the flota's structure, readying it for flight. Though full recovery would take time, the urgency to return to the Purita White Mother Tree took precedence. Marta's earlier premonition, which had cast a shadow over her thoughts, had proven disturbingly accurate. Now, she could sense even greater troubles on the horizon.

Within a few hours, the flotillas reconnected, forming a streamlined formation. Rising higher into the sky, they sought swifter air currents and harnessed the collective power of the buzzy pack, led by Speckle and Grayface. The buzzies, once scattered and enjoying a brief respite in the Meadow and surrounding jungle before the surprise attack, now felt a pang of guilt for missing much of the battle. Eager to redeem themselves, they pulled on their harnesses with renewed vigor, quickly gaining speed.

As the flotilla reached optimal altitude, the mainsails were unfurled, and the Avians surged forward, swiftly heading back home. The wind was at their backs, and though their hearts were heavy, their resolve was unshakable. The journey home had begun, and with it, the hope of re-uniting with their flock and confronting the challenges that lay ahead.

Marta and Jonus quickly reorganized their battered flota contingent, coordinating with General Eldred, Granger, and the rest of their flotilla. The raiders had retreated hastily after their failed attack, leaving the Avians with a brief but crucial respite. Determined to uncover the Othorians' next move and their motives, Marta dispatched a pair of covert scouts to discreetly trail the fleeing enemy.

Though the Avians had emerged victorious, their triumph was tinged with sorrow as they mourned the loss of two beloved flock members. In contrast, they confirmed seven enemy fatalities and suspected many others were wounded. Thanks to the valiant efforts of the Protectors, General Eldred, Marta, and Jonus, the main White Flock flota sustained only minor damage during the ambush, except for the loss of a cherished gasbag.

Jonus, demonstrating his adeptness in communing, promptly began mending the flota's structure, readying it for flight. Although full recovery would take time, the urgency to return to the PuritaWhite Mother Tree took precedence. Marta's earlier premonition, which had weighed heavily on her mind, had proven disturbingly accurate. Now, she could sense even greater troubles on the horizon.

Within a few hours, the flotillas reconnected, forming a streamlined formation. Rising higher into the sky, they sought swifter air currents and harnessed the collective power of the buzzy pack, led by Speckle and Grayface. The buzzies, once scattered and enjoying a brief respite in the Meadow and surrounding jungle before the surprise attack, now felt a pang of guilt for missing much of the battle. Eager to redeem themselves, they pulled on their harnesses with renewed vigor, quickly gaining speed.

As the flotilla reached optimal altitude, the mainsails were unfurled, and they surged forward, swiftly heading back home. Their journey lasted two relentless days and a night. As they neared their beloved home territory, Marta, Jonus, General Eldred, and the remaining Protectors flew ahead of the flotilla, filled with concern for the flock's well-being. As they approached, their ability to commune intensified, proximity making it easier to connect. Jonus, the foremost Communer, discerned escalating waves of distress from home. Flying in formation, Marta led the way with Jonus by her side, the others straining to keep up.

Marta, a striking figure with her pure white plumage and an aura of quiet strength, glanced at Jonus as they flew. It felt exhilarating flying full tilt, lungs burning and feathers slicing the air. She eyed Jonus with pride. His feathers, equally pristine, were complemented by his calm and wise demeanor. Jonus's flight feathers bore a tantalizing delicate metallic tinge, a trait passed down to his son, Caleb.

They flew high and fast, but in perfect unison, so synchronized that Marta positioned just beneath Jonus, her head inches from his.

"Jonus, I can't shake this feeling of dread," Marta sang out, her voice tinged with worry, cutting through the wind with a high pitch. "I sense something terribly wrong. What do you hear?"

Jonus closed his eyes briefly, his brow furrowing as he concentrated. "The distress signals are stronger now, Marta. Our flock is in turmoil. I can feel fear and confusion."

Marta sighed, her wings twitching with anxiety but keeping perfect time. "I hope Caleb is safe. He's so far away on his exploration voyage with Goffry. We must get a message to him somehow. Perhaps I'll summon a swift to carry a message when we get home."

Jonus touched wings with Marta quickly yet reassuringly. "Caleb is strong, like you. I worry more about Irka without any of us to protect her. I hope she is somehow okay. We must stay focused and reach PuritaWhite as quickly as possible."

General Eldred, flying beside them, glanced over. His robust yet thin frame and commanding presence were evident even in flight. "We'll get through this," he sang out, vocalizing notes of encouragement. "The Protectors are ready. We'll do whatever it takes to ensure the safety of the flock and our home."

Marta nodded, drawing strength from their resolve. "Thank you, General. Your presence here is a great comfort."

As they flew on, the landscape below them changed, becoming more familiar—and more concerning. During a brief, much-needed rest, Marta and Jonus perched together on a sturdy branch of a high tree, overlooking their homeland. The sight of their beloved PuritaWhite far in the distance filled them with a mixture of hope and dread.

"Remember when Caleb was just a fledgling, always so curious and eager to explore?" Marta reminisced, a sad smile touching her lips. "He would have flown circles around us by now, trying to get a better view."

Jonus chuckled softly, though his eyes were clouded with worry. "Yes, and he'd be asking a thousand questions. He has always been a seeker of knowledge, wanting to understand everything around him. It's what makes him such a talented all-around Avian. His communion skills are already astonishing for his age—I feel he is truly gifted."

Marta's eyes brightened with pride but shimmered with unshed tears. "I just want Irka and Caleb to be safe, Jonus."

Jonus encircled Marta with his arms and wings, cooing softly into her face. "We will find them both. We will protect our flock. Together, we are stronger than any threat."

They remained together in a loving embrace, calmed by the quiet peace around them, beguiled for a moment by the scents of night blooming plants. Their acute senses could discern thousands of flower aromas, it was intoxicating to them and they gave into it.

Jonus's body involuntarily trembled and ruffled. He groaned; eyes widened as he picked up a particularly strong mental signal. "I see it now, a clear vision. The Othorians are responsible for the attack on PuritaWhite, these attacks were no raiding forays. They have broken our peace accord."

Marta's heart sank. "We need to hurry. If they have turned against us, the flock will be in grave danger."

With renewed determination, despite aching wings and muscles, they took to the skies once more, their hearts united in their mission. As they approached their home, the signals from the flock became clearer, and the full extent of the Othorian betrayal came into focus.

The first close-up sight of their beloved PuritaWhite Mother Tree— burnt and broken—was a heart-wrenching shock. Her lost blossoms and dropped leaves lay like a thick blanket around her scorched trunk. Her branches and trunk, now skeletal, reached for the sky, devoid of greenery. They flew the last distance at top speed, the stench of burning wood and smoke growing stronger as they neared. Several flock members flew out to greet them, serenading them with a mournful ballad detailing the siege of the Mother Tree and the abduction of their kin, including Irka, Caleb's beloved.

Upon reaching the main landing place on the massive tree, Marta clutched Jonus and sobbed deeply into her mate's shoulder, tears streaming from his eyes as well. They embraced closely for some time, breathing deeply from their extreme exertions, despite the commotion from the entire flock around them, they had to take a moment.

Wiping the tears from her eyes, Marta stepped back, shaking out her plumage. "No time for this now. We will find Irka and bring her back. If anyone has so much as bent one of her feathers, so help me, Mother Kondor, they will regret it."

"They will certainly be sorry they tangled with our family, our flock." Jonus let out a loud whistling chirp with his words. "Let's get to it, my love."

As the flock's most skilled Communer, he descended to PuritaWhite's nexus to foster healing, reach out to the other Great Trees in the Grand Valley for information, and focus healing energy where it was most needed.

The synchronized assaults on the flotilla and Mother Tree more than hinted at a hidden agenda. The Othorians' unusual aggression, despite the long-standing peace accord after the Kondorian War, perplexed Marta. Typically, most incidents were isolated raids aimed at procuring food and the precious sappa elixirs exclusive to the birdpeople. Such unsanctioned attacks weren't endorsed by Othorian leaders like the current leader, Thetan, who, at least until now, had been known as an advocate of peace.

While Jonus communed with PuritaWhite, Marta called a flock meeting with General Eldred and the community's remaining Protectors and Workers. They convened at the central meeting place for the flock. A light haze of smoke still hung in the air; without the usual leaf canopy overhead, the area was unusually bright. Tiers of flat seat branches surrounded a central giant bracket fungi floor, with a leather-like softness, now littered with ash and char.

Scouts had reported that the beaten Othorian raiding party that attacked Marta and Jonus at the Meadow had retreated to a hive cave in the Western Othor Mountain Range. From a safe distance, they witnessed the returning raiding party's leader being ruthlessly executed by their superiors while the rest faced severe punishment for their failed attempt. There was no sign of the other Othorians who had attacked their Mother Tree, nor of the captive Avians who had been taken by them.

Marta stood in the center of the floor, other Leaders around her. "My cherished flock," All eyes were riveted on her, no one making a sound. Lifting her head and scanning the audience, she continued, a solemn weight in her voice, "The urgency of our situation demands that we gather intelligence about the closest Othorian hive, that being as you all know Westmount Marketplace. We must discern the Othorian intentions, capabilities, internal dynamics, and vulnerabilities. Most importantly, we need answers about their newfound penchant for abductions. It is paramount that we locate and liberate our ensnared kin posthaste. Time is of the essence, lest further harm befall them."

General Eldred, his demeanor assertive and intent, interjected, "Passivity is a luxury we can ill afford. The Othorians have unabashedly signaled their malevolent intent. It's inevitable that they will redouble their efforts. We must preemptively retaliate."

As they strategized, Jonus joined them, his countenance wearied, bearing an almost ghostly pallor. His visage alone foreboded grim tidings. He strode to the center of the meeting area, eying the flock members seated around him. Marta moved over to greet him, holding his hand in support.

Drawing a deep breath, he began with a small birdsong, an ode to heroes of the past. It took only moments, but everyone stood and joined in, creating a flock chorus that bolstered everyone's lagging spirits. "Upon communing with our beloved Mother Tree and expediting her recuperation, I sought the counsel of the other Great Trees spread across Kondor. The trauma inflicted upon Purita was palpable, yet she rendered her cooperation unstintingly. She will survive the attack and regrow but for the moment remains in a state of dormancy, needed to regain her strength." Jonus's voice broke, he paused, taking several breaths. With the good news that their Mother Tree was okay and would recover the audience became more excited, twitters and musical sighs of relief filled the air.

Jonus looked toward Marta for reassurance; her slight nod and small smile did their work and calmed his soul. He coughed loudly, silencing the crowd. "The revelations are heart-wrenching. The Othorians have laid siege to multiple Great Trees throughout the Grand Valley. Our brethren in the northeastern sector, the Yellow Flock, bore the brunt of the attacks on the east. Numerous of their Avian brethren have been spirited away, while others met a tragic end in these insidious surprise assaults."

He paused again; fatigue evident in his eyes. "Piecing together the details remains challenging. Many of the Great Trees have been damaged and are still in various degrees of shock, however a pattern emerges. An initial assault on the Great Tree serves as a diversion, followed by targeted onslaughts. Certain Avians, for reasons yet unknown, are singled out for abduction, while others face merciless aggression."

Jonus's voice imbued with the raw emotion he'd absorbed from his communion with Purita and the Great Trees, trembled with emotion growing in intensity to a controlled shout. "SUCH audacity, SUCH malevolence, it's INCONCEIVABLE! Were we NOT under the aegis of a peace accord?" His voice again faltered at the end of his tirade, interspersed with desolate chirps and subdued whistling sobs.

Marta lay a comforting arm on his slumped shoulder. "So we must be in agreement; we must plan but retaliate quickly. I believe our next course of action is clear. We'll mount a speedy expedition to Westmount, and unravel their nefarious designs."

The meticulous planning stretched on, with discussions and strategy sessions extending deep into the night. The hive flota, alongside several other larger flotas, underwent significant modifications, transitioning from their customary configurations to battle-ready formations. Extra gasbags were requisitioned and secured to the air battleships. The objective was crystal clear: ascend to a strategic altitude well beyond the Othorians' reach and, from there, mount a surprise offensive.

Communers were rostered into shifts. They were to maintain a continual link with PuritaWhite through her nexus, channeling their energies to hasten her rejuvenation. Simultaneously, all buzzies in the vicinity—those nimble airborne allies—were marshaled to augment the flotilla. Their roles were multipurpose: provide defensive cover, aid in reconnaissance, and, when necessary, launch aggressive counterstrikes.

From the armory, weapons that had not seen the light of day for ages were unsheathed. Among them, the large stinger war crossbows held a place of honor. Alongside them, a plethora of battle bolts and elongated arrows, some imbued with venom and others rigged to detonate on impact, were prepared for use.

In the whole of the White Flock realm, nestled in the southwestern quadrant of the vast Grand Valley, stood seven imposing Great Trees. Still, only four had been repopulated following the Kondorian War: the majestic PuritaWhite, the resilient Primulus, the ever-blooming Wintera, and Clivius, a venerable Father Tree. Jonus, using his unparalleled communing prowess, managed to establish a connection with all the trees and their corresponding flocks.

The intel gathered revealed that in the White Quadrant, only PuritaWhite and Clivius had been hit by the Othorians' assaults, and both trees were struck nearly simultaneously. Recognizing the gravity of the situation, the unaffected white flocks dispatched help, bolstering the defenses around the beleaguered trees and augmenting the ranks of the burgeoning Avian battalion marshaled by Marta and Jonus.

The response was swift and decisive. In a mere span of two days, the ranks swelled to over a hundred Avians, each a testament to their race's courage and resolve. Complementing them was a formidable contingent of buzzies. Including smaller wild buzzies from nearby hives, over two hundred in total flew at the ready, their buzzing wings a vivid expression of their eagerness to confront the Othorians.

As dawn broke on the third day since Marta and Jonus's return, the assembled armada stood poised for action. The sun cast a glow upon the meticulously prepared flotas, their shimmering white sails reflecting the light. Westmount Marketplace, which had served as a nexus for commerce and diplomatic interactions between the Avians and the Othorians for generations, was now their target.

Though this hive marketplace was roughly a three-day journey away, Marta's heart ached to chase after Irka, and she could wait no longer. Forming an elite scouting party comprising herself, the battle-hardened General Eldred, and ten of the fiercest Avians, each hand-picked for their prowess and agility, they were also accompanied by a squadron of fifteen buzzies led by Marta's prime buzzy, Speckle. They were primed with an air of intense focus, their excitement evident by the continuous low buzzing hum as they flew about in small clouds, synchronizing themselves for battle.

The initial phase of the journey was uneventful. The armada scaled impressive altitudes, becoming mere specks in the vast expanse of the sky, rendering them virtually invisible from the ground below. As they drew near Westmount, the atmosphere grew tense with anticipation. When they were close enough, they slowed to a crawl, virtually hovering high in the air. With the decisiveness of falcons spotting their prey, Marta's elite squad sprang into action. In a swift, coordinated movement, they nose-dived from their lofty heights, piercing through the air at breakneck speed.

Their descent was a masterclass in tactical maneuvering. At the bottom of their dive, they expertly weaved through the dense jungle canopy, gliding from tree to tree. Their swift movements created mere blurs against the backdrop of lush green jungle.

Scout buzzies at the forefront began chirping an alert message. From their rapid and synchronized vocalizations, it was evident they had spotted something of interest.

Drawing closer to the indicated location, Marta's advance squad moved even more furtively, their buzzies flying quietly in stealth mode, spreading out to keep watch. Peering through the dense foliage, Marta and General Eldred observed a group of Othorians. They seemed oddly without purpose, pausing frequently to glance back toward the western mountains, an air of anxiety about them.

General Eldred signaled for complete silence as they continued their careful scrutiny. The Othorians were lightly armed, and their behavior was more mysterious than aggressive. Oddly, each one had a bright red mark painted on their faces.

With a nod from Marta, her team, along with Speckle and several buzzies, clearly presenting an aggressive posture, descended from their hiding spots, effectively surrounding the Othorian group.

To Marta and Eldred's surprise, the Othorians didn't react with any aggression. Though startled and caught off guard, they swiftly dropped their few weapons, adopting a submissive yet defensive posture. Most sank to their knees, their hands raised in a universal gesture of surrender.

From their midst emerged a tall, lithe female, her leather skin coal black with gray patches on her arms. A pronounced old scar slashed through her left eye. "Hold," she implored, head lowered and hands raised, palms forward. "We mean you no harm. I am called Lirna, leader of this pack. We are all strongly opposed to the recent onslaughts by our kin and the suffering they have inflicted upon you Avians. We are very sorry, so much so that we have deserted Thetan's army. We are rebels, dissenters against our leader's oppressive rule. We are members of the Resistance. Thetan's power has grown monstrous, worsened by the malevolent influence of his son, Bertran. We wish to ally with you against this common foe if you would have us as partners."

Marta's eyebrows arched in surprise, but her voice remained icy and steady. "Trust isn't easily given, especially in these trying times. Certainly, you must understand our qualms. What proof can you offer?" she continued, stepping forward boldly and peering into Lirna's eyes with such intensity that the Othorian broke her stare and looked down again.

Lirna slowly reached into a pouch on her belt and presented an intricately crafted emblem painted bright red. "This emblem is our bond. It signifies a leader of the Othorian Resistance and our oath, as does the red face painting that we all wear. To betray the Resistance is to face certain death from our supporters."

General Eldred, ever the strategist, stepped forward, standing protectively beside Marta. He interjected in a serious, deep tone, "Your commitment is noted, but information is what we need, which would further prove your allegiance to the side of peace. How can you aid our cause? What do you know about these recent attacks and kidnappings?"

"I am happy to divulge what I know. Whatever helps." Lirna's gaze was unwavering as she quickly detailed the layout of the Westmount caves, the guard rotations, and, crucially, the locations where Avian captives might be held. She also hinted at a concealed entrance, primarily used for illicit activities, which could grant them discreet access to the heart of the Othorian lair.

As Lirna revealed such critical information, the tension slackened. Marta invited Lirna to sit on some logs covered in soft moss where they could parley more comfortably. Eldred and much of the group crowded around to listen in.

Lirna continued, "Our once-esteemed leader, Thetan, has become a mere shadow of his former self. Much of this transformation, we believe, can be attributed to the malevolent influence of his conniving son, Bertran," Lirna's voice was tinged with a blend of sorrow and anger. "In the north, where Thetan's dominion has always been strongest, many blindly follow his orders, bewitched by his powerful oratory. But we in the south embrace and support the harmony that has flourished here for so long. We've basked in the warmth of peace and collaboration post-Kondorian War, thanks to the peace accord." Lirna's eyes flickered with intensity as she continued, "The rapidity and ruthlessness with which these attacks on the Avians were carried out blindsided many of us. We watched in horror as your kin were attacked, abducted, and paraded before us as captives bound for the northern caves. We've heard whispers that their grim final destination is the Northern Keep, located just beside the Highland Plateau near the legendary Three Golden Obelisks."

Marta, listening intently, finally responded, "The transparency and sincerity you've shown in revealing this crucial information only underscores the potential of an alliance. If all you say proves to be true, we can bring about the dawn of peace once again to the Grand Valley."

Lirna nodded gravely. She looked about at her squad of Othorians; each had their heads bowed in silence, clearly saddened by Lirna's words. "Though our assembly is small, we've ventured here fueled by a desperate hope to mend the rift between our races. We hoped to make contact with your people before a bloody all-out war began. Our resistance is led by a fierce and wise leader named Portia. She currently steers the Resistance at Westmount, and by the time we return to that enclave, I believe they will have taken significant steps toward wresting control from Thetan's loyalists. A warm welcome awaits you there if you deign to come with us."

She stopped for a second and reached out for Marta's hand. Touching hands was a sign of friendship between Othorians. Marta hooked her fingers around Lirna's to accept her gesture. Sighs of relief came from the squad; they looked up with more confidence.

Lirna continued, also grasping her other hand around Marta's wrist, giving a final shake and looking deep into her eyes. "Thetan's fanatics still retain control for now, so we must remain vigilant. I am certain that a face-to-face meeting with Portia would undoubtedly cement our nascent alliance. Many Othorians, disillusioned with Thetan and Bertran's despotism, are keen to join forces with you. Together, we can cleanse this land of their malevolence."

"Allow me a moment to confer with my squad," Marta responded after a brief pause, absorbing the information while maintaining a stoic expression. She dropped her hands from Lirna's and turned to her flock mates. Her communication with Eldred and her squad was through a series of secretive whistled chirps and piercing looks that conveyed a depth of strategic understanding. General Eldred, interpreting her signals with practiced ease, nodded subtly in acknowledgment of her command. Among them, a silent consensus was reached: the full might of their aerial armada would remain far aloft and concealed for now, a strategic advantage to be revealed at the most opportune moment.

"Very well, Lirna," Marta responded with a resolute nod. "Time is of the essence, and we must ascertain the fate of any of our people who languish under Thetan's cruel grasp. Speed is also crucial, and if we can free them here, we shall spare ourselves a treacherous journey north."

Lirna gestured affirmatively, her eyes alight with urgency. "Understood. We shall hasten to the secret entrance. Once we breach the hive's confines, with your consent, I will dispatch one of my trusted allies to inform Portia of your approach." Her voice carried firm resolve. "She will undoubtedly endorse your mission and intensify our insurgence against Thetan's dwindling loyalists. Follow my lead; we strike out for the southwestern cliffs. There, a withered colossus of a tree, once touched by lightning, stands as our beacon and marks the entrance we seek."

With an array of silent commands, Lirna rallied her Othorian rebels. They moved with practiced stealth, coalescing around Marta's band with the ease of shadows merging at dusk. Marta offered a sharp nod to General Eldred and two scouts, who immediately took to the trees, their presence betrayed only by the occasional rustle of foliage as they advanced to scout the path ahead, ever vigilant and ready to rendezvous with the buzzies, who remained cloaked in the upper branches.

As the rest of Marta's troops kept to the ground and marched behind Lirna, the tension in the air grew. When they neared the hidden back entry into the Westmount Market hive, the group paused, sensing the change in Lirna's demeanor. With stealth and precision, she and two of her comrades scaled the rocky ascent, confirming her suspicions as an Othorian guard emerged to challenge them. Marta, from a safe distance, overheard the terse exchange of words. This rapid-fire conversation climaxed with a deceptive retreat by Lirna, followed by a swift attack that incapacitated the guard with a blow to the side of his head by her dagger's pommel.

With the sentry now silent, bound, and out of action, Lirna signaled Marta and the rest of the troop forward. They ascended the last stretch to the cave's mouth, concealed behind the dead giant tree. Even after many decades, the charring from the lightning strike still imbued the air with a charcoal odor. Only from this proximity and angle could they appreciate the facade's cunning disguise, revealing a spacious passage just beyond a narrow crevice in the cliff face.

"I attempted diplomacy," Lirna confessed, gesturing toward the unconscious trussed up guard, "but his allegiance to Thetan proved unshakeable. It was prudent to silence him." She leaned closer, lowering her voice. "He did divulge that this entrance is poorly manned, as the guards inside are preoccupied with quelling the insurrection and overseeing the northward transport of captives."

"As for our route, let me explain," Lirna continued, her gaze sweeping over the assembled faces, "we shall traverse a wide corridor leading to a minor cavern used for storage and from there to Westmount's grand marketplace. Let us proceed with the utmost stealth; surprise remains our sharpest blade."

Marta, with a commander's acumen, conveyed silent assent, her eyes briefly touching each member of her retinue, instilling a sense of calm readiness. She sent a psychic ripple to Speckle, reminding the buzzies of the need for silence. The buzzies had joined them, coming down from the trees, much to Lirna's initial surprise but eventual pleasure. Avian buzzies were renowned for their fighting ability, a very welcome addition to any fight.

Together, the whole group silently stepped and flew through the gateway, the passage unfurling before them in grand arcs of stone, the floors beneath their feet polished to a mirror sheen. Bioluminescent lichens and mosses speckled the cave walls, casting a spectral glow that allowed the Avians, with their superior vision, to navigate the dim corridor with ease after a brief moment of adaptation. The rebel Othorians, no longer squinting against the sun's glare, discarded their protective eyewear, their eyes adjusting to the cavern's semidarkness almost immediately.

The group continued through the passageway, the scouts and buzzies sweeping ahead with barely a whisper until they arrived at a large storeroom. Diffused sunlight spilled from a fissure above, painting the hundreds of stacked wooden crates, bins and sacks with muted strokes of daylight. They used the momentary cover to assess their surroundings. The buzzies perched silently overhead, their senses tuned for any sign of danger.

"If it pleases you, Marta," Lirna offered, nodding toward her second-in-command, who stood beside her, "Oboron will reconnoiter the path ahead." She quickly summarized and described the cavernous geography of the Westmount hive, outlining the habitations that lined the main corridor and the vast marketplace cavern that also served as the main entrance at the southern end of the main corridor. Marta remembered the marketplace well—a chiseled masterpiece of commerce and culture, its beauty etched into the stone itself. Not to be outdone, the exterior part adjacent to the main entrance was a breathtaking gorge, beautifully sculpted and modified over the centuries by masterful Othorian masons and builders.

After a tense wait, Oboron returned, his silent entrance announced by a soft whistle and a series of clicks. He reported swiftly to Lirna, his whispers painting a picture of the situation ahead.

Despite not revealing her fluency in Othorian, Marta understood his every word.

"Friends," Lirna translated, her voice tinged with urgency, "there is both good and ill news. Two of your kin, seemingly members of your white flock, distinguished by their white-feathered wings, are confined nearby. Though bound, they seem unharmed. A quintet of Thetan's men watches over them, likely preparing for the journey north." She paused, her eyes flicking toward the passage. "Oboron also encountered Umbra, a comrade in arms, who informed us of a fierce skirmish unfolding in Odin's Hall, the name we give the indoor marketplace. It seems the last of Thetan's loyalists are making a stand there while their accomplices attempt to flee with the remaining captives."

Marta addressed Lirna and the group, her voice a soft yet piercing whisper: "We must act swiftly. General Eldred, one of my Protectors, Speckle, and Oboron shall join me in rescuing our kin. The rest must strike at Thetan's men from behind in concert with the Resistance." Her eyes met each of her companions in turn, her mental message to Speckle reinforcing the plan.

Lirna's nod was slow, her eyes searching Marta's for any sign of hesitation. "Are you certain you would not want more support for your effort, there are five of them Marta?" Her voice held the weight of concern, a testament to the dangers that lay ahead.

General Eldred, with a glint of humor in his eye, quipped in response, "You may not yet know the full measure of Marta's prowess," a wry smirk lifting the corner of his mouth. "Not to cast a shadow over my own abilities or yours, but our Marta could and will dispatch those five miscreants in scarcely more than a moment. However, she graces us with the opportunity to lend her our support, even if not needed. We will not falter. And, Lirna, let's ensure there is a measure of the fray at the marketplace left for us, shall we? A little more exertion would be most welcome." His words ended with a congenial nod toward Marta, who received the jest with a soft chuckle.

Marta's smile was slight but determined as she addressed Lirna. "We will hold our own. Thank you for your concern. After we have dealt with those that hold the captives, we will regroup to help out at Odin's Hall. Let's move." Her voice, infused with quiet confidence, left no room for doubt.

With their course of action decided and their spirits bolstered by the camaraderie that thrived among them, they were ready. Marta's team, lithe and poised for the rescue, peeled away from the larger contingent, moving with the silent grace of a hawk on the wing. Meanwhile, Lirna and her forces steeled themselves for the larger conflict that awaited at Odin's Hall, ready to swoop down upon Thetan's men with unbridled fury.

With Oboron striding ahead, flanked closely by Marta, Eldred, and their elite cadre, they hastened north through the echoing corridors. Less than half an hour had ebbed away before they stood at the precipice of a shadow-laced alcove, which Oboron had pinpointed as the lair where the captives languished, guarded by the five formidable Othorian foes.

Peering around the bend with the stealth of seasoned warriors, they glimpsed their quarry. Then, with a sudden eruption of ferocious war cries and whoops, designed to sow panic in the hearts of their adversaries, they surged into the cave.

The buzzies, with a precision born of nature's own cunning, spat a barrage of venom that struck true, felling two Othorians where they stood. A second wave of deadly barbed stingers flew from their abdomens, the buzzies' unique weaponry further sowing chaos among the enemy ranks.

Marta and General Eldred were a tempest of feathers and steel, laying waste to the remaining three with a grace that was near-artistic in its execution. The conflict was a fleeting storm—over in mere heartbeats. Oboron, positioned as the bulwark at the cave's mouth, found himself a bystander to their swift and brutal efficiency. His dagger, scarcely drawn, seemed an afterthought as the dust settled on the swift skirmish.

Two of the aggressors lay paralyzed and immobilized, venom coursing through their veins, with triumphant buzzies proudly perched upon them like conquerors. The rest of the guards met their demise in silence, one with Marta's thrown talon embedded in his throat, the others peppered with bolts and stingers, their dead bodies looking like pincushions—a testament to the lethal accuracy of the attack.

Oboron exhaled a long, sibilant hiss of awe, his voice a mix of reverence and shock. "Gods of Othor, what a sight to behold," he murmured, his eyes wide. "I have never witnessed a battle's end so swift. To be named your ally is an honor indeed—fortuitous are the gods that we stand on the same side."

"Just as I promised, my boy," Eldred replied nonchalantly, retrieving his crossbow bolts from the vanquished. "These two will be numb for hours but bind them well, so they become no more than a footnote in our future troubles."

Meanwhile, Marta, had glided over to the Avian captives. She had hoped that one of them would be Irka, but the familiar faces of other PureWhite Flock members, Katien and Sebaston, emerged from the gloom, their bodies fettered, poised for transport by their captors. With a tender touch, Marta severed the bonds that tethered them. Embraces were exchanged, the captives' faces blooming with smiles of relief and freedom.

Sebaston, his voice tinged with venom yet suffused with gratitude, began, "We harbored hope that rescue would come from these curs." Confusion clouded his features. "We cannot fathom their sudden malice …" His words faltered as his gaze landed on Oboron.

Eldred placed his hand on Sebaston's shoulder to hold him back, interceding with calming authority, "Fear not, for Oboron is an ally. The hostility stems not from all Othorians but from the tyranny of Thetan and his vile progeny, Bertran. Even now, a faction of Othorians wages battle against their tyranny in Odin's Hall."

Marta, her attention now turned to administering aid, produced a leather skin filled with the elixir of green healing sappa. As she offered it to the weakened Katien, the pair sipped the restorative brew. Vigor flowed back into their limbs, and with a rustle of feathers and an arching stretch of wings, they stood ready, albeit still trembling, weak from being bound for so long.

With the skirmish behind them, Marta rallied her squad. "Let us leave this musty-smelling cave; I yearn to smell fresh air again, and we must hasten to Odin's Hall and join the fray against our oppressors. Katien, Sebaston, stay well behind us. Your courage is undeniable, but you must reclaim your full strength."

Their steps retraced through the main hallway; the troop was now bolstered by the safe rescue of two of their own. Oboron led them once more, his stride infused with newfound respect for his feathered comrades, his demeanor hinting at the pride of one who has witnessed the near-impossible and marched alongside legends.

They surged southward with an urgent pace, and it wasn't long before the main hallway opened up into a vista of grandeur. Ornate carvings now adorned every nook and cranny, interwoven with a tapestry of multicolored, fluorescent mosses, fungi, and mushrooms that cascaded from the crevices and the vaulted ceiling high above. As they advanced, a colossal opening ahead hinted at an expansive cave beyond.

Oboron, with a strategist's caution, had slowed their advance and was hugging the wall. At his signal, they halted. Stealthily, he moved forward, uttering a string of very low clicks to announce his arrival to someone unseen. Uncovering a hidden alcove veiled by drapes of moss and tendrils of vine, they could see Lirna, who, with a silent gesture, beckoned them onward. Inside the camouflaged retreat, the air was thick with the clicking sounds of Oboron's rapid communication, a puff of acidic pheromones punctuating his speech. The air inside the small anteroom was stuffy, filled with other Othorians. None looked like warriors, some holding makeshift weapons, some with dejected faces. As Oboron continued, Marta assumed he was filling them in on the fight they just had; many faces looked up, excited to have such needed help from obvious expert fighters.

When he concluded, Lirna turned to the assembled Avians, crammed together in the entrance, her gaze alight with veneration. "Oboron holds your valor in high regard—a commendation from one who is seldom given to praise," she imparted with a respectful nod. The circle of rebel Othorians hissed and clapped their hands on their thighs quietly, mirroring Lirna's respect.

"We convened here to strategize our assault," Lirna motioned to a slender figure emerging from the shadows. "This is Umbra, our eyes and ears." The pitch-black tiny Othorian might have been mistaken for a child if not for her dignified poise. "Her slight stature grants her passage through forgotten tunnels, a path beyond the reach of Thetan's ruthless sentinels."

Lirna continued, her voice tinged with urgency, "The enemy's ranks are formidable, and they hold the line against Portia's contingent, who, though brave, are but merchants and traders, unversed in combat. They stand ready to lay down their lives to overthrow Thetan's despotism. Now, with your alliance, what was once intended as a show of force and numbers may very well erupt into a full-scale attack,"

Lirna declared. "Once we get into position behind Thetan's forces, we'll signal Portia, who awaits our call, to launch her frontal assault. United, we shall prevail!" Her proclamation, though whispered, carried the weight of an imminent promise.

She then imparted a vital reconnaissance update. "Two of my scouts have sized up the oppressors—thirty-four warriors from the king's army, all skilled and lethal. Their broadswords, laced with a paralyzing toxin, are deadly even at the slightest touch. And take heed, six elite archers are stationed aloft, their eyes scouring the battlefield from their elevated posts, their bows capable of long-range devastation."

The murmurs of planning swelled within their secret chamber. The Avians and buzzies would swoop from above to neutralize the archers with aerial finesse. Lirna and her rebels would attack the ground troops from behind in another surprise attack.

Umbra was entrusted with a pivotal role—to issue the clarion call at the precise moment when the attack became evident. This signal would unleash Portia's forces to engage with full ferocity, trapping Thetan's forces in a pincer of righteous fury.

Their stratagem was set, the legion of liberation, as they had nicknamed themselves, advanced. The cavernous expanse of Odin's Hall loomed before them, where the oppressors stood vigilant yet unaware of the storm that was about to break.

As the first archer crumpled from the unseen assault of the buzzies, the signal from Umbra pierced the air. Together with Marta, General Eldred, and the rest of the Avians, the remaining archers fell like cards before they could unleash even one arrow, plummeting dead among their shocked comrades below. A second wave of stinger crossbow bolts, fighting talons, and buzzy venom rained upon the tyrants below, instantly killing or maiming many more of them.

The frontal attack roared to life, Portia's forces charging with cries of liberation. Thetan and Bertran's soldiers, taken aback, scrambled to meet this sudden onslaught but found themselves caught in the merciless embrace of a well-laid trap.

Swords clashed; arrows flew throughout Odin's Hall. It was clear from the beginning that the remaining soldiers had no chance. Overwhelmed by the unexpected ferocity and precision of the Resistance attack, they succumbed one by one. The once imposing force of Othorian warriors was decimated, their defenses crumbling like sandcastles before the surging tide. The grandeur of the hall, once a testament to the might of Thetan's rule, now echoed with the victorious cheers of the Resistance, their triumph ringing out as a clarion call of newfound hope and freedom.

BERTRAN ON HIS STEED
A HUGE BLACK 'JIANT' USED BY OTHORIANS
FOR TRANSPORTATION AND IN BATTLE

9:
Irka's Captivity

———◇◇◇———

Irka stirred from a pain-laced slumber, her consciousness grappling with disorientation. She gasped involuntarily as she awoke, then spat out remnants of dirt and dry moss from where her face had been planted on the filthy floor. The humid, dirty smell of rotting vegetation and sour earth almost clogged her throat as she took another breath, spitting and coughing. The metallic taste of her own blood made her gag even more.

Attempting to shift her body, she immediately felt the cruel bindings that pinned her wings against her back. Her body ached all over. Enclosed in darkness, her vision gradually adapted. Managing to sit upright, she collided with another body beside her, eliciting a suppressed grunt.

The throbbing in her head matched her quickening heartbeat. The cave's dank, earthy smell mixed with the faint odor of burnt feathers. Irka discerned the contours of the cavern—an expansive space where the ceiling loomed overhead, the bioluminescent fungi that grew on the walls casting a ghostly blue-green light into the oppressive dark.

The figure she had inadvertently bumped into communicated in hushed chirps and faint twittering, warning her to maintain silence lest "they" return with a callous hand. Irka fought back the rising tide of fear within her. "I must be strong, I must," she muttered quietly under her breath, but loud enough for her neighboring captive to nudge her again.

Memories flooded back—the last glimpse she had of her Othorian captors, shrouded in camouflaged garb, their eyes peeking through leather blindfolds fashioned with slits. Confusion welled within her as she pondered the cause of this aggression after years of tranquility between their races.

The soft rustle of movement and subdued murmurs, along with low despondent chirps, confirmed they were not alone. With painstaking effort, she quietly turned herself around to see more of the room, her body protesting with sharp stabs of pain. She surveyed the bleak scene: fourteen of her people, similarly bound—some slumped in unconscious heaps, others sitting with defeated postures. At the cave's mouth, an Othorian guard dozed, his snores punctuating the silence and offering a bizarre counterpoint to the heavy tension hanging in the stale air.

Irka realized that the fellow captive next to her was Precina, a young Brooder from her own PureWhite Flock. Nearby, Yuda and her sibling Ontan, both Workers also from her flock, huddled back-to-back in stoic solidarity.

"Precina," Irka whispered, trying unsuccessfully to keep her voice from trembling, "do you know what is happening? Why are we captives?"

"I have no more knowledge than you," Precina responded softly. "Our capture must have followed the raid on PuritaWhite. The rationale behind our confinement remains a mystery."

The guard was jolted awake by a disturbance at the entrance. His stern admonition to remain silent was a sharp reminder of their plight. "Silence! Any more noise, and I'll make you wish you hadn't squawked," he growled.

His threat was punctuated by the arrival of a young Othorian, Tabor, who hobbled into view bearing a sloshing bucket of water. "My na-name is T-T-Tabor. Please, dr-drink," he stammered, his voice carrying the tremor of anxiety or perhaps empathy. With practiced care, he offered each captive a ladleful of precious water.

The guard, content with the proceedings, began biting his claws idly, unaware of a subtle rebellion by Tabor. With each sip of water dispensed, he surreptitiously slipped small pieces of pollen cakes to the prisoners, his clandestine act of kindness a fleeting reprieve from their harsh reality. The Avians, now mostly alert, received Tabor's furtive gifts in grateful silence, seizing the chance to quench their thirst and nourish their weakened bodies.

"Thank you, Tabor," Irka whispered as he approached her. She could taste the sweet, gritty pollen cake mingling with the metallic tang of her own blood from a cut lip. "What's happening outside?"

Tabor's eyes darted nervously to the guard before he leaned in closer. "I d-don't know mu-much. They're t-t-taking orders from P-P-Prince Bertran. Something b-b-big is happening at B-B-Bison Hive."

Irka nodded, absorbing the information. The mere mention of Bison Hive sent a shiver down her spine. She shared the news with her fellow captives in hushed whispers, trying to piece together their grim situation.

Once Tabor had made his rounds and left, Irka's mind drifted off, lost in the dreary confines of her captivity and total exhaustion. Her sleepy thoughts unfurled, soaring back to the resplendent Avian Western Aerie. It was a haven she longed to return to, not just as a visitor but as a nurturing Brooder dedicated to the upbringing of the next generation. On Kondor, there were only two aeries. The one in the Western Othor Mountains, where Irka had been raised, stood as a testament to natural beauty and wonder, outshining the Eastern Aerie in both size and splendor.

Beyond the hidden entrance, the Western Aerie was immense, the sides of this huge natural cavern rose so high around them that the opening far up ahead went beyond the breathable atmosphere. Down below was a private sanctuary, a microcosm with a perfect microclimate. The flock's communing nurtured the cultivation of trees, lush grasses, and other flora, creating an oasis of serenity amid the rugged grandeur.

Lichens and velvety mosses thrived in harmony with the ambient fluorescent bacteria and fungi, their glow bathing the subterranean offshoots in a soothing, perpetual twilight. The Brooders tended the aerie with meticulous care, ensuring that its beauty was as much a fixture as the rock from which it was hewn. Storage chambers burrowed deeper into the heart of the mountain, preserving precious bounty and supplies in naturally cool recesses away from the sun's heat.

Irka's reverie was shattered, snapping her back to her present predicament. The thumping sounds and vibrations of footfalls signaled the arrival of additional Othorian forces, igniting curiosity and a prickling sense of anticipation. The prisoners stirred from their lethargy, their senses sharpening, more tweets and twitters of fright and concern echoed around the cave.

"Thorag, you lazy fool, wake up!" The command reverberated with authority, shattering the silence. Thorag, the slothful guard at the door, nearly tumbled off his stool in a dance of desperation, his words rushing out in an embarrassed torrent as he struggled to recover his composure before the imposing figure of his captain standing in the entrance. "Sorry, Captain Dagon! I wasn't sleeping, just resting for a second; my eyes burn from the dank smells," Thorag stammered, trying to stand at attention.

The captain, a stern figure, brushed aside the apologies. "We have urgent orders. The prince's impatience is growing. We need to move to the Bison Hive immediately." He entered the cave, and a squad pushed in behind him.

The mention of Bison Hive triggered a flutter of distress and nervous twittering among the captives. Irka felt a cold knot of fear tighten in her stomach, their destination now confirmed. She whispered to Precina, "Do you know why they're taking us there?"

Precina shook her head, her eyes wide with worry. "I have no idea. It can't be good."

The squad of Othorians, with a brusqueness born of urgency, set to work, manhandling the Avians with indifference, pulling them to their feet and shoving them toward the exit. Irka, when her turn came, offered no resistance.

Her breath hitched at the sight that greeted her outside of the cave. A much larger cavern, brighter with somewhat fresher air, awaited them. It was bustling with activity, but what startled Irka to a halt were the grey jiants standing around in the melee, monstrous ant-like relics of war thought long past, looming like behemoths from the shadows.

"Are those … jiants?" Irka whispered, her voice trembling with fear but also with wonder.

"Yes," Yuda replied, his voice barely a whisper. "I thought they were extinct."

The towering animals, with their formidable mandibles and incessantly scanning antennae, were once the backbone of the Othorian war machine. Their six spindly but strong legs, each jointed by articulation of fearsome efficiency, sprouted from a robust thorax, culminating in a slender abdomen from which protruded a lethal stinger.

Harnessed into servitude, the jiants were an imposing sight, each with rope saddle sacs hanging on either side, with an Othorian jockey perched imperiously just behind their massive, chitinous craniums. Their multifaceted eyes reflected a grotesque tapestry of the world around them, increasing their ominous appearance.

Irka, as she was shoved and carried along, could see that the jiants' body harnesses were being loaded with the captive Avians, their forms heaved under the strain, their compliance enforced by the sharp commands and harsh discipline of their Othorian handlers. It was a spectacle of despair—the revival of a once-vanquished tool of oppression that now seemed as vital and formidable as ever.

The captain's hissed decree sliced through the murmurs, squawks, and cries. "Load them up quickly. We don't have time to waste."

Irka found herself confined within the fibrous embrace of a side bag slung upon one of the monstrous jiants. Her restraints had mercifully slackened during the commotion, affording her a small yet significant reprieve. She could draw deeper breaths, a small comfort amid the chaos. The behemoth beneath her lurched into motion, its colossal form moving with a surprising grace that belied its terrifying visage.

As they began their march, Irka whispered to the Avian next to her, "Stay strong. We'll find a way out of this."

At first, their advance was measured, each step a deliberate placement of monstrous limbs. But soon, the pace quickened, the jiants accelerating with unnerving agility. The light clicking of their feet as they ran became a comforting drone. The landscape became a blur as they traversed the uneven terrain at a speed that seemed to defy the natural order of such gargantuan creatures.

Sunlight sporadically pierced the gloom as they emerged onto exposed pathways, throwing stark shadows over the cavalcade of creatures and captives. The jiants navigated with eerie precision, their limbs finding purchase on the scantest of footholds, skirting along vertical cliff faces and through tortuous mountain passes chiseled by time and the elements.

In the clutches of an unchosen destiny, Irka resigned herself to the journey, centering her thoughts and surrendering her body to the rhythm of her colossal carrier. Despite the aches in her limbs, the dryness of her throat, and the gnawing emptiness in her stomach, there was a tranquil ferocity to her spirit. She was now of the White Flock, a lineage not easily extinguished nor broken by fear.

Again, her mind wandered off, seeking reprieve from the present by daydreaming of her new mate and great love, Caleb. She recalled with great fondness their time together as a new couple during the last Pairing. Caressing his downy chest feathers and meticulously preening his coarser hair-like head plumage down to his back, where the larger wing feathers emerged. Irka relived the sensory experience. The musky smell of his feathers reminded her of chocolate mixed with pine sap, with a touch of the sea and fresh air after a rain. The velvety softness of his feathers sent tremors coursing through her being, each stroke suffused with an electric current of affection. The intensity of her love for Caleb was palpable, an emotion that lingered long after their initial encounter.

She had been drawn to him from the outset, captivated by his aura of strength and reliability. In moments when he locked eyes with her and cooed in his intricate, melodic fashion, Irka found herself succumbing to his charm, melting under the weight of his endearing expressions.

To her, his choice to pair with her was nothing short of a profound blessing. The sheer intensity of their physical union and the raw, un-bridled passion of their mating rituals remained etched in her memory. Despite the fact that Avians mated only during the last couple of weeks of every four years, during the Pairing time, the rarity of their physical bond only deepened their connection at the time.

Now, bound and netted like a trapped animal and even as despair sought to take root, Irka nurtured the ember of determination flicker-ing within her. Her people were known not just for their resilience but for their indomitable will—a flame that the damp of her grim circum-stances could not smother. With each jarring stride of the jiants, with each heart-pounding moment of captivity, Irka's resolve crystallized further. She might have been a captive in body, but her spirit soared unfettered, ready to seize the slightest chance for freedom that might present itself.

As they broke out into another open area of the trail, the fresh air full of mountain scents and light floral undertones mirrored Irka's positive attitude. "Do you smell that?" Yuda whispered, breaking the tense silence. He had been loaded in a net bag beside Irka. "It smells faintly of red flowers; we must be approaching the northwest."

Irka inhaled deeply, catching a faint beautiful floral aroma almost overpowered by the musty scent of the jiants and the sharp tang of Othorian leather and pheromones. "Yes," she replied softly. "It reminds me of home."

The comforting smell, although sending a pang of homesickness, also bolstered her determination. She would find a way out, for herself and for her fellow captives.

10:
Caleb's Awakening

Caleb and Goffry made their way back to their flota. To Caleb's elation, the airship was being restored to airworthiness. It had lost some of its size due to the damage it sustained but still hovered defiantly a few feet above the ground, a testament to its resilience. Though the mainmast had been sheared off—a detail Goffry had briefed him on during their return—the storm sail was ready with its modest mast, promising some wind propulsion, albeit at a reduced velocity.

As he looked over the ship, Caleb remarked, whistling a cheerful tune, "Goffry, I must say, seeing the flota like this, still in one piece after all that happened, it's … it's a relief."

Goffry, inspecting a harness and nodding, tweeted in agreement. "It's been a tough journey, Caleb. But look at her, already floating there, still holding up. She's got a spirit of her own!"

Tightening a knot on the rigging and grinning, Caleb replied, "She's more than just a flota to us now. She's part of our story. How are Trada and Pica holding up?"

Goffry responded, "They're strong, like us. They just need time to heal fully." Then, changing the subject, he added, "We will need to find more supplies soon; there's very little to harvest here, and our stores are almost empty."

The scarcity of pollen and nectar in the mountainous region posed a challenge. Yet, they managed to collect water from the pond and gather more organic refuse for the composting chamber of the flota, feeding it the essential nutrients for self-repair.

The remainder of the day saw them both immersed in laborious efforts to bring the airship back to its full majesty. With the aid of Trada, Pica—who were still recovering—and the cohort of buzzies, they meticulously repaired flight harnesses, resecured gasbags to the gunwales, and replenished the storage pantry as best they could.

Linking with the ship's nexus, Caleb tapped into the web of organic beings composing the vessel. His strong communing skills became a conduit of encouragement for the flota's growth, prompting a remarkable spurt that mirrored the ship's response to his unwavering care and potent mental energy. He knew, with joy, that their journey would soon resume.

As twilight embraced the mountains and night donned its dark veil, the small crew, battered yet unbroken, nestled together in the main cabin of the flota. Soon, they succumbed to a profound slumber, serenaded by the gentle cooing and entrancing birdsong duet of Caleb and Goffry.

Caleb felt a mix of relief and exhaustion. The ship's comforting signature smell had returned, with the faint tang of sap and new growth. His muscles ached from the day's labor, but it was a good ache—a reminder of their progress.

Caleb looked over at his companion, who was awake but lost in thought. "Do you think we'll make it back in time to help? I feel so frustrated being stuck here," Caleb asked, his voice tinged with both hope and worry.

Goffry paused, considering the question. "We'll get there, Caleb. We have to. For our flock and for Irka. We'll leave as soon as possible; we must accept that we can do no more."

The mention of Irka brought a pang of longing to Caleb's heart. He could almost feel her soft feathers against his, her floral scent that always clung to her. "I hope she's safe," he murmured.

Goffry placed a reassuring hand on Caleb's shoulder. "She's strong. Just like you. And we'll find her."

They shared a moment of silent determination, holding each other's hands with eyes shut for a short time. Letting go and falling back into their nests, they sighed in unison, both smiling at their synchronicity.

Caleb's dreams were vivid, filled with the scents of the forest—fresh jungle aromas, the sweet fragrance of blooming flowers, and the earthy scent of their home, mingled with the delicate fragrance of white Mother Tree blossoms. These smells always brought him comfort, a reminder of his parents' unwavering support and love. His mind was flooded with sounds: birdsong, thunder, and the wind's rush. He felt the textures of leaves, rock, bark, and soft feathers. Every sense was heightened, painting a world of intense beauty and deep connection.

In the grip of these sensations, Caleb's dreams took him back to his youth. He remembered tales whispered by his parents about his egg's luminous glow and his hatching into the world. Visions of Marta and Jonus, distinguished Communers of the White Flock, filled his mind. They had always known Caleb was special; his egg had shone with an ethereal glow, signaling his innate gifts.

By the time he hatched, his nesting nook had spontaneously grown thick carpets of moss, lichens, and tiny ferns, all interwoven with delicate vines adorned with tiny white blossoms—a sign of his destined greatness.

"Caleb, my special boy," Marta would often chirp, her voice filled with warmth. "Your arrival was marked by nature itself. Never forget how special you are." Her gentle hands would caress his feathers, making Caleb feel safe and loved.

In his teenage years, Jonus would tell him with pride, "Your connection to the Great Trees is unique. You have a gift, my son, one that can change the world."

Yet, with these unique abilities came fears that troubled Caleb. His communion with the Great Trees and other plants extended far beyond what was typical. He kept this secret even from his family, fearing it might set him apart. But his ability to connect with living beings always brought him peace.

One evening, Marta noticed his silence and sat beside him. "Caleb, you know you can talk to us about anything," she warbled softly, her eyes searching his. "Your abilities are nothing to be ashamed of."

"I know, Mother," Caleb replied, his voice barely above a whisper. "But sometimes, it feels overwhelming. Like there's so much more I can do, but I'm afraid of what it all means."

"Be patient, my love, everything will be as it should be," she cooed softly, breaking into a lullaby that never failed to relax him and bring on a deep sleep.

In the White Flock, Caleb's rise as a leader was clear. He started humbly as a Worker, committed to physical labor. But his natural abilities soon led him to the Protector's Guild, where his talent with the talon knife and stinger bow quickly grew, reflecting the prowess of his parents.

Marta, known as Marta the Unbeatable, was a legend among the Avians. She was the epitome of a Protector, her skills unmatched and revered. Under her guidance, Caleb honed his abilities, learning from the best.

"Focus, Caleb," Marta would trill, her eyes intense yet filled with pride. "Feel the energy of the weapon in your hand, let it become part of you. Use violence no more than necessary, but if you must, fight better than anyone else. Only by *knowing* you are the best *can* you be the best."

His father, Jonus, was a leader in the flock, renowned as one of the most skilled Communers of his time. He played a crucial role in revitalizing the PureWhite Flock and repopulating the PuritaWhite Mother Tree grove. Both his parents, along with Granger, a high-ranked Protector, and General Eldred, were key figures in rebuilding after the Kondorian War and the Battle of Bison Caves. Although this war happened long ago, both Avians and Othorians had lost much of their population, and birth rates for both species were low.

Caleb's parents were deeply committed to repopulating the vacant Great Trees in Kondor's southwestern regions. Cultivating and nurturing these ancient white trees, whose saps, nectars, and pollens were vital for enhancing communing skills and spiritual awareness, became their mission—a testament to their dedication to the Avian people's restoration and prosperity.

As Caleb journeyed through his dream, he relived the thrill of his fledgling flights, the joy of soaring skyward and diving down to skim the treetops. Each dream was filled with the exhilaration of flight and youthful joy, filling his night with pure elation.

These intense feelings brought on a deeper level of communing—a depth he had never encountered before. It felt as though he merged with the very essence of all the plants, gasbags, and living beings, as well as the soul of the entire flota and then expanding to the surrounding vegetation, plants, insects, and animals, all pulsating in harmony. His mind began to resonate with their rhythm, the essence of every living thing beating together as one.

Intertwined with their consciousnesses, he was perceiving growth and life down to the cellular level, all at once yet distinctly. This profound union was almost terrifying yet exhilarating; delving even deeper,

Caleb felt so immersed in this state that he almost lost the sense of his own existence, hovering in a space between being and nothingness.

Jolted awake by Goffry's gentle prodding, Caleb blinked open his eyes. "Caleb, you must see this; something inexplicable has happened. You were in such a deep slumber, but please, come—you have to see this. I'm at a loss for words …" Goffry's voice trailed off, his expression a mix of confusion and wonder.

With a series of encouraging chirps, Goffry turned and clambered out into the morning sun. Despite his previous exhaustion, Caleb felt an unexpected surge of energy. He followed Goffry outside, where Trada, Pica, and the rest of the buzzies were perched on the cliffside, overlooking the small plateau where the flota had rested.

"What is it, Goffry?" Caleb asked, still rubbing sleep from his eyes and fluffing his feathers in the morning light.

"Look back at our flota, Caleb," Goffry said, pointing behind him.

As Caleb turned, his breath caught in his throat. He blinked hard, rubbing his eyes again to make sure he wasn't imagining it. The flota, which had been severely damaged the night before, now stood almost fully restored, looking ready to fly. It wasn't just repaired—it seemed to pulse with energy, with shimmering light dancing around the vessel.

The vines, leaves, and branches looked not just restored but rejuvenated, with new blooms scattered throughout the greenery. Although the main mast was still missing, the storm mast and sail stood proudly, surrounded by lush vegetation. Caleb and Goffry stared at each other in disbelief, stunned into silence. The buzzies, unfazed by the transformation, continued their morning rituals with an extra dose of energy.

"Caleb, did you … how did … was this your doing …?" Goffry stammered, staring at Caleb with wide eyes.

After a moment of thought, Caleb replied, his voice steady, "I'm not sure, Goff. Last night, I had these intense dreams—dreams where I was communing with the flota—but this … this goes beyond anything I've ever experienced. You know I have a deep connection, but this … this feels like something out of a myth. And I'm far from mythic. Maybe there's some ancient energy in these mountains that helped us…" Caleb's voice trailed off; his own disbelief clear. "I can't explain it, but last night was … incredible, and I haven't even begun to make sense of it."

"If you're confused, Caleb, then I'm completely lost," Goffry said with a shrug. "Let's just take this as a gift, wherever it came from. This will definitely make our journey easier. For now, let's focus on what's next."

"Give me a moment to fully wake up and gather my thoughts," Caleb suggested. "We're in a race against time, but I need to process all of this first."

They fell into silence, with Caleb preening and smoothing his feathers. As he examined his wings, he noticed with surprise that his flight feathers were regrowing quickly. However, the last great pinion feather on each wing was emerging with a deep gray hue, almost black—a strange anomaly. "Great," he muttered to himself, "just what I needed—another mystery. What's happening now?" He sighed, accepting the change as just another part of the unfolding puzzle. With no immediate answers, he decided to move forward.

After some thought, Caleb made a decision. He knew that at the base of Bison Ridge, where it met the Gorgothon River valley, there stood a Great Father Tree known as Pollitus, Irka's home tree. It was the southernmost of the Red Great Trees and conveniently nearby. Utilizing the updrafts from Bison Ridge, they could glide there quickly, saving more time than if they headed directly south to PuritaWhite.

Caleb knew that the RedBlush Flock, though greatly reduced in number due to the Kondorian War, would still be residing around

Pollitus. They could gather more intelligence from the remaining flock and attempt to reestablish communication. The chance to replenish their provisions was an added benefit, even if it meant a slight detour. Gathering more information felt crucial to Caleb.

Once he had thought everything through, Caleb shared his plan with Goffry, who agreed with the logic. With a mutual nod, they completed their preparations and took to the skies, embarking on the next leg of their journey with renewed purpose, spurred on by the morning's extraordinary events.

11:
MARCUS AND LEURIN

———◇———

Marcus's fingers tapped an irregular rhythm on the armrest of his chair in the Command Center. The room hummed with activity, with rows of machines operating in the background, their lights casting a soft, pulsing glow. The high ceiling arched above, giving the space an airy, cathedral-like feel. Luxurious seating upholstered in velvety materials embraced those who sat upon them, and beautiful art pieces adorned the walls, alongside mesmerizing alien statues and sculptures strategically placed around the room.

The conundrum before Marcus seemed as vast as the void of space surrounding the planet. The flying people of Kondor, with their intricate societal structure and unique abilities, remained a puzzle he had yet to solve. His fleeting connections with them were like glimpses of rare celestial events—brilliant but brief, leaving him craving more.

Marcus shifted in his chair, running his hand back and forth along the plush armrest, a habit that soothed him. The challenge wasn't just about making a connection with the Avians; it was about establishing a stable link that could be maintained over time. He relived that first moment of bridging their minds over and over; the experience had been intoxicating. The emotional high of a good connection was like touching the divine, but it was short-lived. Whatever defensive mechanism the Avians had, it was effective, leaving Marcus frustrated, clawing at mental barriers he couldn't penetrate.

"The Othorians are different," Marcus muttered to himself, his eyes narrowing in thought. "Less complex, more accessible, but lacking the finesse and high PSY aptitude we need." His attention was on several holographic monitor screens in front of him, flickering with streams of data. Sleek, high-tech machines lined the walls around him, their displays pulsating with energy.

Leurin, sensing his master's agitation, entered the room quietly, his mechanical yet fluid form gliding smoothly across the polished floor. "You seem troubled, Master Marcus. Can I assist you?" he asked, his voice a blend of concern and resolve. Little mechanical drones whirred quietly around him, performing precision maintenance tasks wherever they went.

Marcus sighed, running a hand through his sparse, close-cropped hair. "It's the Avians, Leurin. Their minds are … elusive. I must find a way to connect with them, to harness their PSY abilities. The Takers are closing in, and our passive ways won't save us. Countless lives and entire species are being wiped out as I speak. This madness must stop."

Leurin's form vibrated slightly, an indication of his unease. "The plan to enlist the Avians through the Othorians is risky. Are you sure this is the only way?" he queried; his synthetic voice tinged with a hint of hesitation.

"We don't have the luxury of time," Marcus replied, his voice grow-ing more resolute. "The Avians' unique blend of empathy and control over aggression might be the key to our survival. Their PSY abilities and innate flying skills would make them perfect candidates for pilots. We need to act through the Othorians, use them to bring the Avians to us." He stood up, pacing the room, his hand brushing against the cold, sleek surface of a nearby console as he tapped in a brief command.

Leurin's eyes flickered, processing the information. "It goes against our principles, Marcus. We are Creators, not conquerors," he said, his voice low and contemplative.

"I know", Marcus stopped pacing; his voice tinged with frustration, "but our principles won't matter if we're all gone. We must harness every being's best ability, whether for negotiation or combat, to even have a possibility of winning this conflict. We can't afford to be passive any longer." He turned to face Leurin, the determination in his eyes unmistakable.

Leurin nodded, though his hesitation was clear. "If this is the path we must take, then so be it. I will begin preparations immediately."

As Leurin turned to leave, Marcus added, "We need those warships ready, Leurin. The most advanced defense force fields, enhanced inter-dimensional hyperdrive engines, and all the weaponry we can muster." His voice echoed in the high-ceilinged room, filled with urgency.

Leurin stopped, turning back to face Marcus. "I think we also need hope, Master Marcus. Let us hope indeed that the cosmos is attuned to our plight," he said, his voice a blend of reassurance and determination.

Marcus paused for a moment, a small smile breaking his lips. "Agreed, Leurin. I shall retreat once more to my hibernation chamber to enter a state of deep deliberation and meditation. There, my mind is always freer. It becomes easier to commune. I shall endeavor to connect with the Othorian leaders, King Thetan and his son, Prince Bertran. Before my recent awakening, I had planted the seeds of our plan among them; now, I must nurture these seeds to fruition. My aim is to guide their force without allowing them to harm those we might call allies. I am anxious to see the progress they have made."

His gaze hardened with resolve. "While I steer this course, continue the assembly of our fleet, and deploy a stealth communication satellite to relay my message to our Creator comrades and any remaining allies. Perhaps, together, with renewed vigor, we can confront this scourge and halt the relentless massacre. Our longstanding doctrine of passivity ends now.

The empathy I have gained through my mind fusions with the denizens of this planet has solidified my conviction—we have erred grievously by not taking action sooner, and the cost has been unfathomable."

Leurin's eyes met Marcus's with a mix of respect and concern. "Understood, Master Marcus. I will ensure everything is ready for your return."

Marcus nodded, his face softening for a brief moment. "Thank you, Leurin. Your steadfast support means more than you know."

Together, they walked toward his chamber in silence. As they approached, Marcus caught sight of his reflection in the polished surfaces lining the corridor. Stopping for a moment, he examined the image that stared back at him. His age was evident in the sparse, stubbly hair and the many wrinkles that etched his face. Yet, despite the years, his body still looked fit, aided by the advanced body suit that supported him. His muscles had atrophied somewhat during his long periods of intense contemplation. His reflection showed a being who had weathered countless storms, but whose spirit was unbroken.

"Sometimes, I hardly recognize myself," Marcus murmured, tracing the lines of his reflection with a finger. "Time has changed me in ways I never anticipated."

Leurin, standing beside him, placed a reassuring hand on Marcus's shoulder. "Your age is a testament to your resilience and wisdom, Master Marcus. I can program a medial pod to give you a complete physical makeover if you so desire"

Marcus smiled faintly, feeling a surge of gratitude. "Thank you, Leurin. Now is not the time, it takes so long to recover. Let's just focus on the tasks at hand and make sure this chapter of our story ends well."

They continued their journey to the hibernation chamber, a marvel of technology and biology intertwined. Upon arrival, robotic technicians worked with quiet precision, attaching a myriad of electrodes and intravenous lines to Marcus's form, each one a lifeline to his physical self as his psyche prepared to venture afar.

As Marcus reclined into the central pod, the bed's memory-responsive, gel-infused smart foam adapted seamlessly to his form, cradling him in perfect alignment and relief. The viscoelastic fluid within the pod gently enveloped him, creating a weightless sensation that reduced any remaining physical discomfort, while the pod's nano-fiber wrap settled over him like a second skin. Its subtle warmth and controlled pressure gave him the reassuring sensation of floating, as though he were suspended in a tranquil, breathable cocoon.

The pod sealed shut with a soft hiss, and as the ambient luminescence dimmed, Marcus's senses began to recede into the vast, quiet landscape of his mind. Embedded pressure sensors and vibro-acoustic panels activated, emitting a low-frequency resonance that pulsed gently through his muscles, preserving circulation and tone as he drifted deeper into stasis. A delicate hum of neuro-stimuli pulsed from the sensory mesh beneath him, harmonizing with his natural biorhythms, subtly preparing his brain for the cerebral journey ahead.

In the twilight state that mirrored his surroundings, Marcus's mind became a beacon of PSY energy, thrumming with potential as the sophisticated machinery amplified his consciousness to unprecedented levels. The chamber itself, with its blend of futuristic engineering and biotechnological marvels, was an extension of his own being, merging his body with the pod's advanced systems in perfect symbiosis. Here, where thought and distance melded, Marcus's heightened awareness sought out receptive minds across the ether.

In this vast, silent expanse, he would wage his battle—a symphony of wits and wills, a clash of light and dark unfolding in the intangible theater of psychic space, his consciousness tethered delicately to the hibernation chamber. And all of it, every ounce of his energy, was dedicated to the salvation of countless lives.

Back in the Command Center, Leurin observed the chamber monitor, the weight of their mission resting heavily on him. A blend of optimism and unease filled his circuits, the enormity of their work ever-present. "Hope, Master Marcus," he whispered softly, his voice nearly drowned by the steady hum of the machinery. "Hope, indeed.

Hours and days seemed to blend into eternity as Marcus delved into the intricate pathways of Thetan's mind. It was an immense task, like threading the eye of a cosmic needle with his own consciousness. A delicate dance ensued as Marcus navigated the complexities of the Othorian leader's thoughts, seeking a connection without triggering the defenses that guarded Thetan's conscious mind.

One evening, after countless attempts, Marcus finally succeeded. He managed to nestle within the recesses of Thetan's subconscious, becoming a silent observer of the leader's innermost thoughts and memories. As Thetan slept, Marcus carefully studied the Othorian king's recent actions, flinching at the vivid recollections of Bertran's aggression against the Avians. The brutality was staggering, and Marcus's heart ached at the savagery inflicted on the peaceful Avians and their Great Trees. He knew he had to steer Thetan away from further violence.

Marcus began his subtle manipulation, weaving threads of empathy into Thetan's consciousness. He planted seeds of remorse, hoping they would take root in the leader's spirit. At the same time, he played upon Thetan's desires—power, wealth, and the promise of advanced knowledge. He crafted a vision that offered Thetan a glimpse of enlightenment and supremacy, but only if he ceased the violence against the Avians. Marcus embedded a warning in Thetan's mind: any breach of this accord would bring severe consequences.

As dawn approached, Thetan awoke, stirred by the echoes of his nocturnal vision. Feeling a newfound urgency, he quickly dressed and made his way to the King's Hall, the heart of the Bison Hive. The massive chamber, with its towering columns and exalted dais, awaited his presence. Here, Thetan would announce the new edicts that had crystallized in his mind.

In the grand hall, Thetan summoned Bertran, his son and confidant. The space was a testament to Othorian grandeur, with marble columns and polished stone floors reflecting the light from crystalline chandeliers. The hall was filled with the elite of Othorian society, all awaiting Thetan's words.

"My son," Thetan called, his voice echoing through the chamber. The hall, now silent with anticipation, became the stage for the day's strange summons. Two immense black jiants, towering ant-like creatures, stood by the dais, signaling the importance of the gathering. "And all my people," Thetan continued, "I have had a vision—a new path to power, riches, and enlightenment. After I speak with Bertran, I will address you all."

Thetan's fondness for foule, a hallucinogenic drink, was evident as the pungent aroma surrounded him. With a nod, he invited Bertran to join him on the dais, where two thrones awaited.

Bertran, a commanding figure with a noble black hide and powerful wings, took his place beside his father. His wings, a rare and revered trait among the Othorians, marked him as a symbol of power and leadership. Thetan, though aged and scarred, still bore the same wings, now gray and mottled with time. Together, they were the embodiment of Othorian strength—one with the wisdom of age, the other with the vigor of youth.

Their conversation, masked by the low murmur of the court, was a private exchange. "I have had a vision," Thetan confided. "We must continue to collect Avians, but we must do so peacefully. If we bring enough Avians to the Highland Plateau without further violence, we will be rewarded with great riches and advanced technologies."

Bertran's response was cautious, his face betraying no emotion. "So now we must make peace with our feathered adversaries?" he asked, skepticism in his voice. "We started this campaign at your behest, and now we are to change course?"

Thetan, growing impatient, insisted, "We must do this, Bertran. If we don't follow this new approach, we will face dire consequences, not rewards."

Bertran, though ruffled, agreed with a show of deference. "As you command, Father. Let us discuss this further in the war room with our generals."

As he rose to leave, Bertran refilled Thetan's goblet with foule. "Drink, my liege, and we shall convene shortly," he said, his voice loud enough for all to hear.

Marcus, still connected to Thetan's mind, sensed the tension between father and son. But as Thetan took a sip of the drink, Marcus felt a sudden jolt of fear. Something was wrong. He scanned Thetan's vitals, and the realization hit him like a storm: Thetan had been poisoned.

Several minutes later, in the King's Hall, Thetan's collapse was met with gasps and chaos. The once mighty leader, now fallen, left a void in the Othorian empire. Marcus, still in his hibernation chamber, could only watch in horror as Thetan's life slipped away, severing their connection and leaving Marcus with a deep sense of loss.

Jolted from the immersive connection, Marcus found himself suddenly adrift in the stark reality of his pod. His eyes fluttered open, a soft groan escaping his lips as he grappled with the visceral treachery he had just witnessed. The cold clarity of his semiconscious state only heightened the impact of the malevolent act he had been forced to witness. Such a calculated, cold-blooded move was foreign to Marcus;

the harshness of patricide, the ultimate betrayal of familial bonds, was deeply unsettling.

In the dim light of the chamber, his breaths came in short, visible puffs, the shock manifesting in his trembling limbs. Bertran's ruthless deed had violently torn through the fabric of Marcus's moral compass. Yet, amid the turmoil, a steely resolve began to take root. His will to overcome this unforeseen obstacle remained undeterred, resetting itself after a momentary lapse. With renewed determination, Marcus coaxed his racing mind into a tranquil state, preparing to delve once more into the cerebral labyrinth of Bertran's psyche—or those entwined with it.

He needed to wield the threads of influence again, navigating the intricate web of Othorian politics and power. At least the captured Avians, unknowing pawns in a game of celestial magnitude, were already en route toward him. It was now more imperative than ever to secure their allegiance and marshal them against the looming threat of the Takers. The thought of such a union bolstered his resolve, for in the balance hung the very fabric of interstellar harmony.

POLLITUS RED TREE

12:
FLIGHT TO POLLITUS

Caleb and Goffry stood on the brink of a new journey. The air was thick with anticipation, carrying the scent of rain and fresh growth from the north. The surviving members of their buzzy pack thrummed in synchronized formation, their hum a low, comforting drone that filled the air with a sense of purpose.

Goffry broke the silence as their flight commenced. "This is it, Caleb. We're finally on our way. It's a pity about the mainmast, but I believe we'll make good time with the storm sail alone." His voice was steady, though his eyes flickered with concern.

Caleb, his gaze fixed on the horizon, nodded. "Yes, Goffry. Every time I think of Pollitus, I'm filled with memories of serenity. I hope Irka's family and our friends at the RedBlush Flock have been spared from the Othorian raids." His words carried a mix of hope and trepidation.

Goffry, sensing Caleb's concern, added reassuringly, "We've got the buzzies with us, and the southern winds are in our favor. We should reach there in three to four days, all going well." He tightened a strap on his harness, the leather creaking softly.

Caleb took a deep breath, the crisp air filling his lungs as he looked skyward. "Mother Kondor, watch over Irka's kin. Guide us swiftly and safely to them." His voice was barely above a whisper, but filled with fervent hope.

Goffry placed a comforting hand on Caleb's shoulder, his touch warm and reassuring. "She will hear you, Caleb. She always does. Let's set our course and bring some hope back to Pollitus." His tone was steady, a rock in the swirling sea of Caleb's worries.

Caleb returned Goffry's nod with a determined look. He adjusted the storm sail, feeling the coarse fabric under his fingers, guiding their flota toward the Gorgothon River. The landscape below was a blur of green canopies and winding rivers, a patchwork quilt of nature's bounty. His thoughts were a mix of hopes for a reunion and fears for what they might find. The wind whispered around them, carrying their silent prayers and unspoken fears toward their destination.

The voyage to Pollitus proceeded with surprising ease, thanks to the generous air currents that rose with the afternoon's warmth, creating ideal conditions for wind sailing. Caleb and Goffry alternated piloting the flota. Whenever possible, they meticulously applied the healing properties of green sappa to their battered feathers. The salve worked wonders, especially on the primary pinion feathers, which had borne the brunt of their harrowing escape. When needed, Avians could regrow feathers quickly, and combined with the effects of the special sappa, flight feathers would only take days to grow out.

Toward the end of the day, Caleb's new flight feathers were becoming fully unfurled, and his suspicions were confirmed.

"Hey, Goffry," Caleb called out, his tone a mixture of wonder and uncertainty, "take a look at these." He extended his wings, revealing the two ebony black feathers on the tips of either side. They had just opened, now contrasting starkly with the surrounding white plumage.

Goffry leaned closer and whistled in surprise. "Yes, I noticed them growing in, and they were … unusual. Now seeing them opened up, they're even more so, but in a good way. Black feathers? I've never seen anything like it. Could be stress, trauma, who knows? Life has its ways of marking us."

Caleb nodded, his gaze fixed on his wing feathers. "It's strange, isn't it? It's not like I can just pluck these primary feathers out. They feel like part of my story now—a badge of what I've endured."

"Yeah," Goffry agreed, his voice soft but firm. "They're not just plumage, Caleb. Wear them with pride."

Caleb smiled, a newfound acceptance lighting up his eyes. "Thank you, my friend. They're certainly different now, but so are we, after everything."

The conversation lingered in the air, much like the flota itself, as they continued their voyage under the open skies.

Later, in the stillness of the night, Caleb endeavored to rekindle the profound communion he had once achieved with the flota and the life energies surrounding it. Despite his efforts, the depth of that bond eluded him. His mind always wandered back to Irka. He longed to see her again, to hold her in his arms and smell the sweetness of her breath. He tossed and turned in his nest all night. Even the scent of evening-blooming mountain flowers—usually a fragrance he adored— now seemed cloying, an ever-present scent that disrupted his sleep.

The entire next day, Caleb felt heartbroken, unable to shake the sense of ineffectiveness. He just wanted to get back home. Memories of good times with Irka flooded his mind. He recalled his favorite time during the Pairing when they met—not just the passion, but the quiet midnight roost and cuddle they had afterward. Those enchanting full moons shining above seemed to empower their souls, connecting them so deeply they could feel each other's emotions as they snuggled together. Caleb would never forget that.

On the second night, resolved to make headway, Caleb hoped for a restful night, preparing for the dawn when he would launch ahead of the flota to herald their arrival to the RedBlush Flock at Pollitus. Trada, his loyal buzzy, would shadow him, ready to relay messages to Goffry if any problems arose. With plans laid and spirits buoyed, he anticipated the reunion with the RedBlush Flock.

Descending into the heart of the flota, Caleb made his customary pause at the vessel's nexus, where he conducted his nightly ritual, merging his consciousness with the ship to encourage its continued healing and well-being. The flota, though resilient, bore the scars of their tumultuous journey and was not yet entirely whole. Caleb lingered in the transitional space between meditation and full consciousness, attempting to strengthen his mental faculties by further melding with the airship's essence.

This time, he stretched his mind beyond the immediate connection, drawing upon the energy exchange with the surrounding life— receiving and giving in harmonious balance. With each reciprocal flow, he felt his awareness swell, embracing not only the vitality of living organisms but also the latent energy within the inanimate: rocks, air, wind, and even the mists clinging to the valley's contours.

This communion, though less immersive than before, was no less profound. Caleb drifted among the surrounding life forces, even touching deeper dimensions of existence. He became one with the meticulous spider, weaving its web in solitude, and sensed the enduring, sluggish pulse of the rocks themselves.

As the intensity of this shared existence surged through him, Caleb's body responded with a tremble, a visceral echo of the communion's potency. He focused, calming his racing heart, steadying his breath, and preparing to disengage. But just as he neared the threshold of his normal state, he felt it—a probing tendril of consciousness, soft with an undercurrent of curiosity, yet dominant. At first, Caleb was intrigued. He lingered, putting up a wall but leaving wisps of his mind receptive. Just as they were about to connect, his instincts flared. The probe seemed desperate, seeking something from him. He thrust back a sharp jolt of his own energy, a fierce psychic rebuke, an unequivocal "NO." The presence recoiled and vanished, leaving Caleb alone once more.

He surfaced from the depths of the nexus encounter, disoriented, his skin slick with perspiration, chest heaving from the exertion. Staggering away, he felt vulnerable yet invigorated. Without further ceremony, Caleb surrendered to the embrace of his sleeping nest, where sleep claimed him swiftly, a merciful reprieve from the evening's startling revelations.

The crisp dawn air invigorated Caleb as he emerged topside, the first blush of sunrise painting the skies with hues of gold, violet, and amber. The side of the mountain, adorned with massive purple blooms, exuded a scent that had troubled Caleb the night before but now smelled divine—spicy, sweet, and slightly minty. The glorious sights and fragrances chased away the uneasy remnants of the night's communion, replacing them with eager anticipation for the journey ahead.

Goffry, weary yet steadfast, emerged from the cabin below, his eyes bearing the telltale signs of a night spent vigilant at the helm. "Morning, Caleb. You're looking brighter," he said warmly.

Caleb nodded, a smile playing on his lips. "Morning, Goff. Take some more time to rest and refresh yourself. Trada and I will get prepared and ready the flota for the day."

Goffry stretched his wings, a gesture of agreement, and retreated below once more. Caleb turned his attention to Trada, whose vibrant energy seemed to thrum with the dawn. They shared a silent, intimate connection—a brief intertwining of thoughts and sensations that calmed the buzzy's excitement to a focused readiness.

After feeding and taking care of the buzzy pack, Caleb checked all the flota's rigging and equipment, ensuring everything was prepared for the journey ahead. He then outfitted himself in his battle harness, equipped with a small stinger bow, a quiver of bolts, and replenished rations and emergency supplies. He double-checked his harness, making sure it fit snugly yet allowed for the full range of motion his flight would demand. Trada, sensing Caleb's readiness, hovered nearby, his wings a blur of anticipation.

When Goffry returned, he bore a look of stoic assurance. "Fly swift and sure. We will be shadowing you," he said, clasping Caleb's shoulder in a firm grip.

With a nod of determination, Caleb and Trada leaped from the flota, catching the rising air currents with practiced ease. The updrafts were generous, propelling them forward with little effort. Trada darted ahead, a sentinel navigating the invisible pathways of the wind, his excitement now channeled into the task at hand.

Below them, the world moved along faster, lit by the ascending sun. Caleb, feeling the joy of flight returning to his soul and appreciating the freshness of the morning air, allowed a song to rise from within—a ballad of ancient valor, a tribute to his forebears who had defied the Othorians with wing and claw.

The melody lifted on the breeze, a lone, lilting anthem of remembrance and resolve. As they soared on, the landscape began to shift, signaling their approach to the heartland of the RedBlush Flock.

The grandeur of the Bison Ridge gave way to gentler slopes, heralding the transition from high-altitude austerity to the green embrace of the central Grand Valley. With each powerful wingbeat, Caleb and Trada descended, the landscape ripening into a lush tapestry of life as they neared the heartland. The dense foliage below, a riot of green splashed with vibrant colors from a myriad of flora, was a sign of the proximity of the life-giving Gorgothon River.

Caleb's sharp eyes caught the first glimpse of their destination—Pollitus Father Tree of the RedBlush Flock. His immense trunk and sprawling branches were legends themselves, seeming to hold up the sky with ancient grace. Pollitus was not merely a tree; he was a symbol of life and resilience, a natural spire that had withstood the ebb and flow of time beside the Gorgothon's mighty waters.

Sending Trada ahead as a swift messenger, Caleb felt a wave of fatigue wash over him. The thrill of the journey had initially buoyed his spirits, but the undeniable reality of his still-healing body and feathers tempered his excitement. The shorter, newer flight pinions, though strong, demanded more exertion from him than they would when fully grown.

As he drew closer, his heart lifted at the sight of Avians emerging from the canopies to welcome him. The faces within the flock would be familiar—family and comrades whose fates had been a constant weight on his mind.

As Caleb neared the noble tree, its gigantic sprawling branches a testament to its age and wisdom, the air was filled with a symphony of calls from the RedBlush Flock and their buzzies who had come out to greet him. Each song and chirp was an expression of welcome and relief.

The moment Caleb's talons touched the broad landing pad cradled by outstretched flat limbs, the air was electric with a cavalcade of emotions and Avians. The vibrant green foliage seemed to dance in response to the flurry of activity as everyone welcomed one of their own in-laws back into the fold. The buzzies, in their own expressive way, weaved through the air with frenzied delight, their buzzing underscoring and adding to the harmony of welcoming birdsongs that resonated throughout the RedBlush grove.

Glorita, Irka's mother, with eyes that had seen many seasons, was one of the first to bridge the gap, rushing into Caleb's arms just as he landed. Her embrace was an ocean of warmth, her feathers barely containing the tremors of her concern. "Caleb, my dear young man, bless Mother Kondor for bringing you to me," she cried out, her voice trembling with a mixture of relief and worry. She pulled back, her intense gaze locking onto his, her eyes brimming with anxious questions. "How is Irka? And what news do you bring of the Othorians? They are like shadows growing over our sunny days. Tell me, what has the world beyond become?" Her hands, feathered and warm, gripped his shoulders tightly, seeking reassurance in his presence.

Before Caleb could piece together a response, the buzz of conversation and birdsong around him reached a crescendo as others clamored for his attention, their eyes wide with curiosity and astonishment at the sight of his black feathers.

It was the commanding presence of Oritus, however, that cut through the commotion like a sharp wing through the air. The leader of the RedBlush Flock, with a stature that seemed to command the very wind, stepped forward with a deep, rolling call. "Everyone, still your wings and your mouths. Lend me your ears," he boomed, the sea of feathers parting before him.

The crowd fell silent, the only sounds being the rustling of leaves and the distant call of lesser birds and insects in the surrounding forest.

Glorita stepped back, allowing Oritus to envelop Caleb in a mighty embrace that was a testament to their shared history and mutual respect. "Caleb," Oritus murmured, his voice a gentle thunder. "Your journey has marked you, I see. These black feathers … we have never seen plumage of this hue adorning birdpeople. What tale do they tell?"

Caleb nodded, the gravity of his story anchoring him firmly to the present. "We were caught in a vicious tempest in the Bison Pass," he began, his voice steady despite the fatigue that clung to his bones. "The winds showed no mercy, and our flota was shattered against the storm's will. Goffry and I barely survived, and these feathers"—he paused, the memory of that harrowing experience flooding back— "they seem to be a reminder of our ordeal."

The flock listened in rapt attention as Caleb recounted the harrowing events, their expressions ranging from disbelief to awe. As his narrative concluded, Oritus's gaze swept over his flock, his voice resolute. "Caleb brings us not just tales of hardship but also a message of strength. We, the feathered children of Kondor, have weathered many storms. This one shall be no different."

"Oritus, I must implore you to grant me time with Father Pollitus," Caleb pressed. "My heart is laden with dread for Irka and our abducted flock mates. There may be little time left for a prompt rescue."

Oritus, his dark crimson red plumage a vibrant testament to his station within the RedBlush Flock, met Caleb's gaze. His eyes held the wisdom of the ages and the weight of leadership that was his to bear.

"Indeed, the shadow of Othorian aggression looms. It has not darkened our skies … not yet," Oritus responded, his voice tinged with relief yet heavy with the burden of foresight. "Our isolation may have been our shield. But let us haste to the nexus, where Pollitus will be your bridge to PuritaWhite. Though I warn you, we sense a tremendous disturbance throughout the Grand Valley; the ripples touch us even now, we are still sorting out the information."

Caleb's resolve shone through his troubled gaze. "My dreams, darkened by forebodings for Irka's safety, have driven me to action."

A collective breath was drawn as Caleb mentioned Irka—their own fears for her safety momentarily crashing against the sturdy branches of their home. Glorita, amid the crowd, seemed to embody their collective anxiety. "Oritus, enough talk. Go—you must help us find out if Irka is safe. I implore you to take action," she pleaded.

With a decisive movement, Oritus grasped Caleb's hand, his touch a solid reassurance. "Then let us waste no more time with words," he declared. Navigating through the gathered Avians, he led Caleb with swift determination along the arteries of the Father Tree.

Beneath the lush ceiling of intertwined branches and leaves, the path to the nexus was a journey to the heart of Pollitus. As they reached the hallowed site, the solemn figures of two RedBlush Communers were like silent sentinels seated around the nexus point; their meditative poses were a testament to their sacred duty.

Caleb, taking his place beside Oritus, felt the thrum of the tree's life force around him. The hum of meditation vocalizations and the whisper of leaves in the light breeze created a symphony of serenity in this inner sanctum.

Oritus's voice was a soft murmur, encouraging yet somber. "Your innate mental strength has not gone unnoticed, young Caleb. The time may come when you assume the mantle of a full Communer, but for now, let your spirit reach out together with ours. We will guide you, observe and learn."

Settling beside the silent figures, Caleb took a moment to compose himself. The anticipation of communion, of reaching across vast distances to touch the minds of those he sought, stilled his racing heart. He inhaled the musty scent of the ancient wood and fungus around him, the aroma grounding him to the here and now. He allowed a pang of hope to rise in his chest. Together with a group of skilled Communers certainly they would get news about his home flock!

With a collective breath, both he and Oritus extended their hands toward the smooth surface of the nexus. As their fingers made contact with the surface, it instantly grew into their skin, creating a physical bond. The potent energy of the tree surged into them, a conduit for their thoughts and spirits.

Caleb's inner eye opened to the intricate web of communion that connected all of the Grand Valley. His thoughts, honed by intent and need, wove through the tapestry of life forces, seeking the one thread that would lead him to PuritaWhite—and through her, to Irka.

The nexus chamber thrummed, a harmonious echo of energies converging within the heartwood of Pollitus Father Tree and down into his roots. Here, amid the silent communion with the ancient tree, Caleb's newfound potency as an extraordinary Communer was about to reveal itself in astonishing measure.

His consciousness, crystal clear and focused, attuned effortlessly with Oritus and the other two Communer veterans flanking him. Their initial surprise at his mental adeptness was substantial, a shared wave in the pool of their united minds. But there was no time for wonder; Pollitus awaited, his ancient spirit extending a welcoming probe of thought.

"Hello and welcome, Caleb," intoned Pollitus, his inner voice a gentle surge within the mindscape they shared. *"Your communing growth is remarkable, a beacon of potential for us all. But now, let us bridge the expanse to PuritaWhite."*

With gratitude suffusing his essence, Caleb fortified his resolve. The minds of his companion Communers yielded to an unspoken transition of leadership; now they followed Caleb's direction, an un-precedented gesture that acknowledged his astoundingly superior skills.

"Thank you, Father Pollitus. We would appreciate your help in com-muning with PuritaWhite of my PureWhite Flock. Something bad has happened, and I could not communicate through my previous attempt with IrmadineRed. Can you please guide us?" Caleb mentally requested.

"Then let us begin," came the reply.

Drawing a deep, steadying breath, Caleb delved into the deepest state of communion he had ever known, his abilities were growing expo-nentially. His spirit melded seamlessly with the Great Tree, transcending mere messaging. This time, he became a living avatar of the tree's will and way, journeying through the underground latticework of the Grand Valley's roots and mycorrhizae. He traversed this subterranean maze, Pollitus's guidance present but unobtrusive, empowering him to navigate the complex web of life that connected all within the valley.

As Caleb's spiritual quest finally found PuritaWhite, the acute suffering of his cherished Mother Tree lashed at him with a visceral intensity. Yet within the maelstrom of pain and memory, he held firm, fortified by the shared vitality of the valley's network. He bore witness to the ravages that had occurred, understanding not through words but through shared experience—the hallmark of true communing. He now knew all that had transpired.

In the face of such profound empathy, Caleb was imbued with the collective life force of the whole of the Grand Valley. With every ounce of his being, he directed a wave of healing energy, sending it cascading through the interconnected roots to soothe and mend PuritaWhite's wounds and then spreading this restorative energy to all damaged Great Trees. He felt a deep bond with this network of ancient arboreal beings. He was, for an instant, one with them all, basking for a moment in the energy of their combined life forces and yet feeling the hurt and pain of the surprise attacks that many of them had endured.

"Thank you, Caleb," echoed a chorus of gratitude, a symphony of the Great Trees that were impressed and awed by his powerful connection and support. PuritaWhite, once a beacon of despair, now began to shine with a spark of rejuvenated light, her gratitude infusing Caleb with a brief resurgence of energy.

But such an act was not without its toll. As the life force he had tapped into began to ebb, Caleb felt the unmistakable pull of his physical form calling him back. It was an abrupt retraction, a snap of spiritual elasticity that wrenched him from the communion and sent his consciousness hurtling into the vessel of his body.

The impact was jarring. His physical body, unprepared for the velocity of his return, was catapulted from the ceremonial seat in the nexus chamber, launching him into the soft, mossy embrace of the wall. Air rushed into his lungs in desperate gasps, the world teetering on the brink of his senses.

And then, darkness. The strain of such profound communion, the intensity of the healing he had facilitated, drew down the veil of unconsciousness over Caleb's mind. The last thing he felt was the concerned touch of his fellow RedBlush Communers, their presence a fading comfort as he succumbed to the void.

MARTA IN THOUGHT
AI REPLICANT IMAGE

13:
The Resistance

—◇—

Marta emerged from behind the stacks of boxes and crates in Odin's Hall at Westmount Marketplace, stepping into the celebratory crowd of the Othorian resistance. Her arrival, flanked by General Eldred and her flock's squad, accompanied by Lirna and Oboron, gradually quieted the exuberant cheers filling the vast cave.

"I present our allies from the White Flock," Lirna announced, her voice resonating powerfully over the lingering noise, commanding attention. "Despite the atrocities committed by our misguided Othorian brethren, these Avian allies approach us in a spirit of peace, offering their aid in our struggle against Thetan. It was they, along with their extraordinary buzzies"—she gestured toward the buzzies now hovering in a serene formation above—"who ingeniously orchestrated our rear assault, decimating the traitorous forces before they could unleash havoc upon us. Please extend your warmest welcome to these brave souls, my esteemed comrades in arms. Their aid has proven crucial, and they seek our support in return to liberate those unjustly captured by Thetan's ruthless forces."

A profound silence enveloped the crowd, their expressions a mix of awe and disbelief, stirred by Lirna's heartfelt oration. During this moment of quiet reverence, little Umbra quietly moved up behind Marta, gently clasping her hand in solidarity.

"Hail to our new friends!" The sudden cheer erupted from the front of the crowd, breaking the spell of silence. As the crowd parted, a short, rotund Othorian woman with a face adorned in vibrant red pigment stepped forward. "I am Portia, the one they call their leader. It's a delight to meet you, Marta and company. If memory serves me right, Marta, we've crossed paths before on the marketplace floor!" Her face brightened with a wide, welcoming smile. "Let's not stand around like statues, people! Celebrate our heroes!" she bellowed to the surrounding crowd. "Bring forth our best drinks and food; we must rejoice in our triumph and honor our new alliance!"

Portia's enthusiasm was infectious. She approached Marta and enveloped her in a hearty embrace, her words of gratitude lost amid the renewed wave of cheers, clicks, and songs from the jubilant assembly of Avians and Othorians. Above, the buzzies, catching the spirit of camaraderie, performed aerial acrobatics, buzzing energetically, diving, and looping playfully over the heads of the joyous crowd.

Portia led Marta and General Eldred through the rejoicing crowd, triumphantly raising their hands. Her voice echoed commandingly as she directed the flow of food and drinks. "My new friends and allies," she addressed Marta and her companions, "let's step into the freshness of the marketplace canyon. The dusk air will be a welcome relief for us all, and we can converse more freely there."

Approaching the grand exterior entrance to Odin's Hall, the scent of fresh air was indeed a soothing balm to Marta. The sight of the outdoor marketplace, especially at dusk, never ceased to amaze her. Its towering canyon walls, which shrouded the sun during the day, now added a mystical aura to the evening's ambiance. The fluorescent mosses and lichens, along with a profusion of vegetation clinging to the gorge's sides, began to glow softly in the dimming light, their luminescence casting a serene radiance and muffling any echoes.

Far above, the canyon rim was crowned with enormous trees, their lofty canopies nearly obscuring the sky. Carved into the rock faces were imposing statues commemorating Othorian historical figures and heroes. Some were chiseled directly from the canyon walls, while others stood as individual sculptures or busts, forming a silent procession of the past's valor. The canyon floor below was meticulously maintained, its sandy surface artfully raked, interspersed with vibrant gravel designs. Stone cairns, known as prayer stones, balanced in harmonious structures, punctuated the landscape.

As they neared a large oval table carved from a huge slab of ebony stone, Marta reminisced about its significance. Often a focal point for ceremonies and crucial meetings, the ceremonial table now served as a platform for their reception, with plush cushions adorning the stone benches and chairs surrounding it. Marta and General Eldred, at Portia's urging, were seated at its head while the entire surface was swiftly filled with an array of delicacies tailored to the Avians' vegetarian preferences.

Aromatic pollen cakes, blocks of aged milkcheese, and a variety of sappa drinks in assorted colors were arrayed before them. Exquisite pottery and glassware added elegance to the setting, accompanied by baskets brimming with exotic flowers. Even the buzzies were not forgotten, with large bowls of nectar and pollen cakes placed at the table's opposite end for their enjoyment.

As the hostess, Portia dove into the feast with gusto, and the Avians soon joined, relishing the much-needed sustenance. Before immersing herself in the feast, Marta dispatched a member of her squad to guide the main flotilla down to the canyon, having first sought Portia's consent. Portia's approval and evident delight at the prospect of gaining additional allies only enhanced the convivial atmosphere as the marketplace resonated with laughter, clicks, and harmonious hums from their Othorian hosts.

As the celebratory mood began to ebb, Marta, General Eldred, and Portia convened in a quiet corner. The dim, mystical glow of several burning braziers and torches cast dancing shadows across their determined faces. Portia, with an air of solemnity, broke the news that had been weighing heavily on her.

"Our little spy, Umbra," Portia began, gesturing to the petite Othorian who had discreetly joined them, "has uncovered crucial information. It appears the captive Avians, including your Irka, have been taken north to the Bison Hive. From there, Thetan's soldiers plan to transport them to the Northern Keep. The specifics are unclear, but we fear the worst."

Marta's expression tightened, her eyes reflecting a mix of dread and anger. General Eldred's gaze flickered with strategic calculation, contemplating their next move.

"We must act swiftly," Marta stated. "Our people in the Grand Valley must be rallied. With our aerial forces and your ground strength, Portia, we can strike a decisive blow against Thetan."

Portia nodded, her expression fierce. "The Othorian resistance stands with you. We will gather our forces, ready to strike when the time comes. Together, we can end this tyranny and free the captives."

As their strategic meeting ended, a sense of unity and purpose solidified among them. Marta extended her hand to Portia, sealing their pact of friendship and allegiance. Portia grasped it firmly, her grip strong and assured.

"In unity, we find our strength," Marta affirmed. "Together, we will face this storm."

Westmount Marketplace, typically a hub of trade and chatter, had transformed into a bastion of alliance and strategic planning. The newly formed coalition between the Avians and the Othorian resistance devoted the latter hours of the night to discussing tactics and possibilities for their joint endeavor.

As the discussions drew to a close, the Avians' flotilla, though still small, presented a magnificent sight. The armada of airships, with Jonus at the helm, adorned with vibrant colors and fluttering banners, descended gracefully into the canyon. The gathered Othorian crowd fell into a respectful hush as the flotilla's elegant sails, masterpieces of craft and design, billowed in the soft late-night breezes. The ships, each a testament to intricate bioengineering, came to a poised halt, hovering above the ground with regal dignity.

Marta, General Eldred, and their squadron made their way aboard the lead hive flota, pausing to offer a goodnight to Portia and her band of resistance fighters. They would stay overnight in their flotas to rest and then leave first thing the next morning. Portia, her expression one of relief and anticipation, raised her hand in a salute, her eyes reflecting the unspoken vows of victory and transformative change.

Marta, now reunited with Jonus, who had stayed with the flotilla, snuggled together in their shared nest. They were alone at last, and Marta shared her story, punctuated by chirps and tweets, of all that had transpired since she had departed on her mission. Both teared up when Marta confirmed that Irka had been taken north, apparently bound and packed onto jiants. Yes, jiants, Marta had to repeat. Everyone thought them to have been eradicated during the Kondorian War, but obviously not, as several now trusted resistance members attested that they had seen some alive and well. It was now clear that some had survived the viral attack that had decimated them at the hands of the Avians so long ago. The Othorians had kept their survival a secret and had clearly begun breeding them once more, again using them to wage war.

As dawn quickly approached, both Marta and Jonus finally found themselves succumbing to sleep. Jonus tucked in beside her, and they slept together.

Marta's sleep was far from restful. Her mind wandered back to her youth in the Western Aerie, where CeCe, the revered Head Brooder, mentored her. These memories took her to a time when, driven by a mix of youthful exuberance and a thirst for adventure, she and other fledglings would test the limits set by their elders. Once, they ventured into forbidden territory, exploring a network of caverns branching off from the main nursery chambers of the aerie. Their destination was a passage leading to a panoramic view of the grand western Ocean, a sight they had longed to witness firsthand.

This cavern was high up in the cliffs with a wide ledge overlooking colossal waves crashing below. The mighty mega-ocean, covering most of the planet's surface, whipped up formidable winds that spanned across Kondor and its few surrounding tiny islands. The young adventurers, including Marta, reveled in these winds, spreading their wings to glide effortlessly above the ledge, some experiencing the exhilaration of free flight for the first time.

Marta, the boldest among them, soared further out than the rest. The gale-force winds lifted her up high on her small wings, and she belted out a birdsong of conquest and exhilaration, the notes of her melody piercing the gusts. But her audacity turned dangerous as a powerful gust caught her, carrying her up and away. Marta fought to stay aloft but couldn't. After what felt like an eternity of tumbling and twisting in midair, she was swept down into another gorge along the mountainside.

After a tumultuous crash and long slide, Marta came to rest against a rock face, losing consciousness. Upon awakening, she found herself near the bottom of a deep canyon, surrounded by lush vegetation and the echoing birdsong of wild birds. Her pain and salt-crusted eyes testified to her ordeal, yet she was amazed to find herself largely unharmed.

Gazing across the canyon, Marta was stunned to see what she initially thought was an immense Great Tree. It turned out to be two Great Trees growing together. The trunks were entwined, sometimes fused, emerging from separate roots and extending upward along the towering cliff. These conjoined trees were massive, their intertwined boughs adorned with enormous black blossoms, each bloom twice Marta's size, dwarfing those she knew from any other Great Tree. The black blooms had a deep matte finish, seemingly absorbing all light yet shimmering with a metallic sheen.

Driven by curiosity, Marta decided to investigate this wondrous tree. She flapped her damaged wings and glided across the canyon. Upon landing on a large bough, she was immediately assailed by a swarm of wild buzzies, seeing her as a threat. Fleeing from venomous spits and stingers, Marta sought refuge in a crevice within the tree's bark.

Just as she braced for the worst, a commanding masculine voice echoed in her mind from the Great Tree itself. *"Stop, little ones. She is not a threat,"* the voice commanded with authority. The buzzies immediately retreated, and Marta realized the words were a form of communion. Although a skilled Communer herself, she was not normally able to send such clear messages directly from mind to mind.

"And you," the presence continued, *"who are you, and how did you find our secret enclave?"*

Then a second feminine voice, warmer and far more reassuring, joined in. *"Do not be afraid, my child. You are safe with us. It has been so long since we've had a visitor; your arrival is quite a treat. I am Miranda Black Tree with my brother Fraxus."*

"I am Marta. I came here by accident. I do not mean to intrude. Will you help me return home?" Marta spoke aloud to the trees, curious if they could hear her spoken voice as well.

"We know who you are, Marta, and yes, we 'hear' you, either in your mind or through vocal vibrations when you are near enough. Come join us," came the inviting response.

Marta's ascent through the ancient Black Tree was both exhausting and exhilarating. Her damaged wing could not support an aerial ascent. Guided by a now friendly wild buzzy, she navigated through vast branches and boughs, climbing higher up the cliff face. Finally, she reached a spacious hollow, a sanctuary formed by the tree's colossal limbs. This hollow housed the tree's nexus, a sacred spot likely untouched for ages, blanketed with soft mosses and lichens. Marta sank into it, her weariness engulfing her.

As she curled around the nexus, her mind drifted into communion with the two black Great Trees, sharing her memories and knowledge of the Grand Valley and beyond. This communion, though enriching, drained Marta significantly, leading her into a deep, restful sleep. Upon waking, she discovered gifts from the buzzies—globs of luscious, black honey, as sweet as it was nourishing. Miranda and Fraxus encouraged her to also feast on their ripe black macca fruit, its effects potent and transformative. *"This fruit will heal you but also will change you,"* Miranda intoned, *"but fear not. Its power will guide and strengthen you for the challenges ahead."*

Time passed quickly in the nurturing embrace of the Black Trees. Although fascinated by the fantastic lost valley, Marta was anxious to return home. As soon as she regained her strength and healed, it was time to leave.

Miranda and Fraxus imparted a mental map for her journey back to her flock, along with a solemn instruction: *"Keep our existence a secret. You will actually find it impossible to share. Cherish our peaceful sanctuary. But remember, when the time is right, you will feel the call to return to us. Your path is marked for greatness."*

Emerging from the canyon, guided by the map etched in her mind and the company of the Black Tree buzzies for a brief while, Marta's return was a blur of determination and instinct. When she returned to the aerie, she fabricated a tale of being lost in the mountains, a story met with relief and great excitement from her fledgling friends. CeCe, her mentor, gave her a look that spoke volumes—a mix of understanding, love, and disbelief.

Awakening from this vivid dream as the sky began to paint itself with the hues of a beautiful violet sunrise, Marta lay trembling next to Jonus. She had almost completely forgotten that childhood adventure. Over the years, the memory had blurred, and she even convinced herself at one point that it was just a tale conjured by her imaginative young mind. But now the recollection was so lucid, so real, that it shook her to her core.

The words of Miranda Black Tree still echoed in her mind: *"When the time is right, you will feel the call to return to us."*

That moment, she realized, was now. Despite the comfort of Jonus's side and her urge to follow Irka and the captives, Marta knew her destiny was calling. She could not deny it.

As the sun began to crest the horizon, the White Flock flotilla, accompanied by the harmonious thrumming of numerous buzzies, ascended majestically into the sky. Departing Westmount Marketplace, the silhouettes of the airships were etched against the brightening blue sky, leaving behind a scene of jubilant Othorians below. Their cheers and goodbyes echoed through the canyon, a resonant testament to the newfound unity and the hopeful dawn of a collaborative future.

POLLITUS RED TREE
BACK VIEW OF THE GREAT FATHER TREE

14:
RedBlush Planning

Caleb awoke gently, momentarily disoriented in the unfamiliar comfort of a soft nest, with his trusted buzzy companion, Trada, nestled snugly against his side, emitting soft purrs and buzzes. As he reached down to stroke Trada's bristly head and scratch behind his antennae, Trada responded with even more humming, licking Caleb's hand in a show of affection. Trada's relief was palpable, clearly relieved to see his master awake and well.

Stretching his limbs, Caleb's recollection of the previous day's events flooded back, along with a dull ache in his wings from his collision with the communing chamber wall. Shaking off the initial grogginess, he playfully nudged Trada aside and slid out of his sleeping nest, standing up somewhat shakily. After ruffling his feathers and gently flapping his sore wings, he turned to make his way toward the doorway.

Goffry entered the room with a chuckle, his face a mix of concern and relief. "Well, it's about time you got up, you lazy, mangy bird," he teased. "Where do you think you're going?" he continued, gently guiding Caleb back toward the nest. "Seriously, take it slow. The whole of RedBlush is abuzz with your communing experience. The elder

Communers are still reeling and in disbelief at how strong your gift has become. You've been through a lot. Rest is crucial for you now."

Caleb, heeding Goffry's advice, settled onto a soft, moss-covered ledge-like protrusion that grew from the wall instead of returning to the nest. "True enough, Goff," he sighed. "I don't understand what's happening to me. My ability to commune has intensified beyond my comprehension. It seems to take over, and I just flow with it."

As he spoke, Oritus entered the room, his voice booming with astonishment as he noticed Caleb awake. "By Mother Kondor, I've never witnessed anything like this in all my years," he exclaimed. The other two Communers who had been present during the previous night's communion, along with several members of the RedBlush Flock bearing food and nectar, entered the room. They fussed around Caleb, looking at him with a mixture of concern and awe.

Glorita pushed through the small crowd. Ever the nurturing figure, she sang out a shrill whistle, stopping everyone in their tracks. "Enough gaping, everyone," she said in a motherly tone, her voice imbued with pride. "My son-in-law needs nourishment and rest." She approached Caleb, balancing a tray of food and a glass of nectar, which she placed on a small table beside him. With a tender embrace, she stroked Caleb's face and wings with the loving care of a mother.

Oritus, perceiving the necessity for privacy, gently dispersed the crowd. "Please, let's give Caleb some space," he announced.

Caleb, yearning for a moment's peace, requested, "Just my closest family for now." Glorita and Goff, understanding his need, stayed by his side. "I'll address everyone's questions soon enough, at least as many as I can," Caleb assured as the room began to empty.

Previously filled with flock members curious about his transformation, the space quieted down as Oritus's directive was heeded. News of Caleb's extraordinary communion had swiftly spread through the flock, echoed in the songs, twitters, and chirps that vibrated through the Father Tree and its surrounding grove.

Caleb, driven by hunger and thirst, swiftly devoured the food and nectar placed before him. "How long was I out? Any updates?" he asked, a hint of urgency in his voice as he finished his meal.

Glorita, with a nurturing touch, caressed his cheek. "Slow down. Take a moment to digest," she said softly, her motherly tone easing his restlessness.

Goffry began filling him in. He was standing in the doorway blocking access to visitors. "You've been asleep for over a day, Caleb. It's late afternoon now. A quick update. This morning, Oritus and the other Communers managed to reconnect with PuritaWhite. She's on the mend, all thanks to your efforts last night. A young Communer named Joahiem, who was at PuritaWhite's nexus, brought us up to speed."

Goffry's recount of the recent ordeals was filled with detail: the attack, the abduction of four PureWhite Flock members, including Irka, and the prompt counteraction by Marta and Jonus to rescue the captives. His narrative, laden with emotion, paused as he recounted the losses they had suffered—the toll on both the Avians and buzzies, not least the severe injury to Trudy, Irka's lead buzzy.

After absorbing the news in a somber silence, Caleb stood up, his expression resolute. "I will find those responsible for these cowardly acts. They will pay dearly for their transgressions," he declared, his eyes steeling with determination. "We must leave at dawn's first light, Goff. I promise to rescue my love, your daughter, Glorita. I will either succeed or perish in the attempt." He outlined his plan to consult with the RedBlush elders for more information and to formulate a swift, decisive course of action. "I won't let my true love suffer at the hands of these villains a moment longer than necessary. By Mother Kondor, we will have our liberation and vengeance!"

After a few encouraging words and solace to Glorita, both she and Goffry left Caleb to attend to his grooming and personal cleansing. The attached lavatory, ingeniously designed, allowed fresh rainwater to be directed to rooms designated for this purpose, with all waste efficiently piped down to composting chambers located in the roots of the Great Tree. This eco-friendly system ensured that nothing went to waste, and all organic materials were repurposed to nourish the Great Tree and the surrounding grove.

Feeling rejuvenated from his cleanse, Caleb quickly made his way to the general meeting in the upper boughs of the massive tree. Workers of the RedBlush Flock led him upward, with Trada, his loyal buzzy companion, by his side. The meeting area was a marvel, a formed and grown amphitheater within a wide fork of the Great Tree, large flat branches for perches spiraling upward, nurtured over centuries to accommodate such gatherings. The boughs around the bowl were becoming populated with audience members of the Red Flock alongside visitors from the Yellow and even more distant Blue Flocks. The news of Caleb's transformation had traveled fast, drawing many curious onlookers eager to witness his change and participate in the upcoming discussions.

Off to the side of the large central floor of the meeting place was a small, ornately decorated table surrounded by plush chairs, each custom-grown from the Father Tree itself. Positioned near the nexus chamber's entrance, Oritus sat there with two other Communers, General Botus—leader of the Red Flock Protectors—and other key community figures. As Caleb entered, a hush fell over the attendees, and all eyes turned to him. Goffry, who had joined Caleb at the last moment, stood by his side. The silence was soon replaced by applause, singing, and respectful tweets, initiated by Oritus, who stood on a small dais in front of the meeting table. As the applause dwindled, Oritus beckoned them forward. "Come, join us," he invited, gesturing to two vacant chairs.

The gathering was illuminated by the glow of luminescent mosses and plants, enhancing the ambience of the early evening meeting. Oritus opened the session with updated information gathered from across the Grand Valley. "We have good news from PuritaWhite," he announced. "A scout messenger from the White Flock has reported back from Westmount, where Marta and Jonus successfully led a retaliatory raid and initiated a partnership with the Othorian Resistance."

He detailed the events at Westmount, highlighting the successful mission and the formation of an alliance with Portia's resistance movement, now preparing to march north against Thetan and his regime. "We now have allies in many Othorians who oppose the breach of peace by Thetan and his son," Oritus explained to the relief of all present.

Turning to Caleb, Oritus continued, "Marta and Jonus, along with your flock, suffered no casualties during the battle at Westmount Marketplace. Marta has now gone to check on the Western Aerie and will soon rejoin the White Flock's armada, which is in route to assist us here in the north. They are expected to arrive to join us in just a few days. Furthermore, the Blue and Yellow Flocks, who have also suffered brutal attacks and abductions along the eastern side of the valley, are amassing forces to join the battle. We will develop our strategy and soon unite with our fellow Avians. Together, we will prevail!" His voice, filled with determination and enhanced by his Communer abilities, resonated not just audibly but through the collective minds of all within earshot, stirring a powerful sense of unity and resolve.

The night's meeting, a marathon of strategic discussions and heartfelt deliberations, stretched on until fatigue set in. The leaders, after considering the contributions from various attendees, decided that the Red Flock would marshal as many people and buzzies as possible to form an armada of flotas. The Red Flock's numbers were small, and the repopulation process was far from complete. Geographically situated in the northwestern region of the Grand Valley, the Red Flock quadrant was perilously close to the Othorian hives, making them vulnerable. They had almost been obliterated being the hardest hit in previous wars, four Red Great Trees remained, only two currently occupied by Avians.

As the meeting drew to a close, Oritus invited Caleb for a more intimate discussion in Pollitus's nexus chamber. There, with the other Communers present, Oritus expressed his awe at Caleb's unprecedented depth of communing. "Caleb, what you achieved was extraordinary. We were merely passengers on your journey of communion. We've never experienced such a profound mental connection, extending even to the life force of Mother Kondor. Afterwards, while you were 'indisposed,' we tried but couldn't replicate your accomplishment. Any insight you could offer would be invaluable, especially now, as we prepare for war," Oritus said earnestly, reflecting a blend of curiosity and urgency. The other Communers echoed his sentiments.

"I'm willing to try," Caleb responded, his voice tinged with both humility and determination. "I'm still coming to terms with these new abilities myself, but let's attempt another communion. Perhaps together, we can reach out to the Grand Valley's other flocks to gather more information." He proposed that they first commune with PuritaWhite and possibly the Blue and Yellow Flocks.

Joining hands, they gently touched the nexus. Almost instantly, Caleb felt the familiar waves of communion and heard Pollitus's welcoming greeting. Together, they focused their intent on connecting with PuritaWhite and other receptive Great Trees in the valley. Caleb led the communion, a great honor to be bestowed upon anyone, let alone one who was not officially a member of the Communer's Guild. However, he only felt the usual energy flow patterns emanating from RedBlush and branching out across the valley.

PuritaWhite responded weakly with a brief update, still recovering from the recent attack and grateful for Caleb's previous healing energy. A following communion with Darien of the TetriusBlue Father Tree in the southeast was more fruitful, revealing progress in assembling a Blue Flock armada poised to join the northern assembly, and he also was aware that the Yellow Flocks were gathering and would join the coming battle. Darien confirmed to them that several of the Great Trees on the eastern side of the valley had been attacked, with many injuries and deaths, and an unknown number of Avians had also been taken by the Othorian raiding parties.

As the communion session concluded, Caleb felt a sense of disappointment. He looked at the others in the dimly lit chamber, seeing the anticlimax in their eyes. "I'm sorry, my fellow Communers. It seems I can't replicate what happened before. This has been no more than a normal communion. Maybe exhaustion is hindering us all," he expressed, feeling a mix of frustration and fatigue.

Oritus responded with a nod and a cheerful chirp, his voice imbued with empathy and understanding, "Don't worry, Caleb. We appreciate your efforts. Rest now, for tomorrow brings new beginnings."

With these words, Caleb retreated to his chamber, collapsing into his nest, where sleep quickly overtook him, enveloping him in much-needed rest after a long and eventful day.

BERTRAN
WOULD BE KING OF THE OTHORIANS

15:
BERTRAN TAKES POWER

Bertran's smirk shifted into a more serious, contemplative expression as he swiftly exited the King's Hall, fully aware that his father's reign had just come to a quick and dramatic end. The poison he had slipped into Thetan's foule had been carefully chosen—fast-acting, painless, and undetectable. To any observer, it would seem that Thetan had suffered a sudden stroke, with even the most skilled court healers unable to uncover the true cause.

For a long time, Bertran had grown frustrated with his father's insistence on maintaining the peace accord with the Avians. While Thetan had recently been swayed by Bertran's influence to support assaults on the flocks, it wasn't enough in Bertran's eyes. He was driven by visions of grandeur, instilled by his mental connection with the enigmatic entity—promises of unimaginable gifts, immense wealth, and ultimate power for those who were worthy and fulfilled specific tasks. In Bertran's mind, he was undoubtedly both worthy and deserving.

Unlike his father, who leaned toward diplomacy, Bertran had no patience for peace or negotiation. His heritage was rooted in aggression and conquest, a legacy of Othorian rulers who had waged war and sought to dominate the Avians. Now, with Thetan out of the way, Bertran was ready to seize control and fulfill his own ambitions.

During the last Kondorian war with the birdpeople, the Othorians reached the peak of their power in the Grand Valley, commanding a formidable army of enslaved jiants. These colossal creatures were a crucial component of Othorian military strategy, offering rapid transport for troops and supplies and serving as powerful mounts in battle. Their tough exoskeletons provided a natural defense against the venomous stings of the buzzies, who were allied with the Avians. The jiants' massive mandibles and powerful stingers were devastating weapons, giving the Othorians a significant advantage in the conflict.

As the war intensified, the Othorians made significant advances, obliterating countless Avians and buzzies. The western side of the valley, home to the White and Red Flocks, was the hardest hit, being closest to the majority of the Othorian population. Othorians preferred the more arid conditions of the west side of the valley.

Victory seemed within reach until an unforeseen catastrophe struck. Reports of a mysterious illness began to surface among the jiants, but the Othorian leaders, blinded by their thirst for conquest, ignored the warnings of the jiant caretakers. In a matter of weeks, the disease, engineered by the Avians with their expertise in biological manipulation, spread uncontrollably, decimating the jiant population.

The momentum of the war shifted dramatically. Isolated and without their jiants, Othorian forces, now cut off from supply lines and reinforcements, rapidly weakened. The Avians, seizing the opportunity, launched a massive counteroffensive. They rallied vast numbers of buzzies and deployed their battleship flotas, unleashing a relentless assault on the beleaguered Othorians. The Avians and their buzzy allies pushed the Othorians back, mercilessly driving them into their mountain caverns and decimating their ranks.

The final confrontation, known as the Battle of Bison Caves, took place near the treacherous terrain of Bison Pass. In a united, relentless effort, the Avians orchestrated a strategic offensive that proved decisive. This bold maneuver led to the capture of the Othorian leaders, who were swiftly brought to trial for their heinous acts of war and cruelty. Their subsequent execution symbolized the culmination of a long, arduous conflict.

This pivotal moment in history marked a turning point. The once-dominant Othorian forces, now leaderless and fragmented, were forced to come to terms with their defeat. Reluctantly, they entered negotiations for peace, leading to an accord that, while marked by underlying tensions, signaled the beginning of a new chapter between the two races.

For decades, this fragile truce persisted, marred only by occasional rogue raids from some Othorian factions. However, as time passed, a gradual shift occurred. The era of hostility gave way to one of cautious cooperation. Trade and bartering between the Avians and Othorians became commonplace, fostering an environment where even friendships could flourish.

In modern times, this evolution in relations continued to progress. Leaders of both races, once sworn enemies, now convened in a spirit of peace, exemplifying the potential for reconciliation and unity after a period of prolonged strife—at least until now.

As Bertran strode through the dimly lit corridors, his thoughts turned to the failures of Othorian leadership, particularly the memory of his great-grandmother Corra. Once a respected head keeper of the jiants, Corra had warned of the dangers of the mysterious illness that eventually decimated their forces. Her pleas to isolate the infected jiants went unheeded, leading to catastrophic losses. Yet, unbeknownst to many, Corra had secretly saved a small herd of jiants. A handful of Othorians had nurtured them in a hidden cave, far from the contagion, living in complete isolation. Over generations, despite inbreeding issues and limited breeding seasons, this secret herd had grown to over a hundred formidable creatures.

Reaching his private chambers, Bertran stretched his wings, feeling a mix of satisfaction and anticipation. He chuckled and clicked to himself, savoring the distant commotion that echoed through the hallways. He had just administered a lethal dose of poison to his father, ensuring a swift and untraceable demise. Now, as the only heir, he was poised to seize total control.

Bertran's preparations were meticulous. He applied a stinging lotion around his eyes to induce tears, then casually adorned himself in somber yet elegant battle attire. Practicing in front of his ornate mirror, he perfected an expression of shock and grief, every detail honed to convey the image of a grieving son, masking the treachery beneath.

Finally, the moment he had been waiting for arrived. A messenger, flanked by guards, burst into his room, panic etched across his face. "Pr-Pr-Prince Ber-Bertran," he stammered, "you-ou must-st-st come qu-quickly! Something aw-aw-ful has hap-happened. Our es-es-esteemed leader, y-y-your f-f-father, has collapsed in the Kin-King's H-H-H-Hall."

Bertran turned sharply, his face a mask of feigned surprise and concern. "What has happened? When I left him not long ago, he was well. Let me through!" he demanded, his voice booming with urgency as he rushed past the messenger, his wings aiding his swift movement. Guards and onlookers joined him but had to run to keep up, forming a hurried procession toward the great hall. He allowed his well controlled pheromones to indicate anxiety and anger, it flowed around him like an acidic cloud.

Upon arrival, Bertran found a crowd surrounding his father's lifeless body. "Stand aside!" he commanded, expertly faking distress. He swooped over the bystanders, landing beside his father with dramatic flair. "Father, what has happened?" he cried out, his voice laden with manufactured anguish, perfect body language showing distress and grief.

Trembling and sobbing he embraced the corpse, his cries of denial filling the hall, waves of sorrow laden odors filling the hall. Turning to the medical team, he yelled, "Do something, you idiots! Help him!" The team, led by a stern but clearly frightened Dr. Otriss, scrambled around the body, but their efforts were futile.

"It's too late; he's gone," Dr. Otriss finally announced, his voice heavy with defeat and shaking with fear. "Our great leader is gone. We tried everything, Prince Bertran, but his soul has departed."

In a fit of feigned rage, Bertran's eyes, now teary and red from the ointment, streamed with convincing sorrow as he struck Dr. Otriss, sending him reeling backward into the crowd. "By the great god Othor, why now? Why now?" he wailed theatrically, his performance resonating with the crowd, who joined in his grief, lifting their arms to the sky, their cries of grief echoing through the King's Hall. Inwardly satisfied with his deception, Bertran continued his elaborate ruse, unmoved by the genuine mourning that surrounded him.

Seated deliberately not on the throne but on a step below, Bertran projected an image of respect and anguish. His posture was one of a burdened heir, his head cradled in his hands, yet his keen eyes discreetly surveyed the gathered crowd. Among them, five figures stood out— the appointed generals. Three were staunchly loyal to Bertran, but the other two, Generals Tang and Ladlow, stood apart, their mannerisms and demeanor showing a mix of distress and suspicion.

Amid his exaggerated display, Bertran reveled in his own theatrics, savoring every dramatic gesture. Inside, his thoughts raced, his pulse quickened—not from sorrow, but from excitement. As he gazed upon his father's lifeless body, there was no trace of guilt, only triumph. He was finally free. Free from the chains of his father's will. Free to be king.

The weight of his father's expectations had fallen away, leaving only his own desires to guide him. No one could stand in his way.

After enough time had passed, he arose slowly, appearing forlorn and dejected. With calculated nonchalance, he fully stretched out his magnificent wings, eliciting a subdued wave of admiration and envy from the crowd. This display was a subtle reminder of his physical superiority and commanding presence.

Breaking the somber silence, Bertran's voice quavered initially but soon gained an authoritative timbre. "Enough of this," he declared, directing the attendants to prepare his father's body for removal back to his royal bedchamber. His command for a day of mourning echoed with the weight of impending leadership. He concluded with a solemn invocation, "Odin and Othor, save the king and grant his soul peaceful passage to the beyond, to wander in happiness and peace in the great mountains above."

The crowd responded in unison, their chant a mix of mourning and homage. Bertran's three most favored generals, Igor, Morang, and Hathtu, initiated a new chant, subtly shifting the focus to Bertran's impending rule. "Odin and Othor, protect King Thetan's soul," they intoned, seamlessly transitioning to, "Bless our new monarch, long live King Bertran!"

Bertran absorbed this adulation, standing tall, his regal posture signifying his readiness to ascend the throne. As the chant "May Odin and Othor bless our new King Bertran!" filled the hall, he acknowledged the crowd with a dignified salute. With a final, respectful bow to his father's body, he turned and made his way back to his chambers, the echoes of his newly affirmed authority following him.

Once the door to his private chambers closed behind him, Bertran's facade of grief vanished. The new king grinned widely and performed a jubilant jig, his wings vibrating in a display of unbridled joy. His powerful physique, taut and glistening, contrasted with his dark, leathery skin. The play of light across his body accentuated the powerful contours of his form, a testament to his strength and vigor.

His private chamber, filled with the earthy scent of polished wood and exotic herbs, was a sanctuary of opulence and secrecy. The polished stone walls, adorned with tapestries depicting Othorian conquests, glowed dimly under the soft light of bioluminescent fungi. Bertran's every move exuded confidence and dominance, his presence commanding the luxurious space.

Settling into his plush bed, Bertran drew comfort from the presence of Broot, his miniature jiant pet. Broot's unique ability to stridulate, making soothing, humming vibrations, offered a calming counterpoint to Bertran's tumultuous emotions. Although severely stunted and minute in size due to inbreeding, Broot had found an unlikely companion in Bertran. The prince cherished Broot, not just for his unquestionable loyalty and the protection of his deadly sting but also for his chameleonlike ability to blend seamlessly into their surroundings, perfect for spy missions.

"Well, Broot," Bertran said, his voice dripping with satisfaction, "we did it. The old fool is finally out of the way. Can you believe how easily they all bought my act? I almost deserve an award for that performance!" He laughed, the sound echoing off the chamber's high ceiling.

Broot tilted his head, his multifaceted eyes glinting with curiosity as he continued his soothing hum. Bertran stroked the pet's soft, segmented back, feeling a rush of exhilaration mixed with relief.

"Father always underestimated me, didn't he? Thought I was just a spoiled boy with no real ambition. But look at us now, Broot. I've outsmarted them all. And soon, I'll have more power than he ever dreamed of. We're just getting started."

The miniature jiant shifted his shell colors slightly, blending into the rich fabric of the bed, as if in agreement. Bertran's laughter subsided into a contented sigh. He lay back further into the cushions, the adrenaline of his victory giving way to a sense of triumphant calm.

Exhausted from the day's events, Bertran needed to rest, his solitude a fitting guise for his supposed mourning. As he finally drifted off, his mind was filled with plans for the future. Yet, his sleep was soon interrupted by the familiar mental pull of the mysterious entity that had long been guiding him and his father.

In his semiconscious state, Bertran found himself again engaged in a strange communion with this being. Lacking the more skilled communing abilities of the Avians, Bertran's interaction was a swirl of images, emotions, and intuitive understandings. Initially, the entity conveyed a sense of sorrow but was also angered and shocked over Thetan's death. Bertran acknowledged his role while revealing his intent to continue their plan of bringing the captive Avians to the meeting place near the Three Golden Obelisks.

However, as the concept of "captives" entered Bertran's thoughts, he sensed more disappointment and irritation from the entity. It seemed to question his methods and motives. In response, Bertran projected thoughts of the necessity for speed and results, coupled with a request for more details on the promised rewards. Their mental exchange was a battle of wills, with Bertran feeling both the lure of immense treasures and power and the discomfort of being commanded to "obey or else."

Bertran awoke in a sweat, Broot eyeing him from the edge of the bed. The intensity of the mental exchange left him restless, his body tossing and turning as he sought clarity amid the confusion. The promise of rewards tantalized him, yet the entity's insistence on obedience and the undercurrent of threat left him uneasy. As sleep finally reclaimed him, Bertran's dreams were a chaotic blend of emotion.

Bertran awoke with a jolt, his mind still buzzing from the previous night's intense communion. The entity's lingering presence in his consciousness was unsettling, an unusual and disturbing phenomenon for him. Determined to shake off these remnants, Bertran nudged Broot out of bed, his spirits buoyed by the realization of his newfound power.

"I am now the king of the Othorians," he thought triumphantly as he sprang out of bed, eager to embrace the day and his new role.

As he stepped out of his chamber, Bertran noticed new royal guards now posted at his door, a clear sign of his elevated status. His personal groom and assistant, Dorion, appeared beside him—a figure markedly less imposing than Bertran, lacking wings and of lesser stature.

Dorion, with a mix of servility and eagerness, inquired, "What are your wishes today, my liege? The news of the king's sudden passing has grieved us all deeply. There are many urgent matters requiring your attention."

Bertran, without missing a beat, declared, "Dorion, I appoint you to be my royal chamberlain. You will replace my father's chamberlain, but he shall assist you. Compile a list of all necessary duties. I have no desire to be burdened by the daily affairs of running the hive. That responsibility falls to you. Remember, you report directly to me, and confidentiality is paramount. Failure to adhere to this will have severe consequences."

Dorion swelled with pride at his appointment but quickly recoiled at the gravity of Bertran's warning. "Fear not, just follow my commands and stay discreet, and we shall continue to get along fine," Bertran concluded with a dismissive wave.

"Now, leave me. I am off to dine and refresh myself. Summon my generals for an emergency meeting in the Battle Room in exactly thirty minutes. After that, bring me the list of my duties and any other appointments I must honor. You will accompany me to all meetings and ensure a trusted scribe is present to record every word. You are dismissed."

With that, Bertran strode off, leaving Dorion to scramble in his wake, a mix of excitement and trepidation accompanying his new role as the right hand of the new king of the Othorians.

THE BLACK TREE GORGE
HOME OF ANCIENT GREAT TREES
MIRANDA AND FRAXUS BLACK TREE

16:
Back to the Aerie

---◇◇⬦◇◇---

Navigating to the Western Aerie was no small feat, given its strategic design to be both impregnable and hidden. This secluded haven, essential for nurturing young Avians, required a steep ascent above the Western Mountain Range. Typically, the journey was undertaken by riding a gasbag or a flota, and while intimidating at first, it became more manageable with experience and the right starting point.

Once airborne, Avians aimed to pinpoint the aerie from high above, leveraging their innate aerial skills. A swift, diving descent followed, minimizing the risk of being spotted. Avians possessed an exceptional ability: an internal mental map of the entire Grand Valley, ingrained through genetic inheritance, instinct, and ancestral knowledge. This gift made them adept at stealthily dive-bombing toward the aerie's entrance, each employing unique techniques to reach this hidden sanctuary.

Marta executed this maneuver with expert precision, locating the naturally camouflaged narrow landing ledge on the cliffside. The ledge, resembling a natural shelf covered with soft layers of sand, led to the aerie's entrance—a narrow crack barely wide enough for one person. This tunnel, stretching for several feet, eventually opened into a vast cavern. Generations of Communers had cultivated the plant life within, creating a safe, healthy atmosphere and a place of immense beauty, ideal for nurturing and educating the young brood of the valley's flocks.

CeCe, the revered Great Mother Brooder, oversaw this sanctuary, serving as the grand matron for the entire brood. Avians often lived beyond two hundred years, balanced by a low birth rate, with females typically having only one or two successful hatchlings in their lifetime. Multiple siblings were rare, making population growth a gradual, generational process. Consequently, younger fledglings were pampered and educated but kept hidden and safe until they were self-sufficient.

Inside, the aerie revealed a massive circular cavern with steep walls rising thousands of feet. The sky appeared as a small disc far above. Vines, mosses, and lichens covered the rocky walls, the diffused light bright enough to nourish plant life. A band of lush forest and vegetation grew where the sun brushed across the cavern floor. The combination of scents from the varied plant life brought back fond memories to Marta—there was a mosslike plant that covered much of the cavern floor and some of the walls, its minuscule white flowers blooming constantly. The scent was calming, lightly floral with a citrusy note.

The gentle whispers of the young flock members filled the air, cushioned by the dense tapestry of flora. Here, amid the nurturing embrace of the Brooders, Avian offspring were cradled through their formative years, their laughter a melody accompanying the rustle of leaves and the soft glow of luminescent algae and fungi emanating from the darker corners.

One side of the cavern housed the nursery, a hive of delicate life. Private alcoves, carved into the walls, served as cozy sleeping quarters for the young Avians, where they dreamed of the sky, the sky that they would one day conquer. Nearby, larger and more ornate chambers were reserved for the Brooders, their guardians and mentors. On the opposite side, a solemn space for council meetings stood in contrast, flanked by more accommodations for visiting kin and dignitaries.

Marta, always awestruck by the aerie's grandeur, quickly refocused on her mission and swooped toward CeCe's quarters, located in the center of the forested swath. Here, a unique orchard of immature Great Trees representing all four flock colors thrived in a perfectly balanced climate. The leaves were enormous, designed to capture as much sunlight as possible, but they appeared in somewhat paler hues due to the low light. This grove, transplanted a millennium ago by the aerie's founders, had grown a link with the Great Trees in the valley far below. This biological connection, through the roots and mycelium of countless organisms in the rocks, crevices, cracks, and streams, allowed for communing between the aerie and anywhere in the valley.

As Marta approached, the lively sounds of children and their Brooder teachers filled the air. Landing in the largest central tree, affectionately known as the Little Mother Tree, Marta was greeted by two familiar young Brooders with many hugs and excited twitters and chirps. They escorted her to CeCe, who was perched within a natural amphitheater formed by spirally arranged flattened boughs—typical of Avian meeting places—overlooking a lattice floor of interwoven branches. CeCe, the venerable maîtresse of the aerie, greeted Marta with a warm, welcoming smile. Her deeply wrinkled face, covered in fine white downy feathers typical of older Avians, radiated peace and love. CeCe rose and clasped her hands together, lightly flapping her old grey wings in a gesture of joy and anticipation.

"Come, my young Marta, I have missed you dearly and am relieved to see you safe and sound," CeCe spoke warmly, her voice like a soothing breeze, a combination of skillful birdsong and vocalizations. She enveloped Marta in a heartfelt hug who immediately recalled her smell, that warm faint motherly scent that one never forgets. Hanging onto Marta's arm CeCe looked deep into her eyes. "Tell me your worries, though I sense they are many. The valley has been greatly troubled, and we've been anxious for news."

Marta led CeCe back to her comfortable seat before recounting the recent events. Her narrative was filled with much clucking and angry chirps as she detailed the Othorians' renewed aggression and the abduction of many of their people. She also narrated their recent victory at the Westmount Marketplace, a story accompanied by uplifting cheerful birdsong.

"I'm here for another reason, too," Marta began again, seating herself near the venerable Grandmother Brooder, holding her time-withered hands in a gentle caress.

But CeCe interjected with a hint of a squawk, "You still carry the effects of the Blacks with you, child. I sensed it when you returned from your adventure that day, not so long ago."

CeCe gripped Marta's hand with surprising force, pulling her forward. Her penetrating gaze seemed to open Marta's mind to her mental probing, a connection deepened by shared memories and emotions. Marta felt as if she was being examined to her core, uncomfortable but done with good intention. After a moment, CeCe leaned back, releasing the mental embrace and easing her grip. "You know now, don't you? Your visit to the Blacks changed you indeed, as they foretold. I am aware of their rare interactions with our ancestors. It has only occurred three times in recent Avian history, yours being the third. I am certain there were several more going back even further before our recorded history."

"I need to return to the them, I feel obligated to do so," Marta asserted in a hushed yet firm tone, her voice resonating with passion and a sharp resolute birdcall to punctuate.

CeCe, with a gentle chuckle and cluck, responded encouragingly, "Then go, my child. Go in peace. You know the path. Who am I to hinder the journey of a determined Marta?" She laughed softly, her eyes twinkling with affection and understanding. "But what holds you back now? Is it doubt… perhaps, do I see fear?"

Marta hesitated. "I feel torn. Everyone here relies on me, the timing seems off, and yet … I sense a calling, a compelling need to come here, as if it's essential for everyone's good. I'm just … unsure …," she confessed, her voice trailing off in uncertainty.

CeCe looked intently at Marta, squeezing her hand reassuringly and tenderly. "If your heart tells you it's necessary, then you should follow it," she advised with a wisdom that seemed to transcend the ages, letting go of Marta's hands with a final, motherly cluck of acceptance.

"Let us share a meal and some special sappa first," CeCe insisted, gesturing toward a table adorned with a sumptuously laid spread. She reached for a uniquely ornate metallic bottle. "This black sappa is extremely special, a gift from the Blacks, brought back by the last visitor before you—your great-great-great-grandfather Hestor, a PureWhite Avian like yourself. Like you, he was called to visit them at a pivotal time in our history." She poured the ancient, concentrated nectar into an intricately carved glass, its surface glinting in the dim light as she extended it toward Marta. The obsidian liqueur released a scent that filled the air—an intoxicating aroma, sharp and alluring, that stung the back of her nose and flooded her senses. It was a fragrance that seemed to carry the essence of time itself, mingling the whispers of the sea, the echoes of mountains, and the very life force of Kondor in its mysterious depths.

As they drank, Marta felt a surge of energy and clarity. The liquid from the Blacks seemed to unlock something within her, also imprinting a clear map of a pathway back to their lost domain. She felt renewed, her purpose now unequivocal.

∘◇∘

After a heartfelt farewell, Marta embarked on her journey, following the vivid directions now etched in her mind. She navigated through the aerie with a sense of familiarity and purpose, passing the main nursery where she had once been a fledgling. The route took her through a labyrinth of caverns, requiring her to fly over a mountain, squeeze through narrow passages, and dive into a subterranean lake. She moved with unwavering certainty, guided by the mental map.

Finally emerging into the hidden gorge of the Blacks, Marta was greeted by the familiar sight of the colossal, intertwined trees, Miranda and Fraxus Black Tree. Their towering forms, rooted along the cliffside of this vast crevasse, reached skyward, a testament to their ancient and mystical presence. Marta soared along the valley, carried by the updrafts flowing from the distant ocean, and alighted gracefully on the main bough of the mighty twin trunks.

As Marta neared, the familiar, welcoming presence of Miranda and Fraxus enveloped her consciousness. Their voices, gentle and profound, resonated within her mind. *"Welcome back, dear Marta,"* they whispered, *"the time has come for revelations and guidance."*

Instinctively following her now clear memory, she stepped into a cavernous hollow within the tree. Bathed in dappled light filtering through the canopy, she found the Black Trees' nexus. She was surrounded by an array of glistening vines and mosses, their deeply dark green surfaces shimmering with an iridescent black sheen, creating an atmosphere of warmth and mystique.

Settling into the cavity, Marta lovingly embraced the huge node, as she had done in her childhood. The Black Trees' nexus was distinctive, combining nerve points from both Great Trees and featuring two "shades" of black with a barely perceptible difference—almost like a trick of the mind—yet both truly black. "I've returned, Miranda, Fraxus," she murmured, her voice echoing softly in the hallowed space. *"I am ready to receive your wisdom,"* she continued in mind speech.

The Black Trees, in their resonant mental tones, began to unfold their tale. *"Now you are ready to hear all of our truth, Marta. We are the last of the planet's first Great Trees,"* they explained, their voices harmonizing with the rustle of leaves. *"Here, in this chasm, was the origin of all arboreal life on Kondor, emerging from the primordial ocean on the unique tidal plain of this gorge's floor."*

Marta listened intently as Miranda and Fraxus recounted the beginning of the Great Trees' existence and the survival of the Blacks through an ancient deluge that had claimed their ancestral brethren. *"Driven by an innate foresight, we grew upward along the cliffside. We were beyond the reach of the encroaching waters, unlike our brothers and sisters, who all perished. We begged them to reach upward as we did, but they did not listen and grew outward along the bottom of the chasm. We sadly watched them all drown,"* they recalled, a deep sadness tinging their story. *"Since then, we have lived alone, in peace, our essence intertwined with Mother Kondor. Their disintegrated remains created the rich humus that feeds the jungle forest below us now."*

"Throughout the eons, some explorers have found their way to us," Fraxus added, a note of nostalgia in his voice. *"Nine, to be precise. Each left with insights that subtly altered the course of history."*

Marta felt a surge of awe. *"So, my visit here is part of a legacy?"* she asked, her inner voice tinged with reverence.

"Yes, Marta," Miranda replied softly. *"Our black fruits, nectar, and pollen have long possessed transformative powers, heightening spiritual awareness, enhancing the ability to commune with the unseen, and even granting the gift of passing these abilities to future generations."*

As the communion deepened, Marta grasped the profound significance of her presence. "I am part of something greater," she whispered aloud, a sense of purpose swelling in her heart. "This is not just my journey but a continuation of a grander purpose—a communion with the soul of Mother Kondor."

In that moment of profound connection and realization, Marta knew that her path was irrevocably intertwined with the destiny of her people and the planet. The wisdom of the Blacks would guide her in the challenges ahead as she carried forth the endowment of those who had communed with these ancient guardians before her.

As Marta absorbed the gravity of the prophecy revealed by Miranda and Fraxus Black Tree, she felt the weight of destiny upon her shoulders. The ancient trees showed her a future where her son, Caleb, would play a crucial role in shaping the fate of the Grand Valley, the Black Trees, and, indeed, all of Kondor. The details of this future were shrouded in mystery, the trees conveying that more information would unveil itself in due time, as necessary.

They entrusted Marta with two precious metallic bottles, just like the one she drank from with CeCe—inside was the super-concentrated special black sappa. This rare elixir of life was painstakingly produced by the Black Trees at an extremely slow rate, its potency intensified and condensed over decades if not centuries. She was instructed to leave one bottle entrusted with CeCe, to be shared with the next Kondorian destined to visit the Blacks, while the other was for her son, Caleb, to be used *"when the time was right."*

With a heart full of determination and a renewed sense of urgency, Marta prepared to depart. She felt an intrinsic trust in the truth of the Blacks' words and was eager to return and find Caleb. After expressing her gratitude to the ancient trees and promising to play her part in the unfolding events, she stood at the brink of departure, her heart brimming with resolute determination and a newfound urgency. She clutched the vials of black sappa closely, sensing their potential to sway the tide of the ongoing war and bring freedom to the captives. Before leaving, she turned to the Blacks, her voice carrying a mixture of gratitude and resolve. *"I will not let your wisdom go in vain,"* she promised. *"I will play my part in what is to come."*

"We know you will, Marta. Go in peace," a warm and loving voice echoed in her mind as she gazed upon the gorge. The sun illuminated the landscape, glinting off the dark foliage that shimmered with an opalescent energy. The air was alive with the buzzing of countless creatures and the sounds of the jungle below, forming a symphony of magic that reverberated in her ears. The scents—intoxicating and refreshing—brought tears to her eyes, overwhelming her senses. After a moment, she reluctantly tore herself away from the sensory spectacle, a touch of sorrow lingering in her heart as she turned away.

Marta retraced her steps along the hidden pathway she had taken on arrival, but she managed to cover the final stretch by air, gliding swiftly and directly down instead of hiking on foot. On the ascent, the air had been too thin to gain altitude, but descending was far easier. As she flew through the cloud-kissed peaks, the wind whispered secrets about the landscape below. A patchwork of vibrant greens and earthy browns stretched out endlessly, showcasing Kondor's beauty. The sun dipped toward the horizon, casting long shadows over valleys and ridges while painting the sky in shades of violet and pink.

The journey, though physically demanding, was spiritually uplifting for Marta. With each passing mile, she replayed the wisdom imparted by Miranda and Fraxus. Their words resonated within her, echoing the profound connection she now felt with all of Kondor.

As the Western Aerie came into view, nestled among the towering cliffs and hidden from the prying eyes of the world below, Marta prepared for her descent. She maneuvered skillfully, utilizing the thermal currents to glide downward, her approach as silent as the falling dusk.

Back at the aerie, Marta sought out CeCe. In her hands, she held the precious vials, their contents shimmering with a promise of change.

Handing one of the ampoules over to her revered mentor, she began breathlessly recounting the details of her time with the Blacks, her nervous tweets and chirps betraying her excitement. CeCe raised a weathered, lightly down-covered hand to stop her.

"Marta, it is not for me to know the details right now," CeCe spoke with gentle authority, her speech interwoven with birdsong, coos, and motherly clucks. "Your path forward is now clear, and time is fleeting. You must act swiftly."

Marta could see understanding and empathy in CeCe's eyes—a silent agreement that transcended words. "Thank you, CeCe," she replied, her voice tinged with appreciation. "I will waste no more time."

CeCe nodded, a soft smile touching her lips. "Go, Marta. The future awaits your hand."

With these parting words, Marta spread her wings wide, launching herself into the sky. The air hummed through her wings as she flew with a renewed sense of purpose. Each beat carried her closer to her son, Caleb, and the destiny that lay before them. Her mind again replayed the wisdom of the Blacks, guiding her actions with the promise of hope.

CeCe smiled but also sighed deeply as she saw Marta fly away. At times, she wished that she could divulge more information about the Blacks, but they wished that their existence be kept secret. Miranda and Fraxus had insisted many times that there would be a time for all knowing, but not yet. "*Soon*," they said, "*it is foretold.*"

17:
Irka's Plight

—◇◈◇—

As the grueling days wore on, Irka found solace in the companionship of her fellow captives—Precina, Yuda, and Ontan. Irka, with her striking white feathers, though now dirty and sullied, retained a faint pink tinge from her RedBlush lineage. Her poise exuded determination and resilience. Deep blue eyes, filled with worry and resolve, connected with the others, creating a bond that transcended mere survival.

Precina, who normally displayed sleek white plumage, also now bore the signs of captivity—partially plucked and filthy. Despite this, her nurturing aura remained intact. A light band of blue feathers around her neck betrayed her Blue Flock heritage. Her gentle nature and soothing voice, filled with melodic trills, made her a favorite among the younglings in their flock.

Yuda, a robust young flock Worker, had become a willing but inexperienced Protector of their small group. His strength and courage were matched by a fierce loyalty to his friends, his voice deep and resonant like the call of an ancient bird.

Ontan, the youngest and smallest of the group, still had some adolescent brown feathers mixed with his white plumage. His infectious energy lifted their spirits, his cheerful chirps and warbles a constant source of comfort.

In their shared adversity, they formed a covert alliance, gleaning snippets of information from the guards' conversations. Their Avian ability to quickly memorize and reproduce sounds verbatim, even without understanding the language, became an invaluable asset.

One morning, huddled together, they listened intently as their captors spoke.

"Did you hear that?" Yuda whispered, his keen ears catching the guards' hushed conversation. "They mentioned Bison Hive again, but also something about Highland Plateau. Are we really going that far?"

Irka nodded, scanning their surroundings to ensure they were not within earshot of the guards. Her expression was serious yet hopeful. "Let's keep our heads down and our ears open. We need to stay alert, identify their weaknesses, and exploit them when the moment is right."

Precina, always the voice of reason, added, "I agree, and I'm certain that a rescue attempt will be made by our flocks. We're being kept alive, so we must have value to them." Her soothing tones, interspersed with gentle coos, calmed the group.

Through their combined efforts and Irka's basic knowledge of the Othorian language, they pieced together fragments of their predicament: They were indeed headed to Bison Hive, but their ultimate destination was further north, to a meeting spot on the Highland Plateau. Whispers of a growing resistance against Thetan's rule and vague talks of a mysterious exchange for rewards added layers of complexity to their situation.

Their ability to discern which guards were sympathetic to their plight helped them navigate the treacherous landscape of their captivity. They learned when to whisper and when silence was their best defense.

Amid the bleakness, despite her weak communing abilities, Irka's attempts to mentally connect with the jiant who carried her, known as Artula, gradually bore fruit. Drawing on the rudimentary mental exercises and skills she had learned from Caleb and Marta, she reached out to Artula with gentle mind-to-mind touches. This form of communication was alien to the jiants, who were accustomed to the harsh vocal commands and physical coercion of their Othorian masters.

To Artula, Irka's mental overtures were a revelation. Jiants communicated with each other primarily through clicking sounds made by their mandibles, stridulation, and emitting pheromones. When in close proximity, they also rubbed their long, super-sensitive antennae together, thus imparting much more information, utilizing a form of mental communion through physical contact. The jiant's curiosity was piqued by this gentle Avian's kindness and direct, gentle mental probes, a stark contrast to the aggressive physical treatment he usually received. Over surprisingly little time, a bond of trust developed between them.

"Irka"—Artula's mental voice was simple, filled with a blend of curiosity and longing— *"why … different?"* Irka had been quiet that day. Tied and netted as usual, slung over his back like sacks of fruit, she was somewhat despondent. Her bindings were hurting her, and it was a misty day. They were traveling along the side of a steep cliff, supposedly shaving hours off their trip.

"Because I see you as a friend, Artula," Irka replied softly, sending waves of warmth and empathy despite her discomfort. *"We can help each other. We just need to trust and understand one another."* She wasn't sure how much of her message Artula understood, but she knew he got the gist of it.

In return, Artula conveyed some of his race's history to Irka, painting a mental picture tale of contrasting epochs. He fondly reminisced an account, in the form of a generational memory, of a time long in the past when his species was under the compassionate supervision of an elderly Othorian, Corra, whose kindness nurtured a peaceful coexistence. Those were times of mutual respect and gentle care within their gray hive.

"Corra … good. Kind." Artula's thoughts were tinged with nostalgia. *"Now … pain. Hurt."*

Irka's gentle touch and shared visions of harmony between the Avians and buzzies began to reshape Artula's world. Her kindness was a beacon of light in the jiant's existence, long shadowed by the harsh demands of the Othorian masters. Gradually, Artula's demeanor transformed, reflecting a newfound sense of empathy toward the prisoners. He became more considerate in his movements, striving to ease Irka's discomfort. Even his reactions toward the Othorian handlers grew bolder, manifesting open disdain when they mistreated Irka. The silent bond between the Avian and jiant, a dance of thoughts and emotions, remained undetected by the Othorians, who attributed Artula's behavior to mere stubbornness.

As the days passed, Irka's influence extended somewhat. Her efforts to communicate with each jiant, as they sometimes switched who they were hauling, also started to bear fruit. The tender mental nudges and soothing calls began to resonate with more of the gentle beasts.

"Irka, what are you thinking? Are you sleeping?" Precina asked softly one evening, noticing Irka deep in thought, her eyes closed in concentration. They had just curled up to get some sleep, lying facing each other.

"I am connecting with the jiants," Irka explained, opening her eyes. "They deserve better than this too. If we can win their trust, they might help us. I feel like I am making some headway."

Yuda, who also had his head nearby, sounded skeptical, warbling lightly. "Do you really think it will work? The Othorians have them under tight control."

"We have to try," Irka insisted with a convincing chirp, eyeing them both. "If we can turn even one of these poor beasts to our side, it might give us a chance to escape."

"I am certainly not a Communer, but I will be kind and gentle with them. These soldiers are really tough on them. I noticed that the jiants are different somehow, so your efforts are having an effect. This is exciting to hear!" Precina turned over on the hard, stone floor as she responded, trying to find a comfortable position. "By Mother Kondor, these rocks are hard to sleep on."

Irka and Yuda both chuckled with a low series of amused chirps. "I sure miss my soft nest; I will never complain about it again," young Yuda added as they all laughed and tweeted in agreement.

Irka tossed and turned, thinking only of her love, Caleb. It had been too long. She shut her eyes and let her mind's eye reconstruct his face in every detail. She missed him so much, aching to hear his voice or feel his strong arms hold her. One touch was all she needed. She feared for his safety and hoped all her family was unharmed. Irka finally fell into a troubled sleep.

The jiants grew more restless under the Othorians' brute tactics, no longer as compliant as before. The seeds of resistance were sown, and hope for change began to take root. On the morning of the seventh day, the usual rhythm of loading unraveled into disarray. Irka, eavesdropping on the Othorians, had learned that this small outpost cavern where they had spent the night was called Summit Reach, and they were to arrive at Bison Hive by late evening that day. This tight schedule was part of a desperate attempt to appease Bertran by pushing the jiants to their limits. The Othorians also relied on nimble, bat-like creatures known as gnarts for communication. These swift flyers carried written messages attached to them, facilitating rapid information exchange across vast distances.

A recent message, borne by a gnart, had stirred unrest among the Othorians. It became known that their respected and beloved king was dead, and his son, Bertran, the prince, had assumed total control. The news of Thetan's demise under mysterious circumstances had sent ripples of shock and division among the Othorians, with loyalties split between the longtime ruler and the newly ascendant would-be king, Prince Bertran.

At Summit Reach, Artula's unrest also reached a boiling point. As he was ushered into the loading area, his behavior became very unruly. Irka was loaded on his back first, and he remained somewhat compliant as she was being secured onto his back. But then he thrashed and bucked against any other attempts to approach him, showcasing a surprising and uncharacteristic assertiveness.

The tension escalated quickly. Artula's mounted jockey, growing increasingly irate with the jiant's contentious behavior, lashed out with his whip, striking a sensitive antenna. In response, Artula bucked violently, dislodging his rider and sending him tumbling onto the ground. The angered and disgraced jockey jumped up, cursing and swearing. Standing in front of Artula, he thumped his fist down hard on the jiant's head, raising his other hand to whip the rebellious creature again.

Several guards and handlers stood at the sidelines, laughing, hissing and snorting at his misfortune. Artula retaliated in a shocking burst of defiance. With a swift, powerful movement of his head, he seized the jockey in his powerful mandibles. With a sickening crunch and snapping sound, he bisected the man at the waist, cutting him cleanly in two.

The acrid smell of blood filled the cavern as it splashed onto the rock and sand that had been warmed by a morning sunbeam. Artula flung the now detached upper torso into the crowd of stunned soldiers. The dead rider's expression was frozen in a grimace of terror and disbelief, the last fading note of a scream of horror still escaping his gaping mouth.

The ensuing chaos provided a window of opportunity. As the soldiers scrambled to respond, Artula, with Irka aboard, bound and trussed into the net saddlebag, seized the moment. He charged toward the nearest exit, his powerful legs propelling them forward with astonishing speed. The cave walls became a blur as they made their escape, bursting into the daylight. Artula paused briefly, adjusting to the sunlight before resuming his powerful strides.

Irka's heart pounded as she clung to Artula, her mind racing with both fear and exhilaration. The jiant's sudden rebellion had ignited a spark among the others. Several of them, inspired by Artula's defiance, began to resist their handlers, causing chaos among the Othorian ranks and paralyzing any effort to chase after Artula.

As Artula galloped across the rugged terrain, Irka could sense his determination and fear. The gentle creature's mind reached out to hers, a comforting presence amid the chaos. *"Hold on, Irka,"* Artula communicated mentally, his thoughts a calming balm to her frayed nerves. *"We go."*

Irka, her emotions a whirlwind of fear and hope, responded with gratitude, *"Thank you, Artula. I trust you."* Her mental voice, though weak, carried a note of determination.

The landscape blurred past them as Artula's powerful legs leaped over obstacles with ease. Irka, her bindings already loosened in the captors' haste to secure her, clung to Artula's back, her heart pounding in sync with his every move. "We're really doing this," she whispered to herself, a surge of hope rising within her with every stride.

As they journeyed, Irka noticed Artula's keen sense of direction. *"Where are we going?"* she asked aloud and mentally, her voice laced with curiosity and hope.

"Safety, hidden valley, friends, long ago," Artula transmitted back, his mental voice steady, though unclear as usual, still reassuring Irka despite the uncertainty ahead.

The sun beat down on them, marking the progression of the day. Artula's pace slowed, his antennae twitching as he sensed the environment. *"Close,"* he conveyed with a click of his mandibles, to Irka, who had managed to free one arm and reposition herself for a clearer view.

The scene that greeted them as they crested a rocky hill was a stark contrast to the harsh journey they had endured. A lush oasis lay before them, the scent of water and verdant growth invigorating Irka's senses. Artula's labored breathing indicated his extreme weariness; he was spent, but he persisted until he gently lowered himself to the ground in the shade of a large tree.

With meticulous care, Artula used his mandibles to sever Irka's remaining bindings. *"Free now,"* he communicated, his actions tender yet urgent.

As the last rope fell away, Irka collapsed beside Artula, her body overwhelmed by the sudden release. She lay there, trying to process her newfound freedom, her entire body throbbing in pain. "I think my wing is broken," she murmured, the realization hitting her with a wave of dizziness and nausea.

Artula lay collapsed beside her, his own exhaustion taking control. *"Rest, Irka ... safe,"* he reassured her, his mental voice a soothing presence in her world of pain and uncertainty before he fell into an unconscious sleep.

Determined to find relief, Irka spotted a nearby stream, its water cascading melodically over rocks. With great effort, she hobbled to the water's edge and submerged her face in the cool, clear flow. The cold, pure mountain water was revitalizing. She drank deeply, then spent some time washing away the grime and exhaustion of her ordeal, preening and cooing lightly, happy to be free once again.

Returning to Artula with a makeshift container she had fashioned from a large leaf and filled with water, she gently awoke him and lifted his head so he could sip up the water through the tips of his mandibles. After several refills, Artula indicated he had enough and drifted back into a restful sleep.

Irka settled beside her savior, her gentle strokes on his face and antennae conveying her gratitude. She surveyed their surroundings, noting the canyon's serene beauty. Sparse trees, gnarled with age, dotted the landscape, but she spotted ripe fruits hanging just within reach. Despite her exhaustion, hunger spurred her on. The fruit she discovered was gnomples, a tart and sweet nourishing meal, meaty on the inside with a satisfying crunch. She also left a few of the ripest fruits beside Artula's head; he would need nourishment as well if he awakened before her.

As the sun began its descent, casting long shadows across their makeshift sanctuary, Irka realized they were at least temporarily safe. Not knowing their exact location but content in their seclusion, she nestled into a soft nook by Artula's side and succumbed to a deep, exhausted sleep, her sighs blending with the evening breeze.

Turbulent dreams and a heavy burden of guilt haunted Irka's restless sleep. Her mind oscillated between fitful rest and frightening thoughts filled with concern for her fellow captives, left behind to face an uncertain fate. As the first light of dawn pierced the horizon, she awoke with a new resolution to aid her friends and flock mates with everything she had. Sitting up, she noticed the remnants of the fruits she had left for Artula, a small sign of his silent gratitude.

Looking about to locate her new friend and rising with effort, Irka hobbled to the stream, grateful for the chance to cleanse and preen her battered feathers further. Despite the soothing ritual, each movement was a reminder of her abused condition. Her once majestic wings, now devoid of their great white pinions, were a stark symbol of her inability to take flight and locate herself. With only a faint salt scent in the air and the sun's position as clues, she could estimate their proximity within the Western Mountain Range. The exact location remained unclear, certainly not an area she had flown over before.

Lost in contemplation, she found herself longing for Caleb and her new family at the PureWhite Flock, and missing her mother and old family at RedBlush. The weight of worry for their safety was almost unbearable, and she yearned to reassure Caleb and her family of her survival. If only she could bridge the distance with a message to bring some solace to their troubled hearts.

Her musings were abruptly interrupted by a sharp mental command from Artula. *"Irka, come. Slowly."* The urgency in his mental tone spurred her into action. Approaching cautiously, she found Artula alert and protective as he positioned himself as a shield while creating a rhythmic, rattling sound with his body. Sheltered beneath her guardian, Irka cautiously scanned their surroundings, gasping silently as she spotted hundreds of jiants lining the canyon's rim. These new arrivals, slightly smaller and much redder than Artula, seemed to assess the situation with equal parts curiosity and caution.

Artula's message to Irka was brief: *"Friends? Hope? Family?"* His continued defensive posture suggested uncertainty. As a group of the new red jiants descended the cliffside with remarkable agility, Irka sensed a complex exchange of pheromones and antennae movements between them. The lead red jiant ignored the Avian but approached Artula, engaging in a vigorous rubbing of antennae exchange before turning its attention to Irka. Artula's protective instincts flared, his mandibles clicking in a warning tone as he repositioned himself to shield Irka completely.

This moment of palpable tension passed quickly. The newcomers seemed to accept Artula's stance, retreating and lowering themselves in a gesture of peace. Artula, still encircling Irka protectively, relaxed slightly and communicated, *"Accepted. Meet Queen. Go."* Grateful for his continued protection, Irka acknowledged his message and mounted the jockey's saddle still attached to Artula's frontal thorax.

Perched high on Artula's shoulders, Irka absorbed the stunning vista as they crested the canyon's edge. Before them lay an expansive bowl carved eons ago into the mountains, its floor crisscrossed by deep ravines and indentations, each filled with lush vegetation. As part of a long procession of about two hundred red jiants, they followed a trail that snaked westward along the bowl's rim. The path, interspersed with intricately constructed bridges, seemed ancient yet meticulously maintained.

Their destination was clear from Artula's brief mental updates: the main hive and an audience with the Queen. As they progressed, Irka observed some of their procession heading off into the canyons, but the core group stayed its course.

Hours later, as the sun dipped low in the sky, casting long shadows across the mountainous terrain, Irka and Artula approached a massive cave entrance. The mouth of the cave was guarded by several red jiants, their imposing figures standing watchfully. Inside, the immense cavern buzzed with activity, a well-orchestrated symphony of purpose and order, as countless red jiants busily engaged in their daily routines.

The procession came to a halt at the entrance of a smaller cave within the main cavern. This offshoot was adorned with soft mosses and pale, ghostly vines that draped the entrance like a curtain. Artula gently prompted Irka to dismount, and she settled herself protectively in front of him, her heart pounding with a mix of anticipation and anxiety.

A flurry of clicking and humming announced the arrival of the Queen. She emerged from the depths of the cave, a colossal red jiant who dwarfed even Artula. Smaller attendants buzzed around her, tending to her every need and guiding her forward with gentle pushes. The Queen's presence was overwhelming, her massive bulk moving with surprising grace.

"So, what do we have here? A fine specimen of a gray male ... and a little ... tidbit?" The Queen's surprisingly clear communing voice echoed in Irka's head. Her enormous, bulbous eyes shifted from Irka to Artula. *"I see you've brought a small token of friendship. But hardly even a small bite, is it?"*

Irka, taken aback by the Queen's jest—at least she hoped it was a jest—replied earnestly, mustering as much clarity and respect as she could manage. She spoke both verbally and mentally, trying to mask her wounded dignity. *"I am not a tidbit, Your Highness. My name is Irka, and we come in peace, seeking your kindness and asylum."*

The Queen's response was tinged with amusement, though her tone remained focused on Artula. *"How delightful, the tidbit speaks, and somewhat eloquently, though lacking in communing experience, I see."*

Finally, turning her full attention to Irka, the Queen continued, *"You are the one Artula speaks so highly of, aren't you? I am Queen Atoffalita the Thirty-Second of the Red Nest. Firstly, I shall converse with your friend the gray jiant directly, and then perhaps we will commune further with you, my tiny … Irka."* The Queen's tone was regal, with a touch of nonchalance that suggested she was both intrigued and amused by this unusual situation.

Artula crawled forward, low to the ground as a sign of respect. He and the Queen engaged in an intense exchange, their antennae touching in a delicate dance of communication, accompanied by a chorus of clicks and hums. The air grew thick with the sharp tang of pheromone messages, a language of scents and signals beyond Irka's full comprehension.

As the two jiants communicated, Irka took in her surroundings. The cavern was vast, reminiscent of the aerie where she had been raised, but it was filled with much lusher vegetation. The ceiling was draped with fungi, creating a green canopy above, and the red jiants moved with purpose, tending to every surface to ensure the plants thrived. Openings in the roof allowed light to filter through, casting a gentle glow over the flora, which seemed meticulously chosen to flourish in this unique environment.

The air was rich with the earthy aroma of damp moss and fertile soil, mingling with the subtle sweetness of blooming fungi. After so many days of captivity, the symphony of life around her captivated Irka's senses—the soft rustling of leaves, the whispering of petals, the quiet bustle of the jiants, and the distant, soothing trickle of water echoing through the cavern.

After what felt like an eternity, the Queen finally retracted her antennae, and Artula returned to his position beside Irka. The queen moved up really close, her huge face and bulbous eyes were only inches from hers. Irka stood firm, although inwardly nervous over the proximity of her razor-sharp mandibles.

"You have piqued my interest," the Queen declared, her voice resonating in Irka's mind with a mixture of authority and curiosity. *"You are both granted asylum, the fact that your Avian species caused a great catastrophe to befall my brothers and sisters so many years ago caused us to have great concern over your intentions. However, I pardon this, as it is clear that your kin were in jeopardy of eradication, with the unwilling help of the gray jiants. It is understood that your people acted in self-defence during a war that was not of your instigation. We are also well aware of the Othorians' evil deeds and their impact on us all. We will ally ourselves with you, seeking a way to assist our remaining gray cousins and ensure our mutual survival."*

As the Queen's words of acceptance and alliance filled the air, a wave of relief and gratitude washed over Irka and Artula. The surrounding hive members absorbed the Queen's declaration, signaling the dawn of a new, albeit unexpected, alliance.

LEURIN
LERIN'S AVATAR, COMPOSED OF MILLIONS
OF NANOPARTICLES

18:
AT THE THREE GOLDEN OBELISKS

Marcus found himself in a curious quandary, one that almost coaxed a laugh from him despite its gravity. The emotions swirling within him were uncharted yet invigorating. Even this burgeoning frustration and anger seemed to infuse his life with a newfound zest.

For much of his existence, Marcus had delved into the nature of reality, aware that he was living within a three-dimensional, lower vibrational realm. He often yearned to transcend these mortal limits, to explore the higher dimensions where many of his kind had already ascended. Yet something held him back—a sense that he had more to learn within the tangible reality of this current plane.

His understanding of good and evil was evolving. Where he once viewed malevolence as purely negative, he now questioned whether evil served a 'necessary' role in amplifying the experience of goodness. The idea unsettled him, shaking the very foundations of his beliefs.

Marcus pondered: if evil acted as a catalyst for the growth of good, did that make it any less abhorrent? This notion blurred the boundary between right and wrong, forcing him to reevaluate his deepest certainties. He realized that evil's existence didn't make it essential; rather, it was the conscious choice to reject evil in favor of good that infused life with true meaning and purpose.

In this physical realm, duality was inescapable—light and dark, joy and sorrow, love and hate. Perhaps, he mused, evil simply was. It existed as a counterbalance to good, maintaining the universe's equilibrium. Yet acknowledging its presence did not mean condoning it. Marcus now saw that morality's essence lay not in the existence of evil, but in the choices made in response to it. Ultimately, it was only by understanding and confronting darkness that light could be fully realized.

His anger toward Bertran for betraying his father, though seemingly irrational, felt essential, it was a testament to his inherent goodness and capacity for empathy. By embracing these emotions, he hoped to understand the lessons needed to ascend further one day.

In the here-and-now, his journey was not only about confronting evil but about transcending it, transforming darkness into the fuel for positive growth.

Marcus was resolute in his mission to halt the Takers' rampage across this quadrant of space. The plethora of vibrant worlds and diverse races, teeming with life and unique experiences, couldn't be allowed to fall victim to such rampant destruction. He would not accept that allowing such pure wickedness and violence to continue unchecked was the right course of action.

This evil was a force that had grown disproportionately powerful and now required a formidable counterbalance. He felt compelled to act, to be that counterforce.

In his meditative trance, Marcus extended his consciousness, reaching out across Kondor in search of open minds to influence and steer events back on course. His recent attempt to reconnect with Bertran had failed; the Othorian's mind was now a bastion, sealed shut by the intoxication of newfound power. Marcus's PSY abilities, even augmented by his technological arsenal, struggled against such resistance.

A recent mental encounter with Caleb, a remarkably gifted Avian, had starkly reminded Marcus of his own limitations. Caleb's mind had not only repelled his intrusion but retaliated with a surge of mental energy so potent it had disrupted Marcus's equipment. Marcus resolved to keep Caleb within his plans, intent on seeking further contact with him in the future. He sensed that Caleb would play a crucial role in what lay ahead.

An Avian with such formidable PSY power had to be convinced to join the cause.

After repairing his machines, Marcus resumed his outreach. This time, he found more receptive minds: Portia, a respected leader of the Othorian resistance. Portia's openness made her an ideal conduit for his influence. She had already demonstrated her leadership capabilities by liberating the Westmount Marketplace and driving out Bertran's forces from the southern part of the Western Range. Marcus subtly nudged her toward a rapid mobilization and a bold push toward Bertran's stronghold in the north. He hoped that a significant display of opposition might sway Bertran from his destructive path.

Marcus then discovered and managed to connect with Major Jubba, an Othorian who had not only encountered the Avian Caleb but was also an officer in Bertran's army and a significant member of the resistance. Connecting with Jubba proved to be an intricate undertaking; it required careful maneuvering to align Marcus's desired outcomes with Jubba's inherent moral compass. Marcus focused on gently guiding Jubba, steering his decisions in the preferred path while preserving his autonomy.

As Portia gathered her forces in the south for a northern advance, Jubba was summoned to oversee captive Avians now being transported north along the Western Mountain Range as they arrived at Bison Hive.

Marcus grappled with the urgency of the situation, and the dilemma he faced became increasingly complex. He was acutely aware that his actions, while aimed at protecting the planet and its inhabitants, risked estranging the very allies he sought to rally. The balance between intervention and preserving the autonomy of Kondor's races was delicate and fraught with potential missteps.

Taking a break from his communing efforts, Marcus stood at the entrance of his observatory the massive, arched windows framing a vast expanse of the cosmos with a view of the Kondorian Highland Plateau below. These windows were only transparent from within, from the exterior no opening would be visible in the central spire of the Three Golden Obelisks, Marcus's home base.

Marcus entered the room, sitting at a comfortable chair facing the seamless wall of windows, a small table in front of him. The stars flickered against the inky violet blackness, their light reflecting off the polished obsidian floors. The room was cool, the air crisp with the scent of rare, alien flora that lined the walls, their mesmerizing colors and soft luminescence adding a gentle natural glow to the space. Marcus loved his collection of plants and tended to them with an obsession.

Leurin materialized silently in the room, his form coalescing from a shimmering cloud of nanoparticles that shifted and flowed like liquid mercury. His body, though distinctly humanoid, had an ethereal quality—silvery and fluid, with surfaces that seemed to ripple gently with each movement. Despite this mutability, his form was well-defined, with sharp features designed to resemble a humanoid face, his ageless appearance lending him an air of timeless wisdom.

His silver hair, composed of the same malleable particles, was slicked back, giving him a regal yet understated presence. The tight garb that draped his form appeared almost woven from the same nano-material, their texture subtly shifting as if responding to his thoughts.

Leurin's eyes, however, were the most striking feature. They glowed with an inner light, sharp and penetrating, revealing the depth of his consciousness and the gravity of the message he bore. Though his appearance was otherworldly, he had crafted it with care, maintaining humanoid features to offer Marcus a sense of familiarity and comfort.

"Marcus," Leurin began, his voice calm but laced with urgency. He moved to stand beside Marcus, his gaze fixed on the stars. "There's been a development."

Marcus turned to face him, noting the tension in Leurin's usually serene expression. "What is it, Leurin? What's happened?"

Leurin took a deep, his eyes locking onto Marcus's. "The Takers," he said, voice low but resolute. "Their course has altered. They're accelerating toward Kondor. We believed we had more time, but at this pace, they'll reach us within the year—possibly even sooner."

The weight of his words settled heavily, and Marcus felt a chill snake down his spine. His fingers tightened around the edge of the table, a spark of anger igniting in his eyes. "So, they've finally chosen us as their target," he murmured, half to himself. The Takers—beings of insatiable hunger for life force—were the stuff of haunted legends. Entire worlds left barren, civilizations erased as if they'd never existed. Their arrival always heralded nothing short of annihilation.

Leurin's gaze hardened, a look of grim determination now purposely etched into his features. "They're moving with surgical precision, as though drawn to the vitality of Kondor, like predators sensing prey. We've seen it before, Marcus, and it never ends well."

Turning to the observation window, Marcus let his gaze drift to the distant stars. His hand absently stroked the leaves of a favorite plant he had brought to the table, his mind racing between hope and dread. Could they mount a defense powerful enough to repel the

Takers, or would Kondor meet the same fate as so many others? He inhaled deeply; his voice resolute. "We can't waste a moment. If there's even a chance to stop them, we have to seize it."

Leurin stepped closer, resting a soft hand on Marcus's shoulder in reassurance. "Our preparations are underway but I propose we escalate, pushing beyond what we've attempted before. We need to dive deeper into our archives and data bases, resurrect technologies we've barely touched, inventions we've kept dormant. Nothing is off-limits now."

Marcus's gaze met Leurin's, a steely determination filling his eyes. "You're right. This is more than a battle. It's survival itself." He stood and turned fully to face him, his resolve solidifying. "Where do we begin?"

With a swift gesture, Leurin directed him to the central console, where a holographic interface sprang to life, casting shifting blue and green light across the room. Complex schematics of warships, drones, and tactical formations flickered into view as Leurin deftly manipulated the projections. "We've initiated the construction of battleships, but with the urgency, I suggest a fresh start," Leurin explained, his fingers gliding over the interface. "We'll craft an armada—small, but unparalleled in power. I propose twelve core battleships, each shielded by a network of intelligent drones. These won't be ordinary vessels; they'll be hybrids of Creator tech and the most advanced systems from all our allies."

Marcus studied the images, his mind quickening as he took in the advanced designs and possibilities. "This armada... it has to be more than just a line of defense. It should be a symbol of hope for us and a harbinger of fear for the Takers."

Marcus absorbed the information, his mind racing with visions of the new battle squadron in action. "We'll need every advantage—shielding that adapts under pressure, weapons with power that rivals and exceeds theirs. This armada has to be a force they can't ignore."

Leurin's eyes glimmered with determination. "And that's exactly what it will be. Kondor will not go down without a fight. Every ship, every drone, every ounce of technology we have will converge for this. Together, we'll ensure that when the Takers come, they'll find far more than they bargained for."

Marcus felt a spark of hope ignite within him. "What about our manufacturing and assembly plants? Can they handle the new designs?"

Leurin smiled slightly, a hint of pride in his work. "Indeed. I have already begun converting our mining colony on Kondor's nearest moon into a high-capacity production facility. It's primed to produce the alloys and nanomaterials we'll need—materials capable of withstanding the most extreme conditions, and power sources that can fuel battles lasting as long as necessary."

Marcus took a long slow deep breath, letting the weight of the plan settle over him. "So now it comes down to a crew. We'll need pilots—beings who not only have a natural affinity for flight but also possess the PSY abilities to integrate and enhance our advanced AI systems."

Leurin's expression grew serious. "That's why we must also focus on the Avians. Their natural abilities make them ideal candidates. But convincing them to join our cause… that's another challenge entirely."

Marcus's thoughts turned to Caleb, the Avian he had encountered briefly. The strength of Caleb's mind had been formidable, a sign of his immense potential. "I'll work on that," Marcus said, determination coloring his tone. "If we can bring them on board, it could make all the difference."

Leurin nodded, his confidence in Marcus evident. "I'll continue with the preparations. We have a lot of work ahead of us, but together, we can do this."

Marcus placed a hand on Leurin's shoulder, their eyes meeting in a shared understanding of the gravity of their mission. "We will do this," Marcus affirmed, his voice resolute. "For Kondor and on behalf of all life in this universe. We will be ready."

As they stood together, the stars twinkling in the vast expanse beyond the observatory's windows, Marcus felt a renewed sense of purpose. The path ahead would not be easy, but with Leurin at his side, he knew they could face whatever came their way. The Takers might be powerful, but they were not invincible. And with the force they were building, Marcus was determined to prove that the light of life could shine even in the darkest of times.

That is why they needed the Avians; their contribution was critical.

Marcus returned to his hibernation chamber refocusing his efforts, first on Major Jubba, eager to assess the progress made since their last connection. Jubba was now situated at the Bison Hive, preparing for the imminent arrival of the captive Avians from the western side of the valley. This large Othorian settlement with a central fortress, concealed within the mountainous terrain, was now under the direct command of General Igor, a close ally of Bertran. With General Igor occupied in a war council with the new king, Bertran, Jubba had an opportunity to influence the local guards and soldiers.

Accessing Jubba's mind was now relatively straightforward for Marcus. Given Jubba's strong moral opposition to Bertran's continued brutal methods, drawing upon Jubba's admiration for Caleb, Marcus subtly implanted the idea of fostering the resistance movement within Bison Hive. Jubba, already aware of the growing opposition in the south, began to nurture similar sentiments among the northern guards and soldiers. Many of them, disillusioned with Bertran's harsh tactics and uncertain of the rationale behind the treatment of the captives, were easily persuaded to join the resistance. With Marcus's guidance, Jubba skillfully worked to turn the soldiers' loyalty away from Bertran, bolstering the growing opposition to his rule.

Marcus reclined comfortably in his pod; the air thick with the hypnotic scent of a blend of rare herbs designed to sharpen his mental focus. He was not in full hibernation mode so the pod remained open without filling with the usual combination of oxygen-rich perfluorocarbons and cryoprotectant-infused hydrogel. His ultra comfortable bed, made him feel like he was floating in the air. Reaching out carefully, his consciousness left his body behind, astral traveling across vast distances, seeking the presence he had touched before. His control was improving, the result of centuries spent honing his PSY abilities. This was no ordinary communion, it was a subtle art, and he wielded it with care.

Far away, Portia sat on a windswept ridge, her campfires glowing dimly in the twilight below. The cold mountain air filled her lungs, carrying the scent of cactus pine flowers and damp earth. She had been deep in thought, her mind occupied with the growing responsibilities of leading an army, when she felt it—a faint, almost imperceptible presence at the edge of her consciousness.

She froze, her breath catching as a wave of warmth washed over her, a sense of another mind brushing lightly against hers. Images began to form, not her own, but offered by this presence; scenes of battles fought and won, of strength and unity, of a future where her people stood victorious. She knew instantly that this was not just a daydream. Someone was reaching out to her, offering guidance.

"Portia," came the mental whisper, soft and controlled, yet carrying the weight of intent. It wasn't just a voice; it was a blend of images and emotions, pictures of a battle well fought, of a cause worth fighting for.

"Who are you?" Portia thought, her mental voice tentative but curious. The connection was strange, foreign, yet friendly and not unwelcome.

"I am Marcus," the presence replied, and with the name came a flood of reassurance, like a hand guiding her through a fog.

Portia's heart pounded, but the fear that had initially gripped her was quickly replaced by a surge of determination. She could see what Marcus wanted—strength, unity, a swift push against their common enemy. And she understood, on a deeper level, that he intended to help.

Through the connection, Marcus conveyed a vision of the path ahead: details of marching soldiers, the urgency of battle preparations, the need for swift action. He showed her scenes of victory, the calm after the storm, and the vital role she would play in the coming conflict. His influence was gentle but firm, guiding her thoughts toward the actions she needed to take.

"I understand," Portia replied, her thoughts clear and decisive, reflecting the determination she felt in her heart. She shared his goals—a united force moving north, their red-painted faces set in grim resolve. *"We will move quickly, I assure you, Master Marcus,"* she added with full agreement in her voice, finishing with a series of clicks and a wave of pheromones that swirled around her in the night air.

The connection began to fade, Marcus's presence retreating as he carefully pulled back his influence. But before it disappeared completely, he imparted one last thing—a feeling of deep trust, of mutual need, and a future they both sought.

Then, it was gone. Portia blinked, the world around her snapping back into focus. The cold air nipped at her skin, the comforting scent of the night air filling her senses once more. The brief encounter left her with a strange mixture of confidence and clarity.

She rose and began to make her way back to camp, her thoughts buzzing with purpose. The encounter had been brief, the words few, but the impact was profound. She knew now that she wasn't alone in this fight, and that knowledge steeled her resolve. As she descended toward the campfires, the flickering light reflected in her eyes as she prepared to lead her people into the battles ahead, her mind clear and focused on the goal before her. She knew what had to be done.

Meanwhile, Marcus opened his eyes, his breath slow and steady. The connection had been successful; the guidance needed had been given. Portia was moving forward, her mind now aligned with the path he had subtly laid out for her. He had felt her determination, her strength, and he knew she would lead her people well.

As he rose from his comfortable bed, Marcus felt a quiet satisfaction. The pieces were moving into place, the resistance growing stronger. The task ahead was monumental, but with minds like Portia's to guide and influence, the future held hope.

PURITAWHITE
MOTHER TREE GROVE

19:
Summit Reach

Caleb stirred awake, the faint light of dawn filtering through the woven branches of his nesting chamber within Pollitus Father Tree at RedBlush. He had slept fitfully, plagued by restless dreams that left him with a lingering sense of unease. As he lay there, the soft rustling of leaves outside and the distant calls of early birds greeted him, creating a calm that contrasted sharply with his inner turmoil.

He pushed himself up, shaking off the remnants of sleep, and stepped out into the open air. The sky above was a canvas of soft blues and pinks, the first rays of the sun painting the clouds with delicate hues. Caleb inhaled deeply, filling his lungs with the crisp morning air, hoping it would help clear his mind.

As part of his usual morning ritual, he began preening his feathers, meticulously realigning each one with care. The black pinions at the tips of his wings caught his eye, and he hesitated, his fingers lingering on the dark feathers. Up close, they were captivating—a deep black that shimmered with iridescent colors, shifting like a kaleidoscope with every slight movement. The transformation still unsettled him, filling him with a mix of awe and anxiety. He couldn't help but wonder how Irka, his beloved, would react to this change.

"Will she see me differently?" he mused quietly to himself, his mind drifting to thoughts of her. Despite the uncertainty that gnawed at him, he knew Irka's love ran deeper than appearances. She would see beyond the altered feathers—he was sure of it.

Determined to put his worries aside, Caleb finished his grooming, and as he did, Trada, his loyal buzzy, buzzed up to him, his wings thrumming with excitement. He greeted him with an affectionate wag of his abdomen, and Caleb couldn't help but smile, singing a joyful birdsong in response, a melody that conveyed both his affection and his readiness for the day ahead.

Just as Caleb was about to stretch his wings, a low, harmonious birdcall reached his ears. Goffry, his best friend, emerged from the adjacent chamber, his eyes bright with eager energy. "Good morning, Caleb," Goffry greeted, his voice infused with enthusiasm. "Ready to get moving?"

Caleb hesitated, his gaze dropping to the ground. The thought of continuously dragging Goffry into danger weighed heavily on him. "Goffry, I've been thinking," he began, his voice tinged with concern. "I'm not sure I can ask you again to come with me on this excursion. The risks… they're too great. I was planning to go alone; I have put you through enough already."

Before Caleb could continue, Goffry let out a snort and a chirp of feigned annoyance, shaking his head in disbelief. "You honestly think you could keep me from coming? Every Avian in Kondor couldn't stop me from being by your side. Danger be damned, Caleb—I'm with you, no matter what. We'll rescue Irka and our kin together."

Caleb met Goffry's gaze, seeing the unwavering determination in his friend's eyes. A wave of gratitude washed over him. "You're the best friend anyone could ask for, Goffry," Caleb said, his voice thick with emotion and grateful chirps. "But how are you holding up? Are you ready for this?"

Goffry's eyes sparkled with resolve. "Caleb, I'm more than ready. Like you I might not be at full strength yet, slightly battered but I can definitely keep up."

Caleb nodded; relief evident in his expression. "That's good to hear. We will need to move quickly. A flota won't be fast enough. I was thinking of forming a small strike force—something agile that can get to and navigate the Western Mountain Trail northward. The captives, carried by the jiants as we have heard, must be getting close to Bison Hive. If we can find them, we might be able to ambush them."

Goffry's chest puffed with pride as he responded, "I've already been working on that while you rested. I've rallied ten of the finest Protectors and Workers from RedBlush and other Flocks. We've even got volunteers from the Yellow and Blue Flocks, all ready to fight. And with your approval, we've got General Botus and his lieutenant, Maxima. She's a master with the stinger battle bow. They're assembling now, waiting for us at the meeting area."

Caleb couldn't hide his admiration and relief. "You've outdone yourself, Goffry. I'm so grateful for everything. Lead the way, I'm ready. The glorious aroma of the Pollitus's red blossoms grows as the rising sun hits them, filling me with renewed strength. Thank you, Goff."

With a nod, Goffry turned, and the two friends, side by side, made their way toward the team's gathering place, their hearts united in purpose and resolve. They hummed and lightly sang a birdsong of unity they had often shared in the past, the harmonious tune mingling with the other morning Avian sounds in the Great Tree around them.

As they arrived, Botus called out a hearty greeting. "Good to see you, Caleb!" His voice was tinged with both relief and excitement.

"Ready to take on these obnoxious upstarts Othorians!" Maxima added with an almost cheerful squawk, her feathers ruffling in anticipation.

"Let's show them what we're made of!" Adamik, a Protector from the Blue Flock, chimed in, his tone fierce and determined. His flock mate Gregor whistled a note of agreement, his eyes flashing with resolve.

Caleb responded with a confident chirp and a brief song of encouragement. "We will bring our people back. Thank you all for your bravery."

Together they meticulously planned what they hoped would be a swift and decisive counterstrike. If not to rescue their captured kin at least to garner more information. Their strategy hinged on sending a reconnaissance team of buzzies ahead to survey Summit Reach, a minor yet strategically significant Othorian outpost along their route. Information gathered by these stealthy scouts would be crucial to gaining a tactical advantage.

As the planning session ended, Caleb turned to Trada, his loyal companion, and engaged in an intense mental dialogue, conveying the intricate details of the mission. Trada, along with Pica and several other buzzies, had joined them, quietly awaiting instructions. The buzzies, known for their speed and ability to move inconspicuously, would scout the target area and return with vital intelligence, all without attracting attention.

With their resolve steeled, the group set off, navigating the challenging terrain with precision. They traveled along the northern flank of Bison Ridge, heading westward. The journey was arduous, with the unyielding easterly winds pushing against them, but they kept a low profile, hugging the cliffs and utilizing the sheltered canyons to ease their passage.

By the time they reached the halfway point, night was beginning to fall. They found a sun-warmed ledge of rock and decided to rest there. From this near-perfect vantage point, Caleb could still make out Pollitus in the far distance, its branches a dark silhouette against the deepening sky. The stunning beauty of their surroundings captivated them all. The clear air offered expansive views over the Red Flock quadrant of the Grand Valley, and the fresh mountain scents filled their lungs, rejuvenating their spirits. The setting sun cast long shadows across the rugged terrain, painting the landscape in hues of gold and purple.

Despite the physical toll of the prolonged flight, their spirits remained high. Most Avians couldn't sustain such lengthy flights, but this team was composed of strong fliers, their camaraderie and shared purpose keeping morale up. As the evening wore on, they chirped and sang together as they preened themselves, their voices echoing off the rocky cliffs. Eventually, exhaustion claimed them, and they fell into a deep, restorative sleep, their minds at ease and their bodies grateful for the respite.

The next day, they neared Summit Reach by late morning, and just as they approached, Trada returned with crucial intelligence. He hadn't risked getting too close due to the presence of sentries guarding the entryways at Summit Reach. Still, the scout buzzies had observed a significant disturbance at the cavern earlier that morning, marked by angry shouts and, astonishingly, the sighting of gray jiants.

The news left Caleb and his team stunned, the rumours they had heard at RedBlush were true. Jiants—these colossal creatures thought to be relics of the past—were present here and now, alongside a company of Othorian troops. The revelation seemed impossible, yet they trusted their scouts implicitly. There was no time for conjecture; they knew they had to act swiftly to exploit the element of surprise while also contending with this unexpected and formidable threat.

With their battle plan set, Caleb, Goffry, Adamik, Gregor, Trada, and several buzzies prepared to infiltrate the main southern entrance of Summit Reach. Meanwhile, General Botus, Lieutenant Maxima, and the rest of the team would simultaneously strike from the northern exit.

As Caleb and his group approached the entrance, the tension was palpable. Summit Reach, carved into the heart of the mountain, loomed before them, its entrance a gaping maw in the dawn light. The air was cool and damp, carrying the scent of earth and the faint musk of jiants. Surprisingly, there were no soldiers manning the entry posts.

Every muscle in Caleb's body tensed as they prepared to enter the unknown, the scent of the forest lingering in his nostrils as a reminder of what they were fighting for. The time had come to put their plan into action.

Caleb, leading the squadron, paused briefly at the cavern's threshold. Peering inside, Caleb noted the pervasive dimness, broken only by shafts of light filtering through cracks in the cavern ceiling, casting long, dancing shadows on the walls. His heart pounded, a mix of adrenaline and resolve fueling his every movement. As he entered, the sight before him was both confusing and heart-wrenching. Two immense gray jiants dominated the space, their massive forms towering over four trussed and helpless Avian captives lying nearby. One of the jiants lay immobilized, pierced by spears that glistened wetly in the half-light, its mandibles still stained with dark blue Othorian blood. The air was thick with the metallic tang of gore and the acrid scent of fear.

Around twenty visible Othorians were scattered throughout the cavern—some standing defiantly, others milling about in confusion seemingly without purpose. Caleb's sharp eyes caught sight of more figures lurking in the shadows of adjacent cave mouths, their intentions unclear.

Without hesitation, Caleb let out a fierce battle cry. The sound echoed off the cavern walls, a clarion call to action. Goffry, General Botus, Maxima, and their allies surged forward in a wave of Avian and buzzy fury. The Othorians, caught off guard, scrambled to mount a defense. Arrows whistled through the air, clattering against stone or finding their mark with sickening thuds.

Maxima, ever the strategist, quickly began rounding up the surrendering Othorians, her movements swift and precise. She worked methodically, ensuring no hidden threats remained in the smaller offshoot caves.

In a blur of motion, Caleb released a volley of stinger bolts, each one striking true. He then dove toward the trussed Avian captives, his heart in his throat, desperately hoping to find Irka among them. The sight of the jiants—one standing protectively over the other lying on its side, grievously wounded—struck a chord of both admiration and sorrow in him. As he cautiously approached, the protective jiant eyed him warily, yet there was a faint glimmer of hope in its gaze, and it showed no sign of aggression.

"Caleb, it is I, Precina," a weak voice called from one of the nearest bound Avians. Relief and concern flooded Caleb as he recognized her voice from his PureWhite Flock.

"Precina, thank the skies," he replied softly, his voice a mixture of joy and trepidation. "Are you okay? Let me get these ropes off you. But please, tell me—where is Irka? Is she here?"

His hands worked quickly to free Precina, his mind racing as he examined the other bound captives, searching for any sign of Irka. But she wasn't among them.

"Thank you … Caleb," Precina stuttered, wincing and making a low whistling sound in pain. "Irka … she … escaped … I think."

Caleb's heart sank. The cavern seemed to whirl around him as he tried to process the information. His hands trembled. Tears welled up in his eyes, and he let out an involuntary, sorrowful warble of pent-up frustration.

A shout and loud alarm call from Goffry snapped Caleb back to reality, just in time for him to dodge a spear hurled by a surviving Othorian attacker. With agile grace, Caleb countered, launching himself at the attacker. His feet connected with a bone-jarring impact, and the Othorian crumpled to the ground, unconscious.

The cavern was a whirlwind of action—stinger bolts, arrows, talons, and venomous strikes from the buzzies blended into a vortex of conflict. Caleb, amid the chaos, spared a glance toward Goffry, who was diligently freeing the other captives from their bindings.

The battle reached its climactic end quickly, with the remaining Othorian defenders succumbing to the surprise onslaught. Before Caleb could engage another enemy, General Botus's authoritative voice rang out—a victory bird call that echoed through the cavern, followed by a bellow. "Victory is ours! Sound off, everyone!"

A chorus of responses filled the cavern, confirming their victory and the safety of the entire team. The buzzies, with Trada and Pica at the forefront, swarmed overhead, buzzing with the thrill of triumph.

Breathing deeply, his muscles still trembling from the adrenaline of battle, Caleb stood in the dimly lit cavern, his heart a tumult of emotions. Amid the aftermath, he heard a feeble yet unmistakable voice. "Caleb, it is I, Ontan," came the weak utterance from a figure lying beside Precina. Rushing to Ontan's side, Caleb's gaze fell upon another flock mate, a sight that tore at his heart.

Ontan was a shadow of his former self, his once majestic wings now brutally distorted and twisted. His feathers were a mess, coated in dust and stained with blood, signs of their ordeal. The massive injuries he had suffered spoke volumes of the cruelty he had endured. Ontan's pain was palpable, his soft sobs and shivers under Caleb's tender touch laying bare the depth of his suffering.

With a gentle hand, Caleb freed Ontan from his bindings. He then carefully administered a triple dose of green sappa, watching as the healing properties visibly soothed Ontan's pain. "Rest now, my friend. We'll look after you. You're safe now," Caleb whispered, laying Ontan down on a hastily gathered bed of moss and leaves.

Turning back to Precina, Caleb saw her eyes filled with both relief and severe fatigue. He offered her the same healing sappa, which she gratefully accepted, taking a long, reviving sip.

"Caleb, the Othorians … they turned on Ontan when Irka escaped," she began, her voice heavy with a mix of pain and relief. "He bore the brunt of their anger."

Caleb listened intently, a mixture of relief and concern washing over him. "Irka escaped? But where would she go?" he asked urgently, his voice echoing slightly in the cavernous space.

"I ... I don't know, Caleb. She had already been loaded onto the jiant known as Artula, who rebelled and fled with her on board." Precina responded, her weak voice tinged with regret. "It all happened so quickly. Then the six other jiants remaining were quickly loaded with captives, albeit with resistance, and continued on their way north. Most jiants seemed compliant but unruly. We were left behind in the confusion. Our intended mounts lie before you, and they are friendly. Please, treat them kindly; they made our journey easier. I'm so sorry, I'm ... so ... sorry ..." Precina's voice trailed off as the effects of the sappa fully took hold, and she drifted into an exhausted sleep.

Caleb's mind raced with thoughts of Irka's whereabouts and well-being. Despite the uncertainty, a glimmer of hope remained—Irka had found a way out. No matter what it took, he would find her. He scanned the cavern for any more hidden threats or injured comrades, determined to leave no stone unturned in their mission of rescue and retribution.

As Caleb assisted Goffry with the remaining Avian captives, a sense of urgency enveloped the cavern. Two other survivors, hailing from the GoldenRay Yellow Flock, recounted their harrowing ordeal. They were part of a trading delegation when an ambush occurred, and six of their number were taken captive. Their eyes, filled with a blend of relief and trauma, reflected their disheveled feathers and weary postures. They, too, were given a dose of the healing sappa and helped to settle down and rest alongside Precina and Ontan.

Once all the surviving Othorians were rounded up, bound, and safely guarded, the Avian leaders gathered near the two jiants. The protector had now laid down beside the other, neither having moved to interfere during the battle.

Goffry, his brow furrowed with concern, turned to Caleb. "So… What's our best course of action from here?" His voice carried a mix of resolve and uncertainty.

General Botus, tense and with a flicker of nervousness in his eyes, added, "Caleb, do you think you could try communing with these massive creatures? Their kind has a notorious history with our people; we'll never forget how they aided the Othorians in the Kondorian War. But that was long ago, given what Precina said, maybe there's more to them than our old enmities suggest. What's your take?"

Caleb, taking in the general's words, responded with a calm yet firm tone, "Let's hold off on any rash actions. I'll attempt to commune with them. I sense they're not the enemies we've always believed them to be, and Precina begged that they be treated with respect." He scanned the group, seeking their consensus.

Nods of agreement rippled through the team. Caleb, taking a deep breath, cautiously approached the pair of jiants. He already knew their names, identified by Precina—that was a start. The uninjured one, Prudentia the Fast, was vibrating gently, creating a soothing hum. She lay protectively beside the injured jiant, Mikia the Jumper, their antennae tenderly intertwined. Caleb observed Mikia's injuries—a spear impaling an eye and another lodged in his thorax, with clear hemolymph oozing from his wounds.

Maxima had approached clucking in a motherly way, her voice tinged with empathy, asked, "Caleb, should we try to remove the spears? We can't just leave him like this."

"Let me try communicating first," Caleb replied, his tone a mix of determination and concern. As he approached, he extended his hands, and the jiants cautiously wrapped their antennae around his fingers. Through a blend of gentle birdsong and a calming presence, Caleb initiated the communion. The exchange was a succession of images and emotions; words took shape, but it was more a conversation of souls, much like his communication with buzzies.

Prudentia's thoughts were clear and poignant but very direct and short: *"Help, Irka, Nice. Mikia, please, help."*

Mikia's plea was more fragmented, yet his pain and request for assistance were unmistakable. *"Hurt, yes … Irka, nice; Happy, help … help me? Pull, block hole … please, water?"*

Caleb relayed the instructions to Maxima and Goffry: "Pull out the spears and seal the wounds tightly with tourniquets and pads soaked in diluted green sappa. Be ready." He called for the sappa mixed with fresh water to be applied to Mikia's mandibles, where he could absorb it directly, aiding the procedure and his overall well-being. Caleb then dove deeper into the communion, tapping into the life forces around him, collecting and channeling that energy into Mikia's battered form.

As Goffry and Maxima carefully began removing the spears, Caleb felt Mikia's agony and mental convulsions. They experienced it together, which made it just a little more bearable. The extraction was delicate, but with the combined efforts of Goffry and Maxima, the spears were pulled free, and the wounds tightly packed as directed. Mikia's condition soon stabilized. Despite his significant injuries, he showed a remarkable ability to begin his recovery.

This experience not only changed Caleb's perception of the jiants but also deepened his understanding of the interconnectedness of all life on Kondor. Caleb felt a profound connection to Mikia and Prudentia, a bond forged in the crucible of shared pain and healing. He knew them for what they truly were.

Amid the small victorious battleground of Summit Reach, Caleb's mind wrestled with concern and determination. With Mikia resting more peacefully and the extraction process complete, he turned his mental focus to Prudentia. He desperately sought any information on Irka and Artula's whereabouts and intentions. *"Please, I know this is a bad moment to ask, but any knowledge about Artula and Irka's direction would be vital,"* he mentally implored Prudentia, his communion voice laced with urgency and despair.

Both jiants responded, though cryptic and fragmented as usual, suggesting an overly vague direction. *"Lost canyon, the Red ones? Legend. Far from home. Artula knows. Think? South? West? North, not east, maybe. Not known,"* they conveyed, their thoughts a puzzle of fragmented hints. Caleb's heart sank slightly; the information was as vast and unclear as the mountainous landscape around them.

Despite his tracking skills and the concerted efforts of Maxima, Goffry, and the entire Avian team scouring the area around Summit Reach, the mountainside offered no clues. No prints or scents hinted at Artula's path. Jiants moved very stealthily, and he had left no trace of passage. On top of this, the terrain was rocky and smooth in large areas, making it an even greater obstacle.

Caleb and Goffry set out flying in a search pattern, hoping to find some clue, but with so much of a head start, Irka and the jiant were long gone. Without knowing a direction, it was clear that it would be a hopeless task.

The disappointment was palpable, yet Caleb knew they couldn't afford the luxury of despondency. His only thought was to move forward. Perhaps the escaped gray jiant might return to familiar grounds in the north, where the rest of his kind came from. Irka was strong and resourceful, and Caleb had great confidence in her ability to handle herself, but he longed to help her, frustrated that he didn't know how. He had been so close.

Caleb gathered his squad, and together they strategized their next move. They were considering a path northward; so far, that was their consensus, chasing the elusive hope of finding Irka and the other captives or at least gaining insight into the situation at Bison Hive and the intentions of the Othorians.

During their planning, an unexpected source of information emerged. One cooperative captured Othorian, claiming to be part of the Resistance, shared vital intelligence about Bison Hive. He spoke of Thetan's demise, Bertran's ascent to power, and divulged the most strategic entry points into the settlement as well as details of the king's fortress within.

"The Northern Keep and even beyond is their ultimate destination, stopping only briefly at Bison Hive," the Othorian divulged, his voice betraying a mixture of fear and defiance. The Keep, a fortress near Othor's Head in the Northern Mountains, stood as a daunting obstacle, its history etched into its stone walls. It was deemed impregnable, as history had proven many times.

Caleb, though still uncertain, felt a pull toward this direction. As if on cue, a small group of reinforcements from RedBlush arrived with news that bolstered their spirits. A formidable armada was forming, converging toward Bison Hive. Marta and Jonus, along with other White Flock members, were nearing RedBlush and then all together would be pushing north to face Bertran. Simultaneously, the Yellow and Blue Flock armadas were advancing along the Eastern Mountain Range. A flood of resistance from friendly Othorians was also rising, gathering strength with each passing moment.

After further deliberation, it was decided. "We move with purpose," Caleb announced, his voice steady and clear. "Our path is now certain. Let's head north to scout ahead and join this tide."

The two jiants left behind would also help Caleb by searching for any signs of Irka and Artula, once Mikia was sufficiently healed. As Caleb was leaving, he glanced back toward Summit Reach, relieved that he was able to help the jiants and forge a new connection.

He knew this bond with the jiants was destined—to what end, he could not yet foresee.

IRKA
AI REPLICANT IMAGE

20:
RESISTANCE GROWS

Marta and Jonus, having reached the RedBlush Flock's home at Pollitus Father Tree with remarkable speed, now found themselves at the epicenter of a growing resistance. They had missed their son Caleb by just a little over a couple of days. The ancient boughs of Pollitus, draped in rich, crimson foliage, seemed to pulse with the shared determination of those gathered beneath them. The air was thick with anticipation, the kind that precedes a decisive battle.

The plan was bold: to unite their forces with Caleb and his advance squad and then confront Bertran's army head-on. Intelligence reports sent by Portia revealed that Bertran's recent rise to absolute power, overshadowed by the suspicious death of his father, had only intensified the resolve of the Othorian Resistance now moving north on the Western Trail converging on Bison Hive.

Marta, a whirlwind of focused energy, moved through the ranks with a sense of purpose that was both commanding and infectious. Her sharp eyes missed nothing as she coordinated the next phase of their campaign, her mind already several steps ahead, weaving together the disparate threads of their alliance into a single, unstoppable force.

As Marta had journeyed northward toward RedBlush, a remarkable phenomenon had begun to unfold. A large flock of swifts—small, raptor-like birds—started to accompany her. Such occurrences were rare but not unheard of for powerful Communers. These 'familiars,' typically a single species of animal, would rally to those whose strength of will or need was great enough to draw them. In times of crisis or heightened emotion, these creatures became more than mere companions, they were protectors and allies.

For Marta, the swifts were not just companions but a part of her very essence. They flew about her in graceful, synchronized murmuration, a living, breathing extension of her presence. When she rested, they perched nearby, their sharp eyes ever watchful. Often, they would descend to her, perching lightly on her shoulders, arms, and even her head, a constant and comforting presence.

These birds were not only vigilant guardians; they were also unmatched messengers. Their strength in numbers made them formidable, capable of overwhelming threats with their sheer speed, precision and sharp talons as well as a deadly beak. But it was their communication abilities that set them apart. The swifts had a unique talent, known as a "song wave," which allowed them to transmit intricate messages across vast distances.

When Marta and her swifts harmonized their voices, they created a ripple of sound that resonated through the valley. This "song wave" wasn't just a series of notes; it was a complex vibrational message, carrying information to other swifts spread across Kondor. These messages could travel the entire Grand Valley in less than a day, reaching Communers attuned to their unique frequencies. For most Avians, the swifts' song was a background melody, reflecting the emotions and thoughts of the valley. But for someone like Marta, whose connection with the swifts was profound, the song wave was a tool of immense power, one that would be crucial in the battle to come.

As Marta stood at the heart of the RedBlush gathering, surrounded by her swifts and other Avian leaders, she knew they were on the cusp of something monumental. The battle ahead would not just be a fight for territory or power; it would be a struggle for the very soul of Kondor. And with the swifts by her side, their song wave ready to carry her commands across the valley, Marta was prepared to lead them into the fray.

Jonus stood beneath the towering branches of Pollitus, the ancient Father Tree of the RedBlush Flock. The air was alive with the scent of blossoms and the sounds of preparation—wings fluttering, voices and birdsong raised in coordination, and the hum of urgency. He and Marta had arrived only one day prior, and already, the energy around them was palpable, charged with the anticipation of the mission ahead.

As Marta discussed plans with Oritus, the revered leader of the RedBlush Flock, Jonus surveyed the scene. Flotas were already assembling, air rafts were being loaded with supplies, and Avians from across the Red Flock and beyond were gathering for what would be a crucial push north. His heart swelled with pride at the sight but was tempered by a gnawing anxiety for what lay ahead.

Oritus turned to Jonus, his expression a mix of seriousness and hope. "We've gathered as many as we could on short notice," he said, his voice carrying the weight of responsibility. "Over ten flotas are ready, with more arriving."

Jonus nodded, feeling the gravity of their situation. "It's more than we could have hoped for," he replied, a hint of gratitude in his voice. "But we need to move quickly. Every moment counts."

Marta, sensing Jonus's tension, stepped closer and placed a hand on his arm. Her eyes, filled with determination, met his. "Jonus, we're here now. Caleb's out there, and we'll reach him in time. Whatever's coming, we'll face it together."

Jonus looked into her eyes, finding solace in her steady gaze. "I just can't shake this feeling, Marta. Something's waiting for us out there, something we're not ready for."

Marta's lips curled into a soft smile. "That's why we're doing this together. We've faced worse, and we'll get through this too."

Before Jonus could respond, a sudden rustling above drew their attention. From the canopy of Pollitus, a large flock of swifts descended, their small, raptor-like forms cutting through the air with practiced precision. The birds swirled around Marta, their presence a sign of something rare and powerful. They perched on nearby branches, their keen eyes watching, waiting.

Oritus's eyes widened at the sight. "Swifts... I have seen them gathering. It seems they've chosen you, Marta."

Marta looked at the birds, a mix of understanding and affection in her expression. "They've been with me since the Westmount battle. It seems they've decided to stay and increasing in number."

Jonus marveled at the sight; he had seen his mate attract them but never in such numbers. The swifts, known for their fierce loyalty and unparalleled communication abilities, had become a part of their journey, a sign that the stakes were higher than ever. "They'll be invaluable," Jonus said, his voice filled with admiration. "With their help, we'll have eyes everywhere."

Marta nodded, her resolve hardening. "They'll guide us, and they'll carry our messages. We're not alone in this."

With the swifts now a part of their mission, Marta and Jonus took their place at the head of the formation. The flotas and air rafts lifted off in unison, a spectacle of precision and unity. Jonus felt a surge of determination, pushing aside his doubts as they soared into the sky, leading the charge toward the Western Mountains.

The swifts flew alongside them, a living shield and a network of messengers, their presence both comforting and formidable. As they traveled, the winds picked up, challenging their flight, but the swifts expertly navigated the currents, guiding the flotas through the treacherous paths.

Night began to fall, casting long shadows over the landscape below. Jonus and Marta found a sheltered ledge where they could rest, the swifts circling above before settling around them. The stars overhead were shining bright, casting a cool violet light over the rocky terrain. Jonus felt the weight of the day's journey in his wings and bones, but the presence of Marta beside him, along with the swifts' vigilant watch, brought him comfort.

Marta, sensing Jonus's lingering unease, leaned against him. "Jonus, we're doing everything we can. Caleb needs us, and we'll find Irka. I believe that."

Jonus wrapped an arm around her, pulling her close. "I just wish I could shake this feeling that something's coming... something big."

She looked up at him, her voice soft but firm. "Whatever it is, we'll face it together."

Jonus nodded, the comfort of her presence easing his mind slightly. "I know we will. I just wish it didn't feel so uncertain."

Marta smiled, though her eyes reflected the same uncertainty. "Uncertainty is just another challenge, and we've never backed down from one before. Tomorrow I'll assemble another team, let's move ahead of the armada and reach Caleb as soon as possible."

"I agree, and of course I am coming with you." He held his hand to her mouth as she started to object. "I am coming, my love." Jonus finished with a light warble of pleasant reassuring notes and a soft kiss on her forehead. Marta melted into his arms, enough said.

As the night deepened, Jonus closed his eyes, holding Marta close. The warmth of her body, the steady rhythm of her breath, and the soft rustling of the swifts as they settled in for the night began to soothe his troubled thoughts. Sleep came gradually, the tension easing as they drifted off, ready to face whatever awaited them with the dawn.

On the eastern side of the Grand Valley, the Blue and Yellow Flocks had endured their own brutal onslaughts from the Othorians. Similar to the ambush at PuritaWhite and other Western Great Trees, Avian captives were swiftly rounded up and transported northward, their fates hanging in the balance. As word of these attacks spread through the valley via communing, the eastern Avian flocks swiftly united. The call to arms echoed across the skies, and soon their armada was surging forward, a powerful force of unity and determination.

Below the vast expanse of the Highland Plateau, however, a different story unfolded. Beneath the surface, ancient labyrinthine tunnels stretched like hidden veins through the bedrock of the northern Othor's Head Mountain Range. These passages, carved by forces long forgotten, were shrouded in shadows and whispered echoes of the past. It was through these subterranean corridors that the captive eastern Avians were being herded, their destination a secret even to their captors.

The tunnels were a world apart from the open skies the Avians had once known. Cloaked in darkness, the oppressive silence of the tunnels was broken only by the shuffling of feet and the occasional murmur from weary prisoners or their Othorian oppressors. The air was cold and damp, clinging to the feathers of the captives and chilling them to the bone. The walls, rough and unyielding, seemed to close in around them, evoking a sense of timelessness and confinement. Though their spirits were dampened, the Avian captives trudged on, each step taking them deeper into the heart of the mountain and further from the freedom they once knew.

Among the procession were several gray jiants, their massive forms barely visible in the dim light. Too few to transport the captives, the jiants were instead used as steeds for the Othorian leaders, who rode atop them with an air of grim authority. The jiants also bore the personal belongings of their masters, their once-mighty strength now reduced to servitude.

Above ground, the scene could not have been more different. The armada of the Yellow and Blue Flocks painted a vibrant picture against the backdrop of the Highland Plateau. The plains stretched out beneath them like a sprawling canvas of green, dotted with wildflowers that swayed gently in the breeze. The air was filled with the scents of earth and life, a stark contrast to the cold, damp world below.

The eastern armada's journey was both a race against time and a testament to the indomitable spirit of the Avians. With the wind at their backs, they soared over the plains with a grace born of purpose, their eyes scanning the landscape for any signs of their captive kin or their Othorian captors. Scouts flew out in all directions, covering the vastness of the plateau in a tireless search. Though the expanse of the plains threatened to dampen their resolve, hope and tenacity drove them ever onward.

As the armada approached the Othor's Head Mountain Range, the terrain began to shift, becoming more rugged and imposing. The mountains loomed ahead like ancient guardians; their peaks shrouded in mist that whispered secrets of times long past. The Avians knew that the Othorians, along with their captives, would eventually have to emerge from the tunnels at the base of these mountains, just below the ominous Three Golden Obelisks. It was here that the armada would converge, ready to intercept and pursue the enemy into the mountains if necessary.

The tension in the air was palpable, as the Avians prepared for the inevitable confrontation. The weight of the mission pressed heavily upon them, but they remained undeterred. The captives belowground could not see the vast, open skies or the vibrant life above, but they could feel the determination in their hearts. The Avians above were not just flying to rescue their kin—they were flying to reclaim their freedom, to defy the darkness that sought to imprison them, and to restore the light that had been momentarily dimmed.

The stage was set, the forces were in motion, and the battle for the soul of the Grand Valley was about to begin.

Portia's leadership in rallying the resistance movement was nothing short of extraordinary. Her ability to connect with the Othorians, understanding their fears and hopes, galvanized them into a unified force. She led with a delicate balance of strength and empathy, commanding respect while ensuring that each member of her growing army felt valued.

At the heart of Portia's inner circle was Lirna, her childhood friend and confidant. Lirna's sharp intellect and unwavering loyalty made her an indispensable advisor. Slender and quick-witted, with bright eyes that seemed to pierce through any deception, Lirna often provided the voice of reason in their strategic discussions.

Then there was Oboron, a towering figure whose scarred skin told tales of countless battles. His deep, rumbling voice and no-nonsense demeanor instilled confidence among the troops. As Portia's lieutenant, he was the pillar of strength the army leaned on during the most harrowing moments.

Umbra, the master scout, completed the core team. Small and agile, with sharp features and an uncanny ability to move through shadows like a whisper in the night, Umbra had proven invaluable for reconnaissance. Her keen sense of hearing and ability to navigate even the most treacherous terrain made her the eyes and ears of the resistance.

Their journey north along the Western Mountain Range, along the hazardous path known to the Othorians as the Western Trail, was fraught with challenges. The mountains themselves were a labyrinth of grand tunnels, natural passageways, and expansive underground caverns. This hidden route, expertly enhanced over centuries by master Othorian stone masons, revealed the ingenuity and determination of their ancestors.

However, the journey was anything but straightforward. Narrow paths and above-ground shortcuts, while offering breathtaking views of the sprawling valleys and sky-touching peaks, often slowed their progress. The contrast between the scenic vistas and the dark, echoing expanses of the subterranean route only heightened the tension among the troops.

The Western Trail was dotted with Othorian guard posts, small garrisons, and bases strategically placed to control the flow of traffic and provide rest stops for travelers. Many of these outposts had already been abandoned as Portia's army advanced, but one formidable strong-hold remained, Midway Outkeep.

This outpost, held by Bertran's loyal forces, was strategically positioned to control a crucial passage through the mountains. The structure was imposing, with thick stone walls and heavily fortified gates. The morning of the battle found Portia's forces locked in a tense stand-off against the entrenched enemy. The air was thick with anticipation, the mingling scents of fresh cactus pine and the acrid tang of sweat and fear filling the cavern.

Portia called her inner circle together for a quick briefing. "Oboron, take the left flank. Umbra, scout the perimeter for any weaknesses. Lirna, stay by my side and coordinate our forces," she commanded, her voice steady and clear.

Umbra nodded, determination gleaming in her eyes. "I'll find us a way in, Portia," she promised, disappearing into the shadows with the stealth of a predator on the hunt.

Oboron gripped his battle-ax tightly, his muscles tensing in readiness. "We're with you, Portia. Let's show Bertran's men what true strength looks like."

The battle that ensued was fierce. Portia's forces fought with a ferocity born of conviction, driven by the desire to reclaim their land and their freedom. The enemy, though entrenched and well-armed, was caught off guard by a surprise rear attack from defectors who had joined the resistance. The chaos of the battle overwhelmed Bertran's forces, leading to a decisive victory for Portia's army. The Resistance suffered only minor casualties, a testament to their strategy and resolve.

As the dust settled and the echoes of battle faded, Portia stood tall among her victorious troops. She looked around, meeting the eyes of Lirna, Oboron, and Umbra, as well as the volunteer soldiers who had fought bravely. "We did it," she said, her voice a blend of relief and determination. "But this is just the beginning. Bison Hive awaits, and we must press on."

With renewed vigor, the Resistance continued their march northward. The tunnels gradually improved, a sign that they were drawing closer to their ultimate goal. Passing through Summit Keep, already cleared by Caleb and his team, they continued toward Bison Hive, the heart of Bertran's dominion.

21:
CALEB'S FALL

———⬦◇⬦———

At Summit Reach, Camaz, a newly allied Othorian guard, had joined Caleb's squad. Eager to assist, Camaz provided valuable insight into the layout of the community and the most likely location of the captive Avians, who were probably being held in the central stronghold's prison. As a further gesture of goodwill, he offered to guide them through the city and procure Othorian clothes to help the squad blend in with the locals and conceal their identities.

The buzzies, though loyal and keen to help, would have to be left behind; they were just too conspicuous. Trada, Caleb's faithful companion, buzzed his disapproval loudly, his wings vibrating with agitation as he performed his familiar wagging dance of annoyance. Caleb knelt beside Trada, stroking the soft bristles on his back. "I know, Trada," he murmured. "But you need to go back and meet Marta and Jonus. We'll be fine."

Trada's antennae twitched in reluctant agreement, and after a final affectionate nuzzle, he took off, wings beating furiously as he headed back to rendezvous with the advancing Avian armada.

"Let's get moving, everyone," Botus called out. He was always the first to be ready. Standing at the rocky exit to Summit Reach, the general overlooked the squad, assembling all with directing tweets and whistles.

Caleb felt a surge of determination. He couldn't shake the thought that Irka might have been taken to Bison Hive, where the jiants' home was. The possibility filled him with a mix of hope and dread. Could he allow himself to think of her beautiful face and wings? The longing in his heart was a constant dull ache, but he forced himself to focus on the mission. Shaking off his emotions, he jumped up and glided north up the West Trail, leading his elite frontline squad.

The trail was mostly deserted. The normal flow of traders and caravans had dried up, with the impending war disrupting trading, the economy was at a standstill. The guard posts and garrisons along the way were vacant, leaving the squad unchallenged.

On the second day, they encountered a small caravan of traders. Their initial wariness melted into friendliness once they realized that Caleb's squad was not hostile. The traders, relieved to see the Avians, expressed their anger and shame at their leaders' role in reigniting conflict after years of peace.

"We passed a convoy of Othorian soldiers and jiants with Avian captives moving northward quickly. We were shocked to see so many jiants; although they also have made a rare appearance at the palace before," Pablow, the leader of the caravan, explained. Several other members of the caravan began to speak in excited clicks and hisses at the mention of the jiants. Pablow shushed them, calming the group so he could continue.

"Their captain, Dagon, wanted us to turn back and join them, but we bribed him to let us go. There's so much unrest—some say Bertran has lost his mind. Now with Thetan … gone," he stumbled over the word, "his son is becoming more aggressive."

"But why? What have we done to provoke this? What does Bertran want from us?" Goffry blurted out, his frustration evident. He fluttered his wings in aggravation.

"We need answers, Pablow. What more can you tell us about the captives?" Caleb asked with a firm whistling chirp, his pacing on the rocky trail revealing his impatience. "We need to confront Bertran and free our people. This has to end."

Pablow lowered his head in respect, his voice filled with genuine sorrow. "We're deeply sorry. We oppose what our leaders are doing. Anything we can do to help, we will."

The traders shared everything they knew. Bison Hive was in lockdown, with all soldiers called back to reinforce the settlement in anticipation of an Avian rescue attempt. The captives, though roughed up, were alive and about a day and a half ahead of Caleb's force. Pablow and Camaz also provided detailed information about Bison Hive's layout, guard posts, and entrances.

Eager to continue their pursuit, Caleb and his squad quickly resumed their journey.

Finally, the formidable Othorian stronghold loomed ahead, ominously nestled in the north western Othor Mountains. This large community hummed with activity, housing hundreds and now perhaps well over a thousand Othorians. It was the main hive of their people, the capital. Mostly carved within the mountain, it remained hidden from view, revealing only its imposing exterior.

The fortress was a marvel of engineering and security. Several grand gates and entrances, each with high arched lintels and some with metal portcullis gates, punctuated its rugged facade. The meticulously balanced stone doors, each weighing several tons, could be moved into place and securely locked from the inside. High above, a few watchtower guard posts and small battlements stood vigilant, ensuring the stronghold's defense. The entire structure exuded an air of impregnable strength and unyielding authority, a demonstration of the Othorians' architectural prowess and their determination to protect their capital.

Camaz again proved invaluable as he guided Caleb and his team to a less-guarded entrance on the west side of the hive. Hidden behind some trees, they found the clothing Camaz had promised.

"These are just what we need to blend in," Caleb whispered, examining the garments typically worn by Othorians when they ventured outside their protective caverns.

The outfits, complete with large hoods and masks that featured only narrow slits for vision, were unfamiliar and uncomfortable but essential for their covert mission. Camaz confidently approached the gate, engaged the guards in brief conversation, and smoothly secured their entry without any trouble.

As they entered the hive, Camaz turned and murmured, "Follow my lead. We'll circumnavigate the city since the edges are less populated and offer more vegetation for cover."

"Lead on, Camaz," Caleb replied in a hushed tone.

They had timed their entry to coincide with dusk. Although the hive received no direct sunlight during the day, there was always some indirect light brightening the ambience. As night fell, the hive plunged into a deeper darkness, illuminated only by the eerie bioluminescence of familiar fungi and vegetation. The soft glow cast ghostly shadows along their path, adding a layer of surrealism to their stealthy advance. The musty, clammy air deepened as they moved forward, clinging to their sinuses with the added assault of the sharp odour of pheromones and smoke from burning crake stinging their eyes. Crake, a combustible black material mainly composed of carbonized plant matter, was mined from deep within the mountains and was a popular fuel for stoves and fire pits.

The squad moved cautiously, sticking close to the walls and under the cover of overgrown pale, ghostlike flora. Camaz guided them through narrow alleys and deserted backstreets, occasionally pausing to listen for any signs of activity. The quiet was punctuated only by the distant hum of the city's inner workings and the occasional rustle of small creatures disturbed by their passage. It was the evening meal time and Othorians were very regimented with their eating routine making it an opportune time to move about.

As they progressed, the tension among the group was palpable. Each member was acutely aware that the success of their mission hinged not only on reaching their destination undetected but also on the reliability of the information Camaz had provided.

They arrived at the edge of the hive cavern where the walls were adorned with thick moss, super soft to the touch. Moving became much slower as they had to push through masses of vines, pale, long bladelike banners that hung down from the cave ceiling. These leaves slapped at their faces annoyingly as they proceeded.

"It's like moving through an upside-down forest," Goffry commented very softly, whacking at the vegetation that draped down like inverted aerial seaweed. In some spots, this foliage was so thick they had to elbow through with considerable effort, their wings catching and entangling.

General Botus, shoving his way through beside Goffry, muttered under his breath, "I don't like this; I can't see anything through these infernal weeds."

Navigating through this maze and luminescent vegetation, they all felt a mix of wonder and unease. The low light from the glowing plants was difficult to get used to, hypnotically moving in a dizzying manner. Camaz, familiar with these peculiarities, led them deftly, choosing paths that seemed invisible until they were right upon them.

Suddenly, Camaz held up a hand, signaling them to stop. He pointed to a lighter patch ahead where the dense vegetation seemed to thin out. "Beyond this point lies the beginning of the back of the central district where the Palace stronghold is located, the most likely place to keep captives," he whispered. "We must be extra cautious from here. The guards are fewer on this side, but they are still very vigilant and there is less cover."

The squad crouched low, moving forward with even greater care. The sound of their breathing seemed loud in the silence. Every snap of a twig underfoot sent a jolt of adrenaline through them. They moved like shadows, each step carefully placed to avoid making any noise.

Without warning, Camaz let out a loud, clicking vocalization and vanished into the thick foliage. As he went, he released a distinctive pheromone that clung to everyone around him.

Caleb's heart sank as realization dawned on him. "It's a trap! He just marked us!" he shouted, but the warning came too late. Bertran's loyal forces, previously concealed among the camouflaging vines, sprang into action, ambushing the squad.

"Betrayed!" Maxima cried out as she dodged an attack, the shock of Camaz's surprise treachery hitting them hard. The air erupted into chaos, the clash of weapons ringing out in the confined space, reverberating off the cavern walls.

Caleb frantically scanned the scene, searching for a way to regroup. Goffry, forced to retreat, bumped into Caleb. They quickly found themselves fighting back-to-back, their years of practice making them a seamless team.

Camaz, now at a distance, watched the battle with cold detachment. His eyes briefly flickered toward Caleb before he turned and melted into the shadows, leaving them to fend for themselves.

The battle was fierce and chaotic. Caleb and Goffry fought with desperate precision, their movements a frantic dance of survival among the swaying vines that had now become a treacherous battlefield. Despite their valiant efforts, the Avians were overwhelmed by the sheer number of their attackers. Caleb, his talons flashing in the dim light, managed to take down several foes, but the situation grew more dire by the second.

A massive Othorian, his face twisted with malice, stepped forward, wielding a hammer axe in one hand and a curved sword in the other. "This ends now, little birds!" he bellowed, his voice echoing with cruel intent. He hacked at the hanging vines, clearing a path as he advanced, and with a single powerful swing of his hammer, struck down Adamik who was part of their squad, he crumpled to the ground, unconscious.

The giant Othorian turned his attention to Caleb, who had just felled another opponent. With a hiss, he lunged at Caleb with his huge sword. Caleb managed to dodge and parry the initial strikes, but the heavy onslaught forced him to separate from Goffry. A net was thrown over Goffry, who struggled helplessly against it.

Distracted by Goffry's plight, Caleb's guard slipped for just an instant. It was all the monstrous Othorian needed. He swung his hammer with brutal force, landing a glancing blow to Caleb's head. The impact sent Caleb reeling, his vision blurring as he stumbled, and then that was it. It was over. Darkness claimed him as he blacked out.

"Caleb!" Goffry's voice, filled with horror, cut through the din as he watched his friend collapse under the hammer's assault.

The ogre sized Othorian, driven by a sadistic fury, continued to batter Caleb's unconscious form, smacking him with his hammer and kicking him savagely in the side. He glanced around for another target but found only Maxima, cornered and surrounded by several Othorians. Frustrated, he turned back to Caleb, delivering more punishing blows, each one more brutal than the last.

Caleb's body lay limp and broken. His once-proud wings shattered under the relentless assault. The Othorian sneered down at him, his victory complete. "Not so pretty anymore, are you, little bird?" he spat, ripping out several of Caleb's bloodied feathers and sticking them behind his ear as a trophy. With a final, cruel laugh, he stomped away.

As the captors rounded up the defeated squad, including a now-captured Goffry, their wings broken and their spirits crushed, they were cast into the dark confines of the hive's prison, left to ponder their grim fate and the uncertain future that awaited them.

Throughout the night, Caleb and the other captives drifted in and out of consciousness, their bodies wracked with shock and unbearable pain. The once-vibrant and proud Avians now lay broken and defeated, their dreams of rescue and revenge crushed under the weight of their injuries and the overwhelming despair that enveloped them in the cold, oppressive confines of their jail. The smell alone was revolting—a putrid combination of sweat, blood, excrement, and urine mixed with mould and decay. Together it created a humid, musty funk that clung to their feathers and filled their lungs.

In the oppressive darkness of the damp cell, Caleb's spirit plummeted into the depths of despair. Surrounded by the cold, unforgiving stone, his defeat felt all-encompassing. The pain from his injured, battered wings and body was a constant reminder of his failed mission, each throb an echo of his loss. The flickering flames of hope, which had driven him to this daring endeavor, now seemed snuffed out by the overwhelming shadow of defeat.

At one point, the air grew colder and denser as if the very essence of malevolence seeped into the cell. Indeed, Bertran, the embodiment of cruelty, made his way into the holding caves. His presence was like a dark cloud, chilling the already frigid air. The smell of his pheromones adding to the rankness in the air.

The Othorian leader's voice, dripping with disdain, echoed through the cavern. "Look at the mighty Avians," he sneered, his boots echoing ominously on the stone floor. His magnificent black wings, glistening with an almost supernatural sheen, were displayed with pride as he moved among the captives, delivering vicious, calculated kicks to the injured prisoners with each step. The sound of his mocking laughter, a harsh, grating hissing sound, filled the prison.

Caleb, struggling to sit up, caught Bertran's attention.

"Ah, I've been told of you, the great Caleb," Bertran mocked, standing over him with a cruel smirk. "Look at you now, just a foolish little fowl with broken wings. Is this the hero who thought he could defy me?"

Caleb's eyes, though filled with pain, met Bertran's with a defiance that remained unbroken. "You may break our bodies, Bertran, but our spirits will always soar higher than you can reach," Caleb retorted weakly, his voice barely a whisper but filled with unwavering resolve.

Bertran snickered darkly, a sound devoid of any warmth. "Spirits? I feed on your spirits. Your despair is my strength." He delivered several harsh kicks to Caleb's side, finishing with a vicious one to the face. Caleb reeled, his chains rattling as he collapsed, prone on the floor. His head spun, his vision blurred and darkened. The metallic taste of his blood filled his mouth, and he could feel its warmth running down his face, sticking his cheek to the cold stone floor. He was too weak to move, too broken to fight back.

As Bertran continued his torment, strutting from one captive to the next, Caleb lay there, each breath a struggle, each moment an eternity. The sense of hopelessness grew, the weight of their grim reality pressing down upon him like the cold, unyielding rock of the cell. The darkness around him felt deeper as if even the faintest light of hope had been sucked up by Bertran's evil presence. Pain and exhaustion overwhelming him at last, he passed out, his mind devoid of any thought, surrendering to the cold, hard floor beneath him.

The break of early dawn brought with it a flurry of activity as Bertran orchestrated the departure of his prisoners and his formidable host, numbering over a thousand of his most loyal and battle-hardened troops. The scene was one of grim efficiency, with all available jiants being harnessed and readied for the journey.

Towering above them all stood a formidable jiant, the largest and most imposing of the others, over forty in total. Its pure black, darker-than-crake chitinous exoskeleton glistened in the dim light. Two extra-long antennae waved menacingly, while a long proboscis flicked in and out between its threatening mandibles. Its bulging compound eyes seemed to look everywhere at once. Atop this giant sentient insect sat Bertran himself, his figure imposing and dominant as he perched in his saddle on the creature's upper thorax, leading the procession further north.

The loading of the captives was a harrowing spectacle. They were stacked in saddlebag nets without care or consideration, treated as nothing more than cargo. Among them was Caleb, in the depths of mental anguish and horrible physical pain. His ordeal had left him in a state of stupor, a complete numbness, his mind shifting in and out of awareness. At times when he blacked out, his mind would drift back to a carefree time of peace and tranquility in his White Flock's Mother Tree, where the air was filled with the sweet fragrance of fruit and the gentle twittering of his people. But each time, the harsh throbbing pain of reality pulled him back, a cruel reminder of his current suffering.

A familiar mental voice, probing and searching, echoed in Caleb's mind during periods of unconsciousness and feverish sleep, but he felt too broken to respond. It was as if the very essence of who he was slipped away. Even thoughts of Irka, once a beacon of hope, now flickered dimly. He thought of her kind-hearted laugh, her fragrance, her touch, but the idea of being a crippled Avian, unable to fly, love, or function, tormented him. A bird person was nothing without their wings, and Caleb realized he would never regain his ability to fly after sustaining such severe damage. What good would he be to Irka and his flock? Would he not just be a burden? Even if he could be a father, what kind of father could he possibly be?

The arduous and painful journey northward through the Othor Mountain Range was a trial of physical endurance for the captives, especially in their weakened state. As Caleb and the prisoners were transported toward Othor's Head, the highest mountain in the norther range, the climate grew increasingly harsh and frigid, with a biting cold that seeped into their broken bones. The frigid air smelled of frost and snow, and the acrid stench of Othorian smelting from the northern settlement grew stronger with each passing hour. The Northern Keep, perched on the western flank of Othor's Head, marked the end of their northward trek.

As they approached, the views from this part of the West Trail were captivating. From this perfect angle there was a magnificent view of the Three Golden Obelisks, standing majestically below the center of several towering mountains, overlooking the vast plains of the Highland Plateau. These awe-inspiring structures, shimmering with a golden hue that caught the light of the sun in dazzling displays, had long been the subject of Kondorian intrigue and attempts at exploration. Legend held that these peaks were the creation of Mother Kondor herself, formed in an explosive fiery eruption many thousands of years ago. Other stories and folklore suggested a more recent appearance.

The Othorians, renowned for their skill in metallurgy and mining, had spent millennia attempting to penetrate the abnormal surface of these immense golden pillars. Despite advanced smelting techniques and access to the purest ores and minerals made with their extensive mastery over rock and earth, their tools could not so much as scratch the surface of these mysterious peaks. The inability to breach their surfaces only added to their mystique, leaving them shrouded in myth, a constant reminder of the limits of Othorian power and knowledge.

For Caleb, the sight of these legendary golden peaks brought no sense of wonder or awe. As the landscape around him exuded a raw, untamed beauty, Caleb's inner world was a stark contrast, filled with shadows and a profound sense of loss. The journey to the Northern Keep was not just a grim physical trek but a descent into the deepest recesses of his despair. Without his wings and without his love, he felt he had nothing. He was nothing.

NORTHERN KEEP

22:
THE NORTHERN KEEP

---◦◇◆◇◦---

The Northern Keep stood as a formidable symbol of Othorian strength, an architectural marvel that represented centuries of advanced expertise in stonemasonry. Designed as both a fortress of last resort and a sanctuary for Othorian royalty, its dual purpose was well understood by all. Perched solidly on the side of the colossal mountain known as Othor's Head, the imposing structure rose majestically from the sheer cliffs, its towering turrets and impenetrable walls stretching thousands of feet into the air.

At the heart of this massive castle lay a smelter and mine dedicated to extracting the unique, dark, heat-emitting ore called crake. This substance was the lifeblood of the keep, fueling its forges and providing a constant source of power that heated the entire settlement. The heat generated by the crake slowly melted adjoining deposits of ever-replenishing ice, ensuring a continuous supply of fresh water for the inhabitants. Inside, giant natural caverns hosted extensive farm fields, rendering the fortress self-sufficient. These farms, warmed by the castle's internal heat, provided a steady source of food, mostly fungi and mushrooms that thrived in the high humidity and constant temperatures.

Over two hundred workers resided permanently within its walls, tending to the flames, smelting metals, mining, and farming. Their spouses maintained the keep, cleaning and feeding the workforce. With ample food stores and the capacity to ramp up production rapidly, the Northern Keep was prepared for prolonged sieges.

Bertran arrived at the Northern Keep with an unmistakable air of authority. His presence commanded attention, his confidence unshakable even as the whispers of resistance grew louder outside the Keep's walls. His entourage was equally impressive, including Mutilla, his aunt now the Head Keeper of the jiants, as well as his most trusted generals: Igor, Morang, and Hathtu. His loyal sidekick, the miniature jiant named Broot, and his chamberlain Dorion, along with a contingent of Bertran's elite guards, completed the imposing retinue. After disembarking from their respective jiants they gathered at the main entrance of the Keep, keeping a respectful distance behind their leader.

"This fortress," Bertran declared loudly as they passed through the massive front gateway, "has stood unchallenged for centuries. Our enemies will break against its walls like waves upon the rocks." Staff and servants were hurriedly helping the royal party, offering the best drinks and morsels of delicious food. Dirty travelling clothes were quickly exchanged for cleanly pressed interior wear and cloaks made from the finest silks and furs.

Dorion, added smugly taking a large swig of foule, "Indeed, my Lord. The keep's defenses are unmatched. We are prepared for any siege."

Mutilla, overseeing the jiants, nodded in agreement. "My jiants are always ready, my King. They will protect this keep as they have always done."

As they were escorted down opulent halls, draped with tapestries and art depicting leaders and great historical events, Bertran's confidence grew even more. The air was filled with the luxurious scents of masses of potted ferns and trees in giant stone urns, sporting dark purple spiked flowers that emitted a flowery yet musky, astringent odor that cleansed the air. They passed by a luxurious hot bath and spa room, conveniently located near the entry so weary travelers could clean up before presenting themselves. Wafts of floral and camphoraceous-smelling soap filled the hallway with an increase in humidity as they passed, tempting them to linger. But Bertran strode on, and the whole group followed.

"This is not just a fortress," Bertran said, a smirk playing on his lips. "This will be our sanctuary, a testament to my power." He removed his gloves and felt the soft luxurious cloth of one of his favorite wall hangings, rubbing his hands over the familiar delicate weave and patterns. He remembered it fondly from previous visits; it depicted an aerial landscape panorama of the entire Highland Plateau. "But first, we must move on to the meeting place below the Three Golden Obelisks," he said, tapping his fingers on the shiny golden depiction of the obelisks on the tapestry. "There, we shall deliver the captive Avians and receive our just rewards. We will have great wealth and more power; I assure you all. Then when we return, I shall rule all of Kondor—Othorians and Avians alike. Everyone shall bow to our supremacy, and you, my loyal friends, shall all benefit as well!"

General Igor knelt at Bertran's feet, bowing his head deeply in submission. "If I may speak, my King, it is my utmost honor to be here with you. I place my complete trust in your leadership. Command me, and I will serve."

"I wholeheartedly agree, and I am certain all present pledge their unwavering support to you, our esteemed leader, King Bertran!" General Morang added fervently, as Mutilla performed a deep curtsy. The others voiced their allegiance with resounding "Ayes" and "Hear, hear," each offering low genuflections, accompanied by respectful clicking sounds and scents of loyalty and submission filling the air.

Bertran's face twisted into a smile, more a sneer than an expression of gratitude, exuding only entitlement. "Station enough soldiers to secure the Keep, and after a well-earned rest, we shall resume our trek. Mutilla, we'll require the jiants to get us down and across the plateau. Let us reconvene tomorrow to finalize our plans. For now, take a short rest; we'll stay on the move."

With a final good night to all, Bertran turned and went off to get some solitude and sleep. He was anxious to make contact with the enigmatic entity that had been promising him so much. Deep down, he knew he would receive a great reward; when joined in mental union with another mind, the truth was apparent. However, it was time to clarify the deal while he had the upper hand.

As Bertran settled into the royal chambers of the Keep, his confidence remained unwavering. He was convinced of his supremacy, trusting in the fortress's unparalleled defenses. This formidable mountaintop stronghold, renowned across the realm for its unassailable design, offered him a secure base from which he could comfortably rule until the turmoil passed. His messengers would deliver orders, allowing him to maintain control from a distance. The Northern Keep, a masterpiece of Othorian engineering and a lasting symbol of power, was built to endure any assault, providing not only protection but also a level of luxury and comfort reserved for the elite of Othorian society.

Bertran, ensconced in the grandeur of his royal library and parlor, warmed by the glowing coals of crake in his ornate fireplace, prepared himself to communicate with the alien entity of his visions. The room, richly adorned with ancient tomes and lavish tapestries, reflected the opulence befitting royalty. As he settled into a plush armchair, the flickering flames cast dancing shadows that played upon his determined visage. He inhaled deeply, trace aromas of the burning crake tickling his lungs. He closed his eyes, steadying his breath, and entered a deep trance. His mind, though limited in communing skills, opened like a receptive vessel, ready to receive the messages from his benefactor.

The connection came quickly, clear and strong, with a voice that immediately dominated Bertran's mind. Stern yet ethereal, it questioned his actions and the suffering he had inflicted. *"You have done much damage, young prince. Why do you not heed my directives?"*

Bertran, defensive and impatient, bristled at the reprimand, surprised by the unusually clear connection; it had been much weaker in the past. In his self-centered view, he took this as a sign of his growing importance and rank. He took a slow breath, eager for the promised rewards and with little tolerance for sermons. His mental tone, dripping with arrogance and barely concealing a threat, cut through sharply as he declared, *"I am King of the Othorians now, not prince! You wanted the Avians here quickly, and I delivered. Now, let's discuss my rewards. Spare me the lecture about disloyalty. I have what you need, and it's time you uphold your end of the bargain."*

Marcus, the entity behind the voice, recognized the need to tread carefully. Bertran was volatile, and pushing him too far could jeopardize the complex plans in motion. To calm the situation, Marcus shifted tactics, projecting a vision of immense spiritual energy, a glimpse of nirvana that was intoxicating in its intensity. For a moment, Bertran was awash in this bliss, feeling an overwhelming sense of contentment and a taste of power beyond anything he had ever imagined.

The reaction was immediate and profound. The surge of energy that coursed through him left him breathless, his mind ignited with the possibilities that such power could bring. This mental force was something he could harness, something that could grant him everything he desired. The allure of it was irresistible.

Sensing Bertran's newfound eagerness, Marcus played his final card, sending vivid images of precious jewels, metals, advanced technology, machines, and quantum computers far beyond Othorian understanding. These tantalizing visions captivated Bertran, promising him a future filled with unimaginable wealth and complete dominion.

"Are you ready to receive your rewards?" Marcus asked, his tone devoid of deceit but heavy with implication. At the same time, to bolster Bertan's faith in him he added, *"My name is Marcus Trumanian the Ninth and I come from a place far away called Niter 6."*

"Yes, I am. I AM ready, Marcus. Marcus from Niter 6. Now I know your name," Bertran responded aloud, his eyes snapping open with an expression of triumph. A huge grin spread across his face as he stared into the flames, his narcissistic mind racing with visions of power and technological marvels. He could sense the precipice of a new era, one where he could wield unimaginable power and achieve his grandest ambitions. The promise of limitless energy and advanced knowledge teased him, drawing him deeper into the pact with the mysterious being.

As the connection deepened, Bertran felt a growing hunger for the power that Marcus offered. He envisioned himself at the helm of a vast empire, commanding both Othorians and Avians, bending them to his will with the technologies and riches now within his reach. The Keep around him, once a mere fortress, now seemed the foundation of his future dominion—a dominion that would stretch across the land and skies of Kondor and beyond.

The next day, Bertran began preparations for his journey to the final meeting at the Highland Plateau with Marcus. The captives, whom he had previously treated with harshness, were now handled with a surprising gentleness, as if they were valuable goods rather than prisoners. Bertran's mind was fixed on the rewards promised to him, and his eagerness to fulfill his desires had softened his approach.

Gathering his generals, Bertran laid out the plan for the descent. A hidden exit tunnel from the rear of the Northern Keep led directly through the mountain to the plateau far below. This path was the most direct but also the most dangerous, requiring a full day of treacherous descent, that would be followed by two days of crossing the highland plain to arrive at the meeting place.

"The first group, including the captives, will descend tomorrow," Bertran instructed, his voice cold and calculated. "The jiants will carry them down and then return for the rest of our forces. By the third day, we will all be united on the plateau."

The majority of the troops would take a slower, safer route, rappelling down the cliffs of the interior passage. But the captives, strapped into nets and saddlebags on the jiants' backs, would be the first to descend. The agile creatures, with their six claw-like feet, could navigate the sheer rock faces with ease.

As a gesture of his newfound "kindness," Bertran ordered the loosening of the captives' bindings, allowing them to walk about and stretch. Sparse rations of water and food were distributed, providing a small lift to their spirits. Even Caleb, still battered and broken, felt a slight improvement.

In a secluded corner of the Keep's prison, Caleb, Goffry, and Maxima huddled together, speaking in hushed tones as they kept a wary eye on the guards. The cold stone walls loomed around them, casting shadows that deepened the suffocating darkness. Even their whispered words and faint chirps echoed ominously, swallowed by the emptiness. Despite the extra rations, the cold, unforgiving floors offered little rest, leaving them to lean against one another for warmth and comfort in the desolate space.

"Caleb, we can't lose hope now," Goffry implored, his voice a mixture of determination and worry. "An opportunity to strike back will present itself. I'm sure of it. Reinforcements must be on their way."

Caleb's response was tinged with despair, tears in his eyes. "I'm broken, Goff. I fear not even the finest healers can mend my wings. And Irka … my heart aches for her. There's a faint ember of hope, but I feel so overwhelmed, and I'm so, so tired."

Goffry's resolve remained unshaken, reaching forward he grasped his long-time companion's hand with a tender touch. "Caleb, you're stronger than this. We WILL find Irka. She needs you; I need you; your family needs you, and your people need you. The communing powers you now have, Caleb, are invaluable to all the Avian people during this dark time. Don't give up now."

Maxima moved closer, caressing and preening what was left of Caleb's feathers. Sensing the gravity of the moment, she began to sing softly. Her voice, though weakened, wove a familiar melody—a song of a gallant hero from the Kondorian War who had lost all hope but eventually led the Avians to victory. The haunting yet invigorating tune rekindled a faint spark within Caleb.

When the song ended, Caleb sighed, his voice heavy with exhaustion. "I need more time … just a little more time to rest," he murmured, his eyes fluttering closed as sleep claimed him, offering a brief respite from his pain.

Goffry, his heart heavy, whispered to Maxima, "Let him sleep until we leave." He then rose slowly, groaning as his own injuries protested the movement. As he looked down at his best friend, tears also welled up in his eyes. Caleb's once-proud wings, now plucked and mangled, were a heartbreaking sight. The makeshift braces they had applied were a futile attempt to give him some comfort, but Goffry knew the truth—Caleb would never fly again.

As Caleb lay there, enveloped in the dim light, his spirit hovered on the verge of total anguish. The glimmer of hope that Irka might still be alive was like a faint star in the dark expanse of his mind, a distant but constant reminder of what could be. Even in his weakened state, the thought of reuniting with her brought a bittersweet comfort. The possibility of seeing her again, of feeling the warmth of her presence, kindled a weak but persistent desire to fight through the hopelessness that threatened to engulf him.

In the depths of his weariness, as sleep began to take him, Caleb felt a gentle, familiar presence touch his mind. It was a sensation he recognized, yet it felt different now, no longer an invasive force but a soothing whisper, like a tender hand brushing away the turmoil within. The presence radiated a soft, nurturing light, easing the sharp edges of his agony and fatigue.

"It will be alright. I promise I will make it right. Stay alive. You are greatly needed," the ethereal message floated through his thoughts like a feather on a breeze. It was a message imbued with care and assurance, a mental embrace that provided a momentary refuge from his physical and emotional torment.

Caleb's mind surrendered to the exhaustion, slipping into a deep, healing slumber. The gentle mental touch lingered, a beacon in the darkness, promising hope and strength for the trials ahead. In this place of rest, he was momentarily free from the harsh reality of his situation, cradled in the comforting embrace of a compassionate, unseen guardian.

The Northern Keep was alive with urgency. Massive doors, engineered to withstand the fiercest of sieges, were sealed shut with a thunderous clamor. Gigantic metal locking bars, hoisted into place by teams of Othorian soldiers, clanged against their hinges with a resounding finality. The Keep was now tightly shut, its narrow-slit windows allowing only the faintest glimpse of the outside world, too small for any living being to pass through. From within, it was clear that the fortress was under assault—rebel Othorians and Avian flotas had begun to converge outside. Yet, the defenses of the Keep, formidable and unbreachable, stood as a testament to the Othorian mastery of fortification.

The captives, still bound and stashed into net bags were at least granted enough freedom to cling to their jiants. They began their perilous descent through the Keep's hidden rear exit, the journey a harrowing blend of danger and wonder. The jiants, with their agile, multi-legged dexterity, navigated near-vertical shafts with ease. Their clawed feet found purchase on the sheer rock faces, carrying their burden through dark, twisting passageways that plunged deep into the mountain's core. At intervals, the trail opened into vast chambers, where the path spiraled downward like the coiled tail of a serpent, carved into the ancient rock.

Hours into the descent, the path began to ease, the sharp zigzags mellowing into gentler curves. At times emerging from the mountain's shadowy depths, they found themselves in hidden valleys nestled among the lower peaks. The change in altitude brought a rise in temperature, a welcome contrast to the icy chill of the upper heights. The Highland Plateau, still luxuriating in the warmth of the wet season, beckoned them forward. The meeting of cool mountain air and warm, moist plateau breezes created a swirling dance of fog and mist, fragrant with the scent of greenery, rain, and flowers. These ethereal clouds wrapped around the jiants and their passengers, adding a veil of mystery to their cautious journey toward the plateau.

The descent finally culminated at the base of the trail, where a grand natural gateway awaited them. Massive tectonic slabs had split the lower mountain face wide open, forming a colossal gash that now bathed the procession in brilliant daylight. The transition from the shadowy depths to the sunlit world was stark, casting an otherworldly glow over the landscape. The group, weary yet determined, gathered at the mouth of this natural marvel, pausing for a much-needed respite. The Avians, despite their chains, basked in the sunlight, drawing comfort from its warmth. The Othorians, meanwhile, huddled in the shadows, shunning the brightness as they adjusted to the light. Many pulled their hoods low over their faces, seeking shelter from the sun's glare.

The encampment at the foot of the mountain pass was a surreal tableau. The jiants, with their towering forms and seemingly endless stamina, returned upward to retrieve more of Bertran's troops. The captive Avians, though exhausted and battered, couldn't help but marvel at the beauty around them. After so much time spent in dark caves and tunnels, the sight of sun-drenched trees, the smell of fresh grass, and the open sky were like a balm to their souls. Despite being left chained together in a gang, their spirits lifted slightly as they took in the natural splendor.

Bertran, dismounting from his majestic personal black jiant steed, Bishop, surveyed the scene with a smug sense of accomplishment. His gaze swept over the encampment, and a look of self-satisfaction settled on his face. The sunlight glinted off his leathery body armor, casting shadows that danced across his features, forcing him to squint against the brightness. Yet, his eyes reflected the dark triumph that simmered within him, an aura of ruthless ambition radiating from his very being.

"In just a couple of days, I will meet this mysterious being, Marcus, face-to-face," he mused silently. The thought of the victory and rewards that awaited him nearly made his mouth water. He could almost taste the future that lay just beyond his grasp, a future of boundless power and influence.

Around him, the temporary base at the bottom of the mountain pass hummed with activity. Soldiers moved with purpose, setting up a temporary camp and preparing for the next leg of the journey. Yet, amid the organized chaos, there was an undercurrent of tension, a subtle but tangible sense of foreboding that hung in the air like a dark cloud.

Bertran, however, remained blissfully unaware of this unease, lost in his grand visions of glory and conquest. In his mind, he was already a ruler without equal, standing on the cusp of unparalleled success. The world, in his eyes, was his for the taking—a prize to be claimed, with only a few more steps separating him from his ultimate destiny.

MARCUS
AI REPLICANT IMAGE

23:
Marcus Prepares

The pivotal moment in Marcus's intricate plan to align the Avians with his cause was rapidly approaching, yet it was fraught with unforeseen complexities. Determined to ensure their cooperation, Marcus knew he needed to confront the situation personally. The Creator Prime Law forbade direct contact, but the urgency of the moment made the decision inevitable. The Three Golden Obelisks—his monumental spaceship and base for millennia—would oversee this critical encounter, and for the first time on Kondor, Marcus would leave its protective embrace.

As preparations began, Marcus meticulously envisioned the meeting. He would be accompanied by Leurin, embodied in his most recent, highly advanced avatar. Marcus himself would don a state-of-the-art body suit, brimming with advanced technology, maintaining a constant link with his ship and Leurin. Beyond its impervious material, the suit emitted an invisible yet impenetrable force field, safeguarding Marcus from all external threats—whether physical attacks, projectiles, energy weapons, environmental contaminants, or biological hazards.

With the Three Golden Obelisks, in direct sight, Marcus had the reassurance of immediate extraction if necessary. Additionally, he could harness the spaceship's immense power directly, a tactical advantage should unforeseen circumstances arise. Seven shuttles were to be arranged in a protective semicircle around the meeting area, and Marcus and Leurin would make their entrance last in his cruiser.

Marcus hoped that his recent interaction with Bertran would lead to increased cooperation, alleviating the Avians' suffering. The battered and bruised captives were a grave concern, but he was resolute in his belief that he could remedy their situation. The looming threat of the Takers only intensified the urgency of his actions.

The previous night, Marcus had managed to reestablish a brief mental connection with Caleb of the PureWhite Flock, a key figure who had previously resisted his advances. Marcus sensed and felt Caleb's deep despair and physical agony—a traumatizing moment for someone unaccustomed to emotions and physical pain. The realization of the Avians' horrible suffering under Bertran's cruelty moved Marcus deeply. Experiencing Caleb's anguish broke him down; he felt overwhelming guilt, recognizing that he bore much responsibility for their plight. Tears flowed freely down his face, a manifestation of his empathy and regret. Marcus couldn't recall the last time he had cried so profoundly.

After the initial shock wore off, Marcus channeled a potent wave of positive energy—a small gesture compared to Caleb's own mental prowess, but one he hoped would offer some solace. *Just get here, Caleb. It will be alright. I am Marcus and I will fix this,*" he projected, but the communion faded as Caleb succumbed to unconsciousness.

Leurin, witnessing Marcus's emotional turmoil, felt a wave of concern. Despite his logical nature, Leurin's empathic abilities allowed him to share in Marcus's sorrow. He understood why Marcus was so disturbed, having monitored the link with Caleb. Gently guiding Marcus to a nearby divan, Leurin offered comfort and reassurance, sitting beside him and holding his hand.

"We did not predict such deceit from the Othorians," Leurin consoled, his logical demeanor providing a counterbalance to Marcus's emotional state. "This has been a profound lesson in understanding the emotional complexities of this planet's denizens. The silver lining is that we will now have the opportunity to connect directly with the Avians and address the challenges created by these deceitful Othorians." His words, though rational, carried a weight of shared understanding and compassion.

"Thank you for your comfort, Leurin," Marcus replied, his tone reflecting gratitude. "Your companionship has always been invaluable."

Leurin nodded in acknowledgment. "I appreciate that, Marcus. I truly do."

After allowing Marcus a moment to compose himself, Leurin rose and continued working, his avatar's arms moving gracefully as he interacted with several screens, pushing command prompts in the air with a refinement that belied his mechanical nature. Though he had no need to physically manipulate consoles, Leurin understood that Marcus and other organic beings found comfort in this more human-like behavior.

Returning to the settee where Marcus now sat upright, Leurin placed a hand on his master's shoulder. Breaking the silence, he continued, "Now, if we could, Marcus, let's focus on the logistics of our current situation. There have been several developments on Kondor. It appears that one of Bertran's generals has successfully merged the eastern wave of captives. But look at the activity on this live stream." Leurin gestured toward a shimmering holographic display that materialized in the room, projecting a real-time topographical video of the Highland Plateau. The map, sourced from low-flying satellite scans, also included detailed overlays of surrounding areas.

Both of them stood and moved toward the holographic display. It was a marvel of technology, with vivid, three-dimensional terrain features and dynamic indicators representing various forces in motion. The command center's high ceiling arched above them, creating an airy feel. The room was softly illuminated by the glow of the holographic screens and the occasional flash of console lights. Around them, sumptuous seating upholstered in velvety plush cushioning added a touch of luxury, while beautiful art pieces and mesmerizing alien sculptures were strategically placed throughout the space, providing an aesthetic contrast to the technological environment.

Leurin's avatar, fluid yet metallic, moved with calm determination as he pointed to the map, which zoomed in to an aerial view of the Northern Keep. "Here," he began, "this supposedly impenetrable Othorian stronghold has been compromised from within, a recurring theme and a clear sign of the growing resistance against Bertran's tyranny. Major Jubba, your contact, once commanded Bertran's troops but was secretly aligned with the Resistance. He opened a side entrance, allowing a spearhead of rebel forces, including an elite squad of Avians and buzzies, to infiltrate. The takeover was swift and precise, with minimal casualties and injuries, primarily on the Othorian side."

Marcus leaned in to examine the hologram closely, his face, worn with age, reflected both concentration and determination. "And up here," he pointed to the northwestern side of the Highland Plateau, "these are the Othorian forces approaching from the west, headed by none other than Bertran himself." The image again zoomed in, revealing a procession of gray jiants mounted with troops and captive birdpeople, followed by more of Bertran's forces. "The Resistance and Avian forces are not far behind, continuing to pursue him after their conquest of the Keep."

Leurin's avatar stood silently for a moment, processing the information. "They're all converging," he noted, "likely close to our final meeting place. This confrontation will indeed be intense, but we're prepared to take the necessary actions."

Scrutinizing the images further, Marcus pointed out, "The Avians' advance forces from the western Flocks have already taken flight toward Bertran. They're taking the fastest direct outside route, leaving the interior descent for the Resistance army. A descent by air down the flank of the mountains is a risky but daring move."

Leurin nodded, the light reflecting off his luminescent form. "The atmosphere at that altitude is extremely thin, and the winds are dangerous and unpredictable. Diving down, they'll have to go slowly for a time, gliding back and forth between sheltered perches. They'll likely halt their progress at nightfall, given the terrain and the need to circumvent a substantial ridge that poses a difficult obstacle. This is shaping up to be quite a significant assembly of forces."

Marcus's eyes lingered on the detailed topographical image; the holographic terrain alive with the movements of armies. The weight of the decisions that lay ahead pressed heavily on his shoulders, but his resolve remained unshaken. He glanced at Leurin, appreciating the unwavering support of his companion. "Leurin, we've faced many challenges together. This one is different. The stakes are higher, and the cost of failure is unimaginable."

Leurin's nano-mechanical yet sentient eyes met Marcus's, reflecting a deep understanding. "We are prepared, Marcus. We've anticipated every move, calculated every risk. We will succeed."

Marcus sighed, the lines on his face deepening. "I hope you're right. For the sake of all the lives depending on us, I hope you're right."

They stood there for another moment in silence, the weight of their mission evident in the quiet of the command center. The soft hum of machinery was the only sound, accompanied by the gentle pulsing glow of the three-dimensional displays, creating an atmosphere of tense anticipation.

"Let them gather, and let's see what unfolds before we act. Bertran is due for retribution—a reckoning for his vile deeds—and I will not allow more innocents to suffer or lose their lives," Marcus emphasized. "Let's strategize further before the meeting. Everything must be ready; they will all face the consequences they deserve."

As they turned back to the display, the reality of the impending confrontation settled over them. They stood on the brink of a pivotal moment. It was a time for reflection, recognizing the gravity of the situation and the weight of the choices that lay ahead.

After a time Leurin turned toward Marcus, his gaze softened with compassion as he met his Creator's eyes. "I'll ensure our preparations are flawless. Together, we'll see this through."

BERTRAN

HE IS RELENTLESS IN HIS PURSUIT OF
DOMINATION, AN AI REPLICANT IMAGE

24:
Bertran on the Highland Plateau

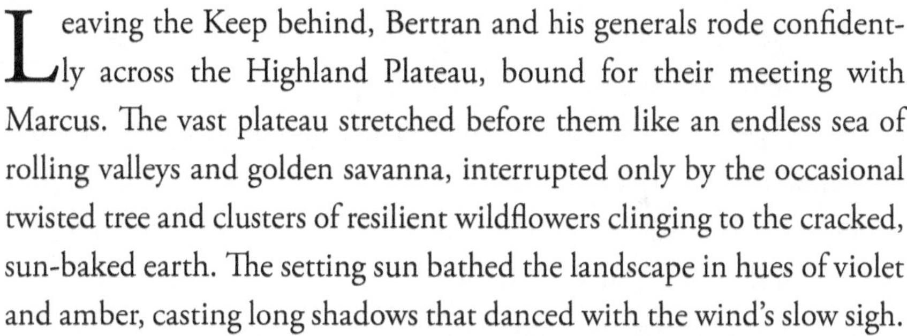

Leaving the Keep behind, Bertran and his generals rode confidently across the Highland Plateau, bound for their meeting with Marcus. The vast plateau stretched before them like an endless sea of rolling valleys and golden savanna, interrupted only by the occasional twisted tree and clusters of resilient wildflowers clinging to the cracked, sun-baked earth. The setting sun bathed the landscape in hues of violet and amber, casting long shadows that danced with the wind's slow sigh.

Bertran, astride his imposing black jiant steed, led the way, his expression one of unshakable confidence. He glanced over his shoulder at his generals, a smirk tugging at his lips. "The Keep is secure, our hold is firm," he said with a sweeping gesture to the land around them. "Let Marcus see what kind of allies he's drawn to his side. Soon, he'll understand what true power looks like."

General Igor rode just behind him, his eyes skimming the horizon. "Yes, Majesty. Nothing stirs here. We've swept this land clean. Any fool still loyal to the rebels wouldn't dare show their face."

General Hathtu, his light-sensitive Othorian eyes narrowing in the evening glow, chuckled quietly. "These rebels are little more than a nuisance. They'll be crushed by our strength soon enough, like insects underfoot."

Beside him, General Morang adjusted his grip on the reins, his scarred face set in a smug grin. "And let them try, if they dare. I've yet to meet an opponent who could match us," he scoffed, his tone filled with a pride that only years of unchallenged dominance could breed.

Bertran nodded in agreement, his gaze lingering on the flat plains stretching endlessly before them. "This plateau is ours," he declared. "Let them cower in the shadows, whispering of resistance. We'll root them out one by one."

They continued on, each word deepening the arrogance that hung over the group like an invisible banner. Their voices carried across the savanna, mingling with the soft sounds of the plateau, the rustling of dry grass, the occasional call of a night bird hidden in the brush.

The moonlight began to cast its silver light over the plateau, illuminating the path ahead as they rode on, still oblivious to the reality creeping up behind them. Far in the distance, a day or two behind, the Resistance forces and Avians pressed forward, closing the gap. Unseen and unfelt by Bertran and his party, they advanced with growing determination.

As the night wore on, the convoy crested a ridge and descended into the next valley. There, bathed in the soft violet light of the moons, they saw the waiting forces from the eastern side of the valley. The Blue and Yellow Flock Avian captives, their figures slumped and weary, were guarded closely by Othorian soldiers. General Po, now one of Bertran's inner circle, led the eastern contingent. As soon as he saw the new king arriving, he rode up to Bertran with a quiet determination, saluting as he approached and bowing his head in respect.

"Welcome, my king and esteemed generals. We have been awaiting your arrival with pleasure." His dialect, marked by more whistling and clicking than the others, was a reminder of his origins in the Eastern Mountains. "All is in order; we await your command."

The sight of the forces combining brought another surge of satisfaction to Bertran. *"Everything is falling into place,"* Bertran said to himself, a grim smile crossing his lips as he surveyed his generals and the scene below. To the others around him, he bellowed out with an undertone of a hiss, "Very well, General Po, your addition to our efforts is welcomed. Let us oversee the quick amalgamation of our troops and proceed on our course immediately."

The merge went smoothly, and the trek continued. The landscape gradually shifted from the flat, green expanse of the plateau to more rugged terrain as they approached the foothills of the towering mountains. The distant peaks, cast long, eerie shadows across the land. The air grew cooler, tinged with the scent of pine and damp earth.

As they traveled, the Three Golden Obelisks came into full view, their majestic peaks rising high against the mountains. The sight of these ancient, mysterious structures filled the air with a sense of awe and anticipation. The obelisks shimmered in the moonlight, their golden surfaces reflecting the light in a way that seemed almost otherworldly.

The convoy pressed on; their pace steady but wary as they neared the meeting place. Confidence held strong at first, their spirits bolstered by the rhythmic beat of marching feet on hard ground and the buzzing hum of insects filling the warm night air. But as they navigated a narrow gulch, the atmosphere shifted abruptly. The night fell silent, as though the land itself were holding its breath. The lively chorus of insects ceased, replaced by a thick, oppressive stillness that seemed to wrap around them like a shroud.

The mood across the entire convoy transformed, an unspoken dread seeping into their bones. One by one, they slowed, a hush falling over the leading group as they edged forward. Even Bertran and his generals, who had led with such confident swagger, found their gazes drifting nervously to the shadows, their initial bravado fading.

"Do you all feel this?" muttered General Morang, his voice a low whisper as he glanced around uneasily. "Something's changed… keep alert. I feel it in my bones."

Even their gray jiants grew restless, shifting and tossing their heads, resisting the forward march with a skittishness that betrayed an instinct for danger.

"Nonsense," snapped Bertran, his voice laced with hisses of irritation as he emitted a controlled burst of pheromones to steady the group. "There is nothing to fear. Look around, cowards. We are the strongest force on Kondor. Who would dare oppose us?"

With a sharp slap, he urged his black jiant, Bishop, forward, forcing it to continue. Yet even Bishop hesitated, its massive legs stiffening mid-stride, antennae twitching as it sniffed the air. Slowly, the other jiants resumed movement, but just as quickly, they all came to an abrupt halt, antennae raised and waving urgently in the night.

Gasps and murmurs rippled through the ranks, the acrid scent of fear growing stronger as the soldiers realized what had transpired. Hundreds of small, crimson-colored jiants lined the cliffs on either side of the gulch, emerging like spirits from the darkness. These red jiants, spoken of only in ancient tales for their unmatched agility and ferocity, stood motionless, their ruby exoskeletons gleaming under the moonlight. Their antennae waved slowly, deliberately, tasting the air with a silent menace that filled every heart with dread.

Bertran's boldness faded entirely as he took in the sight around them, his own breath catching. The eerie silence of the crimson jiants felt like a warning, their stillness more terrifying than any sudden movement. The confidence that had carried the convoy thus far seemed to crumble, replaced by an overwhelming awareness that something powerful, and perhaps inevitable, lay just ahead.

Quickly halting the convoy, heart pounding in his chest, Bertran dismounted his ebony steed, attempting to make sense of the situation.

The air was thick with anxiety as he barked orders to his generals, his voice laced with anger and tension. A mix of odors pervaded the night air—the intense scent of dread, surprise, and shock from the whole procession in sharp contrast with the wafts of confidence, certainty, and sheer electric energy emanating from the red jiants.

"Silence!" Bertran roared, beating and stretching out his wings and hissing loudly. The din had become quite loud as the news of what had stopped them ran through the ranks of soldiers and Avian prisoners.

The generals quickly regrouped around Bertran, each displaying their own interpretation of the situation. Igor, ever the strategist, was the first to break the silence. "We must tread carefully, my Lord. These creatures are not to be underestimated. There are true stories of their aggressive nature that we must heed."

Hathtu's eyes gleamed with fierce intensity, ever the aggressive warrior. "Let them come. We'll show them the might of the Othorians."

Morang, always the voice of caution, urged restraint. "We should attempt to communicate with them first. We do not know their intentions."

Po, with his calm demeanor, added, "We must be prepared for anything. This silence is unsettling."

All eyes turned to their young king. Bertran weighed his options, his mind speeding through various scenarios. Finally, he made his decision. "Prepare for defense or attack, but do not show aggression. I will attempt to communicate with these creatures."

With a deep breath, Bertran stepped forward, leaving his wings partially outstretched, trying to convey strength and fearlessness yet a non-aggressive stance. Being a master at controlling his pheromones, he emitted the odor of self-assurance and superiority.

Despite his outward composure, his heart still raced. He felt sure his troops could handle the situation, but why risk a bloody battle? The fate of the convoy, and his entire plan, draped in uncertainty as he approached the silent, menacing red jiants.

HIGHLAND
PLATEAU

25:
CALEB ON THE HIGHLAND PLATEAU

During the previous night, Caleb's spirit had begun to rekindle. The mysterious mental connection with the entity, Marcus, had shifted something deep within him. He clung to the renewed feeling that Irka was still alive, and this ember of hope ignited his resolve. He realized that his importance extended beyond his physical abilities—his presence, spirit, and communing skills were vital to his people.

As dawn broke over the encampment at the base of the steep trail from the Northern Keep, a small mercy was afforded to the Avians. Their bindings were loosened, allowing a brief semblance of comfort, and they were given food and water. Though each movement brought fresh pangs of pain, any relief was welcomed, even if fleeting.

Caleb, still limping from the beating he had endured, approached Goffry, his face marked by a new resolve. "Thank you, Goff. You've been my anchor through this storm," he murmured, his voice low but filled with gratitude, punctuated by a few enthusiastic chirps that tried to mask his discomfort.

Goffry managed a grin, though the suffering etched into his own face was unmistakable. "We're still here, Caleb. Still standing, still breathing. We haven't had our chance to strike back yet, but it's coming. We're just waiting for the right moment." He matched Caleb's chirps, a hopeful yet restrained echo that seemed to affirm their unbroken bond.

Nearby, General Eldred lay in the tall, sun-warmed grass, his head resting against a smooth rock. "Don't be modest, Goffry," he chimed in, his voice soft but filled with respect. "While Caleb recovered, you held us together. Even with your own wounds, you've watched over every one of us. My thanks, friend, so well deserved."

Caleb placed a hand on Goffry's shoulder, pulling him into a gentle hug despite the pain it caused him. "What would we do without you, Goff?" he whispered, his eyes warm with sincere affection. "I feel… different now, like something's shifted. There's this warmth inside me, like hope, but stronger."

Goffry's eyes sparkled, his tired face brightening. "Thank Mother Kondor for that! It's about time something good found us." He inhaled deeply, closing his eyes for a moment to savor the fresh scents drifting across the plateau. "Do you smell that? The air is free, Caleb. No more damp cave walls, just the earth's warm breath and the scent of wildflowers. I think I could stay here forever," he chuckled softly. "Now, rest while you can. It seems we'll be on the move again soon." With a few reassuring whistles, he hobbled over to help another injured Avian struggling to rise.

As the sun climbed higher, warmth spread over the captives, reviving their spirits as they soaked up the light and took advantage of the respite. The Othorians, still waiting for the remaining troops to descend from the Keep, moved slowly, hiding from the sun's brightness, their pace leisurely, punctuated by frequent stops. By late afternoon, as the mountains cast long shadows, the Avians were rounded up once more, loaded onto the backs of jiants in preparation for departure.

As the sun finally sank below the horizon, casting the plateau in shades of violet and deep blue, Bertran mounted his steed alongside his generals. The entire army gathered behind them, setting off on what the Avians overheard was the final leg of their journey.

The plateau stretched ahead, vast and quiet, its savanna-like expanse undulating in gentle waves. The air grew cooler, scented with the subtle sweetness of wild grass and a faint, earthy musk. Only two of Kondor's smallest moons lit their path, casting a muted glow that painted the land in glorious violet hues.

Late into the night, the convoy from the eastern side of the valley joined Caleb's group, bringing more Othorian soldiers, gray jiants, and, sadly, additional captives from the Yellow and Blue Flocks. These new prisoners were in poor condition, their moans echoing a shared despair as they were reloaded onto the jiants. Among the captives, those who could still move offered whatever aid they could, and with the Avians now all clustered together, the Othorians were somewhat less harsh, if only for ease of handling. Hushed whispers among the captives hinted at a glimmer of hope: the Resistance was on the move, or so they had gathered from snatches of conversation overheard from the guards.

A fragile sense of cautious optimism flickered among them as the convoy resumed its journey. Yet, neither the Avians nor most of the Othorians seemed to know their ultimate destination. Only the vague term "meeting place" surfaced, murmured occasionally by the guards in hushed tones.

They traveled on through a narrow, steep-sided valley, the path a dry riverbed strewn with stones. Suddenly, the convoy came to an abrupt halt. Silence fell over the group as Bertran's stern command cut through the night air, quelling the murmurs, squawking, hisses and confusion that had begun to ripple through the captives and guards alike.

"Do you sense the fear and unease, Goff?" Caleb whispered, turning his head toward his friend, who was bound beside him atop one of the jiants.

Goffry inhaled deeply, a light cough escaping as he tried to clear his nasal passages. "I do," he replied, voice tense. "But there's something else… a strange scent. I can't quite place it. And it seems like we've hit an unexpected obstacle."

Caleb and the other Avians, their senses heightened by the sudden pause, strained to discern the cause of the interruption. The thick dust and tightly packed convoy made it hard to see or hear much. The crowded valley was a haze of mingled scents—fear, sweat, and the unfamiliar smell that Goffry had detected, drifting ominously through the air. Bound tightly and unable to move, the Avians struggled to make sense of what lay ahead, the weight of uncertainty pressing down on them as heavily as their restraints.

In the midst of an uneasy stillness, a sound emerged—distinct, clear, and undeniably familiar to every Avian present. It was the unique call of the PureWhite Flock, carrying a tone that resonated deep within their collective memory. But for Caleb, it was more than just a call; it was a voice that struck the very chords of his heart.

His breath caught as recognition dawned. It was unmistakably Irka's voice! Her birdsong pierced through the background clamor, electrifying the air and freezing the world in place. All eyes turned toward the source, and Caleb's heart surged with hope, longing to be reunited with her.

Struggling against his restraints, Caleb strained forward to witness the scene unfolding before him. Hundreds of smaller red jiants had encircled the convoy, now blocking their path. Bertran, caught off guard, cautiously approached them. From the midst of the red jiants, three imposing gray jiants emerged, each carrying an aura of power. Atop one rode Irka, a vision of determination and strength, her eyes blazing as she guided her steed, Artula. Beside her were Mikia the Jumper and Prudentia the Fast.

Upon seeing Irka, a surge of vitality flooded Caleb's veins, momentarily erasing his pain. Frantically, he tried to break free from his bindings, his gaze fixated on her.

"Irka! I am here!" he called out, his voice strained but urgent, a weak echo amidst the rising cries and squawks of fear around him.

A powerful call from Irka cut through the chaos, and with her signal, the red jiants and the three loyal grays charged forward in a strategic formation. They surged toward Bertran and his generals, catching the Othorian gray jiants off guard. The red jiants swarmed over them, swiftly freeing captives from their bonds, tearing off harnesses, and removing Othorian riders with sharp mandibles and venom-laden stingers. Most of the gray jiants, upon being liberated, made no attempt to fight; relieved of their burdens, they swiftly departed, abandoning their Othorian masters.

Several red jiants rushed to Caleb and the other Avians, severing their restraints with deft bites. Seizing a weapon from a fallen guard, Caleb joined the fray, Goffry beside him, each ready to stand against their former captors.

In that moment, Caleb felt a shift within him, as though his consciousness had expanded. Time seemed to slow, each movement precise and powerful despite his battered state. He drew strength from the earth beneath his feet, from the air, and from the teeming life around him. A rhythmic exchange of energy surged through him, flowing outward in waves that invigorated his allies. It was as if every living thing around him willed him to triumph, amplifying his energy and uniting their spirits in harmony.

His strong energy signature acted as a beacon, attracting a massive swarm of buzzies that quickly gathered around him. Caleb's spirits soared as he recognized Trada and Pica leading the swarm, accompanied by countless wild counterparts, all drawn to the scene just ahead of the advancing Resistance. Caleb now stood at the helm of an immense, harmonized horde of winged allies.

The arrival of the buzzies shifted the battle's dynamic. Their stingers struck with precision, a relentless aerial assault that overwhelmed

Bertran's soldiers. Moving in perfect synchrony with Caleb's will, the buzzies created a defense that the Othorians struggled to counter. This alliance between Caleb and the buzzies deepened his connection with the creatures, blending their individual and collective consciousness into a single, powerful force.

Catching sight of Irka amid the chaos, Caleb's heart swelled with joy and love, the pain of separation forgotten. Irka's presence had completely revitalized him. Behind her, a formidable force of Avians arrived, moving into battle formation. Marta, Jonus, General Botus, and Maxima led the vanguard, Marta's flock of swifts tearing into the enemy ranks with razor-sharp beaks and talons. The battlefield filled with the metallic scent of blood mingled with sweat and earth, a mist of retribution blanketing the plateau.

Caleb and Irka fought their way toward each other, slicing through Bertran's forces in perfect harmony. Finally, the two met, their eyes locking in a moment of pure, wordless connection. They fought side by side, seamlessly coordinating their attacks as clouds of buzzies and flocks of swifts provided cover, while nimble red jiants tore through the enemy lines.

Bertran, flanked by his elite guards, found himself facing Caleb's entire family, who had formed an impregnable circle around him. Marta, a force of fury, led the squad with coordinated attacks that disoriented the Othorians. Irka, guiding her jiants with fierce determination, took down Bertran's last jiant, Bishop, shifting the balance of power decisively in their favor.

Bertran and his remaining generals, Morang and Po, retreated under the onslaught, giving Caleb and Irka the moment they needed. Exhausted, bloodied, and battered, the two rushed into each other's arms, their embrace a tumult of relief and love.

"Caleb, I've missed you so much," Irka whispered, her voice trembling as she clung to him, her grip tight despite their injuries.

"I love you, Irka," Caleb replied, his voice choked with emotion. They stopped, laughing softly as their declarations overlapped. They melted into a kiss, a lingering embrace that felt like the reunion of souls.

Marta and Jonus soon joined them, wrapping the pair in a familial embrace that radiated warmth and solidarity. They held one another close, their thoughts and feelings flowing effortlessly between them.

Marta pulled Caleb aside, her touch both gentle and probing as she assessed his injuries. Her eyes softened with love and concern, yet darkened with sorrow as she noticed the remnants of his once-proud wings, broken and scarred.

"My dear Caleb," she whispered, her voice a soothing balm amid the chaos. She handed him a sleek, dark flask, its mysterious black surface absorbing the light. "This is black sappa," she said, her tone grave. "Its power is beyond our understanding. You'll know when the time is right to use it, but perhaps you need it most now?"

Caleb took the flask, feeling a strange energy emanate from it. "Thank you, Mother. I understand… but I feel it's not time yet," he replied, tucking it safely into his belt pouch. Their moment was cut short as Bertran, rallying his remaining troops and generals, charged once more, his face twisted with desperation and malice.

Caleb, Irka, and their family raised their weapons, their newfound allies at their side, and turned to face the final threat. They were united, their strength a collective force greater than any one of them, ready to confront Bertran and end his reign once and for all.

Suddenly, the chaotic pandemonium of battle was pierced by a commanding presence. "STOP. EVERYONE STOP." A voice, resonant and powerful, echoed across the battlefield, reaching every ear and mind simultaneously. It was a command that transcended language, accompanied by a mental directive, impossible to ignore. Everyone and every being halted in their tracks.

Seven large golden metal objects appeared above in a blur of speed, humming with energy and glowing a radiant blue. They emitted a sharp ozone smell like after a lightning storm. The air seemed to be electrified, sizzling with energy. These sleek airships came to a stop, floating just twenty feet above the stupefied crowd. The sight was awe-inspiring and frightening, as if an ancient prophecy had come to life. Some Othorians, in a futile gesture of defiance, hurled spears and shot arrows toward these otherworldly vessels. But their efforts were in vain, as each projectile fizzled out with a crackle of energy as it neared the ships, disintegrating into nothingness.

A hushed, eerie silence fell over the battlefield. They were all stunned into immobility, with much shaking of heads and rubbing of eyes. Everyone was fixated on the hovering ships, wondering what this new development would bring.

26:
MARCUS INTERCEDES

The atmosphere above the battlefield thrummed with urgency as Marcus and Leurin, aboard their personal cruiser, observed the scene unfolding below. Their fleet of shuttles hovered strategically, ready for intervention. Watching Caleb's forces pushed to the brink, Marcus felt a growing unease; the relentless cost of lives had become intolerable.

"No more of this madness," Marcus declared, his patience shattered. "If they won't come to the meeting place, we'll bring it to them." His decision was final—a daring resolve to intervene directly.

The fleet descended, and Marcus's command, "STOP! EVERYONE STOP," thundered through the air, amplified by Creator technology. His voice resonated with a force of amplified sound waves, energy fields, and powerful pheromones, creating a command impossible to ignore.

The seven shuttles formed a protective semicircle above the battlefield, while Marcus and Leurin descended on floating discs from the eighth ship, Marcus's grand cruiser. The sight was nothing short of otherworldly; the entire field fell silent as soldiers and captives alike instinctively parted into two groups. On one side stood Bertran and his battered forces, still defiant; on the other, the Avians, with Caleb and Irka united at the front, flanked by Marta, Jonus, Goffry, and other Resistance leaders.

Hovering just above the ground, Marcus's presence was magnetic, his authority undeniable. "Greetings to all," he began, his voice carrying an unshakable gravity. "I am Marcus Trumanian the Ninth of Niter 6, and this is my partner, Leurin. We come to end this bloodshed, for which I feel partly responsible." His words cast a spell of silence over the field. "We require the Avians' cooperation," he continued, his statement sparking hostility from the Othorians. "They are a beacon of hope against a common threat to us all."

Bertran pushed his way to the front, his voice dripping with rage and ambition. "I've done as you asked! Delivered these bird people to you!" he spat and hissed, his voice cutting through the quiet. "Now, where is my reward—riches, power, knowledge? Give me what I deserve, or I will kill them all!" His voice seethed with venomous intent.

Suddenly, an Othorian soldier hurled a spear at Leurin. The crowd gasped as it struck him through the abdomen. To their astonishment, Leurin calmly pulled it out, his body reassembling instantly. "A primitive tool," he noted, examining it with detached curiosity. With a flick of his wrist, he sent the spear back, its velocity doubling as it flew into the air and struck its originator, pinning him to the ground by his clothing, sparing his life but sending a clear message. The aggressors among the Othorians lowered their weapons and backed away, a newfound wariness in their eyes.

Marcus, unfazed, extended his hand. "Yes, Bertran, it's time for your reward," he announced. "You and those Othorians who believe themselves deserving of recompense, step forward." Turning to the Avians, he added, "As for my Avian friends and the Othorian Resistance members, know that you are under my protection. I ask you to stand down and I will speak with you shortly. I have something for you as well."

Bertran, alongside his generals and a throng of eager Othorians, surged forward, their expressions a mix of greed and anticipation.

"Now," Marcus intoned, "allow me to present a fraction of the wealth that could be yours." With a wave of his hand, massive floating discs emerged from his cruiser, laden with gold ingots, rare jewels, and precious metals. "But wait," he called, halting the Othorians. "I promised you a reward beyond all material riches. Who among you is interested?"

Bertran, his wings flared with barely concealed greed, pushed to the front. "Of course, I am first!" he announced, shoving others aside.

Marcus's voice dropped to a somber tone. "This reward is truly the greatest, but be warned. It requires you to judge yourself honestly before receiving all you desire. You may take these earthly treasures now and leave in peace, or, if you truly wish for more, you may accept the final gift."

Bertran sneered, glancing toward the riches. "Judge myself? That won't deter me. I'll take what you offer. Others may follow as they wish."

Several Othorians, including Generals Morang and Po, stepped forward with eager cries, positioning themselves behind their king, all waiting for their prize. Then a throng of other Othorians also surged ahead, joining their leaders facing Marcus and Leurin in anticipation, their eyes blinded with the promise of great riches, swirling pheromones of greed and satisfaction rising in suffocating clouds around them.

With authority radiating from him, Marcus raised his arms. Hundreds of ethereal blue beams of light descended from his cruiser and shuttles, each beam singling out an Othorian who had come forward, suspending them midair.

"I offer you the gift of enlightenment," Marcus intoned. "A vision of the One, the truth of our existence, as understood by the Creators." His voice took on a profound resonance. "In this, you may find peace, love, and all you could ever desire."

From the distant Three Golden Obelisks, purple beams of energy erupted, their light visible even from miles away. These beams synchronized with the blue light surrounding the suspended Othorians, creating a deep, pulsing vibration that reverberated through the earth, touching everyone on the field.

"For those who seek this ultimate gift, gaze deeply into the light and be prepared to comprehend the secrets of the universe," Marcus continued.

Thousands of Avians and Othorians watched in awe, captivated by the mystical scene. The ambient spiritual energy being dispensed was intoxicating; Avians instinctively released harmonious birdsongs, while those Othorians with good hearts emitted high-pitched clicks and sweet scents of peace. Night had fallen, and multiple moons cast a violet glow across the low valleys, mingling with the beams of light that now held hundreds of Bertran's followers in a trance.

The beams served as conduits for direct-to-mind enlightenment, a Creator technology refined by Marcus and Leurin, capable of bestowing an intense, spiritual awakening. For those with kind and mature souls, it opened a portal to blissful enlightenment, a realm of peace, health, and love. To those prepared for spiritual ascension, it became a path to a higher dimension, the greatest gift a Creator could bestow.

But for others—those deeply entrenched in malevolence—the experience became a harrowing journey. Bertran and most of his followers, consumed by greed and cruelty, found themselves plunged into the depths of their own souls, forced to confront the full weight of their misdeeds. Faces contorted in agony, they writhed, their minds overwhelmed by the cumulative suffering they had inflicted on others. This was their self-judgment, a penance that exposed them to every pain they had ever caused.

As the truth of "Oneness" dawned upon them, the realization that they were intrinsically linked to every sentient life they had harmed became inescapable. The suffering they experienced grew exponentially, each wave tearing at their physical forms and minds, dissolving them from within in an irreversible transformation.

Bertran, in the throes of torment but still in denial, screamed out to Marcus, "Liar! You promised riches and all that I desired!"

Marcus, with a simple gesture, drew Bertran's floating body closer with the tractor beam that held him. "I granted you riches and, at your behest, the ultimate gift. Your malevolence knows no bounds, Bertran," he declared solemnly, silencing him and the onlookers. "Know that you and your followers will be reborn and by going through this ordeal now you will have less of a karmic load in your next incarnations. For that, you should be happy." Pausing for a slow inhale and tilting his head closer, peering into Bertran's eyes, he continued, "For you, I will show mercy and end your painful existence and relevance right now." With a flick of his wrist, a blazing red beam emanated from Marcus's cruiser and enveloped Bertran. In a mere millisecond, he was reduced to nothing but a wisp of smoke, vanishing into the air. He was no more.

His generals, confidants, and followers who had joined him in receiving the 'gift' lay on the ground motionless. The few living and conscious ones groaning, moaning, and hissing in obvious pain. Some had lost mental stability, babbling incoherently, their bodies shriveled as if with great age. Certain of Bertran's closest circle lay lifeless, strewn around where he had been, some of the worst desiccated into dark, skeletal forms. They emitted a sulfuric burnt smell that now permeated the whole area.

The Othorian leadership lay decimated, their entire command structure shattered. Witnessing the fates of their leaders, the remaining Othorian soldiers dropped their weapons in surrender, bowing their heads in submission. A wave of muted jubilation swept through the Avians and their Othorian Resistance allies, quiet tweets of joy and songs of freedom resonating across the plateau, mingling with the soft sounds of victory.

Marcus observed the scene, the weight of recent events reflected in his eyes. He elevated the floating discs he and Leurin stood upon, ensuring his presence was visible to all. His voice, tinged with both sorrow and warmth, reached the assembled crowd.

"My Avian friends, and all those among you who have shown friendship and loyalty," he began, his tone calm yet heavy with remorse. "At last, I come before you, hoping to be seen as an ally. But first, I must express my deepest sorrow for the unimaginable pain you've endured. It was my desire to bring you here, but not in this way. The suffering inflicted upon you was abhorrent to me, and despite my efforts to intervene, I failed to prevent it. For that, I am profoundly sorry."

A hush fell over the crowd as his words settled, the weight of his regret palpable in the silence. "However," Marcus continued, "I can offer much relief. Within each of these shuttles", he gestured toward the sleek vessels now grounded around the field, "are medical emergency pods, designed to heal your unique Kondorian physiology. Step inside without fear, and your injuries will be tended to. Your feathers may take time to regrow fully, but rest assured, your bodies, wings included, will be restored."

He beckoned gently, encouraging the injured Avians and allies forward. "Please, let those most in need go first. The sooner you begin, the sooner you'll be able to reclaim your strength," he urged, watching as a few of the wounded hesitantly approached the shuttles.

As his eyes swept the crowd, he noticed Caleb and his family huddled together, still bearing the marks of battle. Caleb stood with his arms around Irka, his bruised and battered body marked by broken feathers and raw wounds. Jonus rested a supportive hand on his son's shoulder, while Goffry held him steady from one side. Marta stood in front of Caleb, her posture protective, her gaze uncertain yet watchful.

Marcus lowered his disc beside Caleb and stepped off, approaching with gentle resolve. "My young Caleb," he began, a note of tenderness in his voice. "Though we've only met in dreams, I deeply regret the pain you and your loved ones have suffered. Please, allow me to escort you personally to the medical pod. Bring Irka, your family, and friends. It's time for you all to begin healing."

Marta stepped aside, allowing Marcus to take Caleb's hands. He could feel the young Avian's resistance, the reluctance evident in his stance. "I'll be okay," Caleb insisted, his voice strained but resolute. "Please, take Irka and my family first. They need it as much as I do, maybe more."

Irka touched his arm, her voice a soft reassurance. "Caleb, you've always protected us. Let us do this for you now. We need you whole."

Jonus tightened his grip on his son's shoulder, his voice filled with both pride and a father's authority. "Son, you've given us everything, more than we ever expected. It's time to let us give back to you. Let us see you healed first, and we'll follow."

Goffry nodded, his expression gentle yet firm. "Caleb, we're all here because of you. Show everyone that it's safe by going first, you'll be leading us even now, by letting yourself heal."

Caleb looked around at each of them, his resolve wavering. Marta, her hand resting on his arm, added her voice to the others. "You've carried so much, Caleb, more than any of us could bear to see. Let this be a time for you to receive, not give."

He hesitated, his gaze shifting between his family and Marcus, who stood with unwavering patience. Finally, with a deep sigh, he nodded. "All right," he whispered, the last of his resistance melting away. "I'll go first."

As they neared the shuttle, Irka called after him, her voice filled with love and admiration. "We're right here, Caleb. We'll be whole again together."

Inside, Caleb settled into the pod, his weary body sinking into the soft, supportive embrace. As the pod activated, warmth radiated through him, washing over every bruise, cut, and broken feather, mending his body from within. He closed his eyes, feeling a deep sense of peace overtaking him, as if a weight he had carried for too long was finally being lifted.

As the medical pod's door sealed shut behind Caleb, Marcus reassured his family and the gathered crowd. "He will emerge completely renewed in a couple of hours; I promise. For some of you with lesser injuries, it will only take minutes. I suggest a day of rest and reunion for all of you," he proposed, his voice warm and empathetic. "Use this day to heal and to reconnect with your loved ones. Our situation is urgent, and we still face a formidable challenge ahead. I will return and meet with your leaders at this time tomorrow night to plan our next course of action."

With these words, Marcus and Leurin ascended on their discs, returning gracefully to their cruiser. The Avians below, somewhat speechless, watched in a blend of awe, hope, and uncertainty, absorbing the gravity of Marcus's words and contemplating the miraculous healing that awaited them within the shuttles.

27:
A New Mission

◦◇◦◆◦◇◦

After Bertran's fall, the Othorians immediately embarked on a new era, marking a significant shift in their leadership and governance. The Resistance leader, Portia, a symbol of resilience and hope during the tumultuous times, was unanimously chosen to guide her people through this transitional phase. Her first official decree was one of peace—a heartfelt promise of harmony and cooperation with the Avians. She vowed to aid them in the arduous task of reconstruction, acknowledging the mutual need for rebuilding and healing after the long, harrowing conflict.

The skies above the Highland Plateau, once filled with the imposing presence of the flota armadas, began to clear within hours. The majestic groups of airships, which had valiantly navigated the winds toward war, now embarked on a victorious journey back to their respective homes. This day marked the dawn of a new era, one that whispered promises of peace and tranquility across the planet.

The transformation experienced by those entering the medical pods on the shuttles was nothing short of miraculous. Stepping in battered and broken, then emerging rejuvenated, the advanced technology worked wonders in mere hours, sometimes in only minutes. The same healing grace was extended to everyone needing it and continued all day and night. The previously beaten and damaged Avians and their Othorian friends stepped out of the shuttles feeling renewed, physically at least, with only a few scars and missing feathers to mark their past ordeals.

For Caleb, it was also a wondrous rebirth, physically and mentally. His bones were mended, augmented by biotechnological splices and incredibly light metal alloy plates. His new wing feathers were already sprouting; he emerged feeling almost fully revitalized, albeit groggy and somewhat numb. Irka, Marta, Jonus, and Goffry were waiting for him and marveled at Caleb's appearance.

The large meadow that the fleet of ships had landed in the night before was still filled with Avians and Othorians mixed together but talking happily and certainly in a friendly way. The brilliantly blue sky with its normal violet tinge was stunningly beautiful that day, and the whole plateau was alive and vibrant. The air smelled divine with newly healed senses previously dulled by malice and violence now filled with renewed hope. Fittingly, some wild perennial wildflowers were blooming in profusion, adding light floral scents mixed with a prairie grass undertone to the already clear northern air.

Reuniting with Irka and his family was akin to a first meeting, filled with an overwhelming sense of gratitude and love. The setting was the perfect complement to the mood.

"Caleb, my love, you look wonderful!" Irka exclaimed, leaping into his arms. She had just finished her own healing session, which was shorter than his but equally effective.

Caleb wrapped his sinewy, now unscarred arms around Irka. "My angel, my love." He smothered her face with kisses until she laughed and chirped with happiness and joy.

Overwhelmed with emotions, they broke into tears upon seeing and touching each other. They were both rejuvenated in body and spirit, though still weary from the ordeal. Their new pin feathers remained stubby and patchy as if they had recently molted heavily, but they were otherwise in very good condition. With a few more days of rest and lots of preening, they'd be physically as good as new.

"OK, give us some time," Marta butted in, pulling Caleb away from Irka's embrace.

"Mother, Father, and Goff too!" Caleb's eyes lit up with profound love as they wordlessly locked together in a group hug, with some sobbing, joyful warbles, and warm family birdsong.

After long hugs and joyful greetings exchanged with his family, Caleb and Irka, locked in a tender embrace, left together, flying off to a private tree with a perfect roosting spot. Once settled, they couldn't resist cuddling and kissing, softly cooing and warbling beautiful songs together in hushed tones.

They spent several hours sharing their experiences and just being together quietly. Irka was fascinated by Caleb's black pin flight feathers at the tip of his wings, which, though not fully grown, already displayed a striking deep black color. They tenderly stroked and groomed each other's battered plumage and wounds, applying liberal amounts of healing sappa and Irka's own mix of herbs and tinctures. Irka showed far less concern about his appearance and his odd feather color than Caleb had feared. Her primary concern was that he was now whole and unharmed, healing perfectly, and she felt the same relief for herself.

Sometime later, Caleb took a short walk with his father and Goffry while the females caught up, engaging in a woman's preening and cleaning. This gave the men an opportunity to spend a moment together and release their buzzies, Trada, Pica, and all the others who had connected so deeply with Caleb and helped turn the tide in the heat of battle. Now, they were set free. Although they were always free to go, sometimes they needed encouragement to take time for themselves. There was nothing the buzzies liked more than cavorting and exploring aimlessly, flitting from one flower to another. A slow trip back home through the heart of the Grand Valley would give them all time to heal and renew.

Since the battle, all buzzies regarded Caleb as their cherished grand leader. Like his mother Marta, who had her familiars, the swifts, buzzies were now "officially" Caleb's familiars. Although he always had a great connection with them in the past, his vastly elevated communing skills now made him one of the few great Communers capable of attracting such devotion from another species.

"*Go frolic, my friends. Thank you for your sacrifice and love,*" he imparted to them, sending out a strong mental wave of love and positive life force. He began affectionately rubbing and stroking the heads of all the buzzies who swarmed around him, with Trada and Pica first, of course. Their antennae gently touched him in a display of eternal camaraderie, Caleb laughing as their delicate touches tickled him.

Jonus and Goff had to step back, chuckling and tweeting in wonder as the entire swarm, large and small, crowded around Caleb. The buzzies' strong pheromones filled the air with a scent like warm honey on a hot day. They danced and wiggled around him on the ground and in the air, nearly suffocating him with their numbers. They created a beautiful buzzing harmony in perfect rhythm, signifying their devotion to their leader. After some time, they flew off, not before making beautiful aerobatic murmuration dances as they separated into different groups, with hive mates leaving together in various directions toward their homes.

A bit later, Irka also bid farewell to the red jiants, sending a grateful message of appreciation along with some gifts of rare sappa and fine milkcheeses for Queen Atoffalita. Her little red allies retreated back to their colony alongside Artula, Mikia, Prudentia, and most of the now submissive and friendly grays, ready to create a jiant mother colony together. They would forever after be free, working together with other Kondorian races only whenever they wished and only as equals.

A young, small red jiant called Dexby the Curious had befriended Irka and stayed at her side together with little Trudy, Irka's prime buzzy, who had recovered and joined her as well. A happy trio, now always inseparable.

That evening, as promised, the impressive cruiser of Marcus Trumanian the Ninth descended, an air of expectancy hanging over the awaiting crowd of early gatherers. The Highland Plateau, alive with the vibrant sounds of wild birds and a multitude of chirping and humming insects, was bathed in the golden-violet hues of the setting sun. The flora and fauna painted the scene with a rich tapestry of colors, and the air was thick with the earthy aroma of endless fields of grass and the distinct scent of late summer blooming flowers.

Marcus sent a message requesting an audience within the hour, giving the Avians and friendly Othorians time to gather after their transformative experiences in the healing pods. Endless, warm, trickling showers, as well as food and sweet-smelling fresh nectar, had also been provided by the shuttles, adding to the sense of surreal benevolence that enveloped them.

On the hour, Marcus emerged from his cruiser on his floating disc, with Leurin at his side, commanding the attention of everyone assembled. "I hope you are all feeling as well as can be," he began, his voice echoing with a mixture of hope and regret. "Although we can heal your bodies, unfortunately, we cannot heal the wounds of the mind and heart." He paused, looking sincerely saddened. Taking in a long, slow breath, he continued, "Now it is time to tell our story. To start with, as you can clearly observe, we are not native to Kondor; we come from far away."

Marcus proceeded to explain his identity and mission, describing himself truthfully as a benevolent alien overseer in dire need of assistance against a formidable enemy known as the Takers. The crowd, absorbing this revelation, murmured among themselves in hushed tones, clearly feeling overwhelmed by the enormity of what they were hearing.

Caleb, positioned out front near Marcus and encircled by his family, felt a strong urge to assert himself. His voice, imbued with unwavering conviction, sliced through the ambient whispers and background bird noise. "Your words resonate with truth, Sir Marcus!" he declared emphatically, walking slowly toward them, with Irka and his family following. "The miracles wrought by your advanced technologies have mended our injured, earning not only our collective gratitude but also my individual trust. I stand prepared to offer my assistance, motivated not only by your request but also by a profound sense of duty, I am compelled to help. We must repel these Takers at any cost."

Marcus's face lit up with gratitude as the crowd erupted in cheers of support, the anxiety lifting from his shoulders. "Thank you, Caleb, my exceptional friend, and thank you all," he replied warmly, stepping off his floating disc, which now rested on the ground. The crowd parted in awe and respect.

"We concur with our son and we are with you as well, Marcus," Jonus said, stepping forward. He put his arm around Caleb. Marta, Irka, and Goff joined in, forming a supportive huddle and tweeting their approval.

"Your innate abilities in spatial coordination through a life of flying, plus most particularly your strong PSY energy, are precisely what we need. You Avians possess this rare gift, known as communing, and those with the strongest abilities are ideal for piloting and maneuvering our battleships," Leurin added, placing his hand on Marcus's shoulder.

Approaching Caleb with a broad smile, Marcus felt much more confident. "We understand how difficult it is to leave your loved ones and fight another war so soon after this confrontation with Bertran. However, to do nothing means that we and all this around us would perish. Despite our highly advanced technology, we Creators need your help—your mental skills, fighting spirit, and battle experience, which we lack."

Finally reaching Caleb, Marcus placed a reassuring hand on his shoulder. "Would you accept the role of Flight Commander of the Kondorian Fleet? We know already that your PSY abilities are the highest we have ever observed. With your talents, you could lead our battleships to protect not only this planet but this entire quadrant of space from our enemy."

After a brief pause and an affirming glance at Irka and his family, who beamed with pride, Caleb accepted resolutely. "As long as I am at the forefront of the battle, I accept!"

"And I must be there with my love. Whatever comes to pass, we face it together!" Irka pushed forward and grabbed Caleb by his waist.

Marcus's face brightened with happiness; the relief was openly evident. "Then it is settled," he declared. "You, Commander Caleb, will pilot my cruiser, equipped with the most advanced technology we possess, including self-replicating nanobot technology within the weapons. The defense shields on this cruiser and all the battleships shall be the best that we can provide, designed to withstand and absorb significant force. Your safety is paramount to our mission."

Turning to address the gathered crowd, Caleb's voice boomed with newfound vigor and conviction. "Are we IN?" he shouted, sweeping his gaze over the rapt assembly. He was feeling his old self again, full of nervous enthusiasm, concerned for his loved ones and fellow Avians well-being but eager to help. The response was immediate and thunderous, with cries, chirps, and warbles of "YES!" and "We are IN!" echoing across the field. Numerous lesser birds that had begun roosting in the surrounding trees in the advancing night took to the air, startled by the noise. Even the nighttime eternal beetle chirping ceased for a moment.

As the excitement ebbed slightly, Caleb raised his voice again. "Then let's gather all leaders and Communers around the cruiser. We need to strategize."

Leurin, taking control of the meeting, addressed the crowd. "We invite those with the strongest communing abilities to step forward. We need to administer a test to potential pilots and volunteers. Of course, we have other roles to fill as well, so please, come forward if you are willing."

The response was enthusiastic, with a wave of most of the crowd rising to their feet and moving toward Leurin and the shuttles. With a hint of amusement in his voice, Leurin clarified, "For now, perhaps we should start with Communers first. Please proceed to one of the shuttles, where holographic assistants will guide you." His gentle yet commanding tone guided the crowd efficiently, ensuring everyone knew exactly where to go and what to do.

28:
CALEB MEETS ZOREN

◦◇◦◇◦◇◦

The selection process conducted by Leurin and Marcus proved fruitful, of course confirming Caleb with an off-the-charts high PSY rating and identifying Marta, Jonus, and a host of other skilled Communers as ideal candidates for the crucial roles of pilots, copilots and ground crew in the burgeoning Kondorian Fleet composed of the twelve new battleships plus Caleb's cruiser.

Despite Caleb's direct tutelage under Leurin, he also immersed himself in all the comprehensive training programs available, absorbing the wealth of knowledge from both holographic instructors and direct mind links with an intense focus and determination.

The day Caleb first met Zoren, the EIB that controlled and "was" his cruiser, marked a transformative moment in his education. Seated in the command chair tailored specifically for him, he was surrounded by the finest technology, viscoelastic fluid cushions that conformed to his every movement, an energy-dampening personal defense shield, and its own self-sustaining power source.

Beside him, Leurin's avatar, serving as his first officer, was a beacon of assistance. His role spanned from navigation to gunnery, coordinating attacks and strategies with remarkable precision. Leurin's embodiment could concentrate his entire mental matrix on the task at hand, analyzing millions of strategies simultaneously and providing instantaneous feedback, a tactical edge that Caleb greatly appreciated.

And then there was Zoren. The connection Caleb forged with the cruiser from their very first interaction was nothing short of miraculous. As he closed his eyes in the command chair, his consciousness expanded, seamlessly intertwining with the ship's being.

"*Welcome, Caleb. I am Zoren,*" the ship communicated directly into his mind, its voice a soothing whisper. Encouraged by her presence, Caleb let his mind wander through the cruiser's systems, exploring every biomechanical nerve fiber and nanoparticle. Zoren, observing his exploration, remarked, "*Impressive Caleb, my new friend and commander. We have achieved beautifully seamless integration in such a short time. I am intrigued by your superb abilities. Very interesting, this will go well.*"

Leurin, seated beside Caleb, advised caution. "Take it slowly, Caleb. Normally, it takes several attempts to master control over a spaceship, and we are in a really complex cruiser at that. It was not so long ago you had no idea such things existed so take time to adjust."

But Caleb was sitting upright, his head lifted and jaw firmly set. "I assure you that I am ready now," he declared, releasing a blast from the main engine, shifting the ship subtly forward. "I have complete control. And I have you two to keep things in check. Shall we take it for a spin? I haven't flown in so long. To be free to soar through space as well as above Kondor itself is very enticing and beyond thrilling."

"Leurin, as you can see, his control is superb," Zoren chimed in, almost playfully.

"Seems I'm outvoted," Leurin conceded just as the engines roared to life. The cruiser lifted effortlessly and almost silently from the plateau, rising to an altitude of thirty thousand feet. Caleb steered the ship south over the valley, awestruck by the breathtaking landscape of Kondor that unfolded below him.

Enthralled by the perfect integration with Zoren, Caleb felt every sensor, every scanner, and even the ship's defensive and gravitational fields as extensions of himself. He became the cruiser. Every wire, every biological nerve-like connection, every system was now part of him. The powerful Creator engines harnessed the forces of gravity as well as incorporating plasma drives along with a primary ion propulsion system. Potent and responsive, together they allowed for rapid changes in direction while providing a safe gravitational protective bubble for the pilot and crew.

"Hold on, I've got this," Caleb said with calm assurance, smoothly accelerating the cruiser. He navigated the Grand Valley with a slight detour swerve near PuritaWhite Mother Tree to have a quick aerial glance. His heart ached seeing his home from above, he had not been back for a long time. As he gulped back his upwelling of emotions, he soared out over the Ocean with flawless precision.

"I want to see all of Kondor from above, then we'll head back," he announced, excitement returning quickly to his voice. As the cruiser responded to his will, Caleb found himself absorbing knowledge directly from Zoren about orbits, gravity, and energy fields at an astonishing rate.

Leurin, marveling at Caleb's rapid assimilation of new information, cautioned him again, "Take it easy, Caleb. Absorbing knowledge so quickly can have its costs." However, as Caleb performed a complicated set of barrel rolls and loops, followed by a full 360-degree maneuver, Leurin exclaimed in an uncharacteristically astonished tone, "This is truly remarkable, the ship's response time is actually slightly in the negative! Zoren seems to predict and anticipate your needs even before you express or think about them. Fascinating! This is what we had hoped for, predictive integration. I would venture that our odds of victory have just vastly increased."

Caleb, having brought the cruiser to a geostationary orbit above Kondor, found himself entranced by the planet's vivid colors. He felt a profound connection with the entirety of Mother Kondor's energy, a force so vast it threatened to overwhelm him. Yet, with deep, steadying breaths, he found equilibrium, surfing the cosmic waves of energy, aligning his spirit with the planet's rhythm.

His return to the Highland Plateau was executed with the expertise of a seasoned pilot, the cruiser touching down so smoothly it was as if it were an extension of his own body. After saying his farewells to Zoren and Leurin, both lost in a deep excited examination of a review of the flight data recorders, he flew back to his flota, where Irka awaited him. Their temporary home in Caleb's flota, anchored near the meeting spot, offered a comforting sense of normalcy amid the chaos. There, they spent hours intertwined, sharing stories of their journeys and what they were learning, weaving plans for the impending conflict with the Takers, and rediscovering the intimate bond that had always united them.

Irka, although not on the list for a pilot or first officer role, had been entrusted with overseeing the ground crew operating from Marcus's starship. She had marveled at seeing the Three Golden Obelisks from inside, never before had she even remotely imagined that they were an alien spaceship. Her days were filled with coordinating the crew's efforts, ensuring that the fleet's needs were promptly met, and organizing training sessions. With Leurin's guidance, she adeptly managed these crucial tasks, a testament to her organizational prowess and commitment to the cause.

Upon Caleb's return that evening, Irka's welcoming embrace melted away any lingering concerns. "I've prepared a supper for us," she said, her voice tinged with pride and anticipation. "We've received a new shipment of White Flock milkcheese and nectar, along with many other gifts. The support from home is overwhelming, and it really lifts my spirits."

As they embraced, Irka's vulnerability surfaced. "Caleb, do you think we can truly defeat the Takers? I fear for us, for what we might lose. The thought of being without you again is unbearable. I was hoping to be on the front line with you but now I feel distant."

Caleb, feeling her tremble, held her closer. "Don't worry, my dear Irka. We'll return to our family one day. I can't say how, but I feel it deep within, we will overcome this challenge. Just rest now. Let your worries fade."

Gently, he began to sing a lullaby, his voice weaving a hypnotic tapestry of warbles and twitters, each note cradling Irka deeper into a serene slumber. As her breathing steadied and she drifted off, Caleb continued to sing softly, the melody a soothing balm to his weary soul. Eventually, lulled by the rhythm of his own song, he too succumbed to sleep, their dreams intertwined with hope and determination for the battles that lay ahead.

KONDORIAN FLEET
FIRST FLIGHT

29:
The Fleet Assembles

———◇◇◇———

Over the ensuing weeks, the trainee pilots of the Kondorian Fleet underwent intense mental linking exercises, a crucial process to ensure their compatibility with their designated ships. The rigorous training sessions confirmed the exceptional talents of key figures like Marta, Jonus, and Goffry, each earning the honor of piloting their own battleship. General Eldred, a distinguished member of Caleb's flock, was chosen as Marta's copilot. This meticulous selection process ultimately formed an elite squadron of twenty-four top Communers, two for each battleship, with an additional two serving as reserve pilots.

On the eve of their maiden voyage, a festive air engulfed the entire crew of the Kondorian Fleet, including the ground personnel, as they congregated for a celebratory gathering at the top observation floor of the central golden obelisk. The room, with soaring ceilings and a full 360-degree panoramic view overlooking the Grand Valley and northern mountains, was awe-inspiring. Seamless transparent metal panels allowed for unobstructed vistas, while fresh air from outside—tinged with the crisp scents of snow, rock, and mountain plants—was pumped in, enhancing the atmosphere. Robotic servers dispensed food and drinks to the guests, adding to the surreal yet benevolent ambiance that enveloped them. The mood was celebratory and jovial but underscored with some apprehension for what was to come.

Irka and Caleb, ever the inseparable pair, mingled among the crew, both now fully recuperated from their trials. Caleb's wings, with their distinctive flight feathers at the ends, were fully mature and unfurled—a deep, true obsidian black with a metallic luster that shifted hues depending on the light. They had become a symbol of his heroism and resilience, a mystery now accepted as part of his identity. He was famous all over Kondor, and young fledgling Avians even rubbed crake dust into their plumage to emulate Caleb's black flight feathers.

Marta, with a mix of maternal pride and official decorum, approached her son, with Irka hanging on to his arm. "Commander Caleb," she greeted with a respectful salute, her eyes warm with a proud maternal smile. "Serving beside you, my son, is my honor. We shall prevail, I truly sense that. All of us together." Her eyes briefly met Irka's.

"I'll leave you two to chat for a while." Irka unhooked herself from Caleb, passing his arm to her mother-in-law, allowing her to lead Caleb slightly away from the crowd.

They strolled over to the transparent exterior wall, taking in the breathtaking view. Caleb felt a complex swirl of emotions, triumph and relief mingled with a deep-seated anxiety for the challenges ahead. The weight of his new responsibilities as Flight Commander bore heavily upon his shoulders, yet the unwavering support of his family and Irka provided a comforting anchor.

Marta leaned her head against her son's shoulder and let out a long sigh. "Caleb, about your black feathers," she began hesitantly, "there's something I need to share. In my past, I had encounters with two Great Black Trees in a hidden gorge in the region of the Western Aerie. The black sappa in the metal bottle that I passed on to you comes from that source." She stopped and moved in front of Caleb, clasping his face in her hands. "I believe my time spent there may have inadvertently passed on some unique energies to you, potentially influencing not just your feather color but your whole direction in life. I feel guilty; I should have been more careful."

Caleb, covering her small hands on his cheeks with his large ones, smiled and looked deep into Marta's eyes. "You've done nothing wrong. The only thing you're guilty of is being a great mother! We've touched on your history with the Blacks briefly, but we never seem to find the time to delve into the details. I sense there's much more to reveal." He glanced around and noticed others approaching. "But perhaps it's still not yet the right moment. Briefly though, I did feel and see something when we were reunited during our battle with Bertran—we shared a deep and spontaneous communion. I even shared some of your memories." While he spoke, he retrieved the vial of black sappa still careful ensconced in his emergency pack, turning it over and over in his hands. "I feel that the time still isn't right … not just yet. We will talk more another time. Soon." Tucking the little bottle back into its hiding spot, he leaned forward and kissed Marta on the forehead, giving her a giant hug.

Their conversation was interrupted by the arrival of Goffry and Maxima, a duo whose friendship had deepened over time and who were now pilot and copilot in their own battleship. Goffry, who had initially struggled with the piloting assessments, had been personally coached by Caleb, eventually achieving a high PSY score that secured him a pilot position.

"Here's to the beginning of yet another adventure!" Goffry exclaimed, bringing a couple of extra goblets filled with potent red sappa wine, its pungent, deep citrusy bouquet heralding his arrival. "After all we've endured, this mission should be a breeze!" His laughter was infectious, lightening the mood, echoing slightly in the huge observation room.

Maxima chuckled and chirped out a little well-known Avian bird-song sung at festive events. "I am still amazed that we have adapted to such a different life and so quickly. Cheers to all of us. The occasional brain fog is to be expected!" she added with a laugh with a twitter, taking a big swig of wine.

The group expanded with the addition of Irka, Leurin, General Eldred, and Jonus. Even Portia, now recognized as the ruler of the Othorians, was there with some close friends. Despite her leadership role, she insisted on being part of the confrontation with the Takers. When asked to step back for her safety as the head of the Othorian people, her reply was sharp and instantaneous. "There aren't enough of you to stop me from being there for this pivotal moment in Kondorian history."

Caleb wrapped his arms around his dear ones, and they held a brief silent huddle together. Then, stepping back and facing the rest of the attendees, Caleb proposed a toast, raising his glass of wine high. "I am bursting with pride and gratitude to have so many brilliant and skilled friends around me. To a swift victory against those marauding Takers!" The sentiment was met with enthusiastic cheers and affirmations, the group's spirits buoyed by the evening's fun, allowing them to forget about the future for a moment and simply enjoy some time to socialize and unwind. The gathering gradually settled into gentle, casual conversations before the crew dispersed, each contemplating the significant journey that lay ahead and wanting to rest well before the next day's exercise.

The next day, the crews of the Kondorian Fleet, thoroughly trained and primed for their first space foray, embarked on their inaugural mission with a blend of excitement and apprehension. Caleb's flagship cruiser, now fully refurbished, indeed a marvel of engineering and spirit, took the lead, lifting off into the early morning sky then being quickly joined and surrounded by the rest of the fleet of battleships. Each vessel, meticulously positioned, formed two protective octahedrons, one within the other, then the cruiser at the center, with Marta's battleship at the forefront and Goffry and Jonus's ships flanking Caleb's vessel on either side.

Caleb's voice, resonant and confident, broke through the squad's comm system: "All ships, prepare for combat drills. We're heading to the moon base for a simulated practice battle."

Leurin, ever the strategist, chimed in with his deep, measured tones, "Agreed, Commander. Coordinated defense is crucial. As we approach, let's synchronize our shields and focus on absorbing the incoming fire. Remember, we move as one entity, with Caleb at our helm."

The fleet advanced, slicing through the void of space toward their lunar training ground. Marcus, observing from a distance, had arranged a series of simulated attacks for the fleet to hone their defenses. As they neared the moon, the fleet's defensive prowess was put to the ultimate test. A myriad of protective energy fields, shimmering and pulsating, enveloped each ship and, working in harmony, created an impregnable multilayered shield around the cruiser and the entire squad.

Caleb, at the center, felt the weight of responsibility and the thrill of command. "All ships, brace for action. Let's see what we're capable of!" he declared, his voice carrying a mix of determination and excitement.

The fleet maneuvered gracefully, responding to the barrage of simulated attacks with precision. The multifaceted energy field surrounding the squad of battleship absorbed and deflected each strike easily with not so much as a bump. Inside his cruiser, Caleb could feel the fleet's collective energy coursing through him, each ship adding its strength to the barrier. In a daring demonstration of their prowess and testing their deflectors further, the fleet ventured close to the sun, penetrating four of its super-heated atmospheric layers before strategically retreating.

The practice session ended with the fleet emerging unscathed, their shields having repelled every simulated attack flawlessly, and every single practice target had been obliterated. Cheers and jubilant cries and chirps echoed across the communications network, and Caleb, feeling a surge of satisfaction, pride and confidence, addressed all the crew, "Well done, everyone! Our unity is our strength. This is just the beginning. Together, we will face whatever challenges come our way."

The troop's spirits were high as they returned from their successful exercise, their bond solidified, and their resolve steeled for the battles ahead. The maiden voyage of the Kondorian Fleet, under Caleb's leadership, had proven their readiness!

The most challenging feat, however, was mastering inter-dimensional travel, known as InterDim, a form of space navigation that for most pilots remained elusive to achieve. Only a select few succeeded in creating the necessary portals between dimensions for this mode of travel, and most of those who could, achieved inconsistent results.

Coming as no surprise to everyone except perhaps himself, Caleb proved to possess an innate understanding and deep connection with the fabric of space itself. Together with Zoren he effortlessly opened these elusive inter-dimensional portals. He had continued to grow what was now an intensely profound bond with Zoren. This link that they shared transcended mere mechanical interaction and ventured into the realm of deep, intuitive understanding.

Zoren, an EIB of slightly lower complexity than Leurin, was fully autonomous, equipped with biological neural clusters and synthetic nerve strands similar to a super-charged organic brain. This ultimate Creator design, courtesy of Marcus and Leurin's efforts, allowed for seamless and instantaneous communication with the living minds of pilots, eliminating almost all lag in response time. To everyone's amazement, Caleb and Zoren's predictive integration ability began to improve, now measured by Leurin at nearly a full one-hundredth of a second. It might not seem like much, but this advancement meant that Zoren could anticipate and execute Caleb's commands even before Caleb consciously thought of them.

The stakes of their mission intensified. The Takers were rapidly approaching. The Kondorian Fleet, though vigilant, had maintained a safe distance.

So far, no probes sent out had succeeded in closely surveying the Takers; scouting ships that ventured too near never returned, and those that did return had scant and inconclusive information. Anything that came into close range of the Takers' scans and weapons was hunted down and obliterated with ruthless efficiency.

Caleb convened a general strategy meeting with his crew, Marcus, and all the other air and ground crew at the Three Golden Obelisks, now the center of operations. It had become fondly known as Marcus's House or just the House for short. The entire structure was unrestricted for all, enormous hangar doors opened into a central foyer at its base with large and small gravity discs transporting anyone wherever they wanted to go. At the very top was the Commander's Lounge and Marcus's private area; just below was an expansive command strategy room. It was here that the meeting was being held. The mood was subdued and quiet with large holographic star charts, another area with screens of various engineering renderings of machinery and spaceships. In the center of the room was a circle of soft seats around a massive polished metal-topped conference table.

Walking in hand in hand with Irka, with Goffry and his parents in close proximity, Caleb entered the impressive room. He was never shy to show his love for her, perhaps it was not professional but they ignored that, they would spend every moment they could together. Waiting until more guests had arrived and got settled, Caleb stood up at his place at one end of the table. "We've got a challenge ahead," he addressed the assembly. "These greedy and evil interlopers, the Takers, don't leave much opportunity for close observation. We need to be smart and use our shields to our advantage. I am told that the multi-layered shields of the fleet can make us indetectable to their scans, we will be effectively invisible. This gives us a chance to scout them out properly. I think it is worth the risk. We need more intel to fight them as efficiently as possible before we engage them full-on."

Leurin, with his impressive luminescent silver avatar standing next to Caleb, nodded in agreement. "This really could give us an opportunity to gather the intelligence we need. If we can get a better close-up observation of their technology, it would help us tweak our ship systems tremendously. Yes, our new shields should render us invisible to their scans. These new multilayered and multifaceted force shields actually interact with our plasma engines to…"

General Eldred stepping forward, was quick to interrupt. "Enough, my braniac friend, we don't need a dissertation; I swear on Mother Kondor you could discuss the composition of salt for several hours." He laughed clapping Leurin on his shoulder. "I agree with an observation mission, but couldn't we also test their offensive reaction with a couple of shots, perhaps from an unmanned drone that could draw their attention away from us? It might be wise to understand their defensive and offensive capabilities as well."

Marta weighed in thoughtfully, "I'd advocate for caution. We should only confront them if we're noticed and attacked. Otherwise, our primary and only goal should be reconnaissance. More information will strengthen our position and increase our chances of victory."

"Those are wise words, Marta, I concur," Leurin added, supporting her suggestion.

Caleb, considering the input from his crew, made the call. "I think we're aligned here. Let's undertake a close observation and react as necessary. Thank you, everyone, for your insights. Let's prepare for departure. Once everyone is ready, we'll commence the mission. Let's go get some answers, team."

Cheers and affirmations echoed through the cruiser, with nods of agreement and vocal "yays" resonating as the crew dispersed to their respective ships, united in their purpose.

30:
THE TAKERS

———◇◇◇———

The mission was daring yet seemingly simple: embed themselves within a cosmic debris field to observe the Takers' passage. The fleet's twelve ships plus the cruiser, each manned by a skilled crew, understood the gravity of their task. They positioned themselves inside a massive fragment field, parts of an exploded star, engines off, fully cloaked in stealth mode with all shields activated.

As the Kondorian Fleet lay in wait, hidden in the shadows of the space debris, the enormity of their task became starkly evident. The Takers' 'ship', a leviathan in the vastness of space, soon emerged into view, its gargantuan form dwarfing any spacecraft the Kondorian pilots had ever known or imagined. The colossal entity, a conglomeration of technology and ominous power, had to throttle back its speed to navigate the dense debris field that lay in its path.

To the astonishment of the Avians, they discovered that the Takers' ship was not just a single vessel but an artificial shell formed from a vast array of smaller ships and components. Its surface resembled a living sea, a shifting tapestry of interconnected machinery and equipment, including containers, glass-like protrusions, spheres, and spacecraft of varying sizes. Together, they spanned over ten thousand miles in diameter, making the massive Taker orb rival the size of Kondor herself, effectively turning the ship into a planet.

The crew on the fleet, watching from their vantage point, felt a mixture of apprehension and awe ripple through their ranks. This close observation revealed the Takers' ship to be more than just a formidable foe; it was a testament to a level of technological prowess that was both terrifying and fascinating. Caleb and all the other Kondorian pilots and crew, while dwarfed by this massive cluster, knew that the information they could gather here was vital for their survival and the defense of their world. As they watched the behemoth glide towards the debris field, they continued to gather as much intelligence as possible.

Leurin's voice broke the tense silence. "This is incredible. The insights we're gaining are invaluable. We'll recalibrate our defenses with this data. But let's not overstay our welcome."

Caleb, watching the Takers navigate the debris field, knew it was time to retreat but he wanted to try to communicate. He reached out with his mind, delicate mental probes striving to make some contact with their adversaries. Oddly enough Caleb felt nothing, just a void, it was as if there was no one there, which seemed unlikely considering the size of the Takers 'ship'. He concentrated further, beads of sweat forming on his brow through his intense concentration but all he could sense was a very far-off presence, not strong but unpleasant as it sent involuntary shivers up his back. "Alright, team, let's head back," he ordered as he activated thrusters carefully. "We've got what we need."

Their existence had been concealed, but their exit did not go unnoticed. A small piece of rubble struck the fleet's shield upon their slow movement, causing a tiny energy spike. The Takers reacted swiftly, immediately firing an energy beam from their cluster that struck the fleet's hiding spot. Fortunately, it hit the massive space rock they had been using as cover, vaporizing it entirely and revealing their position.

As the Kondorian Fleet hovered in the dust left behind by their destroyed screen, they braced for impact. The Takers' ship, a colossal amalgam of technology, had already unleashed a second volley of energy blasts, much stronger than the first and from multiple locations. The Kondorian shields, a marvel of engineering and psychic synchronization, shimmered as the dust from the debris impacted them, forming a glowing vibrant barrier around the entire fleet.

The powerful energy blasts from the Takers, radiating at various frequencies and vibrations, crashed against the fleet's protective shields. As hoped, the impacts were absorbed and repelled with remarkable efficiency, reflecting a focused cascade of energy back toward the Takers.

For a fleeting moment, the Takers' defenses wavered under this unexpected counterattack. The first redirected retaliatory energy beam struck their shields and passed straight through. Clearly damage was done, much flickering, explosions and disarray in the massive ship's outer layers were evident. However, they quickly recovered altering their defense shields, revealing an advanced adaptive technology. Further reflected blasts were not getting through.

In response to the counteroffensive, the Takers' planetoid underwent a startling transformation. Like a giant organism performing mitosis, a portion of the huge orb detached, the whole dividing and morphing into two distinct entities. These smaller orbs then rapidly fragmented again into a swarm of even smaller separate parts resembling a cloud of metallic locusts. These smaller globes of space objects, agile and menacing, began to advance toward the Kondorian Fleet, unleashing a relentless barrage.

Caleb was taken aback by the violent assault; he breathed in deeply to steady himself as he realized he had been holding his breath. The metal taste of blood filled his mouth as he had inadvertently clenched his teeth too hard. Relaxing himself back to a calm state he focused on his connection with Zoren and his cruiser. He felt the power and support all around him and his confidence came back in a solid wave.

The Takers' swarm attack was a spectacle of technological prowess and strategic precision. Rather than one target, there were thousands. The individual ships within the swarm fired continuously, their energy beams dancing through space, each pulsating with different frequencies and intensities. The Kondorian Fleet, though initially taken aback by this aggressive maneuver, had swiftly responded. All the Avian pilots, synchronized with Caleb and their ships, maneuvering in a fluid, coordinated dance.

Amid this chaotic battlefield, the Kondorian Fleet's true strength shone. Their shields, pulsating rapidly in response to the barrage, absorbed and redirected the energy, creating a dazzling display of defensive capability that turned offensive in response. The now smaller Taker ships, relentless in their assault, continued to advance, but the Kondorian Fleet matched their aggression with equal tenacity. Caleb did not order a retaliatory assault, he did not want to show their offensive capabilities, just continuing to bounce back what was thrown at them.

Realizing their goal had been accomplished and unprepared for a full-on battle as yet, Caleb had already preemptively decided to retreat to Kondor via InterDim; they could not be followed there. It was time to leave.

"Initiating InterDim portal now," Caleb announced calmly.

As they popped out of existence into that place between dimensions, silence greeted them for a few moments, until they effortlessly reappeared above Kondor.

"That was eye-opening," Caleb muttered, letting out a long breath and an expressive squawk. "We will need a solid plan to face them, but we sure have a lot of crucial intel from that little visit."

"That was crazy!" Goffry exclaimed, also exhaling deeply. "I just want to say a great job, everyone! Amazing piloting, Caleb, wow, that was intense."

Caleb, deep in thought, nodded. "This enemy is relentless. We need to be just as cunning and calculated in our approach. Clearly they can't follow us through dimensional travel, which gives us an edge. We WILL stop them, but we'll do it on our terms when we are fully ready."

"Congratulations to all! You have done what no one has done up to now. We now have a close-up view and scans of the Takers' capabilities. This is incredible!" Marcus's powerful voice boomed over the com system. "I feel elated, truly excited with new confidence that we can stop this invader once and for all. Thank you, thank, you … A million thanks to everyone."

Back on the familiar terrain of Kondor, the atmosphere among the fleet's crew was one of quiet determination and jubilance as they gathered to analyze the wealth of data collected from their encounter. In the calm war rooms, Leurin, Marcus, Caleb and pilots alike poured over every scrap of information, their eyes flickering across screens aglow with alien schematics and energy patterns. The mission had been perilous, but it yielded an invaluable trove of intelligence, offering insights into the Takers' formidable technology.

They rapidly developed modifications and refitted the fleet's equipment, drawing on fresh insights to enhance their capabilities significantly. This allowed them a crucial step forward in their battle readiness, considerably bolstering the strength and resolve as they prepared for an inevitable confrontation.

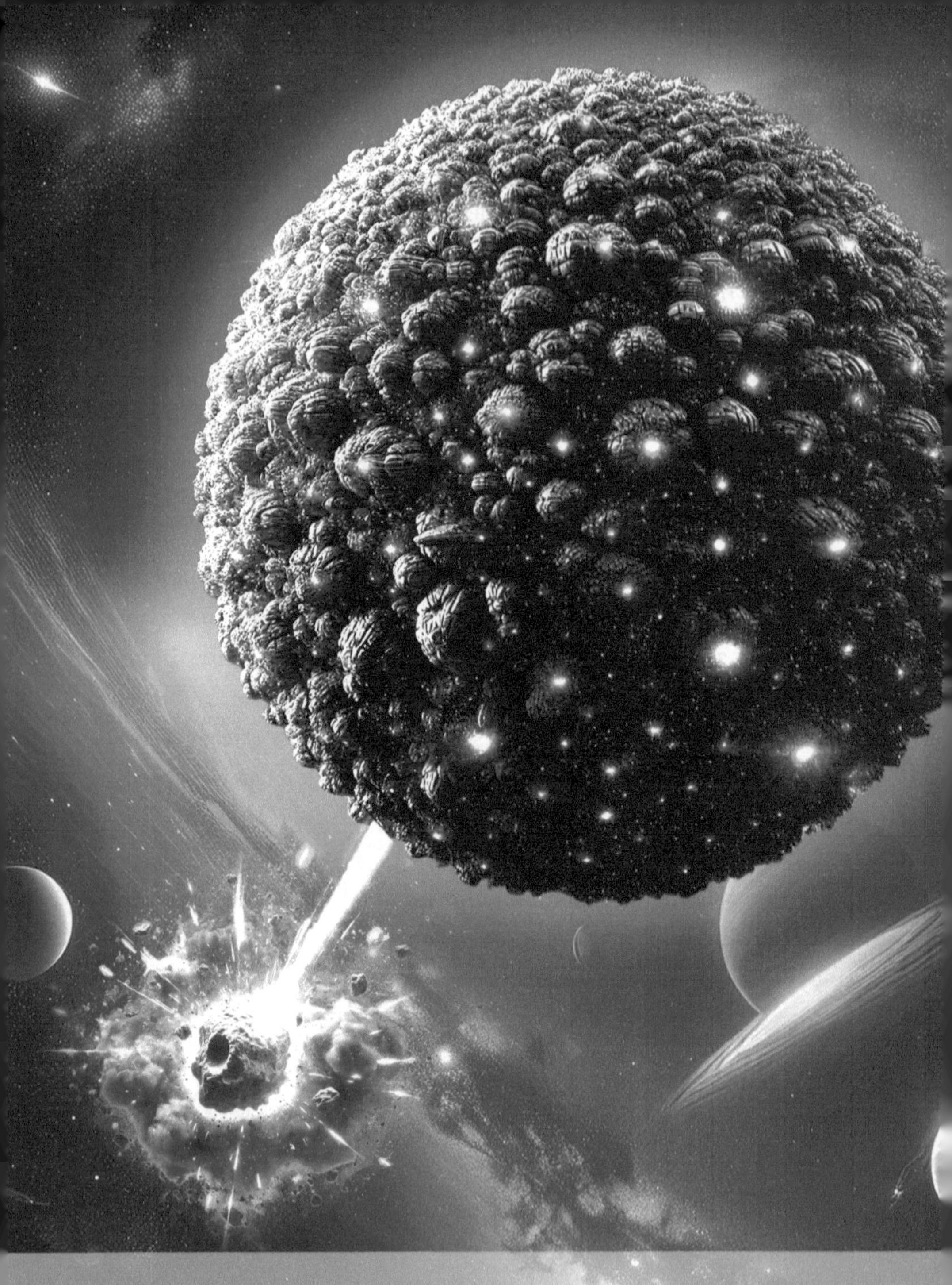

THE TAKERS

31:
CONFRONTATION

The Takers' Cluster, a formidable and relentless predator of the cosmos, set its sights on Kondor. This vibrant blue planet, orbiting the red sun Sol 274 in the Crown galaxy, teemed with an abundance of the life essence that the Takers craved. From the depths of its massive oceans, where colossal octopods and mammoth Cetacea roamed, to the diverse wildlife that adorned its lush landscapes, Kondor was a beacon of life energy. This made it a prime target.

In the bustling strategic command center on that planet, tension and anticipation hung in the air. Marcus, burdened with the gravity of the impending conflict, stood at the heart of operations, orchestrating the planet's defenses. Beside him, one of Leurin's avatars provided invaluable support while a dedicated team of Avian and Othorian ground crew worked tirelessly. Irka, despite her longing to be by Caleb's side, embraced her crucial role as the ground crew coordinator, skillfully managing the team and serving as Marcus's effective Kondorian deputy.

The decision was clear: engage the Takers before they could reach their solar system. This strategy offered a chance to thwart the enemy at a distance, with the possibility of regrouping around the planet if the initial encounter proved unsuccessful. "We won't let that happen," Marcus declared, his resolve evident.

The moment of truth arrived as the Takers came too close for comfort. Caleb, flanked by Leurin's most advanced avatar, took command of the central battle cruiser as usual. As he delved into a deeper communion with Zoren and the fleet, he began to sense the collective emotions of everyone around him—anxiety, fear, insecurity, but also pride, determination, and hope.

He took several long breaths to steady himself, eyeing all the instruments and holographic screens arrayed around him. Catching a whiff of stale metallic ship air, Caleb remarked, "Zoren, how about some fresh mountain aroma to brighten up the cruiser? Maybe with a bit of Irka's favorite white petaled cactus mixed in, please." Immediately, Zoren complied, wafting in the invigorating scent requested, mixed with a special blend of Red Flock nectar essences that provided an instant physical pick-me-up.

His fellow pilots—Marta and Jonus, Goffry, General Eldred, and others, each commanding their battleships—were seamlessly merging their consciousness with their vessels. Darien, General Botus, and Maxima were among the copilots, and Portia had joined the front-line ranks. Her highly superior skills as a gunner complemented pilot Maximillion from the GoldenRay Yellow Flock, at the helm of the rear battleship.

Arrayed in their now familiar double octahedral war formation, the twelve battleships and Caleb's cruiser formed a small but daunting line of defense. At the center of this formation was Caleb, his eyes steely with determination, ready to face the Takers head-on. He felt the energies of everyone and everything around him coalescing, throbbing with an ebb and flow. For a moment, he was dizzy, but then a tsunami wave of determination and support came pouring into him.

It was time to stop them. They must succeed.

Caleb addressed his fleet with a voice that resonated through every ship's communication system, as well as being played to all ground crew. He also used his communion abilities to reach out mentally. His words were filled with conviction, a rallying cry that stirred the hearts of all who heard him. Marta, hearing his voice, smiled with pride. He was using a modification of her battle stealth calls, his voice carried deep into people's core, his vocal modulations were stunningly superb, every note calculated. She was impressed; he was far above her vocal skill level.

His speech, interlaced with an intense deep warble, made everyone stop and listen. "Today, we stand at the brink, not just for Kondor, but for the good of the entire universe. Each one of us carries the hope and resolve of our people and many desperate sentient beings on other planets. Remember, we're not just fighting for survival; we're fighting for a future where peace and good prevail. Let's show these Takers the indomitable spirit of Kondor. Together, we are invincible. For Kondor, for the universe, let's make this count!"

His rallying cry echoed through the fleet, igniting a fire of courage and determination in the hearts of the crew. Indeed, all of Kondor, united by Caleb's inspiring leadership, braced for the battle of a lifetime.

As the Takers advanced, their expected initial response to the seemingly insignificant and insolent Kondorian Fleet parked in their way was to unleash their standard laser and energy-type beams. An opening salvo meant to vaporize any resistance in their path following the same pattern as in their first encounter.

Leurin's calm assurance permeated the neural link connecting the crew: "Nothing to fear. Our defense is secure against this. We'll just absorb this as before. They have been scanning us, but they haven't gotten past our shields."

Despite this encouragement, the crew braced for impact. The shields held firm and soaked up the energy beams with ease. The only effect was a luminescent glow around the fleet, pulsing against the black backdrop of space. As expected, the Takers, only briefly confounded by the resilience of their foes, escalated their attack. They deployed a new barrage of more diverse and higher energy frequencies.

Leurin's voice, unwavering and composed, reassured the crew. "Our shields are holding well. How about we show them some strength, Caleb?"

The fleet, now vibrating slightly under the increased onslaught, still held firm. "Agreed, Leurin. I'm on it," Caleb replied, engaging the fleet's new double reflector mode.

The newly updated shields, equipped with advanced hybrid gravitational technology, bent inward upon impact, collecting and transforming the Takers' energy blasts into more highly destructive focused spheres of intense power. These dazzling ripostes could now be directed at Caleb's will in any direction. They easily pierced the Takers' defense shields, inflicting considerable damage. Although the entire Takers' Cluster kept reforming seamlessly, the aggressive defensive strength of Caleb's tiny fleet clearly made a big impression. The Takers' immense globular structure came to a complete halt, regrouping and pausing the attack.

"Hold off, Caleb. Let's at least try to communicate," Leurin suggested, his voice a bastion of calm amid the chaos. "I have a broadband communication channel open, broadcasting in all known languages and frequencies, including PSY."

Caleb, recognizing the wisdom in Leurin's words, took the lead addressing the Takers. "This is Caleb of Kondor, Commander of the Kondorian Fleet that stands before you. We demand that you cease your aggression. You've caused unspeakable harm. We WILL defend our space."

Again, he integrated an adaptation of Marta's stealth birdcalls imparting an authoritative power into his voice. It exuded extreme confidence and superiority. The words more than a collection of mere syllables. Subtle birdlike undertones resonated in patterned waves that commanded attention and amplified the desire to comply, mentally boosted further with his communing abilities.

A foreboding silence hung in the void of space; the Takers offered no response.

"Not good," Caleb intoned, a sense of foreboding enveloping him. "They might respond aggressively …"

A blinding flash interrupted him, proving his instinct accurate. A coordinated set of numerous blasts from what must have been hundreds of parts of the Takers' Cluster struck the fleet with formidable force. It was quickly followed by another salvo and another. This compromised the shields by over 10 percent, and as the salvos continued, they weakened further.

One of Caleb's battleships had sustained minor damage, resulting in a significant jolt. The entire fleet had tilted over with the ferocity of the renewed attack. A few circuit fuses popped around Caleb in his commander's chair, startling him briefly by sending small sparks into the air of his compartment. The sulfurous smoky smell was quickly evacuated, but after a moment, it actually made him connect more with the battle.

The cluster had just used a different variety of weapons, including nuclear fission and plasma reaction-based technology, hybridizing old and newer tech, trying anything that could work. The barrage continued without pause, modifying and changing constantly. They were searching for a weak spot.

Leurin quickly assessed the situation. "They are quick to adapt, but I shall be quicker. I am recalibrating offense and defense, modulating the shield frequencies and harmonics to compensate for any other surprises." Countless mini-bots were scurrying around, fixing any issues almost instantly. The fleet righted itself, and the vibrations stopped.

Caleb, with the instincts of a seasoned commander, had already re-focused and recalibrated the deflector for the shields, merging Leurin's calculations with his own. The subsequent blasts from the Takers, like before, were absorbed and redirected, now with perfect aim and increased effect.

Despite this the Takers seemed undeterred by their losses and continued their attack. However, the massive cluster began the same transformation as in their first encounter. Their immense globular planet-sized form quickly divided into numerous smaller spherical clusters, morphing into a huge swarm that threatened to engulf the entire fleet. Each newly formed mini-orb fired upon the fleet with continuous rapid-fire energy weapons, modulating across every known frequency.

"Predictable," Caleb muttered to no one in particular. "Leurin, what's our status?" he inquired, his voice embodying both calm and command.

"We have sustained only minor damage so far, Commander," Leurin reported. "I've finished recalibrating our defenses and weapons, but we are still weakening, due to their fierce barrage. We need to go on the offense soon or move away."

"OK, everyone, let's start firing back, not just reflecting their assault. Open fire!" Caleb called out.

"That makes me happy! Thought you would never ask, boss," Goffry snorted with a chuckle and a satisfied chirp.

"Agreed!" Marta added, backed with a chorus of tweets coming from everyone.

The Kondorian Fleet fired back. All guns blazing. It was a sight to see. Needle-like lasers with extreme intensity cut through the Takers' orbs. Intensely damaging blasts from plasma-ion hybrid gravity cannons blasted holes through the advancing globes. The fleet had been outfitted with such advanced weaponry that they were making headway.

The Takers, however, were adapting fast. The seemingly endless clusters were moving further apart to limit collateral damage and make targeting more difficult. Their firing power was still immense, and the fleet's multi-layered shields were still weakening.

Caleb activated the InterDim drives, stealthily repositioning the fleet behind a nearby small asteroid to regroup and recharge the defense shields.

Unaware of their adversary's new location, the Takers commenced a 360-degree blind barrage, obliterating all nearby celestial debris in their immediate vicinity. The swarm of Taker clusters frothed and bubbled, forming and reforming like an angry hive of wild buzzies.

So much had happened so fast. Caleb and all the pilots, staring at the huge oppressive mass that opposed them, couldn't help but feel somewhat overwhelmed and deflated. It was an enormous outnumbering. Caleb felt jaws dropping and disguised discouragement throughout the crew as murmured gasps, nervous twitters, and heavy intakes of breath filled the comm channel.

In that moment, Caleb's hand brushed against the flask of black sappa. He always kept it with him, secured safely in a pouch on his waistband. Spontaneously, a surge of energy erupted through his entire body and mind, invigorating every fiber of his being.

"This gift from the Black Trees, distilled over vast periods of time, is imbued with a potent force. It will give you energy and a burst of spiritual enlightenment that will guide you when you need it most. Trust your instincts to know when the right time has come." Marta's wise words about the black sappa exploded in Caleb's mind.

"This IS the time," Caleb spoke out loud to no one but everyone. Without a second thought, he uncorked the flask and drank deeply, bracing for whatever would transpire.

CECE
HEAD BROODER
AT THE WESTERN AERIE

32:
CeCe

———◇◇◇———

CeCe stood in the shadowy recesses of a cave—geologically speaking, a relatively newly formed crevasse. Unlike other ancient tunnels of the Western Mountain Range, this one lacked the typical organic tapestry that adorned the walls of its older counterparts. Where ancient passageways would be cloaked in a thriving shroud of mosses, lichens, and fungi even in near pitch blackness, here, the stark, bare walls stood as a testament to their youth.

Ever the adventurer since her fledgling years in the Western Aerie, CeCe had a penchant for exploration. In her youth, her wanderlust and bravado often led her deep into uncharted territories, away from the watchful eyes of her Brooder guardians. It was during one of these solitary journeys many years ago that she discovered a secluded hidden chasm, home to the ancient Black Trees, Miranda and Fraxus. Her rare visits to this magical place and these wise entities were always kept a well-guarded secret; they became a sacred pilgrimage she undertook to grow spiritually. Each sip of their mystical black nectar and bite of black fruit deepened her connection to ancient wisdom and enlightenment.

Destined to be the Head Brooder, CeCe embraced her role with a profound sense of purpose. Her occasional secret visits and communions with the Black Trees granted her a rare depth of insight as a teacher. In shaping the young minds and destinies of generations of Avians, she nurtured intelligence, wisdom, peace, and spirituality in her people.

For the Black Trees, she became a bridge between their ancient wisdom and the present outside world. Miranda and Fraxus had long yearned to connect and commune with the other Great Trees and vibrant life of the Grand Valley, craving companionship after eons of solitude. They foresaw the need for a biological bridge—an unbroken organic link—that would enable direct communion with the entire valley. Thus, under their supervision and guidance, CeCe and her Head Brooder predecessors had long ago begun the challenging task of cultivating this elusive connection.

Their goal became more achievable about three thousand years ago when Mother Kondor provided a major earthquake which tore a new passage through the mountains, allowing the first tendrils of life to enter what had previously been an almost impenetrable barrier. All Head Brooders who presided over the aerie had a strong connection with the Black Trees; however, only a few had been privileged to actually meet them in person. Regardless, under the ancient trees' direction, they all willingly harnessed their communing abilities to cultivate this organic link whenever they could spare the time. Miranda and Fraxus also worked from their end, fostering growth from their hidden valley toward the Head Brooders' outgrowth. The work remained as yet unfinished. Creating this living conduit had been a long and arduous journey, demanding patience and unwavering focus over multiple generations.

The 'newly formed' cold, dark crevasse where CeCe worked, smelled of damp stone, must, and mold, but also carried a light mossy, earthy aroma of new growth. The only faint bio-illumination came from the sparse vegetation on either side of her. She stood upright on a ledge, arms and wings flung far out to either side, hugging the damp rock wall. Her face was pressed against the cold stone, furrowed with the intensity of her great effort. One hand, stretched to one side, tenderly caressed delicate pale lichens and algae, while the other hand caressed the mushroom mycelium growth on her other side. Her eyes were closed as she delved deep into communion with these humble life forms.

Completely exhausted, her face and muscles were gaunt and pale. She had spent every moment in this cave since her meeting with Marta many days prior, knowing she had to achieve this goal and complete this vital connection. Her arms shook, she was so tired. Sometimes she just wanted to stop. Sleep, just for a second. But no. She had to go on. She was so close now.

Shaking her head she broke into full birdsong, willing herself into a deeper communion, her eyes tearing with emotion and the physical strain. It was a flawless, enchanting tune, both hypnotic and powerful. Her melodies reverberated through the dark cavern, growing in strength as she synced her voice with her own echoes. The combined resonance intensified until it seemed like there was a whole chorus singing at full volume, the thunderous sound penetrating the stone and plants around her.

The energy from the Grand Valley coursed through one of her hands while the potent life force of the Blacks surged through the other. CeCe became the physical and spiritual bridge connecting these two disparate worlds. Channeling her entire being into the task, she sensed the minuscule rootlets and fungal growths gradually nearing each other, propelled by the strength of her will and the confluence of energies flowing through her.

In a climactic moment, she released a mighty final musical note, unleashing a surge of energy. Instantly, robust roots and mycelium burst forth on either side of her. An extremely rapid expansion of growth ensued with snapping and rustling. A greenish-blue flash of living energy lit up the cave as both sides merged together. This union quickly expanded, forming a thick hybrid rootlike fungal conduit, alive and resonating, luminously pulsating back and forth.

Thrown back by the sheer force of this achievement, CeCe had collapsed, exhausted yet triumphant. Her heart swelled with joy, tears streaming down her face as she realized the magnitude of what had been finally accomplished. This new biological and spiritual link was not just a physical one; it was a union of past and present. Now there was a connection between the ancient wise Black Trees and all the Great Trees on Kondor. Communication was already flowing back and forth, the link strengthening and growing.

CeCe continued her birdsong, now much quieter but with a light, jubilant, joyful tone. With this historic connection now in place, she knew that Caleb and his allies would gain an invaluable advantage in their fight against the evil energies threatening Kondor.

33:
FINAL BATTLE

———◇◇◇◇———

The dark liquid flowed smoothly down Caleb's throat, its immediate effects beyond remarkable.

He felt an extraordinary influx of power, which frightened him at first. Time itself seemed to stretch and contract around him. Voices on the comm and background noises slowed, distorted, and then became inaudible as the speed of sound waves dropped into the infrasound range. Even the normal precisely controlled aromas of the cruiser air seemed weakened and dulled.

However, in a flash of intuitiveness, his fear receded. He knew that he was in control. Bending his subjective experience of time seemed to be a startling newfound ability. Taking in a long, slow breath, Caleb centered and calmed himself, and the world around him slowed to an almost imperceptible crawl, barely a whisper of its former pace.

Deep within, a prodigious surge of his communing ability awakened, catapulting his consciousness to an unprecedented level. He completely merged with Zoren; they were as one. Then he "became" the entire Kondorian Fleet; even slowed to a glacial pace, he experienced all their physical beings, every sense, thought, and emotion of the crew and their vessels, not merely as separate entities but as a unified collective. Caleb could even "feel" the machinery and equipment, following the electron streams and optical laser beams with his mind, sensing its "well-being" almost as if it were living.

Then, like an elastic band snapping back into place, his focus turned inward, connecting to the core of his soul. He felt his very essence intrinsically tied to Kondor and the Grand Valley. Despite the vast distance separating him from his home, he somehow shared a quantum entangled link that transcended the confines of space, enveloping him and his planet in a cosmic embrace. He could feel all the Great Trees, all his fellow flock Communers, and all Avians and Kondorians, drawing immense strength from their collective presence.

A warm, ancient voice, imbued with wisdom and trust, began to communicate with him. "*Hello, Caleb. I am Miranda Black Tree, and here with me is Fraxus, my partner. For millennia, we have awaited this exact moment, knowing you would need our aid. The energies from the black sappa elixir will strengthen you in a profound way. You must be aware by now that you are an integral cog in destiny's plan for the future of Kondor and of the entire Universe. Good has somehow chosen you as its protagonist.*"

Caleb's awe was palpable. "*Miranda… Fraxus,*" he murmured, his voice trembling with respect. "*I feel your presence, your strength. This connection—it's incredible. I can sense everything, everyone. It's overwhelming but … grounding.*"

"*Young Caleb, know that you are where you should be. You are strong. You have already shown that you can master the other gift we have given you. Chronoception, an understanding and mastery of time,*" Miranda continued. "*Existing for over two million years, we have mastered the art of bending time to our will and we have imparted that ability to you. Know that while it is impossible to change time universally, you can alter your perception of it. You can now decelerate your experience of reality; as others experience moments, you experience hours.*"

Caleb's mind raced with the implications. "*This power … it feels limitless. But why me? Why now?*"

Fraxus's mental voice, deep and reassuring, joined in. "*Fate, Caleb. Or call it chance, providence or destiny. You KNOW that it is your path; you must feel that. You have shown courage, wisdom, and an unyielding spirit, and above all, the high sense of ethics and responsibility to wield such power. You are the one who can lead good to victory and peace. You are the bridge between the past and the future, the hope for all.*"

Caleb, struck by the importance and significance of this profound exchange, was feeling a growing weight of responsibility on his shoulders. "*Thank you, Miranda and Fraxus. We have such an incredibly deep bond already, the supportive love I feel and your faith in me is humbling. I won't let you or Kondor down.*"

"*You would never let us down; we know you will do everything in your power and that is all that can be asked of you. Go now, my friend,*" Miranda urged, love and respect evident in her soothing and gentle mental tones. "*Fight the battle you must. We will meet again and commune together soon; we have much to share. Know that Fraxus and I, and all of Kondor, now stand behind you, fully united!*"

Caleb was ready. All his fears had evaporated, replaced by a fierce determination, he was prepared to face whatever lay ahead.

Snapping back to the present, only milliseconds had passed. Caleb still felt the black sappa flowing into his stomach, warming him from inside. His mind remained an oasis of serenity amid the chaos, existing simultaneously in the present and in his own stretched perception of time, a duality that felt natural in this extraordinary moment. He now comprehended the full capabilities of the immense powers he had at his command: an armada of heavily armed ships, combined with his newfound abilities of predictive cognition with Zoren plus his new ability of chronoception time control.

Commander Caleb of the Kondorian Fleet now orchestrated "Caleb's Assault" as it was to be known in the future. A battle that was to be renowned for its breathtaking precision, daring, and innovation.

Caleb confronted the Takers head-on, using InterDim to move and position the fleet directly in front of the bubbling mass. As the Takers unleashed more colossal waves of destructive energy, Caleb piloted the fleet into an extremely complex maneuver—a constantly phasing dimensional shift—using his heightened senses and foresight. The attackers' devastating energy blasts, the strongest the Takers could now muster, passed harmlessly through the fleet's vacated space, leaving them unscathed as they seamlessly oscillated between dimensions in anticipation of each volley.

Caleb continued to control the InterDim shifts so swiftly that the fleet became a blur in space, avoiding every enemy shot. Yet, almost nonchalantly, Caleb turned part of his attention to address the crew. "OK, team," he began, his voice steady, smooth as a hand passing over silk. Caleb had changed and his voice had transformed, more regal now but still humble, certainly magnetically commanding. "It's time to show them our true strength. Strap in tightly and entrust me with your energy and consciousness for a brief moment, if you will."

Turning in his chair to face Caleb, Leurin admitted in awe, "I am struggling to keep up with you, and I am failing. Your abilities surpass my understanding, my friend. I have complete confidence in your leadership, please proceed."

Marcus, communicating from his station on Kondor, added, "Leurin can perform calculations and think far faster than any being or IEB, and if he says you're leaving him in the dust, I am not even in the spectator stand." His unexpected humor brought a chuckle from Irka, easing the tension.

"You have my complete support for anything you wish," Marcus continued, his tone filled with unwavering trust.

"Caleb, we all have your back, and we know you have ours. Go for it," Goffry chimed in supportively.

Over his headset, Irka spoke on a private channel. "My love, we are all one hundred percent behind you. Do what you must to stop this madness, but come back to me whole. I need you to promise!"

"I shall, Irka, my soulmate, my love. I will see you soon, I promise. Warm up the nest for me; I won't be long," Caleb replied with such calm confidence that Irka's fears evaporated. She felt elated because somehow now she knew everything would be okay.

Marta, Jonus, and the rest of the crew also signaled their readiness, trust, and love, the comm buzzing with support.

Caleb refocused his entire being and began to harness the collective consciousness and energy of the entire fleet. Still keeping in perfect formation, he started the entire squad of battleships rapidly spinning. Inside the ships, the artificial gravity systems whirred intensely, working in overdrive to protect the crew from the physical strains of the maneuver. Outside, the fleet became a whirlwind of motion, their synchronized movements unleashing a torrent of firepower.

"So, it begins. We tried to talk. Now, we act," Caleb said, his voice serene against the gentle humming whine of machinery under pressure.

As Caleb delved into the final act of this epic battle, the intensity of his actions reached a legendary status, reshaping Kondorian history. He transported the fleet instantly all over the battlefield, firing on the enemy from within the multitude of orbs and from without. He used InterDim fluidly, and impossibly over hundreds of times a minute, the torrent of gunfire from the fleet seemed to come from everywhere at once, so rapid was their movement.

His tactical mastery over the fleet's maneuvers left the Takers' orbs in disarray, often causing them to strike each other inadvertently or fire aimlessly into the void of space. Despite the fleet's gravity dampeners operating at maximum capacity, the immense G-forces of these intensely rapid, repetitive movements were taking a toll on the crew. The dizzying yet fluid and precisely coordinated movements were far too fast for them to follow or even comprehend; their bodies pulled and battered mercilessly, but their minds remained joined with united resolve and fierce concentration.

The Takers' orbs, unable to withstand the relentless offensive, were being obliterated. Despite their vastly overwhelming numbers, they were no match for the faster-than-thought speed, power, and ferocity of Caleb's fleet.

The diminishing clusters of wannabe invaders were shooting back with utmost fierceness, but the few blasts that managed to connect with the vastly superior battleship formation were of no hindrance. Caleb's relentless attack went on for just over a short hour and only ceased when the Takers were reduced to a few thousand nonaggressive remnants.

As the fleet's rotation slowed to a stop, their barrage ceased also. Caleb surveyed the residue of the beleaguered Taker force, now consolidated into a small, depleted cluster. The entire battleground was full of Taker debris, foggy with tiny floating dust and particles. The fleet's defense shield still hummed and shone as it was hitting and incinerating anything coming into contact.

"Interestingly, and unexpectedly, our scans confirm no life forms—I don't think there ever were any. They're all automated; it was one colossal machine," Leurin announced, allowing puzzlement to affect his tone to accentuate his speech. "I see you're trying to gain control of what's left of them."

"Exactly," Caleb replied. "I'm working on breaching their very alien systems. It was tough to focus on that during the battle, but I am making progress now. I have left enough of them to study, I believe one of these is their equivalent of a command module."

"Making progress? That's the understatement of the century." Goffry chuckled, vocalizing a few sincere notes of birdsong. "Respect, my friend. You just decimated an entire legion, more than an army … a horde, pretty well single-handedly. I'm still reeling from it."

"I am so proud of you, my love; you have saved us all. Now our future children have a chance, and all of Kondor is full of pride," Irka whispered into Caleb's ear on their private comm link.

Muting his mic to others, he privately sent her a big lip smack and a tweet of love, then flipped his link back. "You all helped so much, more than you may know. Thank you, all," Caleb replied, adding to Goffry's song with a few beautiful victorious notes of his own, as he quickly pondered their next move. "We must finish this. These remnant Taker vessels are still linked to their home planet. I have just now gained control of them, but I sense something more insidious behind this attack. I felt and saw an insectoid species reliant on harvesting life force. They are the ones behind this. They are called the Aranchites. These machines we encountered and fought are just their tools, like harvesters, transmitting life energy and resources back across vast distances to their home galaxy."

Marcus's voice boomed with pride over the communications system, "Caleb, let's take a brief moment to acknowledge our victory. You've achieved the unthinkable, Commander. Your actions have not only saved Kondor but countless others. This is truly a monumental triumph."

Marta and Jonus's voices, filled with love and admiration, echoed in agreement. "You've done us all proud, my son," they sang out in unison, accompanied by a jubilant victory birdsong. This prelude was picked up by all the Avians who could hear, followed by a longer verse sung, hummed, and warbled by all in reverence of the moment.

As the others expressed their admiration and support, Caleb, head bowed in humble acceptance of all this unaccustomed praise, focused on the next move. After a moment to allow the wave of victorious feelings to wash over everyone, he felt buoyed and elated but anxious to impart more information. "It is not over, unfortunately." As he quietly yet assertively delivered this news, everyone fell silent again, listening with renewed attentiveness.

Caleb took a moment—leaning forward in his chair to reposition himself, he rubbed his face with his hands, shaking his head a bit to clear his thoughts. "I must follow this connection the remaining vessels have with their home base while it remains active. When I encountered this link, I knew I could use my new enhanced communing abilities to travel back along it to its source. It is like an anchor communication link but also used to transport life force energy. It seems straightforward to navigate it with my own life force, anchored back here. It is imperative to learn more about our true enemy, or I fear they will return with even greater numbers and tenacity. We must leverage this unexpected victory and continue our information gathering and, if necessary, a further assault while they are momentarily vulnerable."

Leurin broke the ensuing quiet first. "Caleb, you speak with logic and wisdom. I see it must be done."

Marcus sighed over the comm, "I see the truth to it, I think it prudent to finish this."

As more opinions and agreement came over the links, Caleb decided. Letting Irka know first. He was going.

"Be cautious, Caleb. Come back to me safe; remember your promise!" Irka chimed in on his private link from the Kondorian ground base.

"This is something I must do, my dear Irka," Caleb replied on the private bandwidth. "I know I will return to you. My love for you is eternal and boundless. That alone will give me the strength I need to come back."

"Go, my darling. I know you must," Irka responded, her voice weaving a few notes of sweet birdsong that carried her support and love through the airwaves.

As he finished with Irka, Caleb immediately prepared for his next step. He leaned back into his plush command chair, Leurin now standing beside him in his copilot role, nodding with approval. "I will ensure all is well on this end, be careful, all of you."

As Caleb was sinking further into his communion, he wondered what Leurin meant by "all of you" when Marcus arrived in his mind.

"Listen, Caleb, I must come, we have no time to argue, let me ride along in your mind. Somehow, I know my presence is important." Marcus's mental voice was insistent yet clearly allowed room for Caleb to decide.

Miranda and Fraxus were also asking for a mental link. *"I agree, and we must come too. It is foretold. Caleb, it is ultimately your call, but we are needed, all of us. That is our belief."*

It took only a second for Caleb to know it was true. *"Let us go then. Together."* With his decision made, Caleb dove deeper into his mind, preparing for an unprecedented venture into the Aranchites' communication link. He felt all of Kondor's energies anchoring him to his reality, along with Marcus and Miranda and Fraxus's presence. Their ancient energies intertwined with his in a transcendental embrace.

Riding the hybrid dark matter and neutrino connection beam from the remnants of the Takers' Cluster to their home galaxy, Caleb journeyed across space and time, finally plunging into the alien hive mind of the Aranchites on their home planet, Klimora.

These Aranchites, an aggressive race of spiderlike beings from the far-off Plexian galaxy, were a highly developed society with exoskeletons and complex, dexterous antennae. They had evolved from physical predators, sucking life fluids from their prey, to a more "advanced" race, prolonging their lives by absorbing collected life force from a network of intergalactic harvesters. They had never lost a battle, always approaching conflicts with an all-guns-blazing method and winning every time.

As one of the oldest and most advanced races in their galaxy, they had succeeded in wiping out and absorbing all entities and life forms with virtually no opposition, becoming the apex predators in their quadrant. They then continued growing and expanding, remotely farming ever more distant areas of the universe for rare resources, new technologies, and most of all, precious harvested life forces that kept them alive indefinitely.

Their feelings of supremacy and arrogant self-assurance now became their downfall. Caleb merged easily with their entire hive mind as they had virtually no defenses from within. Although the Aranchites acted independently, half of each of their brains was always connected together as a race.

In this alien world, Caleb found himself an outsider yet intimately linked for a fleeting moment. But that fleeting moment was all he needed. He slowed down his temporal perception to its maximum and, combining that with his PSY energy, continued to search and spread his consciousness throughout the Aranchite network without significant opposition.

Surrounded by their collective consciousness, Caleb was both isolated and yet covertly woven into the fabric of their immense, narcissistic society. He observed the communal shared memories of the Aranchites, their blind, relentless need for expansion, aware but indifferent to the moral implications of their actions. They operated not out of pure malice but out of a blind instinct to survive and expand.

Time was slipping away for Caleb, even at his ultra-slowed pace. The Aranchite team managing the connection beam with the Kondorian sector had initiated shutdown, realizing something had gone gravely wrong with the harvesting cluster. Caleb knew he had a brief but unique opportunity to influence the Aranchites during the confusion. But how?

"*Caleb, what about implanting some sort of virus from within?*" Miranda suggested. "*We remember when we had a visitor during the Kondorian War. They had a problem with Othorian and jiant hordes attacking. Together we formulated a biological virus that was implanted into the jiant herd and obliterated them in just a few weeks. Could we not draw on that to defeat the Aranchites somehow?*"

"*They have what looks like wide protection from biological viruses, having developed an extremely advanced health-care system like our healing pods. That would not help here; we need something more,*" Caleb responded, feeling somewhat defeated at what he initially thought was a brilliant idea.

Marcus interjected with a quizzical mental hum. "*But wait.*" Pausing to think out an idea, he continued, "*Their minds are all intrinsically linked. What affects one of them will affect all of them. That logically would be an excellent way to distribute something. Not physical, though—mental? What's left?*"

Caleb had a flash of prescience. "*I know why you all are here. You both just gave me an idea. Between you, Marcus, the Blacks, and myself, I see a way.*"

"*We see your idea, brilliant,*" the Blacks clinked in agreement with Caleb's plan.

"*Do it, I say,*" Marcus agreed, understanding what needed to be done despite its consequences.

With unwavering determination, Caleb executed his plan. Using a combination of these innovative ideas, he implanted a "virus" of empathy and self-awareness within the aranchite collective psyche. During his earlier probe of the Aranchite network, Caleb had identified individuals with weaker mental defenses. He strategically planted spiritual enlightenment bombs in these vulnerable links. This insidious payload, once unleashed, would spread through their network like wildfire on a hot, windy summer day.

If the spiritual "virus" took hold, it not only would expose the raw, undiluted anguish of countless planets and beings whose existences had been extinguished for Aranchite sustenance, but it also would compel the them all to experience the pain and suffering from their victims' perspectives. This would be like what Bertran and his cohorts had experienced but, on a species-wide scale.

Caleb then allowed his perception of time to speed up, wanting to see the initial reaction before the link was severed. He had only seconds. On his way in through the link, he had encountered the mind of the Aranchite responsible for keeping the communications beam open and Caleb had been continuously monitoring him. The Aranchite was just birthing the thought to close the connection; only a second or two later, his finger would hit the console. Caleb lingered to the last moment. As he was closing the link, he saw it! The "virus" was working, he could feel it start to grow in that last minuscule part of a second before the connection closed.

What happened next was a great surprise to Caleb and his traveling companions. As Caleb's consciousness recoiled from the alien hive mind and hurtled back to his reality, somehow his perception of the Aranchite timeline sped up for only a brief instance, perhaps as a consequence of the vast distance and temporal differences warping together as they went. In that instant, they saw a brief history of the future of the alien planet, and it was horrifying.

Caleb would later reflect that perhaps this was their karma, having to see what they had done to the Aranchite people.

The revelations implanted by Caleb would strike the Aranchites like a thunderbolt, shaking the foundations of their consciousness. The impact would be immediate and catastrophic. The once methodical and unfeeling hive mind would be riddled with unprecedented emotions.

Numerous Aranchites, overwhelmed by the intensity of shared agony, would quickly fall into a profound depression. The weight of their newfound awareness would drive some to the brink of insanity, their minds fracturing under the burden of remorse and empathy they had never processed before. Amid this tumultuous awakening, chaos would erupt throughout their society. The once cohesive and relentless hive now would grapple with internal conflict and disorder. The revelation of their actions' true cost had irrevocably altered them, sending shockwaves through their entire dominion.

As the hive's consciousness plunged into disarray, connections with the harvesters were severed. These goliath harvester clusters, dependent on the hive link, began to lose cohesion as the connection collapsed, crashing together and eventually dissolving into cosmic debris.

The link collapsed; Caleb was back home. Marcus and the Blacks' consciousnesses had left his mind, each grappling with what they had witnessed in their own way. Caleb was weeping uncontrollably, his hands trying to brush away the flow of tears while pulling at his downy hair. His heart ached with empathy, even for those who had once been the harbingers of destruction across the universe. In his battle cruiser, reality returned in stark contrast to the vast, interconnected consciousness he had just left. He felt alone. He was a solitary figure, racked with sobs that echoed through the silent pilot's chamber.

The sense of victory was laced with profound heaviness. They had succeeded, but at a staggering cost. The realization that his actions would precipitate the downfall of an entire civilization, trillions of lives spiraling into chaos and suffering, pressed on him like a crushing weight.

Beside him, Leurin's avatar stood silently, a steady presence in Caleb's emotional storm. His hand rested gently on Caleb's shoulder, a touch that offered silent support and understanding. Words were unnecessary and perhaps inadequate in the face of such profound grief and moral complexity.

Caleb's mind raced, struggling with the enormity of what he had experienced and the price they had paid for their victory. The room seemed to shrink around him as he grappled with the overwhelming burden of his actions. Caleb took another sobbing deep breath, feeling the weight of his sorrow lift ever so slightly.

Epilogue

The victory over the Aranchites was not just a triumph in warfare; it was a victory for life itself, a testament to the indomitable spirit of those who fought for the sanctity of existence across the entire Universe. Caleb's legend transcended the bounds of his world. The tale of the Avian who bent time, brought enlightenment to a predatory race, and safeguarded his planet and many galaxies against impossible odds became a beacon of hope. His journey, intertwined with the ancient wisdom of Miranda and Fraxus, served as a reminder that even in the darkest times, one individual's resolve could change the course of history.

Upon returning to his home planet and his beloved Irka, Caleb initially fell into a severe depression, both mentally and physically drained from the massive exertions he had endured. Struggling with the weight of his actions, he found solace in the embrace of his family and the largest healing communion ever attempted, which involved Healers from all the flocks of Kondor. This massive effort, lasting several days, was followed by Caleb spending time in a healing chamber specially programmed by Marcus and Leurin to address his mental conflicts and restore his physical health.

Marcus was also struggling to cope. He had been such a pacifist like his brethren Creators, but now he had been at the root of so much pain, hurt and destruction. An entire civilization was decimated, so many had died. What made it right to inflict suffering on so many for the sake of the greater good?

Despite the victory over the Takers, many Creators now shunned Marcus because he had broken their Prime Law and interfered directly with other species. Some thought his actions ruthless and barbaric, and that certainly did not help with his mindset. However, seeing the happiness of the surviving Kondorians and many other species that had been saved by their actions, he felt only happiness and relief. Would he have done it again? Yes, he would.

Hearing of the victory over the Aranchites, numerous species from across the quadrant of the galaxy sent ambassadors and emissaries to Kondor, laden with gifts and heartfelt gratitude to formally thank Caleb and Marcus and all Kondorians, now revered as heroes.

The Avians and Othorians had undergone so much change in such a short period that it was decided to limit contact with alien species for the time being. Marcus and Leurin acted as ambassadors, organizing and receiving envoys while respectfully requesting that the Kondorian people be given time to assimilate all that had transpired. Just the knowledge that they were not alone in the universe was a lot to take in, combined with all the new information, technologies, and spiritual awareness they had gained.

So, Kondorians returned to a semblance of their previous lives, taking all the time needed to reflect and integrate themselves into the new reality without losing the core values they had been raised with. The once-tenuous, then broken, truce between the Avians and the Othorians was now solidified into a robust alliance fostered by mutual respect and a shared desire for a harmonious future.

All over the Grand Valley, the Great Trees, including the newly connected Black Trees, thrummed with a renewed vibrant energy. Now all regions of Kondor were joined together in an intricate web of understanding and empathy. The wisdom of the ancient Black Great Trees, once isolated and distant, now flowed freely, enriching the lives of all who connected with them.

After several weeks, Caleb healed. He had been transformed by his experiences and came to accept that there had been no other options; he had done what had to be done. Standing atop a hill overlooking the vast expanse of the Grand Valley, his black-tipped wings—symbols of his unique journey and connection to the ancient Black Trees—fluttered gently in the evening breeze.

Beside him, Irka, ever the stalwart and loving companion, gazed into the horizon with a mix of renewed awe and contentment. Their bond, forged through trials and tribulations, had grown only stronger. They took a long holiday, accompanied by their returning personal buzzies, Trada and Trudy, to enjoy the beauty of the Grand Valley and revisit cherished places from their youth.

"Caleb, I have something to tell you, some wonderful news," Irka began as they nestled together against the strong winds. "Although it has been so many months since our Pairing before all this commotion started, well, it seems it was a success," she added coyly. "I am now carrying an egg; we are going to be parents, my love."

"What … how could that be? It seems like it was so long ago," Caleb remarked, stammering in surprise but with evident glee in his voice. "Are you sure?"

"Of course, my love. I have been to see CeCe, and my suspicions were confirmed. As you know, it can take a long time for an egg to mature after conception. CeCe feels that my body, reacting to all the stress, kept my fertilized egg in an immature state for a long period. Now, with my body returning to full health, my body is allowing my

… well our egg to reach maturity, and it will not be long before I must lay. I was waiting for you to recover, and I wanted to confirm my pregnancy with CeCe before telling you. Congratulations, my love, you are about to be a father!"

Caleb's mouth fell open in shock, then broke into a huge grin, his face lighting up with amazement and joy. "Thank Mother Kondor!" Caleb let out a long, cheerful song, a series of whoops and joyful calls, embracing Irka in a strong hug and smothering her with kisses. They almost fell off their perch with their exuberance, finally fluttering to the soft ground below in an awkward yet careful tumble of feathers. They came to a stop in a mossy hollow, clutching each other closely and singing a beautiful birdsong in perfect harmony.

After some time, Caleb spoke. "I could not be happier, Irka. My love for you has no bounds, and now, to have this blessing, it makes up for so much of the craziness we have been through. So, when is the date we are expecting this amazing gift? I will construct the softest and most beautiful nest for us and our new egg."

"We still have some time to finish our holiday, my love," Irka responded softly. "CeCe has asked that I go to the aerie to lay, so I thought we could wrap up our vacation there. What do you think?"

"Anything your heart desires is yours, Irka," Caleb responded. With another whoop and loud call, he sprang into the air, flying high and swooping around above his mate. Irka lay in the mossy hollow, laughing and giggling, watching Caleb's boyish antics and flying acrobatics with tears of joy in her eyes.

After several hours of gleeful flying, they nested together in a tall tree covered in scented blossoms. Prepared to spend the night outdoors in a tight cuddle, Caleb covered Irka with his beautiful wings to protect her from the elements. Even if it wasn't necessary, it made Irka feel deeply comfortable and secure, giving her the best sleep she had ever had.

∞◇∞

Over the next couple of weeks, they slowly made their way toward the Western Aerie, using the small flota they had been traveling with. Trada and Trudy, their prime buzzies, joined in the celebration after learning of the good news, harvesting and bringing the most beautiful pollen and nectars for their beloved masters, covering the flota in exotic flowers to celebrate.

Finally, they all arrived at the aerie, where they were joined by Marta and Jonus, the beaming grandparents-to-be, as well as several flock leaders. Even Marcus and Leurin were there to greet them as they arrived. Many of their flock mates, including Goffry, were in attendance, and a large party was held in their honor to celebrate the upcoming new addition to the White Flock family.

Once the festivities died down, Caleb followed through on his promise to Irka. He constructed the most beautiful nest in a secluded back corner of the aerie using the softest materials he could find. He communed with the surrounding vegetation, encouraging the growth of a remarkable canopy of ever-blossoming white flowers that dropped their exquisitely soft petals into the already cozy nest, the whole of which glowed with a beautiful white luminous aura.

On the day CeCe had predicted, Irka was ready. Together with several Brooders, Marta included, she ceremoniously entered the well-prepared nest and waited for the emergence of her egg. Caleb, Jonus, Goffry, and the others waited patiently outside the nesting area for news. Within an hour, a flushed Brooder emerged. "Come quickly, Caleb. You must see … it's … just come," she stammered. "All is well; Irka needs you." Caleb jumped up and followed her into the chamber, followed closely by the others.

As he entered, the whole of the chamber was filled with glowing white light. Irka was cradling the egg, hugging it tight. CeCe, Marta, and the other Brooders looked on with delight, but Caleb felt another emotion—surprise, shock, maybe amazement?

Upon seeing Caleb enter, Irka's eyes filled with tears. She opened her arms, revealing her egg. Perfectly formed, but as Caleb approached closer, he saw … was it just a trick of the light? He blinked and leaned forward, looking reassuringly into Irka's eyes, and then saw what had everyone agape. The egg, beautifully shaped, was not the expected pure white but a lustrous black with hints of a metallic sheen, glowing and scintillating all over.

THE END